"Why did you lie to me?" she asked quietly, without moving her hand away.

"What?" Confusion clouded his mind, the world outside the room suddenly distant.

"During that long night in Africa," she whispered, "you told me that everyone here in Boston was kind and wonderful. I believed you."

"I told you what you wanted to hear."

"You lied."

"You were dying!" The words came out sharply, the tinge of remembered panic lacing the air. "You were dying," he repeated more softly, forcing a teasing he didn't feel into his tone. "I saw no reason to tell you the truth and hasten your demise."

Finnea pressed her eyes closed and laughed, a burst of sound that was filled with relief. "True. If you had told me about Adwina Raines, no doubt I never would have recovered."

"But you did," he whispered.

He stared at her, unable to look away. They were close, so close that if he leaned just so he could kiss her. . . .

Dove's Way

Linda Francis Lee

IVY BOOKS • NEW YORK

This book contains an excerpt from the forthcoming edition of *Swan's Grace* by Linda Francis Lee. This excerpt has been set for this edition only and may not reflect the final content of the forthcoming edition.

An Ivy Book
Published by The Ballantine Publishing Group
Copyright © 2000 by Linda Francis Lee
Excerpt from *Swan's Grace* by Linda Francis Lee copyright © 2000 by Linda Francis Lee

www.randomhouse.com/BB/

Library of Congress Catalog Card Number: 99-91679

ISBN 0-449-00205-5

Manufactured in the United States of America

First Edition: March 2000

10 9 8 7 6 5 4 3 2 1

Acknowledgments

I would like to express my deepest gratitude to . . .

Dr. Scott Joy, M.D., for his help with medical questions;

Dr. Julius Nyang'oro, Ph.D., and Dr. Alphonse Mutima, Ph.D., for their help with Africa;

Shauna Summers, for being wonderful;

Amy Berkower, for her endless kindness;

Jodi Reamer, for Chinatown;

Kathleen Nolan, for sharing her beautiful home on top of the world;

Stef Ann Holm and Kathy Peiffer, for their friendship, for reading everything I sent them, and for always being willing to read more;

Carilyn Francis Johnson, dear friend and sister;

And, as always, to Michael, because I couldn't do it without him.

Part One

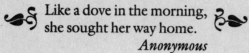 Like a dove in the morning,
she sought her way home.
Anonymous

From the Journal of
Matthew Hawthorne

I met her on a train in Africa. One minute I was alone, the next she was there, the thick green jungle surrounding us in the open-air railcar. Strange how life can turn on end so quickly and unexpectedly, how mere seconds or hours can change the course of a lifetime.

If I noticed her at all when she first walked in, then I'm sure I noticed that she had hair as red and untamed as the setting sun, and eyes as green as the African forest. She wasn't a native; her white skin and light eyes were proof of that. But she was wild nonetheless. Like Africa. A woman so unlike either the Africans I had seen over the six months I had been there, or the ladies of Boston I had known my whole life.

But what I do remember, vividly, is that she didn't so much as blink when she saw the scar that etched my face.

Beyond that, I remember little else of that first moment I saw her. I had no interest. In her. In the surroundings. In anything. I had gone to Africa to forget. All I could think that day was it was a damn shame I hadn't.

Chapter One

Africa 1891

She nearly missed the train.

Finnea Winslet raced across the makeshift platform of the Congo Free State Railway, her hunter's pants and cotton shirt splattered with mud because she'd had to run the last quarter mile to the train. Her father's longtime servant Janji hurried along at her side as they came to the line of antiquated railcars that waited deep in the African jungle.

Only the long, metal scrape of train tracks marred the thick tangle of vines and evergreen trees. And the smell. Of jasmine and damp, mineral-rich dirt. Mixing with the sounds. A nearly deafening clatter of vendors hawking their wares, and of animals—goats, chickens, and even the oxen that had carried many of the travelers to the station.

The oxen could go no farther. The train would take Finnea across the most impassable portions of the Congo to the Congo Free State's major port of Matadi and the steamship that would take her to America. Take her to see her mother and brother, whom she hadn't seen in nineteen of her twenty-five years.

"Tusanswalu," Janji said in Kikongo, telling her to be quick as they ran.

Janji was a powerful man both in size and respect from his tribesmen. His skin was dark against the white of his flowing African robes, his gray hair gleaming in the brutal midday sun. Though years older, he wasn't out of breath and he spoke with ease. "If we don't hurry, the train and the guide I have arranged to escort you to Matadi will leave."

Finnea wasn't particularly happy about the guide, hadn't known about him until minutes ago, when Janji informed her of the arrangement. But she was determined to make this trip, and it was no secret that Africa was not a kind place to a woman alone. And now that her father had succumbed to spotted fever, she was alone.

"The guide will be waiting for you in the second car," Janji added. "His name is Matthew Hawthorne."

"How do you know he will be there?" she asked, her Kikongo as fluent as his.

"Be assured, I know. We made the arrangements just yesterday. And Matthew Hawthorne is a man of his word." Janji hesitated, his face looking distant but determined. "He is also a good man."

"But—"

"You go now," Janji stated in his blunt, forceful way, cutting her off. But then he hesitated, his wizened old face softening. "I will make certain your belongings come to you in America."

Suddenly thoughts of guides and mothers were gone. Her heart kicked in her chest with fear, fear of this new life that both pushed and pulled at her. Without warning, she didn't want to leave Janji or his family. She didn't want to leave Africa. She would stay. She would find a way to make a new life for herself on her own.

Her mind raced with possibilities, but Janji must have read her thoughts.

"You must go," he said, not unkindly. "You are like a dove in the morning that must find its way home. There is nothing for you here."

He was right, deep down she understood that. But that didn't make it easier to accept.

Despite the fact that she knew he wouldn't like it, she flung her arms around him as the train lurched and sent up a great puff of steam. "I will miss you, my friend."

He was stiff and unyielding in her arms, but after a long minute she could feel the tautness of his sinewy muscles ease. One small concession to affection after a near lifetime of seeing to her welfare.

Without meeting his eye, refusing to let him see her tears, she reached down and grabbed her pack, then raced away. Only when she stood on the metal steps as the train pulled out of the rustic, makeshift station, a lump lodged in her throat, did she look back. Janji stood quietly, proudly. No emotion. But just when the train began its first curve out of sight, he raised his hand in silent farewell.

Finnea stood on the steps, her own hand raised, tears streaking her cheeks as she watched until the station was swallowed up by the thick green jungle. Would she ever see him again? Would he send the few belongings that mattered to her as he promised? Could she live without them if he didn't?

With a firm shake of her head, she dashed the tears away. There was nothing she could do about it now. And in that second, she realized she was starting over. With that thought came a flash of emotion. A sweet, exhilarating rush of feelings. A freeing, of things, of the past.

There was truly no place for her in Africa. But she had family a world away in America. In Boston, the town where she had been born. The town from which her father had taken his family and moved to Africa nearly twenty years ago.

But Finnea's mother had hated Africa, her father had explained, hated what she called a "primitive life," and the minute little Nester had become ill, Leticia Winslet had insisted she return to Boston with him to seek medical care.

Promising to return within the year, Leticia had taken her son and sailed to America, leaving her husband and daughter behind. But one year had stretched into two, and two into three, until the promises ceased. Finnea hadn't seen her mother or brother since. Now, in a few short months, she would see the two people who were more strangers to her than family.

Often Finnea had wondered what her brother looked like. Was he tall like their father had been? Full of laughter and kind smiles? But her attention was held by Leticia.

Her mother. A woman she didn't know.

Her father had shared bits and pieces of her mother with her, a sort of jigsaw-puzzle glimpse of a woman, fragmented and incomplete. But soon she would have the rest of the pieces to complete her picture.

Excitement began to drum in her veins as she entered the first car of the train. For years she had dreamed of her mother, in a town house in Boston. Her father had told her of the home he had left behind. A tall, stately structure made from blocks of chiseled stone the color of sand mixed with the sea, and huge windows filled with precious panes of glass. Throughout her childhood he had described the house, the steps built amazingly of granite instead of wood leading up to majestic front doors that clicked open with handles that he swore were made of bright gleaming brass. And inside, more steps, this time made of smooth marble climbing higher in the house. Four floors in all, filled with lights called chandeliers and rugs woven from thick wool instead of dried grasses. After a lifetime in Africa such a place seemed as remote as America itself.

The ivory season was over, so there should have been plenty of empty seats in the open-air car. But she was surprised to find that the first car was packed with people, both natives and foreigners, and small animals trying to settle in.

Finnea refused to think about the descent to the coastal river town. The Congo's train was a rickety affair at best, but it was the only viable means of transportation in the area.

As she made her way through the throng of passengers toward the second car, Finnea spoke to a native woman from a nearby village, pulling out a sweet for the woman's child. She exchanged pleasantries with a brawny man with dark mahogany skin whom she had dealt with at market, joked with a vendor she had traded with for years. She talked and laughed as she made her way through the first car, in no particular hurry to seek out the guide. These were the people she knew. This was where she was comfortable.

She didn't do as well in the coastal towns where small colonies of Europeans had settled. She knew they thought her odd and outlandish. Not that she cared. She never had.

But for reasons she didn't understand, despite the fact that she hardly knew the woman, Finnea cared what her mother thought. She wanted her to be proud of the woman she had become.

Finnea made her way through the throng of people toward the second car. The train rocked and swayed, sometimes jarring so violently that conversation broke off, an eerie silence falling over the passengers. No sooner did the motion of the train smooth out than the conversation flared anew. In Kikongo and Swahili. A smattering of Portuguese and a few other languages. Then sharp, spiking laughter to cover the fear everyone had felt.

When she reached the platform that connected the cars, she was forced to step aside when first one European couple, then another hurried out of the second car. The rush of wind whipped her face, stinging her eyes as she grabbed the rusty handholds for balance. The sound of iron wheels clacking rhythmically over tracks of metal and wood made it impossible to hear what anyone said. But Finnea had the distinct impression that the people were hurrying away disturbed.

She gave it little thought. When the platform cleared, she hooked the straps of her pack on her arm, slid the door open, and stepped into the nearly empty car.

And saw him.

Her head tilted in confusion, and her heart seemed to still.

Unlike the first car, the second was empty except for one man.

He stood like a warrior, fierce and commanding, staring out at the thick, green landscape, indifferent to the reckless way the train hurtled down the mountainside. While the rest of the passengers in the first car shook about like dice in a box, he stood erect, his body fighting the motion of the train as if he could overcome a greater power by sheer force of will.

He stood in profile, but even so she could tell he was more beautiful than any man she had ever seen.

Tall with broad shoulders, a taut waist that tapered down into hard thighs encased in the tightly fitting pants of a hunter. His hair was blond, streaked lighter by the sun, swept back, brushing the collar of his white shirt. He had a chiseled jaw, strong cheekbones, and eyes as blue as the wide-open sky above the African plains. She had never seen a man so perfect.

But then he turned, just slightly, and she saw the scar. Long and angry like the slice of train track carved through the once perfect landscape.

Straightening with surprise, Finnea realized who he was. Janji had called him Matthew Hawthorne. But the natives called him *Mzungu Kichaa mwenye Kovu.*

The Wild White Man with the Scar.

For weeks now, stories of a scarred white man who recklessly disregarded the dangers of Africa had filtered through the Congo. There were stories of the man walking unarmed into a village of Masai warriors. Of him hiking out over the wild grasslands with little more than the shirt on his back, gone for weeks, then amazingly returning unharmed.

But the story that Finnea had never quite been able to put from her mind was of the man sleeping overnight in a native encampment, startling the Africans awake with a sudden, furiously haunted scream. Then silence. When they woke in the morning he was gone without a word, only the highly cherished gift of provisions left behind for them.

A gesture of thanks . . . or apology? The question had circled in Finnea's mind for weeks after she heard the story.

Over the years, she had learned to believe half of what the natives told her, and given the enormity of the stories that had been bandied around regarding this man, in this case she had been inclined to believe none at all. But seeing him now, standing in a train that careened madly down the mountainside, his stance rigid, his face defiant, she wondered if the stories weren't true.

"Excuse me," she said in perfect, though slightly accented, English.

The man shifted from his thoughts, neither startled by her intrusion nor interested as he turned completely to face her.

Finnea could see even more of his scar—an angry slash through his golden brow, miraculously missing his eye, then down to his cheek, giving him a permanently wry expression.

But the scar didn't bother Finnea. A man's fine, smooth face was far more of an unfamiliar sight in Africa. What made him stand apart in this brutal land was the enormity of his escapades—if indeed they were true.

He stared at her, his eyes hard and cold, unnerving, though drawing her in.

"Are you Matthew Hawthorne?" she asked, uncertain if she wanted it to be him or not.

He didn't answer at first, only looked at her, then said, "Yes."

Just that, his voice deep and low, and very unfriendly. She had the fleeting thought that Janji must have been wrong. This wasn't her guide. But she couldn't bring herself to turn around and return to the first car. Pride. Stubbornness. She nearly smiled at her own folly.

She stepped farther inside, and just then the train lurched, jarring her forward. Frantically, she reached out for a handhold, but her hands came up empty. So close, but nothing near enough. Except for the man.

For one startled second she thought he would let her fall. But in the next, he cursed, his arm coming around her. She would have sworn he grimaced as he caught her, but when she looked closer, his face was merely set in hard, forbidding planes.

He smelled of leather and wild grasses, wide-open spaces and sunshine. The muscles in his forearm were rigid and taut like granite. But his shirt was amazingly soft beneath her fingers, with perfect round buttons slipped through perfectly cut holes.

When she realized he was still staring at her, his eyes intense, she smiled up at him.

"I'm sorry," she said, pushing back. "I'm not usually so clumsy."

Still he only glowered.

"You must be angry because I didn't get here sooner," she offered, not understanding the need to wash away his ire. "I'm here now, and rest assured, you'll get your escort fee." She patted his arm as if he were a pet rather than a warrior. "My mistake for worrying you."

"Your mistake was coming into this car in the first place. Didn't you see everyone else flee?"

She blinked. "You ran those poor Europeans off on purpose?"

His face darkened, a flash of an unexpected little-boy emptiness sparking in his eyes.

"On purpose?" he asked finally. Then he shrugged as if shrugging away the emptiness, the gesture cold and indifferent. "I'm not much for company." He looked at her directly. "Theirs *or* yours."

Magnificent or not, he was sorely lacking as a guide.

She started to say just that, but the words died away when he stepped toward her, those hard eyes never wavering, and the truth finally sank in that she didn't really know this man. But he only passed her by, walking with what she assumed was the stiff formality of the Europeans she had seen in coastal towns, his riding pants molding to his muscular legs and thighs as he strode to a long bench.

He reached for a thick canvas bag, flipped back the brass buckles, and pulled out a hand-rolled cigar. Moving with military precision, he clipped the end, put it in his mouth without lighting it, leaned his shoulder against a metal support, then returned his attention to the passing landscape.

She had been dismissed. It was clear he was used to being obeyed, his words a command.

Annoyance flared, and whatever fascination she had felt was forgotten. "I wouldn't have come into this car and sought you out," she stated coolly, holding tight to a rusted pole, "had I not been instructed by my father's servant to do so."

That got his attention, and she nearly smiled when his gaze shot over to her, his blue eyes surprised, his hair golden, his face perfect. Except for the scar.

She took in the whole of him. Even with the angry slash he was more handsome than any man she had ever seen. Rugged and dangerous, sinfully daring. Despite what the Europeans thought of her, she had never been daring; she was only different from them. She had always been careful—always trying to be safe.

But safe didn't exist.

"What are you talking about?" he demanded.

"Janji. A native who has been in my father's service for years, told me that I was to come to the second car to find

Matthew Hawthorne." She raised a brow. "Unfortunately, that appears to be you."

His cool, pale eyes narrowed; then he tossed the unlit cigar onto his bag. "Hell," he cursed, his expression closed. "The little blackguard."

"I don't understand."

"No, you wouldn't." He paused for a moment, his expression growing murderous. "Suffice it to say that I owe Janji, and as payment he asked me to see to an important cargo on the trip to Matadi. He didn't mention that cargo was a woman."

Her chin came up. "Or perhaps your Kikongo is not so fluent and you mistranslated," she shot back.

He studied her at length, bold and assessing, as if he were stripping away her clothes. Her cheeks stained red at the perusal, and she couldn't believe Janji thought highly of this man.

"Hell," he repeated, seeming to engage in some internal fight with himself. "What's your name?"

"Finnea Winslet."

"All right, Finnea Winslet," he ground out. "I'll take you to Matadi, though not a mile farther. Do you understand?"

She regarded him with scathing animosity, that stubborn nature getting the better of her.

"What I understand is you can rot in that hell of yours before I go one inch with you, much less one mile."

He crooked a brow, the flicker of a half-smile pulling at his lips. "Oh, really?"

"Yes, really," she snapped, not liking the way he was looking at her.

He pushed away from the support and her eyes went wide, but before she could move he was in front of her, his hand braced over her head against the metal pole. His body was inches from hers, overpowering, intimidating. So close that she could feel the heat of him.

"I just might rot in *that hell of mine*," he said, his dark voice slightly amused, "but in the meantime, I pay my debts."

His face lightened, his sculpted lips pulling into a smile. The gesture made her heart beat oddly, her irritation sinking away, and she had the fleeting and unexpected thought that this man hadn't always been so fierce. What had happened to him? she wondered. How had he gotten the scar?

"What is that debt?" she asked without thinking, wanting to prolong this glimpse of a different man.

But her words had the exact opposite effect. His eyes went dark, dangerous. And she realized that indeed this was the man whom natives spoke about during long African nights.

This was *Mzungu Kichaa mwenye Kovu.*

"I think there is much more to you than I've heard," she whispered. "Is it true you faced a tribe of Masai and came out alive?"

He cursed, turning his face just so, as if he could hide his scar. Once again he fought the sway of the train, his body tense.

After a moment, his head turned back, his eyebrow arching with anger. "Where did you hear that?"

But she wasn't deterred. "Tell me, is it true?"

"I traded with a Masai gentleman. It was nothing more than that."

Finnea couldn't help her answering scoff. "You use 'Masai' and 'gentleman' in the same sentence? They are fierce warriors, and no doubt they would be insulted to be called anything less. Clearly you haven't been in Africa very long." She studied him closely, considering. "I'm amazed I've heard so much about you in what is so obviously a short period of time."

His gaze grew sharp. "What else have you heard?"

"Many things." She raised a challenging brow. "Like in addition to your run-in with the Masai, you saved a native from a leopard."

"Forget it."

"I won't forget it. Neither will the man you rescued. It is said that once you save a person's life you are bound together forever."

"That's ridiculous. What would you expect me to do?"

"Most white men wouldn't have done anything for a native."

"Hell," he said, raking his hand through his hair. "How in the world did you hear about it, anyway?"

"Word travels quickly here."

"And to think I believed I got away from gossips," he grumbled.

Finnea leaned forward, intense. "My guess is that the natives are wrong. They should call you The Brave Man, not The Wild Man." She said it before she could think, and as soon as she saw the ravaged emptiness that came over his face, she wished the words back.

"Is that what they call me?" he asked quietly, his face etched by more than the scar. "The Wild Man?"

Uneasy, Finnea started to move away. But he caught her arm in a painful grip and wouldn't let her go. She stared at the hand that bit into her flesh before she slowly glanced up into eyes whose innocence was lost forever. "Yes," she whispered. "*Mzungu Kichaa.* That is what they call a white man who they think is crazy. Are they right? Are you crazy rather than brave? Is that why the Europeans hurry from this car?"

He laughed, a hollow, mirthless sound. "Because I'm crazy?" He shook his head as he let her go, his fingers seeming to linger. "Perhaps I am."

His acceptance surprised her. "No, I don't think you're crazy. My guess is that you are simply a man who courts danger— arrogantly and with little regard for the price you will have to pay."

Without another word, she ducked beneath his arm, then hurried to the metal door, aware the whole time of the man's penetrating gaze on her back as she retreated. She wanted away from his darkness, away from his fury.

"Damn it," he snapped, his jaw chiseled, his eyes intense. "Where do you think you're going?"

"To America," she answered boldly.

He started for her when she slid open the door, a sharp gust of biting wind and the deafening sound of wheels over tracks rushing in around them. The wind caught in her hair, pulling it from its binding, and she looked back.

"I don't need your help, Matthew Hawthorne, or anyone else's. I never have."

He looked at her long and hard. But just when he opened his mouth to speak, the air exploded with sound, harsh and staggering, a great high-pitched screech of brakes locking on metal. And the world began to tumble.

Finnea couldn't think, couldn't make sense of the noise that filled the air. The train jerked, throwing her aside, and she grabbed a handrail. But the handhold wasn't enough when the train started to pitch.

"No!"

She screamed the word as she crashed against a metal post. She watched as he leaped toward her, the world strangely disjointed. His face was set in the fierce lines of a warrior's, and she had the fleeting thought that he could save her. But the train buckled before he could reach her, twisting off the tracks, and all Finnea saw was the painfully blue, unrelenting African sky.

Time spun in slow motion as the sound of twisting metal filled the air. Finnea felt weightless. Unencumbered. Before she hit with an agonizing crash as the train came to a shuddering halt.

Then silence.

Part Two

Escape—it is the basket
In which the Heart is caught

When down some awful Battlement
The rest of Life is dropt.
Emily Dickinson

From the Journal of Matthew Hawthorne

After that day in Africa, and the long night that followed, I didn't see the woman again for months. Didn't want to see her. I cherished each day that slipped by without seeing her face or hearing her name. Cherished time slipping away like sand sliding through fingers. Quickly, painlessly. That is why I had traveled to Africa in the first place—to deaden the pain. And my plan succeeded, at least for a while. The gruesome sights and brutal life on the Dark Continent deadened emotion, made it possible to forget that there had been a time when people didn't look away when they saw my face.

But on that day in Africa, Finnea Winslet jarred me back to life. Even months after that day and long night, her face still haunted my dreams.

I remember all too clearly pulling her out of the wreckage. Finding the worst of her wounds. Keeping her alive until the rescuers arrived in the thick, green jungle, who then swept her away before my own weakened body could react.

And I'm sure the feel of her in my arms will haunt me forever.

But one night, as quickly and unexpectedly as she had been taken from me on that fateful day, she stepped back into my life as if walking into my dreams. Sitting down in front of me at a formal dinner table in Boston, so beautiful and alive. Dressed in a decorously proper gown as if she had lived there her whole life. Without uttering so much as a word of explanation or greeting.

As if she had never seen me before on a train in Africa.

But I knew she recognized me. I saw it in the only part of her that remained wild. Her eyes.

Chapter Two

Boston

Leticia Winslet sat in a wingback chair across from Jeffrey Upton, vice president of Winslet Ironworks. His office was well appointed but small compared to the mostly unused office beside his that belonged to Leticia's son, Nester, president of the hugely successful iron foundry. But Leticia knew that Jeffrey had never been a man to quibble about petty issues. He didn't care about the size of his office; he cared only about the success of the company and his part in it.

Winslet Ironworks had been Jeffrey's sole concern since he began running the company twenty years earlier. The ideal person to run a family-owned business.

Jeffrey was a handsome man, with a full head of gray hair that made him look dashing rather than old. He was a widower with grown children well set in their lives.

It went without saying that Nester, who had been named president three years before, was the top man. But everyone, including Leticia, knew that Jeffrey Upton still ran Winslet Ironworks. And it was Jeffrey she turned to when she needed something—advice, an advance on her monthly allotment, or a discussion of any family concern she couldn't discuss with her son or even her own mother, Hannah Grable, who lived in the Winslet home.

Today the concern was the past. Her husband was dead now. A man she hadn't seen in more years than she cared to count. She thought of the one time William Winslet had returned, so different and changed. So African.

She shuddered at the memory, shuddered at how wild he

had become. How he had swept her into his arms and carried her up to their bedroom. His hands so boldly on her, stripping away her clothes, unwilling to turn down the lights. He had wanted to see her, he had whispered, his lips brushing against her skin. Her body tingled at the thought.

But she repressed it adamantly. Fiercely. She had wanted no part of Africa, and she had begged him to return home for good. They had no business in the wilds. They were blue-blooded Bostonians, for mercy's sake. Her own mother the matriarch of good society.

But William had refused, telling her if she didn't come with him then, he didn't want her back.

Finnea was the price she'd had to pay.

Finnea.

Suddenly home. A stranger.

Leticia glanced out the window at the reassuringly familiar streets of downtown Boston.

"I'm not sure I understand what the problem is," Jeffrey said from behind a desk that was too large for the room. But Nester had ordered it, found it not to his liking, then moved it into Jeffrey's office when it couldn't be returned. Nester had a new, perfectly sized desk just beyond the thick plaster wall.

With a minimum of ceremony, Jeffrey straightened paper and pens, secured the stopper in the bottle of ink, sat back, and said, "In the two months Finnea has been here, she has managed to recover her health nicely after that ghastly train wreck. What could possibly be the matter now?"

Leticia smoothed her flowing skirt of rich cashmere, refusing to meet his eye. "Well, she is . . . odd."

Jeffrey rested his chin on his steepled fingers. "What makes you say that?"

"If you must know, the minute she was able she sent the doctor away and requested all sorts of herbs and strange things. The house positively reeks of herbal packs and concoctions that she swears are medicinal."

"Do you doubt her?"

"Well, no. But every time I turn around she is drinking some strange tea, or draping her . . . her . . . person with awful-smelling poultices." Leticia sighed. "Though as you mentioned, she has made a remarkable recovery. But now that she has grown stronger, she has turned her attentions on the servants."

"In what way?"

"She is dispensing concoctions for toothaches and salves for cuts, teas for stomach upsets and tinctures for all manner of maladies as if she were just returning from medical school rather than the jungles of Africa." Leticia placed her gloved hands on either arm of the wooden ball-and-claw chair. "The servants have become absolutely devoted to her."

"What's wrong with that?"

Leticia looked him in the eye. "As my daughter, her place is in the drawing room, Jeffrey, not in the washroom tending the help."

Jeffrey tsked. "Give her time, Leticia. Let her have a chance to become accustomed to Boston and its ways. She has only just recovered."

"But we don't have time! Next Saturday is Bradford and Emmaline Hawthorne's dinner party. I've already sent word that we would attend." Her fingers curled tightly around the wooden arms. "Perhaps it's not too late to send our regrets after all."

"Nonsense. Just watch, Finnea will prove you wrong and be a picture of loveliness."

She worried her lip. "Well, I did manage to find a beautiful gown that will complement her bold coloring." Sighing again, she added, "Even after all this time convalescing in bed, she is still as dark as a native. Good Lord, it will take a box of rice powder to make her look half-decent."

"She has only a hint of gold left in her skin, Leticia. And once you put her in that dress with a touch of powder, I'm sure she will be lovely."

"I've noticed," she said, suddenly coy, "that you certainly have taken an interest in Finnea. Chocolates the other day? Flowers this morning?"

Jeffrey smiled, his spine relaxing against the leather. "I've come to a place in my life where I am thinking of remarrying."

Leticia gasped. "Marry? Finnea?"

"Why not? Older men marry younger women all the time."

His smile faltered and he leaned forward. "But not a word to Nester. At least not yet. I think he needs a bit more time to get used to her."

"I'm not certain Nester will ever get used to her."

Jeffrey shrugged. "Regardless, not a word yet. And you might think about a party yourself, in honor of Finnea's birthday. It's coming up, or have you forgotten?"

"I most certainly have not," she stated, incensed, though in truth she had. "In fact, I was thinking of a party just the other day."

They were interrupted when Nester's fiancée walked into the office. Before the young woman could utter a word, Leticia said, "Isn't that right, Penelope?"

Penelope Manser was a stunning woman with black lacquer hair, pale white skin, and doe-shaped blue eyes. "Isn't what right?"

"That just the other day I was talking about having a birthday party for Finnea," she said with a meaningful look at her soon-to-be daughter-in-law. "A gala," she added, suddenly inspired. She would not be considered lacking in her duty to her child. She put from her mind that she had been lacking where Finnea was concerned for the past nineteen years. She'd had to leave Africa, she told anyone who would listen. She'd had no choice. Nester had been ill. Certainly everyone understood that fact.

"Of course, Mother Lettie. A party for Finnea. It is going to be wonderful." Penelope's rosebud lips pulled into a lovely smile. "Are you ready to go? Nester has left the carriage, and Mother Hannah will be waiting for us."

"Grand. Come, dear," Leticia said, standing and taking Penelope's arm. "We must start making plans. I mean, continue making plans," she amended with a quick glance at Jeffrey. "It will be fabulous. Until then, we shall see you at the Hawthornes' next Saturday, Jeffrey."

Then she stopped at the door and turned back. "I hope you are right about the outcome of Finnea's entrée into society."

Finnea Winslet learned two things on her first night out in Boston Society—that the centuries-old New England town was farther away from Africa than mere geographic miles, and that there was a great deal more to familial ties than blood.

But neither of these infinitesimally complicated facets of her new life daunted her. The long, elegantly set dining table, however, gave her pause.

Finnea sat in the opulent dining room, among some of Boston's most important inhabitants, studying the line of cutlery that was laid out on the white linen tablecloth in descending order like stair steps marching down either side of her plate. Never had she seen so many knives, forks, and spoons on any given table, much less for a single place setting.

Outside, the city stood frozen. It had begun to snow, foreign to her, but beautiful in an eerie sort of way. The muffled quiet. The giant white snowflakes crystallizing on the windowpanes, dusting the streets and bushes like powdered sugar on a cake.

So different from Africa.

That was what she loved the most. Boston was so very different from her beloved Africa. Worlds apart. A lifetime away from belongings that had not yet arrived. Carved wooden toys and hand-sewn little dresses. A lifetime away from the memory of a tiny little voice as soft and sweet as butter candy.

Oh, Isabel, her mind cried. *Your mama misses you so.*

Her throat tightened and her eyes burned with emotion. But she shook memories away, concentrating on the newness of this strange city with its odd and baffling ways.

Like cutlery.

Relief washed over her as Africa faded from her mind and she focused on a fork. What exactly she was supposed to do with each piece of the glistening line of silverware only God and her hostess knew. Or so she assumed until she glanced down the long table and found that not a single other guest looked as dumbfounded as she felt. They all talked and smiled, clearly undeterred by the staggering array of eating utensils.

But then her gaze halted, as it had so many times that night, on Matthew Hawthorne. A rush of blood made her heart pound. He was strong and chiseled. Fierce and warriorlike just as she remembered him, just as she remembered the rock-hard strength of his body when she had fallen against him on the train.

Her breath grew shallow and her lips parted, followed quickly by the sting of red in her cheeks when she remembered those hours after the wreck.

"Don't you dare die on me!"

His words. Bold and demanding.

She pushed them away.

Finnea had wondered about him often, wondered what had happened to him after the rescuers arrived, carrying her out of the tangle of trees and vines. She could think about that— about the *after*. It was only those hours between the wreck and when the rescuers arrived, that dark space of time, that she couldn't think about without emotion threatening to overwhelm her.

Later in the thatch-roofed hospital, when consciousness had returned full force, she learned he had been there asking after her. She had left the hospital early the next morning without a word. She didn't want to see him. Couldn't see him because he made her remember. The jungle. That long night.

"Try, Finnea. Just try."

"Leave me alone," she moaned.

"Damn it, Finn, don't be such a coward. Let me help you."

She tried to turn away, seeking the soft confines of that dark, soothing place behind her eyelids. "Go away."

"I will not go away," he replied fiercely. *"You're going to fight."* His voice quieted and he pressed his forehead to hers for one brief moment, the sounds of the jungle surrounding them. *"You can't die on me, Finn. I won't allow it."*

"I hate you, you know that, don't you?" she bit out, but the need to drift away had been pushed back.

Matthew only smiled. "Yes, I know that. Now help me."

She had cried desperately when she boarded the ship for Boston, determined never to see him again—as if suddenly withdrawing from a potent drug.

But she was better now. Or so she had thought until she found him unexpectedly sitting across from her, his deep blue eyes taking her in, as if looking for scraps of a woman whose shape and texture he would recognize beneath the unfamiliar velvet gown and elaborate curls of her red hair.

Over the months she had begun to discount the effect he'd had on her. But she knew now she had been wrong. It was hard to understand the impact of this man unless a person saw him for herself. The startling perfection of his face—until he turned. The scar slicing through such beauty, as if the gods had been jealous of what they'd created and wanted to even the score.

She closed her eyes, attempting to close out that day and the long night that had followed. But she couldn't forget his face any more than she could forget how he had held her close, touching her.

"Finnea, don't hide from me."

His voice so caring. His hands gently capturing hers when she tried to cover herself as he pulled the blood-soaked material away from her skin.

She had turned her head away sharply, staring into the thick vines, feeling his hands.

"I'm so glad you could join us, Miss Winslet."

Finnea blinked Africa away, then looked up and found Mrs. Bradford Hawthorne smiling at her. Matthew's mother.

Not knowing that Matthew was from Boston, Finnea hadn't put them together until he had showed up at dinner, stilling her heart in her chest. Making her want to reach out to him, despite her need to forget she had ever seen him before.

Emmaline Hawthorne was a lovely woman, one of the few women Finnea had met in the short time she had been in America. Her husband, Bradford Hawthorne, was dark and forbidding. He reminded her of an African, a warrior—bold and direct, fierce. Not a man to cross lightly.

They lived in a spectacular house on Beacon Street in the part of town known as Beacon Hill, one of the oldest and finest addresses in all of Boston. With meandering streets lined with neat brick walkways that matched the redbrick facades of the prestigious row houses, Beacon Hill was very different from the newer section only blocks away where her mother lived. The Back Bay was made up of an orderly grid of streets where town houses were generally larger and didn't conform to the redbrick sameness of Beacon Hill.

"Thank you, Mrs. Hawthorne," Finnea replied. "You are kind to invite me."

She glanced across the table, candlelight reflecting in the long, flat knife blades of European silver. She looked at the woman who sat before her. Her own mother. A woman who seemed more distant to her now than she had when time and an ocean separated them. Finnea was mesmerized by skin as white as a fragile bowl of cream, fascinated by the ways of a woman that were so foreign to her.

Leticia Winslet chatted amiably, a winsome smile animating her face. She wore a shimmery gray satin gown, with a single strand of pearls around her neck. Elegant but understated, her grandmother had pointed out. Never screaming to be noticed, rather drawing people in with her whispered beauty.

Finnea glanced down at the fine-jeweled bracelet her mother had insisted she wear that evening.

"Your father gave this to me," Leticia had said as she gracefully fixed the bracelet on Finnea's wrist. "And tonight for your first evening out, I want you to wear it."

The gold was cool against her skin, warming to her touch. But a borrowed bracelet wasn't enough for her to feel close to her mother. Finnea glanced at the silvered mirror at the end of the dining room. She looked at her eyes, her face, to find some glimmer of proof in the reflection that indeed she bore some relation to the beautiful woman who sat across from her.

"So tell us, Miss Winslet, it must be a tremendous relief for you to be back in civilized society," stated a woman named Grace Baldwin.

The dinner party consisted of twelve people. The host and hostess. Finnea, Jeffrey Upton. Her mother, Nester, and his fiancée, along with several other people Finnea had never met. Grace Baldwin. Another woman named Adwina Raines. A flighty couple called Dumont. And of course, Matthew.

Finnea shifted her gaze and tried to make sense of the woman's question. Relief? Back in civilized society? She hadn't lived in Boston since she was six, and those early years were nothing more than a distant haze.

"Tell us, Miss Winslet," Adwina Raines began, one arched brow slightly raised, "where exactly did you live? With some tribe of sorts, I hear."

Mrs. Dumont gasped, peering closely at Finnea. "A tribe of savages?"

Finnea sat very still, unable to think, much less respond.

"Those heathens are carnivores, you know," Mrs. Dumont added in a breathless rush. "Flesh-eating savages."

"*We all* are carnivores, Mrs. Dumont. Each and every one of us at this table."

All heads turned to Matthew, his abrupt words rumbling through the room, surprising the occupants, since he hadn't spoken thus far. He had sat quietly all evening, a barely contained violence shimmering about him like a mist over the sea.

But Mrs. Dumont only sniffed and glanced meaningfully at his face with a brittle tilt of brow. "Speak for yourself, Mr. Hawthorne."

An embarrassed silence descended about the table. Matthew only stared, his spine rigid. Finnea suddenly remembered the Europeans hurrying from the second car. Could people truly run from a face that would be merely beautiful without the dignity of such a scar? Were these Americans no different?

"Miss Winslet," Mr. Dumont chimed in too brightly, breaking the quiet. "Please tell us about the beauty of Africa."

Before she could answer, Adwina Raines interrupted. "I hear there's no beauty about it, Mr. Dumont," she stated with a superior nod. "All wild jungles and heathens, as your own wife just pointed out. Naked heathens," she added with a knowing and impugning glance at Finnea.

Finnea began to simmer.

"Africa, I hear," Mr. Dumont stated, "is called the Dark Continent."

"The White Man's Grave."

Their tones were accusatory, and Finnea tried to think of words to defend her beloved land. But what they said was true. Africa was a dark, forbidding place, though beautiful beyond words. She knew instinctively that these people with their clothes up to their chins and servants to do their slightest bidding would not understand its unforgiving beauty.

"Yes, heathens the lot of them," Grace Baldwin breathed, her eyes growing wide with excitement. She glanced from side to side, blotted her lips delicately with her napkin, then leaned forward, her sapphire-and-diamond necklace catching the light from the chandelier. "I heard the Dutch heiress Alexine Tinne sailed up the Nile to some desolate place and attempted to cross the Sahara desert—"

"To hear it told," Adwina interjected yet again, pulling the attention back to her, "the fine woman's attempt was sabotaged by her native guides, who slashed off her hands and left her to die in the desert while they made off with her provisions and money."

The women blanched and even the men gasped.

"Proof," Adwina stated with a confirmatory nod, "that Africa is a land of barbarians."

"I would wager it was those cannibals who did her in," Mr. Dumont stated, leaning back in his chair, grasping his lapels importantly.

"No doubt," confirmed another.

"Is that true, Miss Winslet?" Grace asked, her voice a mix of disgust and fascination. "Do the heathen cannibals really eat people?"

"I don't know if it's true or not," Finnea said tightly, her head beginning to throb, "but I do know that their *manners* would no doubt keep them from discussing it at the dinner table."

This time it was the men who blanched and the women who gasped, outraged and embarrassed at the same time.

"You are so right," Emmaline Hawthorne interjected smoothly. "We *have* forgotten our manners."

Adwina harrumphed. Grace barely stifled her sigh of disappointment that she wasn't going to get a firsthand account of the sordid tale that had made its way around the globe.

Finnea was baffled by these people, not understanding the dictates they expressed, though seemed to forget when it suited them. It was like trying to learn the rules to a club of which she wasn't a member. Secret handshakes and unvoiced sentiments that everyone in society understood but her. It made Finnea's head spin.

But when she looked up, she caught sight of Matthew. He looked at her, his blue eyes boring into her, and somehow her thoughts calmed.

"We especially wanted our son to be here," Emmaline explained, "because he has recently returned from traveling in Africa."

Matthew's expression turned dangerous, and he reached for a tall-stemmed goblet filled with red wine. But somehow he stumbled, his hand banging into china and crystal, almost spilling the wine. The group looked on, startled.

His eyes flashed with sudden rage before he covered it by sitting back with a casual grace and self-deprecating smile. "My apologies for my clumsiness," he said, though he made no other move to reach for his glass. "You were saying, Mother?" he prompted, his face a study in calmness, unless someone looked very close.

Bradford looked at his son, his eyes filled with disdain. Emmaline appeared uncomfortable and worried.

"Well," his mother began, seeming to search for her train of thought. "We invited both you and Miss Winslet because we were certain you would have much to discuss."

"*Invited,* Mother?" Matthew's tone was clipped and wry. "As I recall, I wasn't given a choice."

Emmaline blanched, then forced a laugh. "We thought you might have traveled to some of the same places," she persevered awkwardly.

"Actually," he said, glancing across the table to meet Finnea's eye, "I met Miss Winslet in the Congo. On a train."

Finnea looked at him, her heart suddenly pounding.

"I have to touch you, Finnea."

"You've met?" Emmaline gasped, surprised. "Matthew, you didn't tell us you had already met Miss Winslet."

"There is nothing to tell," Finnea interjected quickly. Nothing but hours of frantic struggle. Hours of fighting to survive. Then hours longer as they waited through the night, hours of him holding her close and talking. Of her telling him her secrets. Of her telling him her dreams, the jungle and the trauma lending the night an intimacy she wished she could forget. No, she wasn't interested in sharing that. She wanted nothing to do with Africa any longer. Or Matthew Hawthorne.

Matthew raised a brow. She could read the sarcastic tilt as if it were a page in a book, and she turned away, thankful this time when Grace interrupted.

"Ah, look at this!" the woman exclaimed. "Turtle soup. How divine."

Stiffly uniformed footmen appeared at the table, their steps muffled by the thick Aubusson rug. They carried ornate tureens of soup, silver platters of bread, and dishes of herbed butters shaped like tiny shells. A footman came up to Finnea's side, and stopped abruptly, his whole body seeming to stiffen as he stood next to her.

Finnea glanced to her side, her eyes going wide. "Are you all right?"

Then silence, people startled and confused.

"Of course he is all right," Adwina stated with a twist of lips that was tight and condescending. "He is offering you soup."

Finnea felt her answering blush, a blush that grew worse when she saw her mother's flash of embarrassment. Mortified, Finnea turned to the footman and nodded.

Soon everyone was served and Finnea had no choice but to eat, though which of the slew of spoons she was supposed to use she had no idea. Not wanting to make another mistake, surreptitiously she tried to see what everyone else was using. But given the assortment of flowers and tall stemware dotting the table like trees in a forest, Finnea couldn't make out which spoon the others had picked up. Her only clear view was of Matthew in between three towering crystal goblets. But he wasn't eating at all.

With no help for it, hoping for the best, she made a choice. Choosing the closest to her hand, she picked it up and waited. Then she sighed her relief when no one said a word.

"Matthew had a wonderful time in his travels," his mother said, her tone soft and loving. "He brought back the most interesting gifts." She sighed unexpectedly, her eyes clouding in sudden memory. "I remember a silvered mirror Matthew brought me from Venice years ago. I still have it. Do you remember that, Matth—"

As soon as she looked up at him, her words cut off and her gaze grew startled, as if both surprised and devastated by the sight of her son.

Finnea knew in that second that she had been right on the train: He hadn't always been so fierce, or so scarred.

What had happened to him? she wondered. What had changed his life so drastically?

No one spoke. They watched as the careless disregard that had marked Matthew's face all night long evaporated into the candlelit night. Finnea wanted to weep for this man when he looked at his mother with grim devastation of his own.

But after a moment passed, it was her own mother who broke the awkward silence. "I hope everyone here has received their invitations to the gala ball we are having to honor Finnea's birthday."

Penelope sat forward, excited. "It's going to be a grand affair. Mother Lettie and I have been making the most wonderful arrangements."

Mother Lettie.

As if Nester's fiancée were the daughter instead of Finnea.

Leticia toyed with her pearls, then glanced at Jeffrey with a meaningful smile. "We are hoping Finnea will have some joyous news to announce at the ball."

Finnea's head shot up. *Joyous news?*

Jeffrey reached over and discreetly squeezed Finnea's hand beneath the table, and she understood very suddenly what she should have understood earlier when he had placed a possessive hand against her back as he led her to the dining room. From the minute she had met him he had shown her nothing but kindness and consideration. He had made her feel cared for and welcomed. And now she realized that he was going to ask her to marry him.

Hot embarrassment shot through her when she glanced up to find Matthew pinning her with a penetrating gaze, and she looked away.

Nester straightened in his seat. "What news? I haven't heard a thing about any news."

"Now, dear," Leticia said, her voice cajoling. "I can't say. It would ruin the surprise."

"I think I have a right to know, Mother."

"Nester, please." She gave him a pointed look, tempered with a smile.

Soon the soup bowls were cleared from the table. Thankfully, this time when the footmen appeared Finnea wasn't expected to do anything. A plate was simply set before her. A large plate covered with food. Though the only things she recognized were the gossamer-thin petals of a nasturtium.

But at least she recognized that. With a silent sigh of relief that there was something she knew what to do with, she picked up the long green stem of the umbrella-shaped flower and bit off the top.

It wasn't until she glanced up, one betraying petal stuck to her lip, the stem still held in her hand, that she realized everyone, including the statuelike footmen, had stopped to stare at her, their mouths agape.

Adwina's hard brown eyes cemented with knowing disdain.

With a silent groan, Finnea wondered what she had done this time.

Moments passed before she noticed that not a single other person there had touched the flower and she understood her mistake. Americans, apparently, didn't eat nasturtiums.

Her mother's slightly rouged lips rounded with humiliation; her brother groaned. Emmaline stammered.

But it was Matthew who spoke.

"The nasturtiums are a special surprise, Miss Winslet," he said, his voice low and deep, commanding. "I told my mother they are a delicacy in Africa, and she served them in your honor. Isn't that right, Mother?"

"Ah, yes, dear," Emmaline said, her pale gray eyes flashing with quick understanding.

Matthew looked at Finnea, his eyes intense. She didn't know what to make of his actions, and her embarrassment grew. She wanted to leap up and run from the room. But then, with his gaze never wavering from hers, he picked up the flower from his own plate and bit off the petals.

Finnea's eyes suddenly burned as she watched this man, such a contradiction. One minute fierce, the next so caring. Just as he had been in Africa.

She forced herself to finish chewing. And after a moment, Emmaline picked up her own nasturtium, eyeing it dubiously. "I hope they are as good as what you enjoy in Africa, Miss Winslet. I've been looking forward to trying them myself." And she did, chewing carefully and swallowing.

One by one, the guests murmured doubtfully but followed suit—every guest but Adwina Raines. She sat in her chair with a suspicious scowl.

"Eat!" Matthew bellowed, his fist crashing against the table, silverware clattering against china and wood.

A startled moment passed before Adwina picked up the stem and bit off the top.

Matthew focused on his plate, but after that he seemed to understand Finnea's dilemma. After each new course was set before her, with barely held patience, he very discreetly, though emphatically, showed her which utensil to use.

There were forks for salad and forks for meat. There were knives for cheese and spoons for coffee until all fourteen pieces of silver were gone and Finnea felt she would burst from so much food. But at the end, she felt proud. She hadn't made a single other mistake the rest of the evening.

At least she hadn't until the guests began to depart, and she noticed that the bracelet her mother had given her to wear was missing. She glanced back toward the dining room. But just then Grace Baldwin extended her hand to shake in polite farewell.

Without thinking, Finnea extended her own, placing her left hand under her armpit, as was her custom.

First Grace's then Adwina's eyes went wide. Her mother groaned. And the pudgy, old Mr. Baldwin couldn't seem to help himself. He laughed out loud.

Finnea forgot about the bracelet as she realized it was her hand in her armpit that was causing the consternation.

Nester made a harsh, frustrated sound, then snatched his coat from the footmen and bid a tight good evening.

Shaking her head, Finnea dropped her hand and forced a smile, hating the sudden threat of tears that burned in her eyes.

Chapter Three

"I think it's time you remarry."

The words stopped Matthew cold in his tracks.

It was the next day, Sunday, and he was exhausted. The dinner party last night had taken its toll. It was getting harder and harder to hide the fact that the injuries that were only hinted at by the scar on his face were getting worse, not better.

He stood in his parents' foyer, having just arrived from his town house on Marlborough Street. At the sound of his mother's voice he looked up to see her standing at the top of the stairs. Her hand rested on the mahogany banister that stretched out atop white spindles that looked like soldiers lined up in a row.

Hawthorne House was what most prominent Bostonians considered an exemplary home. Large, but not too large, as some Back Bay residences tended to be, and built by Charles Bulfinch in the early part of the century.

The rooms were exquisitely detailed with fine woods and oriental carpets. Elegant and refined, but never ostentatious. Porcelain Ming vases stood on high pedestals. Priceless paintings lined the walls. One could spend money on art. That was an investment. But gold-gilt crown moldings or marble balustrades were an extravagant waste of a man's good, Puritan money. Or so his father had always said.

Matthew waited, silently, not trusting himself to speak. His head pounded, his arm and shoulder ached, making it difficult to think. Anyone who looked at him could see the scar on his face. But no one except the doctors had seen the scars on his shoulder and forearm, left from the accident that made him a widower a year and a half ago.

Sometimes in the night he found it hard to believe how much his life had changed.

"I've made you uncomfortable," Emmaline said, descending the stairs with regal grace and a desperately loving smile.

When she stood before him, she placed a hand on his wrist. Pain shot up through his arm to his head. It took every ounce of his control not to suck in his breath.

He thought of the doctors. The looks on their faces, the concern in their eyes. But Matthew was never quite sure how much of their concern was about his condition and how much was due to the fact that they had to tell one of the wealthiest, and once one of the most powerful, men in Boston that he wasn't getting better, as they had assured him he would.

When they first voiced their concerns, Matthew had refused to believe. But he was finding it took more and more strict concentration to make his wounded arm work properly. The arm was growing weaker, and just like last night, if he didn't focus, he fumbled around like a schoolboy. But if he did pay careful attention to each task, he moved through life with a large degree of normalcy, making it possible to hide his growing weakness from his family.

"Oh, Matthew, I just hate to see you so unhappy." Emmaline hesitated, then added, "And marriage would do you a world of good."

"I will never remarry, Mother," he said, his frustrations seeping through, his normally ironclad control strained.

"Stop living in the past!" she suddenly cried. "Kimberly is gone. You have to accept that!"

His throat worked as he thought of his wife. They had been married seven years earlier. He had known from the minute he saw her that she would be his wife. Now she was dead, he was scarred, and he would never marry again.

"I think Finnea Winslet would make a wonderful wife."

She had caught him off guard with her talk of marriage, but this stunned him. "Marry Finnea Winslet? That's crazy!" And it was. He hardly liked her, much less wanted to marry her. Or so he told himself over the sudden rush of sound through his head.

Emmaline's face was riddled with uncertainty. "I don't know. It was just a thought that came to me last night at the party."

"I can't imagine why. Finnea and I hardly spoke."

"I noticed, as no doubt everyone else did." She sighed. "Even though your behavior makes it easy to forget, I still remember a day when you made everyone around you smile. Gracious, you had all of Boston dancing attendance on you. Women followed you with simpering looks, and men courted your favor. Everyone you knew, and many you didn't, adored you." She looked him straight in the eye. "Now you slam your fist down on the table to deal with those very same people."

He bit back embarrassment over the truth of his mother's words. Futile embarrassment. Just as wishing life hadn't changed was futile.

Showing none of the turmoil he felt, he crossed his arms on his chest and leaned back against a Roman column. "You mean I wasn't charming last night?" he asked, teasing, as he once did so often and so well.

"No you were not, as well you know," Emmaline snapped. "Act as you want; that's your right. But the least you could have done was be civil to Miss Winslet."

He came away from the column in a flash. His pain was pushed aside by a sudden, intense fury—a fury he had never known until his life had changed so drastically, a fury that was now never far away.

"Civil? I was more than civil." He had saved her ungrateful life in the jungle, then led her through the intricacies of dinner etiquette like a guide leading the blind.

"You may have saved her from that embarrassing flower debacle," his mother continued, "but boorishly ignoring her the rest of the evening hardly constitutes civil behavior."

"If you believe I was so terrible to her, then why in the world would you suggest marriage in the first place?"

"Because Finnea Winslet is the first person I've seen who pulled you out from under that steely facade you have built around yourself." Her gently lined face softened. "You've locked yourself away, Matthew. But for one fleeting moment last night when she walked in, life filled your eyes."

His heart hammered in his chest as the sudden glimpse

of naked white skin flashed through his mind. And blood. Everywhere.

"She's such a nice woman, Matthew. I liked her instantly."

Ripping his outer shirt. Pressing piece after piece to the jagged wound in the soft flesh of her inner thigh. But the blood hadn't stopped, seeping into the material, staining it red. Again and again, white turned to red until his shirt was completely spent. Working ceaselessly. The powerless feeling of her growing weak in his arms. Life draining away. Frigid, aching cold seeping into his soul when he knew she was giving up.

"I think she would be good for you, son."

"No!" The word exploded, echoing against the silk-lined walls and twenty-foot-high ceilings.

He blinked and sucked in his breath, the sound of his heartbeat rushing through his ears as he looked at his mother's startled expression.

"You're wrong, Mother," he managed to say, forcing his mind back to the present. "I don't want a wife, nor do I need one."

"But what about your daughter!" Emmaline demanded, anger flaring in her eyes.

Matthew flinched, jerking away to look out the long windows that lined the front door, the simple movement making his head swim. *Mary.* His precious six-year-old daughter. She was the only reason he had come back from Africa at all. But his homecoming hadn't gone as he had hoped.

"Mary has you and Father to love her," he answered.

"She needs *you* to love her."

"I do love her!" The words were torn out of him. "God, I do," he whispered. "But she needs a woman to guide her. And I can't do that."

"But a wife could."

He met her gaze and very slowly said, "I am telling you for the last time, I will never remarry. Not Finnea Winslet, not some other woman you get it in your head would make me a good wife. I was married once. I will not marry again." He searched for control. "Is that why you sent for me?"

After a long moment, she sighed. "Actually, no. I wanted

you to return this bracelet." She hesitated uncertainly. "It's the one Miss Winslet wore last night."

He prayed for patience. "Isn't that convenient."

"Now, Matthew. I just want you to return the bracelet so they won't worry about its whereabouts any longer. I had a note this morning."

Matthew could imagine the note, just as he could imagine Finnea wanting to make up some reason for seeing him.

"Will you do that for me?" she asked.

"Fine, I'll return it. Then I'll leave. That's it."

"Fair enough."

He glanced toward the study. "Is Father here?"

Emmaline looked at her son for several moments and said, "No, he's out."

"Tell him I was here and wanted to know if he would like to meet me for lunch on Friday. At Locke-Ober's." His voice quieted. "Just as we used to."

Emmaline pressed her eyes closed for a fleeting second, then seemed to pull herself up. "I know he plans to travel out to Worcester next Friday to look at some property."

"Then the following Friday."

She nodded her head. "All right. I'll tell him. I'm sure he'll send word when he returns this afternoon."

"Thank you."

"Here's the bracelet."

He sliced her a grim look, took the piece of jewelry, and slipped it into his pocket. Leaning down, he brushed a quick kiss on her cheek.

"I will expect you tonight for Sunday dinner," she added.

He made a noncommittal sound, then turned to depart.

"Aren't you at least going to say hello to Mary before you leave?"

Matthew stiffened. He didn't want to see Mary, he told himself firmly. But a pang of yearning wrenched his heart. He cursed himself for a fool. He knew what would happen, but still he couldn't bring himself to walk out that door without at least trying. Maybe this time would be different.

"She's in her room."

Carefully he took the wide curving staircase that led to the upper regions of the house. Walking down the long, spacious hall, he passed his brothers' childhood rooms, nearly stopping when he came to his own. But he forced himself to continue on, down two more doors, where he knocked.

"Come in."

Sweet and gentle Mary.

His heart surged as he turned the knob and found her sitting in the window seat. Lace curtains framed her tiny little-girl's body, making her look like a cherished princess. Her dress was full and ruffled, as she liked, her hair curled and pinned back. She had white-blond hair and huge blue eyes. A beauty already. For a moment he forgot the past, forgot that everything had changed, and he started toward her.

But when she turned and saw him, her sweet angel's face tensed, first with surprise, then with fear. He stopped dead in his tracks. She hadn't been able to look at him without crying since the accident.

His heart plunged and naked despair snaked through him. But he blocked it out. "Hello, Mary," he said softly, his voice steady by sheer force of will. He turned his face just so, in a way that minimized the sight of his scar.

But it did little good. The look in her eyes grew distant, and she started to hum, quietly, with determination, stroking her doll as if soothing it. He wanted to cross the room and pull her into his arms. He wanted to bury his face in her soft shoulder, hold her close, tell her everything was going to be all right.

But everything wasn't going to be all right. He couldn't erase the scar. And as weak as he was today, he doubted he could even hold her close.

His heart turned to stone, and it was all he could do to contain himself. He held on by a thread, focusing as he left, shutting the door with a barely controlled violence. At the bottom of the stairs he stopped in front of his mother. "One of these days you're going to accept that I do more harm than good."

He slammed out of the house, white dots dancing before his eyes when he hurtled into his carriage. He jerked up the reins, taking to the streets as if he were back in Africa, heedless of the mammoth dray wagons carrying their heavy loads. He threaded in and out of traffic, snowflakes the size of silver dollars catching in his hair. He barely missed light posts and granite curbs as the wheels of the two-seater skidded, then caught, then skidded again, slipping along over the cobblestone street as he turned left off Beacon Street onto Arlington toward the Winslet home on Commonwealth Avenue.

Rage and despair ticked like a clock inside him. He moved on the seat, and the bracelet bit into his leg.

Finnea.

His heart beat oddly at the thought of her—this strange woman who had come into his life so unexpectedly, twice now. He wanted to see her. Just look, as if by doing so it would give him some clue as to why unwanted thoughts of her circled in his mind.

But he tamped down the desire. He knew he was being set up.

He could just imagine Finnea firing off a note with some trumped-up excuse to see him. Then his mother had insisted he personally return the bracelet to her. Of course Emmaline had said the Winslets and not specifically Finnea, but Matthew was wise to his mother. First she had demanded he attend the party; now she insisted he return the bracelet after receiving a note.

Finnea wanted to see him, and his mother was making it happen.

Well, he had news for both of them. He had not been amused when Finnea walked into his parents' house last night and allowed herself to be introduced to him without so much as a blink of recognition. And now this blasted bracelet. He was not a man to play coy games, as Finnea Winslet was about to learn.

Marry Finnea.

A flash of unexpected desire swept through him. He cursed into the wind and wrote the desire up to rage. He would never remarry. He would make that clear to his mother and to Finnea Winslet.

Matthew entered the Winslet home. The house was new by Boston standards, no more than thirty to forty years old. It was ostentatious as well. Imported marble floors in the central hall, receiving rooms on either side with plush upholstered furniture and extravagantly draped windows. Fluted door casings and crenellated, gold-gilt crown moldings. A marble staircase ascending to the upper floors, and a lavish crystal chandelier to highlight it all.

After seeing Finnea last night, Matthew had learned that her mother and brother lived off the income of Winslet Iron Works, as did Finnea. The company was a prosperous family concern with shares controlled equally by Nester and a board of directors in trust for Finnea.

But it wasn't income or trusts that he was thinking of when he entered. It was the smell. A curiously pervasive odor that filled the house that he couldn't quite name. Like the outdoors, or a garden. Or cooking, perhaps, with ingredients not normally used in Boston.

Matthew was shown into the east receiving room on the right. But before the butler had a chance to announce him, Finnea dashed into the room.

As always, she had the infuriating ability to take his breath away. She was all dazzle and shimmer, movement and light. She was dressed in a perfectly proper gown, but even the most expensive silks couldn't quite hide the wildness about her.

He forgot about his aching shoulder. He forgot about his frustration as he felt an insane desire to dip his head to her lips and taste her.

But he stopped himself short. He was not interested in Finnea Winslet.

He cocked a brow and studied her. "I see you were expecting me," he drawled insolently.

His words brought her up short, and she whirled to face him, her eyes widening as if she were surprised.

"A nice touch, I have to admit," he stated. "You look quite fetching standing there acting as though you have no idea why I'm here."

"Why *are* you here?"

His eyes narrowed with impatience. "Enough of your games, Miss Winslet. I'm here because you sent word."

"I did?"

A fissure of doubt crept in, but his jaw tightened against it. "Stop playacting. I've brought your bracelet. Now, why did you really want to see me?"

The sudden sound of heels clicking on marble echoed in the high-ceilinged foyer.

"Who are you talking to, Finnea?"

Leticia's voice echoed much like her heels as she came to the receiving room. Nester and Hannah followed in her wake.

"Mr. Hawthorne," Leticia called out in an excited rush. "Your mother is so kind to respond to my note so quickly. Did she find the bracelet?"

Matthew watched Finnea, who stood to the side, an unrelenting glimmer suddenly sparking in her eyes, one graceful brow raised in challenge.

He cleared his throat. "Ah, yes, Mrs. Winslet, she did." He extended the jewelry in a stiff, clipped movement that had little to do with pain and everything to do with the fact that he didn't like the smug look on Finnea's face.

"Where did you find it?" Nester asked, his voice scathing. "In the soup tureen?"

"Nester, please," Leticia admonished.

Matthew saw the teasing gaiety in Finnea's face grow brittle. But he was surprised when she seemed to swallow back one of the sharp retorts he had become well acquainted with on the train, and merely smiled.

"Again, thank you, Mr. Hawthorne," Leticia said. "We were just about to have luncheon." The woman's body tensed, and Matthew knew she felt the need to invite him to join them but didn't want to. "Would you care to stay?" she offered belatedly.

"No, but thank you."

Nester shook his head. "He doesn't want to stay because the whole house smells to high heaven from all the tinctures and concoctions Finnea has been making to heal anyone and everyone who comes within a mile of her. Before we know it, she'll hang a sign out front to advertise. If I had somewhere else to go, I would. In fact, I think I'll have luncheon downtown on my way to the office."

Moments later he strode from the room, his mother and grandmother following.

Matthew turned back to Finnea. "You're a healer?" he asked, an odd pounding flaring in his head.

Clearly distracted, she shook her head. "Not really. I simply learned a bit about herbs from Janji." She looked at him. "Janji is the healer."

"Ah," he said as the pounding ceased. "Well, I suspect I owe you an apology for the . . . misunderstanding."

"Misunderstanding?" The mischievous gleam returned. "I'd say you didn't misunderstand; you out-and-out jumped to the wrong conclusion."

A slight smile tugged at his lips and he stepped closer. "Perhaps."

She was like a flame, drawing him in. Her form was slender but curved. His hands itched to trail across her body to cup her breasts, full and rounded; to brush against the rosebud nipples to bring them to taut peaks beneath her proper gown.

In that second, he gave up trying to understand why he wanted her. He only knew that he did.

"Jumping to wrong conclusions appears to be a habit of yours." Her expression was impish. "As I recall, you did the same thing on the train."

But at the mention of that day, her lips straightened into a bloodless line and she looked away.

Thoughts of kissing her fled. "So you still don't want to talk about the train."

"There's nothing to talk about," she answered, her chin rising as she busied herself brushing nonexistent wrinkles from her gown.

"So you said last night."

A stillness came over her as she drew a deep breath. She gave one final dash to the soft cashmere, sighed, and looked him in the eye. "Oh, all right, if you must have it. You saved my life. I'm indebted to you. I can never repay you, but I suspect I'll have to try. There, do you feel better now?"

He stepped back sharply, his reaction swift and angry. "I don't want payment." He wanted her out of his thoughts, out of his life. "That wasn't what I meant. I was simply inquiring after your well-being."

"I'm fine. Perfectly fine." She moved her leg around in proof. "See?" Then she met his gaze. "And I *will* repay you, somehow. Just like you said about yourself in Africa, I repay my debts, too."

He wished he had never brought her the bracelet. "Forget it," he said tightly.

Finnea pressed her eyes closed. "If only I could," she whispered, surprising him with the despair he sensed as much as recognized.

"Could what?"

She didn't answer at first. "Nothing. I just wonder if I'll ever get used to it here," she equivocated as she walked to the window and looked out. "Buildings everywhere. People racing about. Carriages hurtling through the crowded lanes. And not a goat roaming the streets, or a chicken in a yard. It is all so strange." She paused. "But intriguing," she added with an unexpected laugh.

It had been that way last night at dinner as well. One minute she was filled with delight over some new discovery. The next, she looked like a doe, startled by the dazzling lights around her.

And if she was unsettled by Boston and its inhabitants, there was no doubt that Bostonians were equally unsettled by her. If he hadn't already been indoctrinated by the custom in some parts of Africa of placing a hand under one's armpit when shaking hands, he would have been shocked as well.

But it went beyond mere differences in customs. People were intrigued by her, or rather, people watched her like passersby watch a terrible accident. They didn't want to see but couldn't look away. And in truth, Matthew understood. Her boldness had surprised him in Africa, but seeing her here, in Boston, made her seem even wilder—standing out so sharply in contrast to the restrained ways of this puritanical town.

"I'm intrigued, but that isn't enough," she said quietly. "I don't fit in here, and I'm afraid I never will. I don't know how to learn what is expected of me."

She swayed from side to side and did some sort of dip that he could only guess was supposed to be a curtsy. Practicing. Trying to learn. Beneath her sheen of wildness there was a raw, stunned quality about her, as if she were trying hard to be strong but not quite succeeding.

He hated to see her like this, and before he knew what he was doing, he said, "That's not true." The words amazed him, but he couldn't seem to stop himself. "Of course you can fit in."

She didn't look convinced, and why should she, he thought grimly. Based on what little he had seen of her behavior, he stood a better chance of becoming a proper lady than she did.

But his tongue and his brain seemed to be out of touch. "If you want to be a lady," he told her firmly, "you can."

She bit her lower lip. "Are you sure?"

"Of course I'm sure." He nearly choked on the lie, but then she smiled up at him with such innocence and purity and a desperate desire not to give up hope that he found himself adding, "You can learn everything you need to know."

"Oh, Mr. Hawthorne," she cried out with joy, "I take back every unkind thing I ever thought about you!"

His brow furrowed indignantly.

But she only laughed. "Thank you, thank you! And thank you for returning the bracelet. Now I must go. I have a million things to do."

She flew out of the room much as she had entered, in a whirl of skirts. Matthew was left alone in the receiving room with a wry grin and a shake of his head.

He left the house, taking the three steps down to the walkway before he stopped beside his carriage, which waited at the curb. He turned his face into the winter sun as it broke through the pewter-gray sky. It was at moments like this that he felt almost normal again—the past pushed back.

A smile broke out on his face. She did that to him. Despite his determination to put her from his mind, Finnea Winslet had the uncanny ability to make him smile. And he couldn't imagine why. She wasn't a beauty by Boston standards. She was too vibrant for that, her hair too red, her manners too bold.

But somehow she made him forget about the ache in his

shoulder and the stabbing pain in his head. All he could think about when he saw her was the sheer mesmerizing force of her eyes when she made—no, forced her way through every encounter like a wave crashing onto the sand.

He shook his head and chuckled, then started to turn. But he was caught off guard when a rock hit him in the head. Pain flashed white in his eyes, blinding him, and he staggered back. Through the fog in his mind he saw two young boys hiding behind a bush just beyond the walk.

"You touch him," one hissed.

"No, *you* touch him!"

"Baby!"

"I am not a baby," the second boy cried.

"Then touch him!" the other taunted.

"Not on your life! He's a monster!"

Unsteady, Matthew stood like stone as a wave of icy humiliation raced through him. He forced himself to breathe, the boys' bickering and taunts a backdrop to the returning hardness in his heart. He tried to block them out, telling himself he didn't care. But another rock hit him, and the scar that ran down his arm beneath his shirt and coat turned to fire, making his head spin.

He fell back against the carriage, his horse tossing its head when its guide reins jerked. Matthew counted. He breathed. He had to get home before someone saw him like this. But when he tried to straighten, a wave of stomach-churning heat washed through him and sweat sprang out on his forehead.

Breathe, damn it, breathe, he told himself.

He concentrated, aware of nothing other than steadying his mind, and he didn't hear the boys whispering. It wasn't until he felt another rock pelt him in the back that he whipped around with a roar of frustration and pain.

The boys were right behind him. Their eyes went wide with fright, and they screeched, knocking each other over in their haste to be gone.

Two women, dressed in elegant winter day gowns and heavy capes, must have heard the boys' bellows and hurried toward them from around the corner, their eyes wide with fear. At the sight of their terrified sons and of Matthew standing there like a wild man, they gasped and grabbed the boys' hands, racing away as fast as they could go.

Matthew's mind reeled. Humiliation snaked through his pain. He had known both of the mothers for a lifetime. Nan Penhurst and Corrine Adams were women he had danced and laughed with for more years than he could count. Their boys were friends of his daughter's. Now he scared them away.

He started to shake. Breathing deeply, he threw himself into the carriage, steadying himself on the plush leather seat. His entire body burned, pressing in on him. The glimpse of sun was gone, the sky closing up. The wind gusted, ringing in his ears. He turned the horse by sheer instinct toward his house on Marlborough Street, barely noticing the people who hurried out of his way—barely noticing the tiny little girl wrapped tightly in a coat and hat who stared at him in shock.

He sped along with no thought for traffic, ignoring the shouts and curses when he cut in front of careening dray wagons.

Mere blocks seemed like miles, but finally he crashed through the front door.

His butler rushed forward. "Mr. Hawthorne!"

At the sight of his employer, the man gasped. "Dear God, let me get the doctor!"

With a ravaged remnant of strength, Matthew grabbed Quincy by the lapels. "Tell no one," he commanded through the blinding pain. "I'll be fine; do you understand?"

"Yes, yes, sir," the man stammered.

Matthew spun away, then jerked into his study, slamming the door shut and locking it. When he turned back, his head spun and he fell, catching himself against a burled-wood credenza, sending decanters of hundred-year-old brandy and finely wrought crystal goblets flying before he collapsed on the floor.

Chapter Four

Mary Hawthorne stood on Commonwealth Avenue, watching, stunned, long after her father's carriage had careened out of sight. Thankfully he hadn't seen her. No doubt he hadn't recognized her because of her big-girl double-breasted cheviot sailor's coat with painted buttons shaped like boats that floated across the front. But not even her favorite coat could make the fear she felt at the sight of her father go away.

Cold surrounded her, but she hardly noticed. She had walked the whole way there, as she did whenever she could slip away unnoticed from her grandmother's house. Her old house was only a few doors down the street. But suddenly she didn't want to go to her old house. She wanted her grandmother to wrap her in her arms and hold her close.

Fighting back tears, Mary whirled around and headed in the opposite direction.

"I will not cry," she whispered desperately with each step she took, dashing her tiny, gloved hands across her cheeks.

She hurried down the street before anyone noticed her. She had become quite good at slipping away from adults ever since her life had changed.

She didn't understand how her world had been turned upside down, or why. Her grandmother had explained that her mother was sitting with God and angels, and wouldn't return. Mary knew that her mother would be pleased to be visiting such important people. But she was angry that her mother had left her behind.

And her father. Her throat tightened at the thought of this new man. He had left, gone as suddenly and as unexpectedly as her mother. But he had returned, a scar on his face. And his body. No one knew that she had seen his arm with its spider-web of cuts. No one knew that she had seen how he couldn't move quickly anymore, no longer able to sweep her up into the air for big hugs and kisses. Or how he couldn't catch her when she ran away.

Nor did anyone know that she had heard the whispers about the scandal. But she wasn't even sure exactly what that meant. She only knew that everything had changed.

Not willing to take any chances that her father might come back and see her, Mary didn't slow down until she was well along the granite walkway. But she hadn't gotten farther than a few houses when she saw some of the children she had played with her whole life gathered on the front steps of Thaddeus Penhurst's house.

Stopping dead in her tracks, she tried to dart across the street without being noticed. Since her mother had gone to heaven and her father to Africa, none of the other kids liked her anymore. But she had gone to live with her grandparents on Beacon Hill and it hadn't mattered. And every time she had come to her old house before, she had managed to avoid them.

"Look! There's Mary!"

Mary kept walking down Commonwealth Avenue toward the Public Gardens, pretending she didn't hear. But in a few short seconds, the children raced up to her.

"What are you doing back here, Mary?" little Harry Adams demanded, his voice muffled beneath a thick scarf.

"We thought you were gone for good!"

Seven-year-old Thaddeus laughed harshly, his woolen hat sitting at a jaunty angle over sandy blond hair and a face full of freckles. "Do you want to hear the poem we made up for you while you were gone, Mary?"

She continued on, nearly slipping on a patch of ice, keeping her eyes determinedly focused straight ahead.

"Sure she does," another stated.

But Mary didn't stop.

Surrounding her as she walked, they began to chant. "Mary, Mary, monster Mary, where did your father go?"

The children repeated the words over and over, their chime of voices echoing against the snow- and ice–covered street.

Mary's lips started to tremble, and it was all she could do not to slap her hands to her ears. Instead, she started to run, never stopping until she skidded through the tall wrought-iron gates of the Public Gardens, the children thankfully left behind.

She fell back onto a bench, wanting her mother, wanting her father—wanting her old life back.

Closing her eyes, she felt the bench slats bite against her spine as she willed herself to be stronger. But when she opened them again, she saw a mother and her daughter hurrying through the park, their hands clasped together. The tears she had fought back slipped down her winter-reddened cheeks.

"Oh, Mama," she whispered, "why did you leave me?"

Chapter Five

It was the pounding on the door that woke him.

With a hoarse groan, Matthew moved his head experimentally. He felt as if he had been run over by one of those dray wagons.

Bleary-eyed and weak, he pushed up into a sitting position on the divan. White light flashed in his head from the movement. He barely remembered collapsing on the floor, didn't remember at all having moved to the divan.

His breathing was shallow but steady as he looked around the room, taking in the upended furniture, the shards of broken glass, and the smell of liquor that overpowered the space like an unwelcome guest.

The pounding came again, making him flinch at the noise. Someone was there. He could just make out the heated exchange that was taking place beyond the study walls.

"Damn it, Quincy. Step away from that door."

"But sir! Mr. Hawthorne doesn't want to be disturbed."

"First you tell me he isn't here, and now you tell me he is unavailable. What is going on here?"

The thick velvet draperies were pulled nearly closed, only a sliver of the world outside showing through. Matthew had no idea how much time had passed since he staggered home and holed up in the study. And based on the voices just beyond the door, he thought to hole up a little longer.

But he knew who was there, and knew as well that his older brother would not be turned away. Too bad it wasn't his younger brother who had arrived. No doubt Lucas would be more understanding of the disarray Matthew found around him. As the black sheep of the family, Lucas had been in more than his share of predicaments over the years.

Matthew fumbled with a damnably tiny knob on the lamp next to the divan, then stood and straightened his rumpled coat and tie as best he could. With no help for it, he unlocked and opened the door. As soon as he appeared, silence descended in the foyer.

"Good afternoon, Grayson," he said pleasantly, as if nothing were amiss.

But no one was convinced, least of all his brother.

Matthew bit back a curse when he saw shock crease his brother's face. Grayson had spent a lifetime acting more as father to Matthew and Lucas than as brother. He took his responsibilities to his family seriously in an attempt, Matthew was sure, to please their father.

It had always been that way—Grayson seeking their father's approval but never seeming to get it, Matthew having it without even trying, and Lucas tossing it back in Bradford Hawthorne's face so often, and with such relish, that he had ultimately lost it forever.

"Interestingly enough," Grayson said with a slant of dark brow, his shock now contained behind an implacable mask, "it's morning, not afternoon, but who am I to quibble about details."

Unlike Matthew, Grayson had hair as dark as midnight. The tall, forbidding older Hawthorne glanced around the room, no doubt noticing the tumult. "I take it good help is hard to find these days." He glanced back at Matthew, taking in his appearance. "It also must be hard to find a good bath and a shave. No wonder you missed Sunday dinner."

Sunday dinner? He had missed Sunday dinner?

Matthew's head spun. What day was it?

Just beyond the multipaned window, he could make out snow drifting down from the cloud-laden sky.

A whisper of something teased at the back of his mind. He thought about what the doctor had told him. *We would assume the weakness in your hand and shoulder was due to the wounds. However, accompanied by the insistent pain and oc-*

casional slurred speech and blindness, we are forced to con-sider other problems."

The man had been reluctant to expand, but in the end he had said if the pain did not recede as was expected, perhaps the pain was due to a progressive degeneration of nerves and tissue.

"If it is this deterioration, as you say," he had asked care-fully, "what do you do?"

The man had grown truly uncomfortable then. "Let's cross that road if we come to it."

"Let's not," Matthew had replied through gritted teeth. "Tell me."

Long, painful moments had ticked by. "There is nothing we can do for you if that is the case." The doctor looked at him closely. "But let's not think about that now. Let us monitor your progress."

Matthew understood his progress. None.

"Are you all right, Matthew?"

Matthew dragged his attention back to find Grayson study-ing him.

"I'm perfectly fine," he said with more force than was nec-essary, clenching his hand at his side. But he couldn't seem to stop the anger, or was it fear? His family couldn't know what was happening to him. No one could know. There had already been too much heartache and scandal. He wouldn't let there be any more. "Can't a man enjoy a bit of peace and quiet without being interrogated like a common criminal?"

For the first time, anger marred Grayson's face. "Don't snap at me. What was I supposed to do? Mother is worried sick that you didn't show up last night for Sunday dinner, and here it is well into Monday morning without a word from you. She said you stormed out of the house yesterday and she hadn't heard a word from you since." His anger turned to something more elusive, dark, and troubled. "And when she sent a note to in-quire after you, Quincy here, guard dog of your privacy, only responded with a curt, 'He is unavailable.' "

Matthew's sigh was weary, and a needle of biting pain began to resurface. "Tell her there's no need to worry. Really. I had other plans that I had forgotten about."

He hated the look that came over Grayson's face, the same look he saw in his friends' and family's eyes.

Horror.

The golden boy was no longer golden. And they had no idea how to deal with a man who was so changed.

"You had no other plans. You were hiding away." Grayson gestured to the mess in the room. "In here, from the looks of it. God, Matthew, if only you would try, get out more, see people. Give them a chance to get used to you."

"I will not go out and socialize," Matthew replied with a deadly calm, remembering the dinner party at his parents' house. "I already tried that and I only made people uncomfortable."

"Damn it, I'm not asking you to socialize. I'm asking you to start living again."

"Living?" he suddenly raged, the violence that had become his constant companion erupting. He slammed his fist against the wall, and welcomed the pain that shot up his arm. "Look at me!" he demanded. "I scare young children and innocent women. I am a freak!"

"A scar doesn't change a person, Matthew."

"Tell that to Father," he spat unexpectedly.

Grayson went still, then sighed. "Give him time."

"Time isn't going to erase this scar. He only cares about the Hawthorne name."

It was no secret that Bradford Hawthorne was a man obsessed with appearances. He had been born with a fine old name and the respect that name provided, but when he grew into adulthood there had not been a penny left of the Hawthorne family fortune. So he had chosen a bride for a good deal more than her looks and her ability to bear him sons. He chose Emmaline Abbot for her wealth. Her renowned beauty was nothing more than an added bonus. He would have married her regardless of what she looked like.

In the years since, Bradford had restored the family coffers and built an empire based on the family's good name, Emmaline's wealth, and three strong sons. Grayson, Matthew, and Lucas.

Years ago, despite Emmaline's protests, Bradford had forced his oldest son to make his own way from an early age. However, when first Matthew, then Lucas had come to that turning point in their own lives, Bradford had suddenly been willing to help. But each of them had turned their father down.

Solidarity among brothers. And all three had succeeded, though not all of them had done it in ways Bradford had approved of.

Grayson had become a lawyer—the most respected in Boston, but a lawyer all the same. Lucas had opened a gentlemen's club, fast becoming known for the finest liquors in town, not to mention the finest women. Matthew had been the one who made Bradford proud.

Matthew had made a fortune in railroads and shipping. And because of that success, he had been invited to lunch with his father every Friday at Locke Ober's. Until the accident.

Matthew thought of the message he had given his mother for his father.

Before he could stop himself, he strode to the door and bellowed for Quincy.

"Have I received any messages?"

"None, sir, other than from your mother regarding your, er, schedule conflicts," he finished with a stubborn look at Grayson.

Matthew's face went hard at the thought that his father hadn't replied. It had been no secret that he had been the favorite of his father's sons. But the accident had changed all that.

"Matthew, don't do this to yourself," Grayson said. "Regardless of how Father feels, the rest of us love you."

Matthew's throat tightened. "I think you should go."

The hard lines of Grayson's face eased, shifting into lines of concern. "I think you should see a doctor."

A pulse drummed in Matthew's temple, and he focused on the clock across the room, steadying himself with the regular tick of the second hand. "I have already seen a doctor, Grayson, several in fact. The best in Boston."

"I want you to see someone else, a doctor Mother has learned of who might have more answers."

Matthew looked at him, a flicker of hope sparking to life. "Who?"

For the first time since arriving, Grayson looked uncomfortable. "A man at Southwood Hospital."

Matthew's breath came out through his teeth in a hiss.

Southwood Hospital was an institution for the mentally unstable.

"It's not what you think," Grayson added.

"Isn't it?" Matthew asked coldly.

"There are doctors there who are experts in head trauma." He shifted his weight. "I took the liberty of talking to a Dr. Samuels last week."

Matthew's throat tightened as if a vise circled his neck, but he didn't speak. Couldn't.

"And the fact is," Grayson went on in a reasonable tone, unaware of the turmoil he was causing, "as Dr. Samuels and I discussed, if your head wound was severe, it is possible that you've sustained a trauma to the brain." He hesitated. "Which would account for this erratic behavior of yours."

"I am not insane!" Matthew snarled, hating the shake he could hear in his voice. "And despite what little children think, I am not a monster. I might look like one, but I'm not."

"This has nothing to do with your face. Look at you!" Grayson exploded, gesturing to Matthew's appearance. "You're a mess. This place is a mess. You lock yourself away, won't let your own mother know what is going on with you when she inquires. What would you call it? Normal behavior?"

Matthew counted silently, concentrating. "I did not sustain a severe head injury. I have been to plenty of doctors, and they all say the same thing. I just need time to heal," he lied, unwilling to believe anything else but that he would, given time—just as all the doctors had said in the beginning. And until then he needed to keep to himself.

Grayson sighed. "I am just trying to help."

The thick haze of Matthew's fury began to fade. He knew that his family was only thinking about what was best for him. But he couldn't allow their best intentions to land him in a place like Southwood Hospital.

He had heard about the haunting screams and wild shouting or, perhaps worse yet, the vacant stares. Matthew's good hand curled into a fist at his side. He would not end up in a place like that.

"I don't need your help," Matthew said, forcing a calm he didn't feel into his voice. "I'm fine. Beyond which, you mistake an aversion to parading out in society and having people stare at me like I'm some sort of curiosity, such as me being a lunatic."

"I never said you were a lunatic!"

"Of course you did, just not in so many words. And isn't that what you think?"

Grayson looked directly at Matthew. "In truth, I don't know what to think."

The regret and sincerity on his brother's face sent a shiver of foreboding down Matthew's spine.

Was he crazy? Was his brain deteriorating? Was that what the doctors had really meant by deterioration of the nerves and tissue?

He thought of the way he had to concentrate to eat a simple meal without spilling food like a child. He thought of the way he sometimes couldn't get his hand to work correctly, or the blinding light in his head. He did feel crazy sometimes. Crazed with anger and fury and pain.

A soul-deep shudder began to work its way through his body. He wanted his brother gone.

Grayson ran his hands through his dark hair. "God, what a debacle." He strode to the mantel, where a fire was burning itself out. "It used to be so good. The three of us, bound together."

"All for one and one for all," Matthew whispered, suddenly remembering carefree childhood days of hope and glory, nothing more taxing than adventure and fun.

"Yes, the Three Musketeers. Always standing up for each other."

"Always in trouble."

Grayson chuckled. "Speak for yourself. *You* were always in trouble. You and Lucas. Though I'm convinced that it was that best friend of yours, Reynolds, who was the ringleader of it all."

Matthew studied Grayson. The eldest son had worked hard at staying out of trouble but somehow had always managed to make their father angry. As with so many things, Matthew had taken his life and all the golden glory of it in stride, never questioning, never thankful. Taking it for granted.

He didn't know then how easily it could be swept away.

One false move. One tiny slip. And all the world came crashing down as if his life hadn't been any more real than a flimsy house of cards.

What stores of energy had gotten him this far in the day dwindled. Despite the fact that Grayson was still there, Matthew couldn't stand any longer. As casually as he could, he sat down on the divan, pressing his head back, closing his eyes. Without warning, memories swirled, leaping like flames in the fireplace. He thought of the intensely gratifying article that had run in the *Boston Herald* nearly two years ago. He had reread it just the other day, stared at it for hours, remembering the grand gala given in his honor that had followed the article. But it hadn't been the gala that he had cared about. Only the reason for the event had mattered.

He felt the strain sink out of his body, his back relaxing into the thick cushions, despite the fact that he told himself to get up and deal with his brother. But the ease was too enticing, beckoning him down.

"Matthew?"

"Matthew!"

He shook his head with effort, realizing he must have drifted to sleep. Hell.

His eyes flashed open, and he nearly jumped out of his skin when he came face-to-face not with Grayson but with Finnea Winslet, who peered close, her eyes narrowed with worry.

"Is something wrong?" she demanded. "Are you ill?"

He didn't move a muscle as his mind tried to make sense of where he was and why she was there. "No, I am not ill," he stated. "And yes, something is wrong. You are here."

Finnea's brow eased and she smiled. "Good. I'm relieved to see you're back to normal. Ill-humored and pesky as a mayfly."

"Just yesterday you said you took back all the unkind things you thought of me."

She tossed him a crooked grin. "I take that back, too."

She walked away, an odd green-and-gold gown billowing

around her ankles. He watched despite himself, feeling the intensity that she always managed to make him feel. He remembered all too well the shape of her long legs that now hid beneath her skirts. He remembered the feel of her abdomen, gently curved beneath the palm of his hand. Remembered the smell of her wild hair and golden skin, like jasmine just after a rain. But then, as always, he remembered the rest of that day.

When he found her in the wreckage, she had been unconscious and covered in blood. Anyone who could walk away did, disappearing into the thick jungle with a man who said he could lead them out. Matthew had been able to walk but he hadn't been able to leave Finnea. He didn't understand then or now the feeling that came over him—the desire, the yearning. The need to save her.

He explained it away as simple decency. A debt owed—to Janji, if no one else.

"Where's my brother?" he asked caustically, looking around the study for Grayson.

"If you mean that stern-faced, stiff-upper-lip sort that I saw slamming out your front door minutes ago, I'd say he's gone. Looking none too pleased, I might add." She ran her fingers through the long tassels of silk that hung from the drapery, and shot him a bemused smile. "You have a way with people, don't you?"

He only muttered and dropped his head back against the divan. "Why are you here, Miss Winslet?"

She didn't answer at first, and just when he would have asked again, she said, "I need a favor."

He opened one eye. "Why do I get the feeling that I'm not going to like this?"

"Now, now. Don't go jumping to wrong conclusions again. It's nothing much, really." She hesitated, running her fingers over the hand-carved ridge of a hardback chair, before blurting out, "I need you to teach me the ways of Boston."

Chapter Six

Matthew came off the divan as if a lightning bolt had shot down his spine. "What?"

Finnea's eyes glimmered a deep, excited green. "It's the perfect solution. It came to me last night while I was lying on the floor. . . ." She blushed. "I mean the bed, the bed on the floor. Anyway, you know the rules of these Americans. You know which spoon must be used and when. You could teach me the workings of this difficult place!"

"No." He said the word simply, forcefully, sweat beading on his forehead. He would not teach her. He would not be entwined in her life. Would not feel that frantic urgency to save her.

But then she touched him unexpectedly, her fingers running along the scar on his face. Her fingertips sent fire racing through his body. Fire, frustration. And yearning.

"Does it hurt?" she whispered.

The words spun in his head. It hurt nearly every second. "No," he said simply. "I give it little thought."

She looked at him. Into him. As if trying to determine if he had lied.

Left off balance by the concern in her face, he fought the insane urge to turn his lips into her palm. He wanted to hold her, bury his head against her breast. Tell her about the pain, about the fury. Tell her that his family thought he was going insane.

"So will you help me?" she asked.

His eyes narrowed at her sudden change of subject. "What?"

"Will you help me, show me the ways of these people? I can learn, really," she whispered, the words emphatic.

It was her tone that snagged at him, not the words, making

him think that she was trying hard to convince herself but not succeeding.

"You need an etiquette teacher, Miss Winslet, not me."

"But no one can know that I'm doing this! Not my mother, not my brother. When I arrive at my next party I want to be perfect. I want to know what to do. No one will be able to laugh at me." She looked at him hard. "Besides, you said I could learn. You said you believed in me." There was a flash of darkness in her eyes before she scoffed, "Or didn't you mean it?"

As always, Matthew hated the look in her eyes. Only minutes before she had been charging through life, excited about the prospects for the future. But he knew Bostonians weren't so easily swayed. He needed to tell her that it would take more than learning to use the right spoon for this city to accept her.

But the words wouldn't come.

"You learning and me teaching you are not the same issue," he equivocated.

He saw the relief, saw the flicker of hope rekindle in her eyes as she laughed. She turned away in a twirl, her strange gossamer skirts billowing like waves of green and gold.

But her smile trailed off into startled surprise when she suddenly noticed the broken glass and overturned furniture. She stood for a moment before she tilted her head, then shrugged, as if finding a room in such disarray was not such an odd occurrence.

"It would be pretty in here if it wasn't for the mess," she stated.

"I hardly think 'pretty' is the appropriate word to describe a man's study."

She glanced back at him as if amused, seeming to give no notice to his disheveled appearance. "All right, it would be *handsome* in here if there wasn't a mess. Do you feel better now?"

A muscle began to tick in his jaw. "No, I do not feel better, Miss Winslet. And if you truly want so desperately to fit in with Bostonians, you'd best learn that ladies do not call at a gentleman's house for *any* reason, much less do they come to call alone. You could be seen by anyone, including my brother."

She raised a brow at him, and he could just imagine the thoughts that were running through her head. He sounded like an arrogant fool. Not so long ago he would have laughed aloud at such dribble coming out of any man's mouth. But that was before. Now he wanted her gone, and he'd say whatever was necessary to get the deed done.

"Well, there you are," she offered. "Your brother *didn't* see me, so luck was on my hip."

"Hip?"

"Yes, you know. Your American saying."

Matthew hung his head. "Side. Luck was on my side is the saying."

"Hip, side? Whichever. With a bit more good fortune it's possible that before long Bostonians will be shaking hands with a bit of meaning and eating nasturtiums at fancy meals. . . ."

Without warning, she grew flustered, her words trailing off. She seemed to fidget. But she got ahold of herself and raised her chin in that defiant way she had about her. "I never thanked you for . . . eating the flower."

Matthew groused. "It was nothing."

"It was not nothing. It was terribly kind."

Before he could respond, she turned away, an odd assortment of metal bracelets jangling on her wrists as she made her way through the wreck in his study. She picked up a statue of George Washington and studied the bronze face closely. Matthew watched, mesmerized in spite of his determination not to be, as she walked the stately figure along the mantel like a toy. Suddenly bored, she returned it to its spot and continued her inspection of the room and his belongings.

"Miss Winslet, I'm not in the mood for this."

"I thought that is what a woman is supposed to say to a man."

Matthew raised a brow, the scar pulling in surprise. "I'm not in the mood for *that* either."

Finnea sliced him a castigating look, then turned her attention to a hand-etched crystal egg. "I wasn't offering."

Matthew felt a deep growl rumble in his chest. "God save me from meddling brothers and women. All I want is a little peace and quiet. Is that too much to ask?" he muttered grimly.

"Apparently so. Enough of your games. I'm busy. It's time you leave."

"I can't. Not until you agree to teach me."

"I will not teach you, Miss Winslet," he stated, his patience strained. "But if I were, I would start with a lecture on pushy women."

"Then you'd better trot on over to Adwina Raines's house, as she could certainly benefit from a lecture or two," she stated, leaning over to peer at a quaintly built wooden clock.

Matthew gritted his teeth. "Someone should tell you that part of the fine art of being a lady in Boston is knowing when you have been insulted so you can act incensed."

Still bent at the waist, she glanced back at him curiously, an errant strand of silky red hair escaping from her loose chignon. "Have you insulted me?"

"Three times since you got here."

"All right, consider me incensed," she stated, then jumped back with delight when the cuckoo popped out of the clock. "How clever! I've never seen such a thing!"

From the clock, Finnea moved to a vase, studying it with great curiosity. From the vase, she moved to a carved ivory box, and from the box she found a long line of books on a shelf, her fingers gliding over the gold-embossed titles.

"Hmmm," was all she said.

Before Matthew knew what was happening, Finnea walked out of his study into the foyer and glanced up at the ceiling. He could hear her startled gasp.

Even he had felt a shimmer of surprise when he saw the mosaic in the vaulted ceiling for the first time.

"What is it?" she asked, her head tilted back so far on her shoulders that he thought she would tip over.

"A mosaic."

"Of a warrior," she added, her voice awed as she turned to look at him. "With a dove held gently in his hand."

"The house is called Dove's Way."

She stood for a long moment, staring at the mosaic, and whispered, "Because the dove found its way home. To the warrior." Then she scoffed at herself. "Paintings in ceilings and real life are two different things."

He looked at her. "What are you talking about?"

But she had already moved on, turning her attention to the huge pieces of bronze sculpture and oil paintings, leaving him with his brows peaked in surprise.

She studied the Venetian glass with the close-eyed scrutiny of a scientist. She ran her fingers along the draperies with their heavy tiebacks, gray satin balls hanging from them like Christmas ornaments on a tree. She didn't stop until she came to a wall covered by large rectangles of smoky mirror. He watched as her footsteps faltered, her fingers reaching out but not touching the silvered glass. She studied her reflection, seemingly unaware that he watched her, until she pressed her fingers against the mirror, tracing the image of her cheekbones and lips as if she had never seen herself before.

He thought of Africa. With lakes as calm and clear as mirrors but rarely a looking glass to be had. A world away in more than simply distance. Most Africans had never heard of, much less seen, the modern conveniences most Bostonians took for granted. Velvet-lined carriages, paved streets, gaslights. But they were curious men and women, eyeing and boldly touching anything new and intriguing. Just as Finnea did now.

"Look at this!"

Finnea's blunt declaration brought Matthew out of his reverie. Only then did he realize that she was no longer in sight. He headed in the direction of her voice and stopped when he found her in a room off the back of the house that was filled with windows.

"This is a wonderful place! What do you call it?" she asked.

"The garden room."

Finnea tsked. "There are no gardens in here."

"No, but you can *see* them just beyond the glass."

At this she snorted. "All I see is this snow."

"True, but in the spring and summer the yard will be filled with flowers."

"I don't believe a word of it. I can't imagine how it ever gets warm enough for flowers to grow in this city. All I have seen since I arrived is snow. Great mounds of it, making it impossible to get out."

"You are out now," he noted.

"Yes, but my fingers and toes are frozen. I don't like it at all."

"Rest assured, Boston will warm up."

She walked over to a stack of boxes that sat in the corner, clearly not believing a word he said.

"What is this?" she demanded.

"Nothing."

"You and your nothings. Do you ever answer a question directly?"

"Do you ever demur and hold your tongue?"

Finnea laughed appreciatively. In the next second her eyes sparkled. "Look at this! Painting tools. Why are they in boxes?"

"Not everything has been unpacked since my return," he replied, his voice growing taut.

"You seem to have unpacked everything else."

"The servants did that."

"Then why didn't the servants unpack these?"

His jaw muscle ticked again. "That is none of your concern, Miss Winslet."

"Why not?"

Why not? He hung his head in frustration. "Because I sent instructions telling them not to be unpacked. Is that good enough for you?" he demanded.

She picked up a long, thin paintbrush that had been left out on the table, and ran her fingers through the bristles. "I forgot. You told me that you once painted."

During those long hours in the jungle, he had told her about his love of art. Capturing the soul on canvas. He would have said anything to keep her mind alert. "As I recall, I told you that I wanted to paint you."

High spots of color flared in her cheeks. "And I said no."

Suddenly her gaze caught on a crumpled piece of paper on the floor. She reached for it, but he leaned over and snatched it up first. He didn't want her to see it, didn't want her to see his pathetic attempt to capture Mary on paper. His sweet child. God how he loved her. He woke up at night wanting to insist she come to live with him in this new house. But in the morning he always remembered the look on her face whenever she saw him.

Lost in thought, it was too late to do anything when she saw the article lying on the table. Unlike the sketch, he couldn't get it away from her in time, and she began to read out loud.

" 'Prominent Bostonian to Show Artwork, by Justine Crowleigh.' " She glanced at him with a look of surprise, before returning to the article. " 'Boston's very own Matthew Hawthorne has always been a man of many talents. And now we learn he is an artist as well. But don't make the mistake of thinking that this rich man merely dabbles. He is a master at his craft, painting in a way that both awes and disturbs, provokes and titillates. Regardless of what his art makes a person feel, there is no doubt that the man is talented. And now he will have a show.' "

The article went on, but Matthew no longer listened. He could have recited the article from memory. He knew each line by heart. Making his first million hadn't thrilled him half as much as the prospect of that show.

Was it possible it had been written only a year and a half ago? It felt like a lifetime had passed since then. And in truth, it had. His art had been taken away just like the rest. Thinking about it made the fury tick to life in his mind—the supplies sitting before him but beyond his reach.

"Did you have your show?" she asked, her voice soft, as if she somehow understood.

"You ask too many questions."

She studied him for a long time, seeing too much.

"Did you have your show?" she persisted.

"No, it never happened," he said sharply.

She started to reach out, and he knew she was going to touch him again. But he was quick this time, and he lifted his hand to stop her. He didn't want her to touch him; he didn't want her to feel him. But he was unprepared when their hands met, palm to palm. Large to small, narrow rays of winter-gray sun drifting in through the high glass windows.

He watched as she stared at their hands, hers so tiny against his, making her seem fragile and delicate—as if she weren't as bold as she appeared.

"Why did you lie to me?" she asked quietly, without moving her hand away.

"What?" Confusion clouded his mind, the world outside the room suddenly distant.

"During that long night in Africa," she whispered, "you told me that everyone here in Boston was kind and wonderful. I believed you."

His brow furrowed in memory. "I told you what you wanted to hear."

"You lied."

"You were dying!" The words came out sharply, the tinge of remembered panic lacing the air. "You were dying," he repeated more softly, forcing a teasing he didn't feel into his tone. "I saw no reason to tell you the truth and hasten your demise."

Finnea pressed her eyes closed and laughed, a burst of sound that was filled with relief. "True. If you had told me about Adwina Raines, no doubt I never would have recovered."

"But you did," he whispered.

He stared at her, unable to look away. They were close, so close that if he leaned just so he could kiss her.

As if she had read his thoughts, a surge of red stained her cheeks. He touched the stain, trailing his fingers to the delicately soft skin under her jaw. He could feel the flutter of her heart as she went very still, and he fought the urge to pull her even closer.

He understood suddenly why he couldn't forget her. He had been mesmerized by her from the minute she walked into the railcar and fell into his arms. The feel of her fingers, the intoxicating smell of her hair, as if she had washed it in springwater and long grasses. That was it. She made him feel. After more than a year of being dead inside, she made him feel.

And he had no interest in feeling, he thought with cold finality.

"I must go," she whispered, stepping away from him. She started to leave, but stopped. "I will return tomorrow."

"No, Finnea."

He was as surprised as she was that he had used her Christian name.

"I will not teach you," he stated clearly.

She smiled at that, her equilibrium resurfacing in that quick and sudden way she had about her. "Of course you will. Because just like in the jungle, you won't let anything bad happen to me."

Her presumption left him speechless. And before he could find the words, she turned away and strode out of the room. He was dismissed, just like that. Not because of his scar. Not because she couldn't look at him, like so many others. But because she was done, the matter in her mind decided. She would return tomorrow.

Her self-confident assurance would have made him smile if he weren't already so annoyed.

Matthew followed her, intent on issuing a sharp set-down. But when he found her in the foyer, Quincy extending her cape, the words broke off.

He took in the black velvet against red hair and burnished skin. The contrast, her beauty.

She was Africa in Boston. It was what he sought, he thought fleetingly. What he needed. Not her, but the escape he had found in the wildness of Africa.

He hadn't painted since he had been wounded. Thought he never would again. But since he first saw her on that train, the need had begun to circle inside him. He hadn't been able to put her from his mind—not Finnea, not Africa. There were times when he could still feel the quiet of that dark land, a quiet so real that it wrapped around his soul—making him whole.

The first time he noticed the silence it had been night, the sky black and smooth, dotted with thousands of brilliant stars, the only sound coming from the occasional beat of drums, slow and pounding. Like a secret heart beating in the distance.

The sound had drawn him, just as Africa had drawn him. Just as Finnea Winslet still drew him with her ways that contrasted so sharply with the very ladies she sought to fit in with.

For reasons he didn't care to think about, he knew he would teach her.

As if she understood, she glanced back at him. He expected her to smile triumphantly, but she surprised him again.

"You will paint again, Matthew Hawthorne. And then you'll have that show."

His lips drew into a hard line, blood rushing through his heart so hard that it sounded like drums beyond the trees.

"Now get this place cleaned up, and you might even consider a bath," she said with the lack of decorum he was rapidly growing used to. "I'll be back tomorrow."

She was gone in a rustle of wind and jangling bracelets. A flicker of something sparked in his mind. Was it hope?

She had been so confident, so sure that he would paint again.

He returned to the garden room. With trembling hands, he retrieved a pencil and a new sheet of paper from one of the boxes. Tentatively he started to draw. He ignored the pain, willed it away as he moved the charcoal tip. He could feel the need, feel his fingers itch to put image on paper. But he couldn't get the grip right. His fingers stumbled clumsily. He counted and concentrated, then tried again. Sweat broke out on his brow. His arm began to jerk, and his head swam until he suddenly roared his frustration, snapping the pencil in two.

Raging, he crumpled the paper and threw it savagely across the room. With a curse, he stormed out of the garden room and took the stairs as fast as he could, up and up until he came to a solitary room at the top of the house. When he walked inside, only a weak stream of winter sunlight brightened the room. Dust flew up in tiny puffs with each step he took, but he didn't stop until he came to a back corner. There he found rows of covered canvases. Despair threatening, he pulled the drapes away from first one painting, then another, until all of them stared back at him, exposed.

His work, his art. The striking beauty.

The past.

"No, Miss Winslet, I will never paint again." He whispered the words, making him remember the night everything had gone wrong.

Matthew strode through the front door. The house glittered like a jewel, lights glistening, crystal dripping from chandeliers like teardrops. Music swept through the air, and just beyond the reception hall, double doors spilled open to the grand hall, where people danced. A party to celebrate his upcoming art show. A gala celebration and all of Boston was there.

He was late for his own party, but he had wanted to make sure each painting was positioned just right. Now everything was as he wanted it. Tomorrow was the show.

His boot heels echoed against the alternating squares of black and white marble that covered the foyer floor as he scanned the throng of guests for his wife.

"Matthew! There you are, old boy! Let me be the first tonight to offer my sincere congratulations. I look forward to seeing this artwork of yours."

Matthew turned his attention to a short balding man. "Thank you, Walter," he said, his smile easy and warm as they shook hands. "Have you seen Kimberly?"

"Well, yes. I saw her a while ago with that sweet child of yours. Matching gowns and even matching dancing slippers. They caused quite a sensation. I think little Mary has since been put to bed upstairs." He chuckled. "Though your young daughter didn't want to go. I wouldn't be surprised if we saw her sneak back down those stairs at any time."

Matthew smiled. "That's Mary. I'll go up and see her. But first I need to find my wife."

Walter turned to search the sea of faces. "I don't see her."

"That's all right. I'll find her. It's good to see you, Walter."

Matthew took the marble steps from the landing to the spacious reception hall, his tall broad form standing in contrast to the other, much shorter men. He didn't get very far before he was stopped by an elegantly dressed woman, her jewels stunning, though subdued enough for Puritan Bostonians' tastes. She was also his wife's closest friend.

"Matthew, darling," she said, extending her hands. "You naughty boy. You're late."

With a gallant bow, Matthew took her fingers and smiled. "You are a vision, Celia," he said warmly.

"As are you," she said, stepping closer.

He chuckled, the sound deep and sultry, as he firmly but politely pulled away.

"Where's Kim?" he asked, scanning the crowd.

She huffed and smoothed her hair. "I haven't seen her for a while," she said, her full lips pouting. "Why don't you dance with me until she turns up?"

Matthew smiled. "I think it's best that I find her."

The woman snapped open her fan and waved it quickly. "You should have married me."

"So you've told me, Celia," he said, tilting her chin with the crook of his finger. "And I've told you that any man here would be happy to have you."

"Every man but you," she sniffed.

"You're a heartbreaker, Celia. I've known that since I was fifteen. I'm not one to tangle with that," he said with a good-natured laugh.

"You're the heartbreaker, Matthew Hawthorne, as well you know."

After she left in a whirl of skirts, Matthew raked his blond hair back from his forehead as he worked his way through the throng of guests.

"Have you seen my wife?" he asked an older woman who had been a family friend for years.

"Kimberly?" The woman turned to another who stood next to her and raised a brow. "He's looking for Kimberly," she stated in a way that made his thoughts go still. "Does he also want to know that when we saw her a few moments ago, his wife was upset? I wonder?"

She looked back at him, her face pulled into sharp lines of disapproval as if he had done something wrong. "Has it occurred to you that your wife is your first and foremost responsibility?"

"Margot, really," her friend interjected nervously.

"Well, someone has to tell him."

"What are you trying to say?" he asked.

She tilted her chin like a schoolmistress. "Far be it from me to intrude in other people's concerns. But I suggest you go to *the back cottage and see to your wife. I saw her head that way."*

Not liking the sudden ticking in his mind, Matthew shut the terrace doors as he walked out into the nighttime air. He strode across the gray slate tiles, the party raging on behind him. Without a word, he made his way down the curved granite steps to the narrow path leading to the cottage that stood at the back of the property.

With every step he took, his pace increased until he came through the lattice-covered passageway and tall box hedges that separated the front gardens from the back. The cedar-shingled, white clapboard cottage stood quiet, and frustration kicked harder when still he couldn't find her. He started to turn away, but then he noticed one low light burning inside.

Without warning he saw a flash of color inside the cottage. A shimmering blue gown. And white-blond hair.

He felt his answering smile. The relief that he had found her. He would apologize for being late.

He headed toward the tiny house, not stopping until he stood in the doorway. His smile froze on his face.

Her back was against the wall. Literally.

Her long, fashionable gown of crepe de chine and gossamer voile was bunched carelessly around her waist, her naked back pressed along the wood paneling.

At the sight that met his eyes his mind closed with the surety of a steel trap.

In a rustle of fabric, Kimberly cried out, her bare legs wrapped around the strong, lean hips of the man before her. His long, thick shaft teased at her swollen wetness, entering her, though barely, before pulling back, only to tease again.

She groaned her frustration and he kissed her breasts.

"Always so greedy," the man murmured, a smile in his voice as he pushed into her further, though not enough.

"Stop tormenting me," she moaned, her head falling back.

He laughed out loud. "Is this what you want?" the man asked as he plunged deep, his laughter trailing off to his own heated gasps as he sank into her tight sheath.

"Yes, Reynolds! Dear God, yes!"

Chapter Seven

Finnea woke up on the floor.

It was the following morning, and she lay in a bundle of linen sheets and white woolen blankets that she had taken from the bed and spread out on the plush deep blue carpet. Her red hair spilled across plump feather pillows.

She still couldn't get used to the overstuffed bed standing so high off the ground, though she had tried, night after night, only to wake up cross and ill-rested.

She threw back the covers, and quickly smoothed them over the bed before a maid entered to stoke the fire. She had found since moving to America that her family and their friends lived in stately homes with uniformed servants to tend their every need. Finnea was alternately drawn in and repelled by the wealth and privilege, an ostentation, she had heard, that would have been considered modest compared to some cities. But there was nothing like it in Africa. Floors made of dirt, walls made of mud or thatch. The house her father had built, with its rough-planked floors and multiple rooms, was considered the finest for miles around. But it couldn't compare to the likes of Boston town houses with their marble floors, brass handles, and velvet as fine as any gown lining the walls.

Yesterday, Finnea had promised the underbutler that she would mix up a fresh batch of eucalyptus salve for his aching joints. This morning she was going to do it, and while she was at it, she planned to make a restorative tea of dandelions for Matthew, all before she went for her lessons on Boston. The underbutler's hands should do remarkably better after a week using the salve, and no doubt Matthew could use a good cleansing herbal after what must have been a drunken binge, based on the disarray and reek of liquor in his study. If ever anyone could use a purifying tea, it was Matthew Hawthorne.

Thankfully her brother generally went to work, and her mother and grandmother left the house daily for an assortment of meetings, luncheons, and who knew what all, making it possible for her to slip out of the house unnoticed.

Wanting to look perfect for her first day of lessons, Finnea took extra care with her ablutions, pulling on one of the spectacular gowns she had found at the most wonderful little shop she had run across downtown. The store had been in a tiny corner of a cramped street, filled with clothes hanging from racks, and shoes all in a row. No measuring, no pinning. A person could simply buy what she liked on the spot, without waiting for a gown to be made. It was amazing.

Just before she hurried down the grand staircase, she plucked out a few cherished photographs from her bag. She had thought about it last night as she drifted off to sleep, thought about how the photos from Africa might serve as some sort of peace offering to Nester.

The house ran with a precision that both astounded and impressed her. She had learned in the short time she had been there that the *Boston Herald* was delivered to the Winslets' palatial home on Commonwealth Avenue at five minutes past eight, at which time Bertram, the family butler, would take the folded pages to the pantry, where an aproned girl spent the next half hour ironing it into long flat sheets.

At five minutes until nine, a line of serving maids would march up from the basement kitchen and set out the breakfast items. Eggs, ham, porridge, and freshly baked bread with a silver dish of butter. It was always the same; it never varied.

Slowing her pace, Finnea strode to the elegantly decorated brocade-and-velvet-lined parlor and found her mother.

Finnea stopped just outside the room as if peering through a looking glass into a foreign world, taking in the woman who sat so gracefully in a finely crafted wingback chair with a notch in the middle. Chippendale, her grandmother had called it. Finnea only knew that it was beautiful.

As always, her mother's gown was of a soft, subtle color,

nearly blending in with the winter white of the seat cushion. Her skin was creamy, and her hair, barely brown, more like sand, was pulled up in an elegant twist at the back of her head.

Just then Leticia turned, her sky-blue eyes finding Finnea in the doorway, and the woman smiled—a gentle mix of surprise and uncertainty, but pleasure and delight as well.

Her mother. The one person she *should* confide in when she needed help in learning this world. Not Matthew, not some stranger.

Finnea decided in a staggering rush of hope and love that it was foolish to have asked Matthew Hawthorne for help. It was time she told her mother the truth of her situation and gained her assistance. It was ridiculous to think that she couldn't turn to the woman who had given birth to her for guidance.

"Mama," Finnea said, "you look lovely."

"Please dear, don't call your mother 'mama.' It is so common."

Finnea turned with a start to find her grandmother standing behind her in the foyer. Disdain lay below the surface of the woman's smile, barely hidden, like rocks unseen beneath a murky waterline, and a piercing thought leaped out at her.

Was she willing to pay the price of fitting in with these people?

Finnea shook the thought away. There was no price for fitting in, there was only reward, she told herself firmly. That reward was acceptance from her mother.

But could she learn all she needed to know?

Slowly Finnea turned back to the woman she had come clear across the world to see, to love, and her determination to confide faltered. She couldn't utter the words that would confirm that indeed she was lacking in the finer points of American society. More than once since Finnea had arrived, Hannah Grable had made it clear that she had thought little of William Winslet before he left for Africa, and thought even less of him now after meeting the daughter he had raised.

Pride and protectiveness surged. She would prove them wrong. But the only way to do so was to learn the ways of this town inside and out. Which meant she needed Matthew to teach her. Or was that just an excuse? To be seen. To be touched by him again, she thought suddenly. So she wouldn't be lost.

Her mouth was swollen and dry. Matthew gently rubbed water from a rustic pouch over her lips, slowly, with infinite patience, then dripping water onto her tongue.

She was propped between his legs, her back to his chest, his knees up on either side of her. Protecting her.

"I can't swallow," she choked.

"Yes you can."

He tilted the sack so the water came out, but she turned away, the flow washing down over her throat, soaking into the tattered remnants of her hunter's shirt. He jerked the bag up so as not to lose more.

"You are going to drink, Finnea. I will not let you die. You are going to survive this."

Her head was still turned so that her cheek was against his chest, the water on her face mixing with sudden tears. "But I don't want to be saved."

He was quiet for a long time. "Sometimes we are saved whether we want to be or not."

"What is this you're wearing?"

Finnea nearly jumped when she found Hannah standing so close, her plain gray eyes surveying Finnea's gown.

Finnea glanced down at the beautiful dress of vibrant red velvet.

"I think you look fine, Finnea," Leticia said quickly.

Hannah Grable let a long, disapproving minute reverberate through the silence before she smiled tightly. "Fine, Leticia? Of course. Who am I to turn up my nose at leftovers from a thrift shop meant for paupers? What do I care if Grace Baldwin or perhaps even Adwina Raines notices Finnea wearing one of their New Year's masquerade castoffs?"

"Really, Mother," Leticia said uncomfortably, "you don't mean that."

"I mean what I say, daughter," Hannah stated with a crystalline smile. "Now come along. Breakfast is being served."

Nester was already at the table when they entered the dining room. Finnea was surprised to find Jeffrey Upton there as well. The men were huddled over a series of papers. Her brother looked irritated, Mr. Upton looked impatient. The minute they entered, though, the older man stood and smiled.

"Good morning, ladies."

The night he escorted the Winslet women home from the Hawthornes' dinner party, he had asked Finnea to call him Jeffrey. Her mother had made it clear to her that this man would make a fine husband.

In truth, he would make a fine husband. He was older, a widower. Refined and proper. Kind and respectable. A man who already had full-grown children. A man who wouldn't need more.

Beyond that, she liked him. She could trust him. And she knew that was worth a lot.

Jeffrey was what her mother wanted for her. Finnea knew it was the ideal solution. She could please her mother and gain a new life—a safe life. No more uncertainty. No more emotions that threatened to burn her up with intensity and fill her body with heart-racing desire.

She pulled her shoulders back. Exactly, she thought. No more feelings she couldn't afford. This was just the sort of thing she wanted. Though she couldn't quite shake the emptiness that came over her at the thought.

Jeffrey took Hannah's hand and kissed her knuckles. "Good morning, Mrs. Grable." He nodded to Leticia, then turned to Finnea, and a kind and gentle smile pulled across his face. "Good morning, Finnea."

"Good morning," she answered, silently repeating all the wonderful attributes Jeffrey Upton possessed.

"I haven't seen you since the Hawthornes' party," he added.

"Speaking of which," Hannah interjected, glancing at her granddaughter, "have you sent your thank-you note yet?"

Finnea blinked. "Thank-you note?"

Hannah's lips pursed. "For the Hawthornes' dinner party. Surely you have sent your thanks by now."

Finnea felt a traitorous blush sting her cheeks as she glanced between her mother and grandmother. She had never heard of a thank-you note. "I will send it right away."

Hannah stared at her with a disapproving scowl.

But Leticia came around the table, her eyes alive with excitement as she took the seat a footman held for her. "Emmaline Hawthorne is a delightful woman. I'm sure she won't mind that the note is a bit late. But enough of that. All the arrangements for the party are falling into place. It's going to be fabulous."

Nester sat at the head of the table and unfolded his napkin with a snap. "Ah yes, Finnea's birthday party? That should be interesting." He chuckled. "What will you do to entertain us this time, little sis? You've already exhausted the handshake trick, and you can only eat shrubbery every so often before the novelty wears off."

Finnea blanched, but Nester was relentless. "Perhaps you could bark or growl? Maybe chant or dance?"

Jeffrey sat forward in his chair. "You're out of line, Nester."

The younger man's eyes narrowed. "You are the one who's out of line, Upton."

A silent, awkward moment passed.

"I have a photograph of Father that I brought with me," Finnea hurriedly interjected.

Nester jerked around to face her, and something odd showed in his eyes. A flash of yearning, excitement? But before Finnea could make sense of it, the look was gone.

"Let me see that," he stated with a sniff of disdain.

She handed him the photo of their father, tall and broad-shouldered, the red of his hair masked by the sepia coloring, but his wonderful smile looking nearly as real as it had been when he was alive. Her heart twisted with love at the sight. God, how she missed him.

Nester sat for a minute, just staring, that look returning to his eyes, before Hannah reached over and took it.

"He always was a handsome fellow," she observed when she peered at the photo. "I'll give him that."

"Yes," Leticia said, her voice slightly breathless, staring at the photo when it came to her.

Nester took it back. "What is this he's standing in front of?"

Finnea leaned over. "That's our farm."

"Farm?" he demanded indignantly. "Our father was an explorer, not a farmer."

"Yes, he was an explorer, but we owned a farm as well. A rubber farm."

"A rubber farm? Good God, what is that?"

"Three thousand acres of wild rubber-producing vines combined with several hundred more acres of land that Father cleared and planted with rows of tall, thin rubber trees."

Nester was stunned. "Why haven't I heard of this before? Upton, have you heard of this rubber farm?"

"No, I haven't. But that doesn't mean it's not there."

"Well, it must be a disaster. I've never heard of any kind of prosperous concern in Africa—unless it is mining gold or diamonds. Tell me he had a bit of either of those and I might be impressed."

"Actually," she stated, pride getting the better of her, "the farm is quite a successful enterprise. We are one of the largest exporters of rubber in the world."

"That is outrageous," Nester barked. "A prosperous concern that I have never heard a word about. What has happened to it now?"

"It is being run by the Katsu, who have been there hundreds of years."

"A farm turned over to a bunch of savages? You can't just turn over something like that to a pack of heathens!"

"Nester, please." Leticia reached over and rested her hand on his.

Like a mother soothes a child.

Finnea felt an unexpected tightening in her throat.

"Who is this man?" Hannah asked, pointing to another in the photograph.

Finnea dragged her eyes away from her mother and brother and looked. The image was crisp and close up. "That is Gatwith Neilander." She stared at the photo. "He came from Belgium with new ideas about rubber extraction."

"He is a handsome fellow," Hannah remarked.

"Yes. Father treated him like a son."

The room went still.

"And who is this?" Leticia asked quickly.

Thankful for the diversion, Finnea said, "Hatabe, a highly respected man of the tribe."

"What did he do?" Nester scoffed, his anger suddenly more intense. "Have a run-in with a plate-glass window? Look at that hideous scar on his face." He laughed under his breath. "He looks like Matthew Hawthorne."

With the quickness of lightning, the room went silent. In that second Finnea couldn't hold it back any longer. She hated Nester with a passion she thought impossible, and the world seemed to tumble in on her.

"That scar is no accident, Nester," she said. "It is a mark of great bravery. In Africa it is the scarred man who is revered, and the pretty man who is scorned."

Nester laughed. "Thank God I didn't stay in Africa, then."

"Yes," she bit out, "you would have easily fallen into the cowardly segment."

Shocked silence sizzled through the room.

"How dare you!" Nester exploded, leaping from his chair, his fist banging on the hardwood table.

"Nester," Jeffrey warned.

Nester whirled around to face him. "I've had enough of your tone. Remember who you are talking to. You might run Winslet Ironworks, but I own it."

A hardness came into Jeffrey's eyes. "How could I forget."

Finnea couldn't take any more. She had to get out, into the fresh air. Away from these people who thought so little of her and her past, away from a life that was going so wrong.

"If you'll excuse me," she said, each word spoken carefully for fear she might break as she quit the room.

Sitting at his desk, Matthew knew the moment Finnea arrived at Dove's Way. He could hear her, and he suspected he would have heard her had he been up in the attic. She wasn't exactly loud, more that her voice was filled with energy. Talking as soon as the door opened. Greeting the servants.

With a wry smile, he watched a moment later, when Quincy showed her into the study. He had finally slept last night, hadn't passed out, hadn't been on fire with pain. He had dreamed of her, had woken with blood rushing low, desire sweeping through his body with an aching burn.

Just the sight of her now made him grow hard as she

marched through the room, her green eyes flashing, her red hair wild. He wanted to taste her. He wanted to feel the sweet kiss of her skin against his.

But then he looked closer, and this time it was her face that gained his attention. It was red. Bright and splotchy in a way that made him realize she wasn't just angry, she was crying. Really crying. And it wasn't some coy display meant to manipulate a man.

He had the sudden thought that Finnea would sooner wrestle a man to the ground than manipulate him with fake tears. The realization pleased him immensely, then aggravated him in turn.

What was it about this woman that filled him with heat in one second and protectiveness in the next?

"Now what's the matter?" he snapped, disgruntled.

"Nothing," she stated, the sharpness of the word undermined by a sniffle. "I meant to bring you some cleansing tea, but things kind of . . . got away from me, and I forgot."

She grabbed up a pillow and punched it in what Matthew could only guess was meant to fluff. Another punch like that and he expected feathers would fly.

"Hell," he muttered, hanging his head, before coming around his desk to stand before her. "Something happened, and it has nothing to do with forgetting to bring tea," he replied gruffly, though he gently nudged her chin until their eyes met.

She jerked her head away from him.

"You can tell me, Finnea." He hesitated, that protectiveness surging stronger. "It's not like I'm a stranger."

Blood rushed to her cheeks. "Thank you for reminding me," she snapped, but her bottom lip quivered.

With a curse about stubborn women, Matthew closed her in his arms. The feel of her filled him, and for a moment he forgot about everything. It was always that way with her. She settled him somehow.

He shook his head and his hand came up to stroke her hair. "Ah, Finn. What am I going to do with you?"

She let him hold her, and he could feel when her tension eased and she leaned into him. "Talk to me," he said, feeling the tears that suddenly seeped into his shirtfront. "Tell me why one minute you're dancing and laughing, then in tears the next. In some ways it's like I know you so well. But when I think about it, I don't really know you at all."

"After that night in the jungle you know me like no one else," she sniffed, pushing back.

He touched her chin, forcing her to meet his eye. "Clothes aren't the only thing that hide a person. I've seen your body, yes. . . ."

Red surged to her cheeks, and she tried to pull away from him, but he wouldn't let her go.

"Perhaps I've even seen a bit of your soul," he added, memories of Africa swelling in his mind. "But I don't know the things that make you happy or sad. Tell me what happened, Finn, tell me why you're here."

"I told you. Nothing happened," she repeated adamantly, jerking away.

This time he let her go, but she didn't leave as he had thought she would. She grabbed up the brocade pillow, then dropped down to the divan in a billow of skirts.

"I'm here for my lessons," she stated doggedly, hugging the pillow to her chest.

Matthew studied her for a long moment, taking in the stubborn tilt of her chin and the obstinate set of her shoulders, and decided not to push. The fact was, he wasn't certain he really wanted to know what was the matter with her. "Fine. Sit up straight."

"I can listen to your lessons and lean back at the same time."

"That *is* the lesson. Sitting up straight, as in shoulders back, spine erect, knees together, ankles crossed, hands demurely in your lap."

"Good Lord. What kind of a rule is that?" she muttered, dashing her hand across her eyes.

"A rule about posture, and if you sit like a slouch, you'll be tossed out on your ear at the next social event you're invited to."

Her scowl grew fierce, and she tossed the pillow aside.

"That won't do. The next party is the one my mother is giving for me."

"Ah yes, the birthday gala. I would think you'd be happy about that."

Finnea scoffed indifferently, though her chin started to tremble again. "Happy? Happy that Nester is certain I will make a fool of myself in front of all of Boston? You can bet he is counting on it!"

She swiveled to look at him, her eyes pleading, making him uneasy. How could he possibly fix what was wrong? And why did he feel the damnable need to do so?

She was determined to look Bostonians in the face, unafraid. If a woman could conquer Boston by sheer will alone, Finnea would be Queen of Society in a matter of weeks. But Matthew knew that *will* was not enough in the centuries-old town. The only thing that mattered, that would help, was lifelong, endless repetition and submersion in a way of life that could mold a person as surely and as indelibly as a potter molds his clay.

As if reading his mind, and refusing to believe she couldn't do it, she quickly sat up straight, pulled her shoulders back, clapped her knees together, crossed her ankles, and folded her hands in her lap like a debutante.

"I can do it," she said fiercely. "I just need you to teach me the things I need to know."

Suddenly his patience came to an end. He hated the way she wanted to please her family.

An image of his father flashed in his mind, but he pushed it away. "It's ludicrous to want to fit in so badly," he snapped.

"I don't care about fitting in. Not really."

"Liar! You told me yourself that you do." He grabbed her arms and pulled her up from the divan until the scent of her wrapped around him. "Finnea," he whispered on a harsh breath. "Why do you care so much?"

She tried to pull away, tears springing back to life in her eyes.

"No," he said, not letting her go. "Damn it, tell me why you care!"

"Because I don't want my mother to leave me again!"

The words burst out of her, leaving her still.

They stared at each other, her eyes wide, her breath shallow and fast.

"I mean, I mean—"

His anger hissed out of him like air from a child's balloon. "Ah, Finn."

She tried to jerk away, but he closed her in his arms again and stroked her hair with a gentleness he thought long gone.

Long minutes ticked by, sunlight wrapping around them until she started to explain. "She left me there and didn't come back," she said in a choked whisper. "Is it so wrong to want her to love me now?"

He wanted to say that Leticia Winslet had had her chance to gain her daughter's love and had let it go. But he didn't.

"Why, Finnea?" he demanded instead, as if her answer could somehow make him better understand himself. "Why do you need her love?"

She looked at the wall, and he knew she wasn't seeing the velvet-flocked paper or oil paintings. She was seeing something entirely different, something far away.

"I dreamed of her for years," she said finally, "dreamed that she returned for me, dreamed of the feel of her kiss against my cheek, the feel of her arms holding me close."

Suddenly he didn't want to hear any more. He wanted her gone with an intensity that left his heart pounding.

But then she looked up at him, and he couldn't turn her away.

He pressed his eyes closed as if to banish her from his mind. Is that how it would be between them? Drawn together because of the past, but unable to come together because of who they were now?

She who wanted to fit in, and he who no longer could.

"You must have been disappointed when you finally saw her again," he said finally.

Her eyes widened with surprise, and she pushed away. "Disappointed?" She smiled, though barely. "No, I was proud. This beautiful woman was my mother. How could I be anything but thrilled to see her?"

Matthew could think of many things she could have been—angry, hurt—but he held his tongue.

"A woman is so much her mother," she continued, her smile faltering. "A little girl learns who to be when she grows up from her mother, by watching her, by being near."

Sharply, she turned further away, pressing her fingers to her temples, then whirled back. "No one taught me about all those things women wear beneath their gowns, or even to *wear* a gown! No one taught me about jewelry or fashion. Or about thank-you notes!"

Matthew tried to make sense of the rush of words. "Thank-you notes? What does that have to do with anything?"

"Everything! No one ever taught me that I am supposed to write them."

"Thank you for what?"

"For the dinner your mother invited me to, to begin with."

"My mother won't mind. She knows how appreciative you are."

"Your mother might not care, but my grandmother cares, and Nester cares. And you can bet Adwina Raines and her ilk care."

"You can't lose sleep over the Adwinas of the world."

"I don't give a fig about Adwina Raines or her like! It's my family I care about," she stated with a groan of frustration. "And my family cares about thank-you notes."

He ground his teeth. "All right," he conceded. "But now you know to write them."

Her head fell back. "Yes, I do know . . . now!" She raised her head and looked at him. "But only because my grandmother made some snide remark about doing it. What else is out there that I don't know about? How long will it be before I make another mistake? I'm nearly twenty-six years old, and my family looks at me like I'm some sort of dim-witted child. All because I don't act like them."

She looked at him with such bewilderment that he felt as if she had struck him physically.

Her voice softened. "Little girls look to older women to see who they will become," she explained. "But I saw only tribal women whom I loved and who taught me the ways that I have—ways that make me somehow less of a woman here."

"Surely you saw European women."

"Of course, when Father brought me into town. I used to watch them, but if I got too close, they looked at me like I was some sort of oddity." She stared at the thick velvet of her gown. "I'm an outsider. I never truly fit in as a tribal woman; I knew that. It was one of the reasons I came here, to a place where I have family. But I don't fit in here either. And if I have any chance of gaining my mother's love, I have to learn to be like her."

Matthew raised a brow. "I have met many women who swore they would never be like their mother."

"But I *want* to be like her! I want her grace and her refinement! And even if I didn't want that, don't you see, every woman has to have somebody to measure herself against."

He brushed a long curl gently behind the tiny shell of her ear, the touch like fire to his skin. "But you knew your father. Not many women are lucky enough to have a close relationship with their father."

"Yes! And I loved him dearly. But a woman identifies with her mother."

Matthew had thought that somehow she seemed different when he saw her again in America. When he met her in Africa she was scrappy and fearless and spoke her mind. But here the wildness was tamped down, muted, as if she had put pieces of who she really was and who she wanted to be in a bowl and stirred them up. Only the mix wasn't smooth like batter, more like oil and vinegar that separated no matter how many times you stirred.

He thought again how he didn't think she could fit in to this world.

Or if he wanted her to.

He wanted her like she was in Africa. Wild and free.

He could no longer deny that he wanted her. To lose himself in her body. But he didn't want her for his own. He had meant what he had said to his mother. He had no interest in marrying again. Not Finnea Winslet. Or perhaps especially not Finnea

Winslet. He had given his heart once before, and he had the scars to show for it. He would not lose his heart again.

The clock tolled the hour, each bong resonating through the house, the sound seeming to swell beneath the skies that were rapidly growing murky, closing in the windows.

With a shake of his head, his face darkened. "Sometimes there are circumstances beyond your control that people will never be able to embrace. You should accept that fact."

"My mother isn't like that! She can't be! I'm her daughter!"

But he wouldn't let it go. "Has she seen beyond the girl from Africa yet?"

"No. But only because there is nothing more to see yet." She stepped closer. "You will teach me to be more. I have to make my mother proud. And the only way to do that is for your lessons to work."

He stared at her long and hard, watching as the darkness flared in her eyes, and he finally understood that he truly couldn't turn his back on her—just as he couldn't in the jungle.

He nearly laughed his dismay but cursed instead. Gruffly, he pulled her close and pressed his forehead to hers. "All right, we'll see what we can do."

Chapter Eight

He slipped inside as quietly as a thief. The moon was high and full, lighting his way. All was silent except for the rhythmic tick of clocks scattered about the house.

He didn't hesitate in the foyer; he went straight to the stairs, the sound of his boots muffled by the thick carpet runner. At the top, he paused and listened. But still he heard no sound. No one was awake.

Heading down the hall, his heart began to race. He told himself to turn back, but he needed to see her.

When he came to her room, he turned the knob and the door clicked open. Moonlight drifted through the high windows, and he could see that she slept.

Careful not to wake her, he crossed the floor, then silently lowered himself into the chair next to her bed. She lay curled on her side. He took in her delicate face, soft in sleep, and her hands, fingers slightly curled. He wished he could cradle her to his heart, feel her arms wrap around his neck as she squeezed him tight. But he remained silent. It was enough just to see her. To be close.

"I love you, Mary," he whispered, willing her to hear him in some recess of her mind.

He settled back in the chair, unwilling to leave just yet, needing to watch over his child in the only way that was left to him.

She sighed in her sleep, but she didn't roll away. Only then did Matthew feel peace, sweet and intense, settle over him.

Chapter Nine

Lessons began in earnest.

Each day Matthew taught Finnea what he could, while each night he slipped into Hawthorne House to sit with Mary as she slept. He brought little things with him. A new toy. A new book. All left behind when he made his way back through the darkened hallways before anyone woke.

After a week of this schedule, Matthew was exhausted, and Finnea wasn't much further along in her quest than she had been at the beginning—though not for lack of trying on either of their parts. But if she was aware of that fact, she didn't let on, showing up at noon each day with a precision he could set his pocket watch to, after having given who knew what excuse to her family as to where she was going. But Matthew didn't ask what she told them. Like so many things regarding Finnea, he didn't want to know.

Refusing to give up, they went over everything from sitting to standing, starting to stopping. When she sat, she reigned like a queen. When she stood, she commanded attention. A far cry from Boston's dictates that a gentlewoman never demand anything, much less anyone's focus.

When she spoke, her voice filled the room, and when she laughed her green eyes glittered like jewels. While everything she did would send proper Boston matrons fleeing, those very same traits made Matthew want her more.

As a result, the second their lesson for the day was done, he sent her on her way with a grim-lipped dismissal that had her brow furrowed in confusion. He hated the look, but it was either her on the front stoop with the door firmly between them or her beneath him, his body sinking into hers.

To make his frustration worse, he still hadn't heard from his father.

On Thursday, the day before the lunch was supposed to take place, at noon precisely, Quincy showed Finnea into the study for the day's lessons. Though not twenty minutes later, Matthew muttered a curse, swearing he would toss her out on her ear.

"I still don't understand why it matters what the card looks like. A card is a card," she snapped peevishly.

Matthew dropped his head onto the desk with a thud.

"Now really, Mr. Hawthorne, don't you think you're being a tad dramatic?"

Matthew raised his head and gave her a noxious glare. "I'm learning from you."

Finnea straightened in her chair indignantly, but she didn't respond.

Matthew's expression was strained. "Can we continue now?"

"Of course," she said with a haughty lift of her chin.

"The card you are referring to is more properly known as a calling card," he explained tightly, "and I didn't make the rules, I'm only trying to teach them to you." He drew a deep breath. "Let me read the explanation again."

Finnea rolled her eyes.

"Do you have a problem with that?" he groused.

"No, no, read away."

Matthew eyed her with not a little menace in his heart, then flipped open a book he had found in a box in the attic. *Our Deportment* by John H. Young, A.M.

"I quote," he began, " 'To the unrefined or underbred, the visiting card is but a trifling and insignificant bit of paper . . .' "

Finnea snorted.

Matthew determinedly ignored her. " '. . . but to the cultured disciple of social law, it conveys a subtle and unmistakable intelligence.' "

"All right, all right, I got that part. I'm a heathen unless I carry a card."

"A calling card."

"So you've said."

"Tomorrow remind me to deal with polite forms of conversation."

"I will. No doubt you could benefit from a lesson or two," she replied with a scowl.

His jaw muscle ticked. He counted to ten, then back again. "Now, for folding the calling card."

"Are you saying that not only do I have to *leave* a card, but I have to *fold* it, too?"

"Yes," he stated, a sharp pain beginning to stab in his temple—a pain that had nothing to do with his injuries and everything to do with the irritating woman who called herself a student. "If you leave the card in person," he explained through gritted teeth, "you should turn a corner down. As an example, if the call is made on all or at least several members of the household, the card is folded in the middle. If you're calling for a simple visit, you fold the right-hand upper corner. If you're calling for some sort of felicitation, fold the left-hand upper corner. A condolence call, the lower—"

"Stop!" she screeched, slapping her hands over her ears. "I can't take any more!"

"Neither can I." He slammed the book shut, then pushed up from the table.

"Where are you going?" she demanded, her elbows still on the table, her hands still covering her ears as she peered up at him.

"Away."

Her hands came down and slapped against the table. "But we haven't finished!"

"But we are finished, Miss Winslet, and if you don't leave now and give me a chance to regain what little good humor I have left these days, I might be inclined to be finished permanently," he warned.

"That is not fair!"

He slashed her a crafty look. "Hasn't anyone ever told you that life isn't fair?"

"You can't quit now," she cried out, leaping up from the table.

His raised brow flattened, and he heaved a weary sigh. "And why is that?"

Suddenly she dropped her gaze to the floor, shuffled her feet, and bit her lip. "Because you promised to discuss my walk."

"Your walk? What are you talking about?"

Her head shot up. "Yesterday! When I was leaving, remember? You said I walked like a horse."

Matthew grimaced. "Oh, that."

"Yes, *oh that!* And you said we would deal with that another day. Well, this is another day, and I refuse to go another second without knowing what I am doing wrong."

He *had* said she walked like a horse, but only because he had been badgered enough for one day with questions about etiquette and the reasoning behind it that didn't have answers. At least there were no answers of which he was aware.

A woman sat up straight . . . because.

A woman put her ankles together rather than crossing her legs . . . because.

A woman never spoke to a man who was not first introduced to her by someone else under any circumstances . . . because.

Everything was just *because*. How was he supposed to know why women were supposed to do the senseless things they did?

He didn't like the fact that she had caused him to question yet another facet of the life he had lived so happily before the accident. And when she had reminded him that she would be back the next day, his mood had grown less than charitable.

"What kind of a horse?" she persisted in all seriousness, breaking into his thoughts. "A stock horse, an old swaybacked horse?" She groaned. "A clompy old dray horse?"

Instantly, the image of a massive, huge-footed dray horse came to mind, and he chuckled. "Actually, I was thinking more along the lines of a racehorse, if you must know." And it was true.

She moved like the wind, a wisp beyond reach. Like a fast-moving storm or a whispered breath against skin—depending on the day and the depths of darkness that scudded through her eyes. To a man, it was stunning to watch her. But to Boston society, she simply walked much too fast.

It was one of the many things that made her so fascinating.

One of the many things she wanted to change. Though why she wanted to change so badly, he wasn't altogether certain. Was it simply because she wanted acceptance from her mother? He had the feeling that there was more to it than that.

What was that piece to her that he sensed but could never grasp? Or put into words? That piece that somehow seemed to be the key to both of them?

He didn't like the thought, never did when he felt they were tangled together inextricably.

"What do you mean, a racehorse?" she demanded, her eyes narrowed suspiciously.

"You move too fast."

Her suspicion turned glum. "Oh yes. I know I do, though even when I think I've slowed down, my grandmother gives me that displeased look that says I haven't."

"Slow down, yes. But it goes beyond that. Think of it as carrying yourself. Walking into a room like you are a gift to all those present. A vision to behold."

She gave an unladylike snort. "Gift? To all those present? I think not. I might be a vision, but as far as Nester is concerned, the vision is a nightmare."

"Don't think that way," he commanded. "Don't defeat yourself before you ever walk into a room."

"Then tell me how!"

She stood erect. Always proud. Always brave. But she couldn't quite hide the fear that raced through her eyes. It never ceased to amaze him how sometimes she seemed a woman, other times a child.

As always, the contradiction in her brought a reluctant smile to his lips.

"For starters, keep your arms at your side rather than swinging them."

She held her arms up and looked at them like she had never seen them before. "I swing them?" she asked, seemingly dumbfounded.

"Yes, you do," he said, his lips crooking.

"Hmmm." Her brow furrowed in concentration; then she nodded her head and she started to walk across the room, her arms plastered to her side, making her look like a swiftly moving upright stick.

He had to bite his lip to keep from laughing.

"How was that?" she demanded, whirling around to face him.

"Well . . ."

"It was awful! I can tell by the look on your face."

"I wouldn't say awful. Just don't be so stiff."

"Don't move, but don't be stiff. Grrr."

"Just move naturally. Think of it as flowing, keeping your arms relaxed at your sides rather than swinging them like windmills."

"Stiff? Windmills? Aren't we full of compliments today," she bit out caustically.

"You asked," he replied with an amused shrug.

She glared at him, forced out a breath, closed her eyes, and concentrated. "Okay." She rolled her head around as if to relieve tension, then started off across the room. "I'm flowing, how does it look?"

Like her body had lost its bones and she was some sort of palsy victim. "Better," he lied.

"You don't mean it!"

"Actually, no, but I was trying to be polite."

"Why start now?" she snapped.

"Tsk, tsk, tsk, Miss Winslet. What do we say about women with sharp tongues?"

"That they are smarter than the lot of Boston women thrown together, who, I might add, could stand a month or two learning a bit about life in Africa!"

"Hmmm, that wasn't exactly the line I had in mind."

She glared at him.

"Are we going to deal with your walk or not?" he asked.

"Yes! But you're going to have to show me how to do it."

"Me?" he blurted out.

"Yes, you. You walk across the room like you are trying to describe."

"Not on your life."

"What do you mean? You've been telling me how to do it for the last twenty minutes. Why not just show me?"

"Telling you is one thing. I see women walk all the time.

But doing it is another thing entirely. I'm a man, for God's sake."

"Which means?" she asked sarcastically, dragging the words out in question.

"That I am not about to parade around this room walking like a woman."

"Who's going to see you?"

"You will."

"That's the point."

"I won't do it."

"Oh, come on."

"No!"

"Are you afraid?" she asked, her brow raised in challenge.

His stare was murderous, and he muttered expletives that made her blush. "I am not afraid, Miss Winslet."

"Good, then show me."

He stood for long seconds, glowering; before turning on his heel and starting across the room. He tried to do just as he had instructed. Hell, it was hard.

Once, twice, hanging his arms at his sides and walking in a way that felt like a flow. Swish, swish. Head held high. He turned back. And stopped.

"You're laughing!" he accused.

"Me?" she asked innocently. "Never. I've got something caught in my throat."

"You're going to catch something else. A door in your face with no hope for another lesson from me if you're not careful."

She smiled at him, trying her best to look contrite. "Not another word, not so much as a smirk."

"That's true," he began, taking her hand and pulling her toward the door, "because you're leaving."

She stopped abruptly, the motion pulling him back, bringing them face-to-face.

He forgot about what she was saying as his thoughts swirled around this odd woman who stood before him.

She was dressed in a beautiful deep blue silk today, no doubt a gown chosen by her mother. Her hair was pulled back in an elegant twist at the back of her head. Demure. The perfect lady. Except for her eyes.

He had the fleeting thought that no matter how refined she became, if indeed she did, her eyes would always betray her. For a moment, all good humor fled, and he saw someone as lost as he was and just as determined not to show it.

"What made you change your mind about teaching me?" she asked, so quietly he almost didn't hear.

His gaze drifted to her lips. "Your dogged persistence."

"That wasn't it."

He reached out and brushed her lower lip with his thumb. "In truth, I still owe Janji," he replied, hardly thinking about his words. "I didn't get you safely to Matadi."

And he hadn't. As soon as the rescuers had arrived, they were separated. He hadn't seen her again until the night of the dinner party, though he had tried to find her. But she had disappeared from the hospital. He hadn't tried after that, telling himself it was for the best.

"That wasn't your fault," she said.

"A debt is a debt. And I still owe him."

"You never told me why you owe him."

He chuckled at this. "You don't let anything go, do you?"

"Just tell me."

"It was nothing," he said, forcing a casualness into his voice that he didn't feel. "He shot a lion that was showing an overzealous interest in me."

At the words, she stiffened. "A lion that was about to attack?"

Matthew shrugged with practiced indifference, blood rushing through his veins as he remembered. "So it appeared."

"Janji told me about that day."

His indifference fled and he froze.

"He never mentioned your name, but he told me the man stared boldly, straight into the lion's eyes. That was you."

"What else did he say?"

This time she hesitated. She looked up at him, studying him, before she said, "That he was never sure if you were going to raise your own gun to save yourself. Were you?"

He looked away.

"Matthew. Were you?"

No. He wasn't.

His heart pounded, the sounds of rustling long grasses filling his ears. The heat. The constant despair. Then the lion, suddenly there, standing as still as Matthew, each staring at the other. Each understanding in some primal way that one of them wouldn't survive. The odd second of relief that it was finally over. But in the next second, it had come over him, swift and intense. Mary. He couldn't do this to Mary.

He remembered the surprise of the thought, the overwhelming intensity of the love he felt and the need to get home, to make everything right.

At that point he tried to lift the gun. He had. But by then it was too late. Just when he felt the lion's hot breath on his cheek, regret and despair for a little girl across the sea swept through him. But regret froze in his mind when a shot rang out and the lion dropped at his feet. He couldn't move. Couldn't think. Until finally he turned and found the regal black man standing twenty paces away, his gun still smoking, studying him.

Janji had saved his life, but more important, he had given him a second chance to make things right with Mary. If only things had been different when he returned.

"Matthew, talk to me."

Finnea stood before him, proud and determined. She was so strong, stronger than he was. She was lost, for reasons he didn't understand, but she fought on—to fit in, to not give up. He nearly smiled at the thought that *she* was the warrior, not him. He wanted to give up, would have if it hadn't been for Mary. And now he didn't know where to turn, since the one reason he had to live was afraid of him.

He drew a deep breath. "There is nothing to talk about." He stepped closer, needing the feel of her, the strength of her.

His gaze drifted low, catching on her mouth, and he felt the swift rush of blood through his body. God how he wanted her.

He told himself to step away, but his ironclad control deserted him. He couldn't stop himself from touching her any more than he could stop himself from breathing.

His hands came up to frame her face, and his thumbs gently trailed over her lips, her mouth opening on a trembling breath. Her warrior's stance wavered. Her eyes filled with uncertainty.

"I don't think this is wise," she said, her voice hoarse as he leaned down to her.

"I haven't done a wise thing since I met you," he replied, the whispered words fanning her face.

With that, he kissed her, brushing his lips against hers. Just a touch, he told himself. Just a touch to sate his curiosity.

But the touch only made him want more. Yearning raced through him like a torch. His manhood swelled, and he leaned back against a table. With an exquisite slowness, he pulled her between his legs. Desire, hard and raging. And she gasped.

But he wanted her as he had wanted little else in his life. Just as he had wanted her in the jungle.

He realized the truth and muttered a curse against her skin. But he couldn't stop. "God, how I've wanted this."

His hands held her face as he kissed her eyelids, his lips trailing down until he captured her mouth once again in a delicate dance. He gently tugged at her full lower lip, his tongue coaxing her to more.

"Open for me, Finn."

And she did. She sucked in her breath when their tongues touched, and his hand drifted down her back, pressing her close, cradling the rise of his male flesh against her softness. Innocent and unaware of what she was doing to him, she moved slightly, brushing the gentle curve of her abdomen against his hardness, making him suck in his breath at the intensity.

She melted into him, as if becoming a part of him, and all sense of time and place vanished, sensation building like waves.

Suddenly her hands tangled in his shirt, and she pulled, making it clear she wanted him as much as he wanted her. They gave in completely, their kiss becoming something wild, something primitive. She licked his lips and he gently bit her tongue. Her fingers sought skin; then she gasped when he brought his hands around and raked his fingertips sensually over her nipples beneath the bodice of her gown.

Lost to the feel of her, he was unaware of the discreet knock that sounded on the door, unaware still when the door opened.

But Finnea heard and she jumped away, her startled gasp penetrating the desire-filled recesses of his mind.

His jaw tight, Matthew stepped in front of Finnea protectively as she hurriedly adjusted her gown, and found the butler, tripping over himself to back out of the room.

"You better have a damn good reason for this, Quincy," he demanded.

"A note, sir," the man choked out, then clumsily extended a silver tray. "From your father."

Chapter Ten

"Frankfurters on a street corner," Matthew said, his words crystallizing in the frigid air as he stared in disbelief at the nickel dog-in-a-bun the swarthy, dark-haired little vendor had just handed him.

It was the following day, Friday, and Matthew forced a laugh. He had set out from the house in a grand mood, but his excitement was quickly dying a harsh death. "Quite a change from Locke-Ober's, Father."

Bradford Hawthorne and his son stood amid the nearly deafening din at the bustling corner of Tremont and Winter Streets, not fifty yards from the long, narrow alleyway that led to Boston's bastion of male dining called Locke-Ober's. Friday luncheon at the exclusive men's club had always entailed a small, select group of men, muted voices, stuffed leather chairs, a quartet playing Bach in the corner, and some of the finest food in Boston. Matthew and his father had held a standing reservation for years. Had always sat at the same table.

Today they stood on the sidewalk, jostled now and again by the throng of pedestrians, suspect meat in their hands, and a hurdy-gurdy man playing his traveling piano with a tin can set on top to encourage people to toss change his way.

Beyond that, it was cold. Much too cold to be standing outside. Matthew's scars began to throb, his hand started to ache, stabs of pain shooting down into his shoulder, making it difficult to hold his meal. But his good hand held a cup of hot cocoa, giving him no way to shift the burden.

Burden.

His breathing grew harsh. A five-inch, feather-light dog-in-a-bun had become a burden. Inadequacy raked over him.

He told himself to concentrate. This was not the place for his body to turn on him. But the cold was making everything more difficult, and people began to stare. He tried to ignore them but couldn't, and neither could his father.

Bradford grumbled and awkwardly balanced his own frankfurter and cocoa in thickly gloved hands.

"Perhaps we could go someplace where we could sit down," Matthew offered, forcing the words carefully through rapidly numbing lips.

"I don't have time. And this is close to my office."

So was Locke-Ober's, but Matthew didn't say that.

The older Hawthorne looked at his lunch as if he had never seen such a thing in his life, and undoubtedly he never had. Even as children the Hawthorne boys weren't allowed to buy food from street vendors. Matthew's jaw hardened at the thought that suddenly it was good enough now.

Shame spiked through his mind. His nostrils flared on a deep breath as a crisp winter breeze wrapped around him. His hand fumbled, and he dropped the frankfurter on the ground. Mortified, he reached down too quickly, the sudden movement sending sparks of pain shooting through his side, and he lost his balance. Dropping to his haunches, the cup and cocoa spilling from his hand, he balanced himself on the cold grimy walkway.

Passersby craned their necks to get a better look at what was happening.

"Get up," his father snapped, his eyes darting around to see who was watching.

Breathing deeply, Matthew forced himself to stand, forgetting the food that lay on the ground.

"What's wrong with you?" his father demanded, his voice low and harsh. "Your behavior is appalling."

A small, wiry man had stopped and looked on with blatant curiosity.

Bradford wheeled around to face him. "What are you staring at?" he bellowed.

The man's eyes widened and he hurried away.

Bradford cursed, then tried to contain himself. "What do you want, Matthew?" he demanded, no longer pretending to be anything but impatient. "Your mother said it was important."

"What do I want?" Matthew asked, startled.

"Yes. Is it money? Women problems?" He narrowed his eyes and looked at his son before he quickly dropped his gaze. "Are you in trouble?"

Matthew gritted his teeth, pride surging, mixing with the pain. "I thought now that I was back from Africa," he stated, with a casual indifference he didn't feel, "we would start having our Friday lunches again."

Bradford met his eye for a long drawn-out moment, and a world of something—regret, anguish ... anger—flashed across his face before he looked away. "While you were gone, I made other commitments, to the historical society. They meet Fridays at one."

"Then we can lunch another day." He couldn't stop the words. Matthew knew he should have kept to his resolve not to see his father, since the man had made it clear he no longer wanted to see him. But somehow he couldn't let it go. Somehow he thought he could make things right again by spending time together, by letting his father get used to his appearance.

"The thing is, Matthew, my days are filled." Bradford shifted his weight.

Matthew straightened. "Why?" he demanded, his lips feeling thick and awkward. "Why can't we go back? Pick up where we left off."

"Because the past is just that. We've started new lives. We all have new lives since the ... since you've been back," he said curtly, glancing at the spilled cup of cocoa on the ground.

"No!" Matthew snapped, his jaw clenched as rage flashed quick and hot. "Just say it! It's because you're embarrassed of me. Of this face."

His father's head shot up, and he stared at him with blazing eyes. "Yes! Yes, I'm embarrassed of you!" The words exploded into the cold. "But not because of your face."

The older man's countenance went red, a telltale vein

bulging out on his forehead. Matthew's spine stiffened with sudden dread.

"I won't go to lunch with you to a place like Locke-Ober's or anywhere else important because everyone will see you and remember your wife!"

The words slashed Matthew with the sting of a whip. He couldn't move as he watched his father hurl his own frank-furter and cocoa into a wire mesh bin, then turn back to meet his eye.

"Kimberly used you, for your money, for your position, but you were too blind to see it. You failed this family!" Suddenly he became aware of the people who had begun to stare at him, so he leaned close. "That reflects on me!" he hissed. "Me, Bradford Hawthorne. After I spent my life rebuilding the family name, I have to endure the shame of being tied to the worst scandal to hit Boston in a hundred years! I was willing to tolerate your painting fancy, but I will not tolerate a dis-grace." Bradford leaned even closer. "Hawthornes satisfy their women, and if they can't manage to do that," he added with a derogatory sneer, "then they keep them in their place. You did neither." His eyes narrowed. "Your scarred face is simply an unavoidable reminder to me—and to everyone who sees you—of a scandal that will be remembered by all of Boston for the *next* hundred years. *That* is why I can't stand to look at you."

Bradford was breathing hard, his face florid. Visibly he at-tempted to regain his composure. "I believe we are both through with this lunch. Now, if you will excuse me."

With that, Bradford walked away, disappearing into the crowded streets as Matthew stood, too stunned to move.

A sickening fury rose up inside him. He concentrated, forcing himself to breathe. He turned away sharply before he could do violence, but as soon as he came around he saw Finnea. She stood several yards away at the street corner looking between him and the retreating back of his father, her brow furrowed in confusion.

For one brief moment, caught in her dazzling green-eyed gaze, he felt like the man he used to be.

But that wasn't true. His father had just made that perfectly clear.

He felt the burn and itch of his scars. On his face, down his arm. The pain that never went away, that kept him up at night. Made him weak and inadequate.

Without a word, he strode past her on the granite walkway, forcing himself to concentrate on anything besides his father. He held his arm close to his side, minimizing the movement. He needed to get home.

But the walkway was crowded, and people ran into him, jarring his shoulder. White dots flashed and for a moment he had to stop and steady himself.

"Mr. Hawthorne."

He didn't open his eyes, but he could tell she was right next to him, could feel her without touching. He felt a swift stab of longing to turn his face into her shoulder, to pull her close and forget.

The weakness stunned him and angered him in turn.

Biting out an expletive, he started forward. When the throng of pedestrians got too thick for him to maneuver, he stepped down the granite curb to the cobbled street, mindless of the traffic.

"Mr. Hawthorne, please."

He didn't slow down.

"Damn it, Matthew, stop!"

He halted dead in his tracks, as did just about everyone else within earshot. Turning slowly, his gaze was deadly. Finnea elbowed her way through the men and women until she came to his side.

"What do you want?" he demanded.

"I want to know what is wrong."

With a curse, he started walking again. After a startled second, she hurried after him along the brick-lined walkway that bordered Tremont Street. She came up to his side but he didn't stop, so she fell into step beside him. The farther they walked, the quieter it became as they left behind the bustle of downtown. Quiet, but no peace.

"Why won't you talk to me?" she inquired, having to run

every few steps to keep up. "Did you have a fight with your father?"

Still he ignored her.

Tree branches coated in ice formed a weblike canopy over their heads when they cut through the parklike expanse of the Boston Commons toward Charles Street, their footsteps echoing on the recently plowed path. The air was filled with the smell of birch and pine, burning in fireplaces in the houses that bordered the park like a redbrick and sandstone frame. It was a sunny day, the long rays making the ice glisten like crystal.

As usual, she wasn't careful where she stepped, and when she hit a slick of ice, she gasped, her arms flailing at her sides to regain her balance, to no avail. She started going down, but Matthew caught her.

And sucked in his breath.

They stood for long seconds, clasped together beneath the canopy of ice and branches. She could feel his heart pounding in his chest, saw his eyes pressed closed tightly.

"Matthew, what's wrong?"

He inhaled sharply and opened his eyes. He didn't let go of her, and she had the fleeting thought that he couldn't as their breaths curled white between them.

With effort, he cursed and set her at arm's length. When she stood back and looked at him, she had to swallow her startled cry. His countenance was ravaged, the muscles in his jaw leaping beneath his skin.

"Don't you ever stay home?" he snapped.

The question surprised her. "Not if I can help it," she answered too honestly, then quickly added, "I mean, I need to get out to shop."

He cast her a baleful glance. "You mean shop for some more of those bizarre gowns you wear?" he asked unkindly.

Her mouth opened and closed, her eyes blinking.

He started away.

Finnea watched him for a few seconds, then hurried after him.

They exited the Commons, then crossed Charles Street to the Public Gardens. The elaborate, wrought-iron gate that marked the Charles Street entrance stood open, the tall carved granite posts stoic like guards to the wide-open path. Finnea followed him doggedly over the footbridge that stretched over the lagoon, ice-skaters speeding by below. Every time she came here, she marveled at the men with heavy woolen mufflers wrapped around their necks, gliding over the ice like sleek, long-legged birds.

She yearned to leap out next to them, glide along, fly across the smooth surface—to empty her mind. But she ignored the urge and hurried over the bridge.

"Matthew, talk to me! Tell me, what is wrong?"

Minutes later, she nearly ran into the back of him when he stopped short in front of Dove's Way.

"Nothing is wrong, Finnea. Now, go home, or go buy more dresses, or go do whatever it is you do. Just leave me be."

He took the granite steps, and Finnea could have sworn he was counting. But when he tried to slam himself inside the house, she followed.

"I just want to help!" she pleaded.

But his expression transformed from annoyance to outrage, though he was no longer looking at her.

For the first time, she took in the surroundings inside his palatial town house. Quincy stood proudly in the foyer, the servants lined up beside him. The cook, several maids, the groom. All looking starched and proud.

"I hope you don't mind, sir," the butler said, his chin held high, "but I took the liberty of rehanging the paintings I found in the attic that you had uncovered. They look splendid, don't they?"

Finnea's mouth fell open in silent awe at the paintings. Some large, some small, all exquisitely detailed works of art.

"You painted these?" she asked with a gasp, walking into the house uninvited.

Matthew didn't answer, only stared.

"Indeed, madam," Quincy boasted. "An impressive lot, to be sure. Everyone said so."

Matthew stood like stone as Finnea moved from piece to piece, stunned, catching glimpses of other paintings hanging in startling vividness beyond the foyer. She had never imagined the caliber of his work.

With breath held in wonder, she recognized his mother and what had to be his brothers. His father, so finely wrought that Finnea felt as though the man would step off the wall at any moment and comment on the work himself. But it was the portrait of a woman who held her eye. White-blond hair, ice-blue eyes. Stunningly beautiful, carrying herself so properly. She was everything Finnea was trying so hard to be.

"Who is she?" Finnea asked, her mouth going dry.

Matthew didn't say a word.

Quincy grew solemn. "That is Mrs. Hawthorne, God rest her soul."

In that instant everything made sense. Matthew had been married and lost his wife. He had gone to Africa to forget.

He had been married to a perfect lady.

The knowledge embarrassed her—the realization that he had known she was lacking from the second she stepped on the train.

She turned to face him, but Matthew didn't notice. He stared at the work, his eyes traveling from canvas to canvas, his expression closed. He turned to the line of servants, his body rigidly held, though Finnea could see the veins standing out on his temples.

"Please go," he told the staff, his lips thinned, his face deeply etched with lines of strain.

The cleaning maids and footmen exchanged nervous glances, then hurried away. But Quincy stayed, the pleasure on his face disappearing.

"You, too, Quincy."

The man remained at full attention. "I am sorry if I have displeased you, sir," he stated. "I thought . . . I just thought that . . ." His words trailed off. "You left in such a fine mood this morning, and when I found the paintings uncovered, well, I took the liberty—"

He cut himself off.

"I understand, Quincy," Matthew said, his voice tight, though not unkind. "I appreciate your efforts."

The butler immediately raced to a painting and started to

take it down. "I'll have each and every one of them put away within the hour."

But Matthew stopped him, his control barely held. "Please leave, Quincy."

"But sir—"

"Leave!"

Quincy scampered away.

Finnea stood to the side and watched as Matthew closed his eyes. When he opened them, he looked at the painting of his wife. Never had she seen such utter despair in all her life.

"She was beautiful," she whispered.

He wheeled around as if he had forgotten she was there. "Beautiful?" he raged. "Yes, she was beautiful! But she used that beauty to get what she wanted, as my father just got through pointing out. That, Miss Winslet, is what I was just discussing with my father. Are you happy now? Will you finally stop badgering me?"

"I was not badgering you!" She blushed because of course she had been. But how could she help it? "I was concerned, that's all."

He jerked away, but everywhere he turned, he stiffened at the sight of another painting.

"They really are stunning, Matthew. Truly, you should take up your art again. You are an incredibly talented artist."

"I am not an artist!" he shouted, his voice breaking. "Not any longer!"

Without warning he picked up a vase and hurled it, the china connecting with a brilliant portrait of himself. The frame crashed to the ground, and before Finnea knew what was happening, he took to each work with a manic strength, tearing each piece from the wall and crashing it violently to the floor.

"Stop!" she cried, racing to him.

But he only shook her off, the crash and clatter of noise echoing against the high ceiling as he continued his destruction.

"Good God, what are you doing?"

But Matthew wasn't listening. He went from piece to piece like a madman, sweat breaking out on his brow, his step faltering until he stumbled, only to pick himself up and go to the next. He didn't stop until there wasn't a painting left on the walls.

When he turned back, his eyes were wild, as if daring her to say a word.

Matthew leaned back against a marble column, his breath coming in sharp bursts.

They stared at each other, both wary.

"Why?" she whispered finally. "Why do you act this way?"

He gave her a negligent shrug. "It's no act, sweetheart," he drawled, insolence marking his tone. "That's me."

"It is not!"

His insolence evaporated and he stared at her.

"Stop acting like some crazed warrior." She felt as if all of Africa were threatening her. "I happen to know you are not really like this. You are a wonderful man. Stop pretending to be otherwise."

He laughed at that, a cold hard sound that sent a shiver down her spine.

"A wonderful man? How little you know."

He started toward her, his steps slow, and he never took his eyes off her.

"What are you doing, Mr. Hawthorne?" she asked, her blood beginning to rush.

"I'm going to show you exactly how wonderful I am."

"I don't like the look in your eyes."

His gaze was menacing. "You shouldn't."

"Matthew," she said, forgetting to be formal, holding out her hand to ward him off.

"Yes?" he asked, taking another step closer.

"Don't do something you'll regret just to prove some idiotic point."

His eyes bored into her with murderous intensity. She turned to flee, but it was too late. His hand snaked out and grabbed her wrist in a punishing grip and he pulled her close.

Sparrows chirped madly outside, flying in and out of the snow-covered bushes in some sort of game.

"Don't do this," she pleaded.

But his mouth came down on hers, painfully, slanting and

ravaging. He punished her with his lips until she went limp in his arms, her body trembling, though not with desire.

Pulling back, he looked into her eyes, his own tormented. He didn't move. Didn't seem to breathe. Their gazes met and held as she looked close, so close she could see the dark flecks that made his eyes so blue. With effort, she pushed away from him.

"You might be able to prove to yourself that you are a monster," she whispered fiercely, "but it will take more than that to make me believe."

His face hardened, and she could tell he was going to pull her back, intent on proving the worst once and for all. But this time she was too fast for him, and she leaped away.

"This isn't about being a monster," she said when she was well beyond him. "This is about fathers and sons." Her head snapped back in thought. "I think it must be the same as mothers and daughters—only the opposite. Sons love their mothers but see their worth in their father's eyes."

He went still.

"You're angry because of it. And lashing out." Her eyes flickered as another thought occurred to her. "That must be what's wrong with Nester, why he's so angry. He didn't know his father's love."

She started to pace. "And that must be why Jeffrey is so kind," she added, her brow furrowed as her mind circled with insight and understanding. "He must have had a strong relationship with his father."

Matthew stiffened. "Jeffrey Upton?"

"Yes, the gentleman who sat next to me at dinner."

"I know who he is."

The green of Finnea's eyes clouded. "He is nice, and he's handsome."

"I'd hardly call him nice, and I certainly wouldn't call him handsome. I'd call him old. Old enough to be your father."

She scowled. "That isn't true. He is mature, not old. And he is a terribly kind man."

His eyes narrowed dangerously. "Why should it matter if he is kind or not?"

She suddenly remembered where she was, in Matthew

Hawthorne's house, with paintings ripped to shreds all around them. "Because," she said uncomfortably.

"You think he's going to ask you to marry him, don't you?" he demanded, his gaze penetrating. "Whose idea is it? Yours? Upton's? Or is this something your mother wants you to do?"

She tried to turn away. "Stop this!"

In a few bold strides, he came up to her and grabbed her wrist once again, turning her to him. "Does Jeffrey touch you this way?" he demanded in a hoarse whisper, pulling her close. "Is that why you are thinking about marrying him?"

Furtively, she pushed at his hand, but he only persisted, his strong fingers running down her cheek to her jaw. "Or like this?"

"Stop it, Matthew."

"Why?" he rasped against her skin.

She pulled a deep breath when he pressed his lips against her hair, gently, with infinite care, no longer punishing.

"Does he touch you like this, Finn?"

"Don't call me that."

"Call you what?" His fingers trailed to her neck.

"You know what. Don't call me Finn."

"You didn't object before."

"I'm objecting now."

But the words were barely out when his fingers tangled in her hair, and he tilted her head as he leaned down to her.

Their lips met and she groaned. This time the kiss was long and desperate, filled with quaking need.

He captured her against the wall while his hand trailed down her side. He touched her breast, his thumb brushing the tender peak, and she stiffened, trying to step back, but there was nowhere to go.

"Shhhh," he murmured, gentling her, stroking her hair, "it's all right. I won't hurt you."

Drawn into his spell, she started to ease. It was always that way when he touched her, seeking his warmth. But then he cupped her round bottom and molded her against his hardness.

"Matthew," she cried softly, concerned.

He lifted his head with a groan. She could tell he was

reining in his desire. He reached up and gently brushed his thumb over her full lower lip, and she shivered with longing.

"God, you make me forget." He kissed her forehead. "I want to taste you." He kissed her cheek. "Hold you."

She could feel him tremble as he trailed his kiss down her jaw to the curve of her throat, tasting a glimpse of skin beneath the layers of her gown.

"Let me touch you."

Those words. The endless, slow-looping replay of the night in the jungle, the memory filling her mind. But this time the words weren't from memory, they were real. And her breath caught.

"Yes, Finn, let me touch you."

She whimpered and her hands pushed hard against his chest, pushing him away.

He stopped, his breathing ragged, but when he started to concede, her fingers curled into the fine linen of his shirt.

And they were lost.

His mouth covered hers, desire raging unchecked. He cupped her again, pulling her up, moving her against him in slow, torturous strokes.

She wrapped her arms around his shoulders so tightly, afraid that she wouldn't be able to let go. She could feel the beat of his heart, the hard planes of his body.

She understood then how inextricably she was linked to him. Bound together by that day on the train when he could have left but hadn't. Bound to him because he had saved her life. Bound to him because he had treated her with honor. She didn't just owe him, as she had told him, as she had thought. She was bound to him as surely as she was bound to the earth and not the sky. As his lips pressed against hers, she couldn't deny it any longer.

He pulled her closer, his hard muscles beneath her hands, beneath her palms, which only grazed the material.

"Touch me," he rasped.

He pressed her hand to his chest with his own, a dance of fingers and lips.

She needed him as if in him she could find something of herself, something of Africa. But then Africa was the very thing she needed to extricate from her soul. Just as she needed to extricate Matthew from her mind. He was too strong, too forbidding. Too much of *Mzungu Kichaa*. They could be friends, as she had tried to convince herself they were, but she couldn't allow herself to think about the way he had made her feel that night in the jungle among the thick, green leaves and deafening silence. Or here. The yearning. The need.

She might be drawn to this man, but she had no place in his life. Just as he had no place in hers.

With a sound that started deep in his chest, he pulled back and looked at her.

"Do you actually think he loves you?" he asked, his voice ragged.

She tried to look away but he grasped her chin, gentle but determined.

"Why do you even think about a man like Jeffrey Upton?"

"That's none of your business."

"You say that because you don't know why you would consider him," he said, pulling her back.

"That's not true." But she hardly understood what she was saying when his lips brushed against her neck.

She told herself to focus. "Jeffrey is perfect for me."

"Liar," he replied on a stroke of breath against the collarbone beneath her velvet gown. "Unless you mean he's perfect because of the way he condescends to you," he added, his voice sharp as he grazed his teeth against the curve of her ear.

Her head fell back, her lips parting in a gasp. "That is not true."

He stopped abruptly and held her by the shoulders. "Isn't it? I saw the way he treated you at my parents' party. Like you were a child, not like the woman you are."

She tried to move away, but he held her secure. "Tell me, Finn," he demanded, his voice a raw edge. "Do you love him?"

No sound. A quiet that seeped to the soul. Not even a faint rustle of the thick, succulent leaves in the jungle.

The pain receded, floating at the back of her mind like a ship at sea. Matthew held her close. This perfect man with his warrior's scar had saved her. Had cared for her. Pressed his strong, bold fingers to her skin to stop the bleeding, bound her thigh with a long swathe of material he had found in a satchel, securing it around her hips, then wrapping her nearly naked body in one of his shirts he had pulled from his pack. His ministrations so caring. So gentle. So different from how he had been on the train.

Tears burned in her eyes at the thought of him leaving her.

"Hold me," she whispered.

His arms tightened around her and he settled her against his chest.

"I am holding you, Finn. You're going to be fine."

But that wasn't it. That wasn't what she wanted.

Her throat tightened. She curled closer, a desperate yearning seeping deeper than she understood. It was as if she couldn't get close enough to him, close enough to sate this desperate need for a man she hardly knew. It made no sense, she realized that. But still she needed a word, a promise. She needed something to make her heart calm in her chest.

"Will I see you again?" she said softly. "After this. After we get to Matadi."

He looked away from her. Tried to move away, but they were tangled together.

"What's wrong?" she asked, hating the unsteadiness she heard in her voice.

"Nothing," he said, but she could feel tension fill his body.

Despite his sudden harshness, she took his large hand, stared at his long chiseled fingers still stained with her blood, then laced them with hers. Only hours before she had wanted to let go, drift away, but he had pulled her back, forcing her to survive. She felt overwhelmed by emotion, flooded by feelings for this man who had seen her, touched her, held her life in his hands—feelings she hardly understood.

"Will I, Matthew? Will I see you in Matadi?"

She held her breath, needing to know. But the look on his face made her heart drop.

His blue eyes were wild, his face etched in hard, fathomless planes. "No," he said. No feeling. No caring. "No you won't. I have no place for you in my life."

Finnea blinked, the tiled warrior and snow-white dove in the high ceiling staring down at her, mortified as she remembered how he had seen her without clothes, had touched her bare skin, had listened as she foolishly bared her soul. Then turned her away. The one person she had felt connected to, the one person who somehow had made her feel safe, hadn't wanted her.

In that moment in the jungle she had finally and completely faced the fact that there was no place for her in Africa. Her home had to be put behind her. Africa was her past, and she had to move beyond it. But then she had found him here. In a house called Dove's Way.

"Do you care if I love Jeffrey?" she asked in a hoarse whisper, unable to help herself as a tiny spark of hope flared that not all of her had to be wiped away.

Matthew didn't reply. He stood very still, too still.

The harsh stab of desolation snaked through her embarrassment, draining the life from her cheeks just as it had in the jungle. After a moment she stepped away, and this time he let her go.

"It doesn't matter," she said, trying to believe, understanding then that her mother was right. Jeffrey Upton would make an ideal husband for her in this new world of Boston. "And if he proposes, I'll say yes."

She waited a moment longer, but still he said nothing. For reasons she wouldn't let herself think about, she felt as if her heart were being ripped from her chest once again.

Gathering what little dignity she had remaining, she started for the door. But at the last minute she couldn't help herself and she looked back.

"Did you love your wife so much? Is that why you went to Africa? To lose yourself? Is that why you hurt so badly now?"

She saw that her words caught him off guard. He looked at her long and hard, emotion scudding across his face.

"Just tell me," she demanded, needing to know.

"Love her?"

The words were spoken with venom, and a chill raced down her spine. He looked her straight in the eye, and she would have sworn in that moment that he hated her.

"I found my wife making love to my best friend."

Her head came back.

"Surprised? I certainly was," he stated derisively. "It was the night of the party announcing my show. I thought Boston turned out to wish me well. As it happened, the cream of society actually turned out because my wife and her lover were the best show in town. I was the only person who didn't know."

"Oh Matthew, I'm sorry."

"Sorry? Why? Because I was a fool?"

"No—"

"I was a fool. I loved her! I would have given her anything. But all she wanted was my name and my money. She had no interest in my love."

Finnea tried to absorb his words, and she noticed how his hand clenched, then slowly came up to trace the scar on his face.

"Is that how it happened?" she asked before she could think better of it. "Is that the night you were scarred?"

His hand dropped to his side, and he glanced at the tattered remains of the painting of his wife, his face filled with blind despair. "Yes. It was the night I killed my best friend and my wife."

Then he began to talk, the words spoken in an eerie monotone as he told her of that night, told her how he flew into the tiny house, blind with rage and fury, the door crashing back on its hinges.

Kimberly and Reynolds jerked in surprise. In a tangle of arms and clothing, the lovers tried to disengage themselves. But Matthew was on them. He tore them apart, flinging his wife aside, then taking to his best friend like a man possessed.

"Matthew, stop!" Kimberly cried, grabbing his arm.

Reynolds did his best to defend himself, but Matthew had always been bigger, stronger. Richer, wealthier. More handsome.

"She loves me, Matthew," the other man spat out, scrambling to his feet. "She's mine! Should have been mine all along."

But Matthew wasn't listening; he roared his fury, picking up a chair and tossing it aside with a crash of glass and splinters. Kimberly screamed. An odd scream. But he ignored her.

He started in on his best friend, each man's fists finding the other. They fought with years of pent-up emotion. Time passed in a punishing flash before Matthew smelled the smoke.

Abruptly he let go. Reynolds fell back against the wall just as flames burst all around them. The kerosene lantern had ignited the draperies. The sprigged muslin went up like kindling, and within seconds the house rocked and shuddered.

Matthew grabbed his wife again, this time to get her outside, and hauled her toward the door. But she clawed and fought him until they staggered like two drunken revelers into the hearth, now blackened and barely distinguishable. For one brief second Matthew caught his reflection in the massive mirror that hung above the mantel.

But the second flashed by, bursting away as the wall collapsed, beams crashing down from the ceiling. He heard Kimberly's scream and he lunged for her, but just before he got there, the world exploded, sending jagged shards of glass flying through the air.

The cut of glass. The feel of splintered wood. He felt the force of impact, sharp, incisive, knocking him to the floor. His head swam and when he tried to grope his way to his knees from beneath the glass and wood, the room seemed to shift around him and he fell back. His arm ached and he couldn't seem to move it well enough to push himself up off the floor.

But then he saw Kimberly. The sight cleared his mind, and with a roar, he staggered to his feet. Pain swept through him, and when he touched his face, his hand came away slippery with blood.

But he gave it little thought. Stumbling over to his wife, he pulled her up into his arms and carried her from the cottage, blood blurring his vision. Stumbling through the doorway, he came face-to-face with a crowd of guests and his family, wild with grief.

People were everywhere, their jewels and waistcoats streaked with soot and smoke. But Matthew's mind froze at the sight of two men staggering out of the cottage with Reynolds's limp, barely clothed body carried between them.

Matthew tried to make sense of the sight.

"Oh God, he's dead!" someone cried out.

"I told you no good could come of this. Those two have

*been sneaking out of parties all season," one woman said
snidely, unflinching in the face of tragedy. "The least they
could have done was be discreet."*

*"Discreet? Good Lord, Kimberly Hawthorne has been
anything but discreet. And from what I've heard, there have
been many who have caught her eye."*

*The women's gazes suddenly locked on Matthew, who held
his wife in his arms, blood covering most of his face and torso.
He turned away slowly, every movement an agony, to look
down at the woman he had loved since he was a boy.*

*"Kim," he whispered, dropping his head to her breast, tears
mixing with blood. "Why?"*

*But later, after his wife had been pronounced dead, the
tears were gone.*

*The easy charm. The golden smiles. The quick laughter. All
gone. He felt nothing more than a cold hardness in his heart. The
scar on his face a constant reminder of what a fool he had been.*

"Oh, Matthew," Finnea gasped. "I'm so sorry. But it wasn't
your fault. You didn't kill them."

He blinked and only slowly seemed to recognize her. "Get
out, Miss Winslet," he said, his expression murderous.

But she didn't move. "Matthew, please. Don't do this to
yourself."

He started toward her. "Get out!" he raged, the words reverberating against the walls and ceilings in a horrifying echo.

And this time she took heed and dashed from the house.

"Damn you!" he bellowed, his voice deep and wounded.

His throat worked and his eyes burned as he pounded his
fist into the door. "Damn you," he choked out, pressing his
forehead against the wood, welcoming the bite of pain against
his skin.

Chapter Eleven

Jeffrey was sitting in the west receiving room when Finnea rushed through the front door of her mother's house, her cheeks pink from much more than the frigid February air. She tried to sneak across the foyer to the grand stairway, to no avail.

"Don't you look lovely," Jeffrey said, standing up and extending his hands to her. "You look like you've been enjoying yourself today."

"Yes," Penelope agreed from where she sat on the chaise, giving her an interested appraisal. "Where have you been that put such a glow in your cheeks?"

If possible, Finnea felt her face grow even redder, and she stammered. "Out."

"Just out? Hmmm. Sounds mysterious."

"Nothing mysterious about it," she added quickly. "I was shopping."

"Oh yes," Penelope said politely, her dark hair pulled up in an elegant chignon, her gown of the finest silk. "Shopping. You do a lot of that these days. And without a chaperone."

Finnea lowered her head. When she did, she found herself looking at her hands, which were clasped in Jeffrey's. Although his hands were impeccably manicured, his fingers were thick and blunt, the hairs on his knuckles gray.

He *was* old enough to be her father, she thought with a start, just as Matthew had said. She snapped her head up. He was mature, she clarified.

As always, he was neatly attired, from his tie to his trousers, never a cuff or a shirt tack out of place.

Nothing rugged or dangerous about him, she thought with relief.

It was his elegance and sophistication, as much as anything, that she admired most about him.

She wanted nothing to do with a man like Matthew Hawthorne and his barbaric ways, she thought as she remembered the shredded paintings strewn across the floor.

No, she didn't want Matthew. She had only thought that in a moment of vulnerability after a long, harrowing night in the jungle.

Suddenly the front door slammed open and shut, bringing Nester into the house. He stormed into the room, his starched white collar high around his neck, his tie askew, his morning coat improperly unbuttoned, his face mottled and red. "What is the meaning of you signing the Kendall contract?" he demanded of Jeffrey.

Finnea felt Jeffrey tense. He dropped her hands and faced her brother.

"Is there something wrong with the Kendall contract?" he asked coolly.

"I don't care if there is or isn't! That isn't the point. It could be any contract."

"Then what is the point, Nester?"

"That you have no right to make decisions without my approval."

Nester began to pace the room, the sound of his steps reverberating on the hardwood floor, shaking off Penelope when she tried to soothe him.

"If I'm not mistaken," Jeffrey said carefully, his anger only a flicker beneath his calm exterior, "it is my job to make these decisions. Moreover, it is only a decision regarding the purchase of the new casting machine. We have discussed for months now that the one at the foundry had to be replaced."

"Only?" Nester snapped, coming face-to-face with Jeffrey. "Only a casting machine? Well, it is *only* my money that you are spending. *Only* my company that you seem to think is yours."

"I think no such thing, Nester. But must I remind you that I control half of the stock? That, combined with the fact that I do run the company makes it possible to sign contracts without your approval."

"Not for long!" Nester blurted.

But as soon as the words were out, he seemed to wish them back.

"Maybe, maybe not," Jeffrey stated cryptically as each man eyed the other.

Finnea had no idea what was transpiring, but she didn't like it. She liked it even less when Nester's face curved with a snide smile.

Out of seemingly nowhere, he said, "Finnea will never fit in here, Upton. Face it."

She didn't understand what made him suddenly turn on her. Regardless, the words seared her to the core.

"That's right, little sis," he added, his voice low and angry. "You think that you're going to come back here and take your place as the daughter of the house. Well, you have another think coming. You will never fit in here."

Jeffrey stepped forward. "She will if she marries me."

This time Finnea gasped and Nester scoffed.

His face grave and serious, Jeffrey shocked both Nester and Finnea.

"My dearest Finnea, will you marry me?"

She was unable to think, much less speak.

"I know, I know. I just blurted it out, and that was foolish." Jeffrey bowed his head and focused on her fingers, his thumbs brushing over the back of her hands. "It would mean a great deal to me to have you as my wife." He raised his head. "And if you say yes, I will do my best to make you a worthy husband."

Leticia strode into the room. "What is going on here? I can hear your shouting all the way upstairs."

Nester pointed his finger at Jeffrey. "He wants my business!" he shouted.

"What are you talking about?" Leticia demanded, trying to understand.

But Nester wasn't interested in explaining, and Finnea couldn't get a word past her aching throat.

"How could he marry her?" Nester continued in a rant. "She's a heathen!"

Jeffrey reacted in seconds, whirling around, and before Finnea knew what was happening, he slammed Nester up against the wall, paintings and sconces rattling in protest. "Don't you ever say that about Finnea again, do you understand me?"

Finnea's hands flew to her mouth, astonished. But somehow her heart surged with gratitude and heartfelt appreciation for this man who cared about her.

Leticia began to sob quietly and Penelope gasped.

"How dare you!" Nester screeched.

"I dare because I'm sick and tired of you treating your sister with such horrible disregard. She is not a heathen!"

But Nester hardly cared what Jeffrey had to say. "You are no longer employed! Do you hear me, you are fired!"

"But he isn't, Nester," Finnea said without thinking. She stepped forward, looking at Jeffrey rather than her brother, her brain trying to assimilate all that was happening. Her brother's fury. The proposal. But her decision had already been made—in Matthew's foyer with paintings lying in ruins around her. "Because I am going to marry him."

"Oh, Finnea," Jeffrey breathed, taking her shoulders and pulling her close.

"This is absurd!" Nester raged, rubbing his neck.

"I disagree."

They swiveled around to find Hannah in the doorway.

"I couldn't help but overhear," she said. "I believe congratulations are in order."

"Thank you," Finnea whispered, her heart beginning to pound.

Jeffrey took her hand and tucked it into the crook of his arm, then whispered, "You won't regret this."

Regret?

The thought of Matthew flashed in her mind. His pain. His bellowing anger.

His kindness when he had saved her life.

But this, Jeffrey and Boston, was what she wanted. Not Africa, she reminded herself. Africa had nearly defeated her. Took all she had until she had nothing left to give.

Jeffrey gave her renewed hope. He cared for her, he was

kind to her. But most of all, it was his full-grown children that swayed her in the end. Children not her own.

Isabel, her mind cried.

Tears threatened. She would have no more children, because she couldn't bear to love some other child. Africa had taught her that most of all.

The days flew by with anticipation and preparation for the party, giving Finnea little time to think. It had been decided that they would announce the betrothal the night of her grand birthday gala.

Word had begun to filter through Boston's inner circles of an impending engagement. The party was shaping up to be the premier event of the winter season. Her mother was beside herself with joy, and it was all a result of her.

For the first time since Finnea had arrived, she felt close to her mother, and she cherished the moments they shared.

Truly, life was finally falling into place. It was as if by becoming a bride-to-be she had finally been granted admittance into the secret club of Boston society. She told herself she was doing the right thing by marrying Jeffrey. He was mature and kind, and he adored her.

Everything was perfect. Everything, that is, except for the knot of apprehension growing inside her that refused to ease when she thought of the man she was going to marry.

It was Friday, her birthday, the day of the party when Finnea and Jeffrey rolled along Boylston Street in his black enameled landau. She had taken great pains with the errant curls of her red hair and had even dusted her cheeks with the horrid rice powder her mother insisted made her look more presentable. She should have been giddy with excitement. But the knot rose in her throat, choking off excitement.

"I'm so glad you are finally going to meet my mother," he said, patting her hand.

Since their engagement two weeks ago, she had anticipated meeting the woman and having with her own mother-in-law-to-be exactly what her mother and Penelope shared. But day after day, Jeffrey had made one excuse after another until Finnea had begun to grow concerned that the meeting would never take place. She suspected it would have been put off even longer if this night hadn't been the night of the announcement at the grand gala.

Finnea's doubts and concerns must have shown on her face, because Jeffrey put his arm around her and said, "It's going to be fine. What could possibly go wrong?" He patted her hands. "You know that I adore you, don't you?"

Did he really? she wondered suddenly. And even if he did, was it enough?

Despite her intentions never to see Matthew again, she had gone to his house repeatedly since that fateful day when he met his father on the street corner, and every day she had been turned away. He was either out or unavailable, or simply sent word that he didn't want to see her. And no matter how she had tried, Quincy hadn't let her in.

She hated that it bothered her. But it did.

She couldn't have said why she had gone, only felt the need—as if somehow Matthew could ease the knot that lodged so tightly in her throat.

And the truth remained: At night it was Matthew's broad chest that she dreamed of, not Jeffrey's. It was the memory of Matthew's kiss that woke her—disturbed her. But she was going to marry Jeffrey, wanted to marry Jeffrey, she told herself firmly. He made her feel cherished, normal. Like the lady she wanted to be.

And when Jeffrey said, "Mother is going to love you," she wanted his words to be true.

They pulled up in front of a house that would be considered tiny compared to wealthy Boston standards, tucked into a small street on prestigious Beacon Hill. The glass-paned windows, like many in the area, had turned a light shade of violet from exposure to the sun. No one knew why the glass had turned colors, but no one replaced it. It was beautiful and unique to this part of town.

Squaring her shoulders, she pulled her woolen shawl close, then picked up the skirt of her beautifully cut blue silk gown and allowed Jeffrey to help her down from the carriage.

The front door was answered by a stooped butler, his face lined with age, his hands swollen and curled.

"Your mother is expecting you, sir," the man said, his demeanor haughty, his voice imperious.

He led them to a drawing room. Finnea took in the small house. Though everything was meticulously clean, it was impossible not to notice that the once beautiful rugs were worn, their edges frayed. The flocked wallpaper was no longer flocked, and a few of the windows were cracked. But despite the cracks, there was not a speck of dust nor a single smudge on the panes.

The drawing room was small and filled with all the trinkets that had become so popular during the last few decades. Shelves full of music boxes and row after row of small framed portraitures. Collections of thimbles and china dolls. Large flowing ferns in every window and potted palms in the corners. Finnea didn't dare turn too quickly for fear of knocking something down.

For the first time she wondered where Jeffrey lived, where *they* would live. The thought of living in this house made her grimace. But surely not. There would be no room.

"Hello, Jeffrey."

A woman stood in the receiving parlor like a queen at a ceremony. She was tiny, much like her house, but didn't look at all close to her seventy years. The woman was dressed in a voluminous gown of stiff brown taffeta, her shoulders covered with an autumn-colored paisley shawl. She wore a single brooch on her high, prim collar, and her fingers were crowded with gaudy baubles, much like the room. And her face, milky white with two bright spots of rouge on either cheek, made her look like a porcelain doll.

"Jeffrey, dear," the woman said, extending her tiny hands to her son.

Then the woman turned her attention to Finnea, the smile that had curved across her porcelain features melting away. "And who have we here?"

Finnea barely contained her surprise.

"This is Finnea, Mother. Finnea Winslet."

The woman raised a charcoal-penciled brow, her demeanor much like the butler's, but didn't say a word.

"Mother," Jeffrey added with a fond chuckle, "I told you we were coming today."

Regina Upton's lips pursed as if she'd taken a bite of something distasteful. "Well, it hardly matters if you said anything before or not, dear. What matters is that you are here now."

Jeffrey kissed his mother's cheek indulgently. "I can't imagine why you're behaving this way."

His mother straightened, pulling herself up to her full four feet eight inches. "Which way is that, Jeffrey? I'm happy you brought your little friend." She turned to her guest, her sharp eyes running the length of Finnea. "So tell me, Miss Winslet, what brings you to my home?"

Finnea's mouth all but fell open, dread ticking to life in her breast like a mantel clock. But she was saved from answering when Jeffrey sternly tsked at his mother.

"You know perfectly well why she is here. To have tea. We discussed this."

"I thought you said you were bringing that wonderful Seton woman. Melvin Seton's daughter, if I recall correctly. You know, when Melvin was alive he was quite partial to me." Her hand fluttered at her neck. "I'm certain he would have asked for my hand if your father hadn't asked first." She sighed her smile. "I had gentlemen callers every day. Dozens of them, really." She focused on her son. "I think that Seton woman is so very nice."

"Mother," he said, his tone stern. "It's Miss Winslet who is here."

Regina turned back to her once again, her face set in a polite facade. "Yes, of course. If only Jeffrey had told me you were coming. But no matter. Come, let us sit down."

Jeffrey's smile thinned; then he showed Finnea to a quaint little love seat. But just when he started to sit next to her, his mother said, "Jeffrey love, could you please help me with this chair. I'm feeling a bit frail this morning. It is so trying getting old."

The anger left him in a rush and he laughed, taking his mother's hand. "You don't have a frail bone in your body, Mother. And you certainly don't look older than a maiden."

The compliment made her look years younger, like a

schoolgirl with a crush. "Don't be silly," she said with a chirping giggle. "Maiden, indeed."

But it was clear she was pleased—at least she was until her gaze caught Finnea. Jeffrey's mother sat up straight and motioned to the chair next to her for her son to sit.

Jeffrey gave another little laugh and shrugged at Finnea, then sat next to his mother.

Pleased, his mother looked back at Finnea. "Now, what is your name again?"

"It's Finnea, ma'am. And it is a pleasure to meet you." She forced the words from her mouth.

"Yes, of course. Odd name, Finnea. Sounds Gaelic. Is it a family name? Jeffrey is named after his father, God rest his soul, and his father before him. An old family name. The Upton ancestors came over on the *Mayflower*. Who is your family, child?"

"Mother, this is Finnea Winslet, Nester's sister." He shook his head and chuckled. "Stop acting like this."

"Oh yes, the girl from Africa." She looked away dismissively. "Jeffrey, I've been invited to Sarah Chambers's music soiree on Monday. You'll be able to take me, won't you?"

"I'll be at work on Monday, as well you know. But you can take the carriage. I'll catch a hired hack downtown. Maybe you would like to take Finnea with you."

Mrs. Upton looked her over, really looked at her for the first time. Finnea sat very still. Her unsuitability drifted through the proper, overstuffed Victorian room like a foul breeze from the harbor. Finnea sensed it, felt it like a slap of disapproval across her face. Her sun-golden skin was mostly a memory now, but even the rice powder couldn't give her the translucent white of all the women she had met.

Regina smiled, her lips parting like fissures in ice, her pale gray eyes as cold and as biting as the winter wind outside. "Take Miss Winslet with me?" She turned to her son. "I hardly think that is appropriate, Jeffrey. The invitation is for family."

"Which is exactly what Finnea is about to become. Remember?"

"Ah yes, you did mention an engagement. Though I was certain it was to that nice Seton woman."

"Mother," he warned.

Regina Upton sat very still and let her displeasure simmer through the room. "Perhaps Miss Winslet and I *should* go to the party." She patted her son's hand. "You are right to suggest it. Now, I know you have to get back to work. And I would love to spend time with my future daughter-in-law. So why don't you run on ahead."

Jeffrey's face eased, though Finnea could hardly believe it. The last thing she wanted to do was stay here with this woman by herself. She didn't think for one second that Regina Upton really wanted to spend time alone with her future daughter-in-law. No doubt she wanted to malign her without her son to interrupt.

"I had better be going as well," Finnea said.

"So soon? You just got here. And look, Phillips has just brought in the tea," Regina said, her china-doll face looking truly sad and disappointed.

And when Jeffrey encouraged her to stay, Finnea didn't know how to refuse. Perhaps she could win the woman over. A true lady would at least try.

Jeffrey left the house and headed for the waiting carriage. Just when he would have jumped inside, he heard his name called out. Looking up, he found Penelope hurrying toward him, wrapped in a fine ermine coat and matching hat.

"Jeffrey!"

"What are you doing out in this cold? And where is Nester?"

"I don't know where Nester is, but I was just at Diana Greenway's house and when I came out my carriage was no-where to be seen. Do you mind terribly giving me a ride home?"

"No, of course not. You live on Marlborough Street, don't you?"

"Why, yes, I do."

Jeffrey gave quick instructions to the driver, then helped Penelope in, and they settled across from each other. She sat back and sighed, pulling her thick lapels of fur close around her body. "When will this horrid weather ever cease? I hate to think of the months we have left of piles of snow that will only get higher and dirtier."

Jeffrey chuckled. "Finnea is just about at her wit's end over this weather as well. I know she'll be thrilled when spring comes so she can get out of the house more."

"Finnea," Penelope said, her tone questioning, "not able to get out? Surely you're mistaken. She's hardly ever at home."

"That's impossible! She is nearly always there when I call."

"But you're at the office most of the day." She chuckled. "You men. Always thinking that women just sit at home when they aren't with you."

"Well, I . . . I guess I didn't think. Perhaps she does get out on occasion."

"More like every day. In fact"—she glanced down at her kid-gloved hands that lay politely in her lap before she glanced up at him—"I was under the impression that she has been visiting her friend Mr. Hawthorne most of the time."

"Mr. Hawthorne?" he asked, his tone stiff. "Bradford Hawthorne?"

"Well, no. It's Matthew Hawthorne she goes to see."

Tension sizzled through the close confines of the carriage. "How do you know this?" he demanded.

She sniffed delicately into a fine lace handkerchief. "I've seen her myself. Mr. Hawthorne lives on Marlborough, a few doors down from me."

"Why didn't Nester tell me?"

"Actually, Nester doesn't know."

"You should have told him the instant you realized!"

"Then what would Nester think of me, telling on his sister like that."

"He needs to be informed."

"Perhaps, but why don't we keep that to ourselves. No sense in getting everyone worked up. I'm sure if you have a little talk with Finnea the problem will be solved quickly enough."

Phillips brought a tray of tea items into the parlor and placed them on the table next to Mrs. Upton. "So, you want to marry my son," the older woman began without preamble.

Finnea studied Regina Upton and saw no malice. "Yes, I do. Your son is a wonderful man."

"Yes, he is. I raised him to be a wonderful man. An important man. His father always had dreams that he would take his rightful place in society."

"And he has. He is fine and upstanding."

"Yes," the woman said dryly, all signs of the giggling maiden gone. "But an upstanding man needs a genteel wife."

Finnea felt her palms grow moist.

Regina made a great show of serving tea, pouring cream and sugar without bothering to ask, then handing Finnea a cup. Finnea concentrated on being as graceful as she could. But just when she took a sip, Mrs. Upton asked, "Do you think it at all possible that you could make my son a genteel wife?"

The tea was hot, burning Finnea's tongue. Surprise as well as heat made her jerk back. She gasped as tea splashed down the front of her gown, staining the silk.

Regina raised a brow. "Are you always so graceful?"

Finnea fluttered with a napkin, trying to blot up the tea.

"Perhaps you'd like to go upstairs and tidy yourself," the woman said.

Mortified, Finnea set the napkin aside. "Yes, thank you."

The serving maid showed Finnea to the upper regions of the house. Regina watched her go. Seconds later, the front door opened and Jeffrey strode into the parlor.

"Where is Finnea?" he demanded.

"What is wrong, son? You look furious."

He quickly searched the room, then looked at his mother hard. "You are avoiding the question. Did you run her off?"

"What if I did?" she asked with a pout.

He strode into the room with demanding steps. "Damn it, Mother, how could you?"

"Who said I did anything! She is an odd one, Jeffrey. I deserve better." She smoothed her skirt. "You deserve better."

Jeffrey held his patience, but barely, the reason he had returned momentarily forgotten. "That *odd* one is part owner of the company I work for, as well you know. And when I marry her, *I'll* gain control of her shares."

"As a member of the board of directors and vice president

of Winslet Ironworks you already have control of those shares. You told me so yourself!"

"Not for long. If Finnea is not engaged by the end of this day, the control of her shares shifts to Nester."

"What?" Regina demanded.

"It's true. William Winslet sent a copy of his new will to America just before he died."

Jeffrey leaned forward, his gaze intense and unrelenting. "This is my chance. I've been at Nester's beck and call for the last three years. I ran this business when no one else cared. William only cared about Africa. Nester was too young. I made Winslet Ironworks what it is today. And by marrying Finnea, I'll no longer have to kowtow to the blasted man."

Regina's knotted fingers fidgeted with her handkerchief. "Then you don't love her?" she whispered like a simpering belle.

"Love her? Who could love her with her outlandish ways? But I want her! I want to marry her. In fact, I think you should send a note over to her house this instant to apologize for whatever you said to run her off."

"She didn't run me off, Jeffrey. I'm right here."

Jeffrey wheeled around to find Finnea standing in the doorway, misshapen stains of brown covering the bodice of her light blue gown like continents on a map.

"Finnea!"

"Yes, Jeffrey?"

"How much did you hear?"

"Enough," she replied, her voice wooden and emotionless.

"You don't understand!"

The air in the room seemed sharp and stagnant. Finnea felt as if she couldn't breathe. All she could think of was getting away from this house, this woman, and this man in whom she had trusted.

"I believe I do," she said. "No doubt these are the first honest words I have heard from your mouth. If you'll excuse me."

"Damn it, Finnea. We need to talk. Mother, please excuse us."

"There is nothing to talk about, Jeffrey," Finnea said.

"Oh yes, there is."

He took her arm and led her to the murky depths of a man's study. The room smelled faintly of cigars.

"Tell me it's not true," he demanded.

She forced herself to focus. "What are you talking about?"

"Tell me you don't go to Matthew Hawthorne's house."

Finnea's heart seemed to stop beneath her stained gown. "Where did you hear that?"

"From Penelope. Why would she tell me such a thing if it's not true?"

"It hardly matters." And she realized it didn't matter because there was no explaining her visits to Matthew, just as there was no explaining Jeffrey's words about what he really wanted from her. "It doesn't matter because our engagement is off."

"Off?" he demanded. "It can't be off!"

She headed for the door.

"Where are you going?"

"Home to tell my mother there will be no announcement this evening."

"You can't do that!"

"I can't?" she asked, her voice suddenly impatient.

"No! Everyone is going to be there. Everyone is expecting our engagement. I'll be a laughingstock if you back out now."

No apologies, no remorse, simply concern for himself. And to think she thought he was different from Nester.

"I'm sorry, Jeffrey. But the engagement is off."

"You'd rather be at the mercy of your brother?" he demanded.

The words gave her pause, sending a shiver of uncertainty through her.

"Yes!" he exclaimed, pushing his advantage. "Not such an appealing idea."

"But perhaps not much worse than being at the mercy of you. He, at least, has never lied about his feelings for me. Now, if you'll excuse me."

Finnea didn't start to shake until she felt the solid front door close behind her. Cold dread wrapped around her heart. She was a fool to have thought a man like Jeffrey would truly want to marry her—or at least marry her for herself.

She concentrated on the feel of the cold against her cheeks.

No more than a few steps away, she realized she had forgotten her shawl. But she would freeze before she returned to that house.

Finnea hurried down the sloped walkway, the hem of her dress dragging in the plowed snow and ice. She strode through the maze of Beacon Hill streets without knowing where she was going. Sights and sounds pressed in on her. The colors seemed vibrant and shocking compared to the calming greens and browns of Africa.

She gritted her teeth and gave a cry when her feet slipped again and again on the hard-packed snow. It was cold, a cold that seeped through everything, even windows and walls. In Africa it was warm, blissfully warm and beautiful, she thought, rubbing her hands vigorously against her arms. In that second, she missed her home with an intensity that left her gasping for breath.

She didn't know where she was going; she only knew she had to get away. She wanted to think. She wanted to talk it out. She wanted to throw herself into her mother's arms and hear that everything would be all right.

Finnea fought back a sob, pushing at strands of hair that had shaken loose from her chignon.

There wasn't a hired hack to be seen when she finally came to Beacon Street. Rummaging through her reticule, she pulled out a nickel and raced to catch the trolley. After she paid, she fell back on a hardwood bench and stared at the passing house fronts through the murky windows. She didn't think, couldn't think for the jostling and the nearly deafening noise of iron wheels over tracks laid down in the cobbles.

She jumped down at the corner of Beacon and Arlington, before the trolley continued west to Brookline. Without thinking, she headed south, then turned right a block later when she came to Marlborough Street instead of continuing on one block farther to her home on Commonwealth Avenue. With each step she took, she went faster, until she was practically running, never stopping until she came to Dove's Way.

Chapter Twelve

The heavy brass knocker fell insistently against the thick-planked front door. Matthew was certain he knew who it was.

Finnea.

She had come to him every day for the past two weeks, and he had sent her away each time despite the fact that he wanted to see her, more than was good for either one of them.

When he had heard the rumors that indeed she was going to marry Jeffrey, a hard coil of anger twisted in his chest. But he knew it was no business of his. He might want her, but he didn't want another wife.

Matthew tried to focus on a small carved-wood mask he had brought back from Africa. But Finnea would not be banished.

What was it that had really brought her to Boston in the first place? What had sent her in search of her mother after nearly two decades? he wondered again. Was it simply a need for family after the death of her father?

That seemed plausible—until the dark emptiness in her soul flared in her eyes.

When he heard Quincy head for the door, Matthew called out. He could hear the man's footsteps falter, then veer toward the study, bringing the butler to stand at attention in front of him.

"Sir?"

In the distance, the knock sounded again, this time harder.

"I'm not in, Quincy."

The man sighed. "But Mr. Hawthorne—"

"I'm not in," he bit out coldly.

Quincy hesitated before he gave a slight bow of his head. "Of course, sir."

After Matthew heard the sound of muffled voices, followed by the click of the shutting front door, he waited thirty minutes, then called for his coat. Lately he only went out at night, to slip in to see Mary, or when the snow that made his arm ache and his hand fumble was piled high, allowing him to walk alone in the deserted Public Gardens. Today, however, despite the winter sun and crowded streets, he had to get out, away from his thoughts. But as soon as the front door shut behind him, he found Finnea sitting on the steps. He would have cursed her stubbornness had his heart not slammed in his chest.

She was huddled over, no doubt freezing. Stiff with cold, she craned her neck to look at him. He saw the darkness instantly, that stain on her heart that showed through in her eyes.

His brow furrowed. Finnea always came to him when she was upset. He wondered if she realized it, the way she ran to him when things were difficult, the way she looked at him when she was holding on by a thread.

"Do you ever take no for an answer?" he demanded, resisting the urge to take her gently in his arms.

She smiled at him despite his harsh tone, or perhaps because of it, and in that second it seemed the darkness began to dissipate.

"R-r-rarely," she said, her teeth chattering.

"I should let you freeze out here."

"But you won't."

"Hell." He took her hand and pulled her inside. "Quincy!" he called out.

Within seconds the man hurried from the kitchen, conveniently carrying a silver tray.

"Some hot cocoa to warm you, Miss Winslet?" the butler asked solicitously.

"Y-y-you are a d-d-dream, Mr. Quincy."

"You are a nuisance," Matthew grumbled to the man, but not quite convincingly.

In the few minutes Matthew had been outside, the fire had been built up in the study, and a blanket had been retrieved. Finnea was quickly wrapped in the thick wool and seated next to the hearth with a steaming cup of cocoa in her hand.

"Why are you here?" Matthew asked her bluntly.

She eyed him from over the rim of her cup. "Do I need a reason?"

"Yes."

"All right, then, I'm here for another lesson."

Doubt raised his brow. "On the day of your gala?"

The ease she had gained died at the mention of the party. The emptiness flared, sharp, intense.

"Ah, Finn," he whispered, unable to help himself.

He took her cup and saucer and set them aside. When she had nothing to hold, he could see the slight tremble of her hand.

"What is it?" he asked, this time softly.

Her gaze found the African mask on the shelf. "They disapprove of me, down to the core, don't they?"

He could lie, but that would do her no good. "Yes."

"Why? I'm trying. Don't they see that? Don't they care?"

The words tore at him, but he hardened his heart. "You are different from them. That's all they see. You don't fit into their preconceived ideas about how a woman should act. But what I find more telling is that somehow no one looks askance at your mother."

Confusion marred her brow. "She is the very image of what they hold dear. Why would they?"

"Because she is a mother who left her child and didn't return."

Sharply Finnea pivoted away.

Matthew knelt before her and took her hands in his. "If they have to blame someone, they should blame her, Finn, not you."

She suddenly looked at him as if something just occurred to her, something new beginning to spring to life in her eyes. She wanted something from him, he could see it, but what he didn't know.

"Say you'll marry me!"

Matthew froze, his long fingers growing still against her skin. He sat back on his heels, paralyzed by awful, heady longing, until slowly he forced himself to stand up with a curse. He had said it before: He didn't want a wife or need one. Especially this one.

But then he saw her chin tremble, and that dreaded mix of protectiveness and indulgence came over him. He covered it with irritation. "What has happened now?" he asked with a calm he didn't feel.

Her eyes burned with tears, but she raised her chin. "Jeffrey was only interested in marrying me so he could gain control of Winslet Ironworks."

He started to say he could have told her that weeks ago, but held his tongue. She was hurting badly, and he felt the damnable need to slay Jeffrey Upton for causing her pain. But he tamped down the emotion, refusing to feel anything.

She wiped angrily at her eyes. "And if I'm not engaged by tonight, apparently my shares of the company will shift from Jeffrey to Nester. I can't let that happen. I have to be engaged or I will be at the mercy of my brother."

"Ah, hence your preemptive proposal to me."

She started toward him. "Say you'll do it."

His heart began to pound.

"I know such a favor is a lot to ask," she rushed on, "but it would just be for a short time."

His eyes narrowed, perplexed.

"Just until I can figure out what to do. You know, a fake betrothal to buy me some time."

His heart hardened, and his jaw went tight. "No."

Her footsteps ceased. "Matthew please—"

"No, Finnea."

Embarrassment surged in her cheeks; he could see it, hot and bright.

"Do you hate me so much?" she whispered, choked.

"Hate you?" The words startled him. "I could never hate you."

A sigh ran through his heart and he looked away. "I have never met anyone like you. Grasping at life, tilting at windmills. Even now you're still fighting, still filled with desires."

"I don't want so much! And the day I get what I came here for I'll be satisfied."

"No. You've been filled with wanting since I met you on the train. You want everything."

"That's not true!"

"But it is, Finn. It is one of the things that draws me to you. And the day you run out of desires to chase and dreams to wrap your arms around is the day you die."

"You're wrong! I'm not here to chase dreams!"

"Then why?" He grabbed her arms and pulled her to face him. "Why did you run away from Africa?"

"I wasn't running away!"

"Damn it, don't lie to me. Say anything, but don't lie!"

She tried to turn away, but he held her secure. "Why, Finnea?"

She stared at him, her gaze mutinous. "If you don't want a lie, then it is none of your concern."

He let her go immediately. "Fine, don't tell me. But you will have to fight your battles on your own. I no longer want to fight, and I don't want to dream. I simply want to make it through each day."

He expected her to concede, to leave. Instead, she caught him off guard when she grabbed his arm and forced him to meet her gaze, her green eyes filled with emotion. "Coward," she bit out.

His face grew taut.

"You're afraid to live anymore," she said bitterly, tears mixing with her anger. "Just like you're afraid to paint. You're not the wild man or even the crazy man. You're a coward."

His mind reeled, and the fury that was never far from the surface these days surged to life. But before he could utter a word, she was gone.

His hand fisted at his side, his jaw tight. What did she expect of him? She made him want to dream. There were times when he was with her that hope burgeoned inside him. But then reality crashed around him when he scared little children in the streets, stumbled clumsily, or collapsed with fatigue.

No, he was no coward, he told himself firmly. He was just a man trying to accept life for what it was and learn how to continue on with a modicum of pride and dignity.

But regardless of what he told himself, he couldn't quite

forget his anger over the fact that she had called him a coward. Nor could he forget the desire.

The walls pressed in on him. The large, high-ceilinged room suddenly seemed small. He had to get out.

He strode past a startled Quincy, jerked on his coat, and slammed out the door without a word. Ignoring the cold, he started walking. Ignoring the people who did double takes when they saw him, he continued on. He hailed a hired hack on Arlington Street, and seconds later he strode up the steps to his parents' home. It didn't matter that it wasn't dark with everyone asleep. He needed to see Mary.

Without bothering to knock, he stamped his high-polished boots on the horsehair mat to clear the ice and cinders, then entered Hawthorne House. It was Friday afternoon, and Matthew knew Mary would be in the sunroom at the back of the house reading. His daughter loved books, had demanded he teach her to read as soon as she could hold a book. He had cherished those hours of sitting close, her concentration mixed with her cheerful giggles over the stories they read.

Sure enough, he found her in the sunroom curled up in an overstuffed chair, a book in her hands, her white-blond hair catching a long ray of sun. He didn't go in, and when a maid started to announce him, he pressed his index finger to his lip. She nodded her understanding, bobbed a curtsy, then went on with her work.

Matthew stood there, just stood, taking Mary in, feeling the ease he needed so badly wash over him.

But quick on the heels of the ease came frustration. How was this ever going to change? he wondered, leaning his shoulder up against the doorjamb. How was he going to move beyond just watching his daughter from a distance?

As always, he saw no answers.

Voices sounded in the foyer and he turned away, not wanting Mary to look up and see him. He was nearly to the front door when his mother's voice stopped him.

"Matthew?"

He turned to her as she came down the stairway, dressed to go out. "Hello, Mother."

She took his hand, her beaded reticule swinging on her out-stretched arm. "What are you doing here?"

His shrug was casual, and he pushed a lock of blond hair back from his forehead as he searched for a smile. "I was in the neighborhood and thought I'd drop in and say hello."

She looked at him askance. "I haven't seen you in weeks. You're here for some other reason." She studied him. "You look upset. Are you perhaps unhappy that Finnea Winslet is announcing her engagement tonight?"

He felt stung by the words.

"I heard it's true. Everyone is talking about it," she said.

"Actually it isn't true. At least not anymore. Her engagement to Jeffrey Upton has been called off."

"Really? How do you know?"

A wry grin pulled at his face. "She came by the house and asked me to take his place."

Her grip tightened on his hand. "Do it."

Matthew sliced his gaze over his mother. "We've been over this. You know I can't."

But Emmaline didn't back down. "What I know, son, is that you never loved Kimberly in the way you should have loved the woman of your heart."

Matthew's breath hissed in through his teeth, but Emmaline was relentless.

"You looked at Kimberly as the perfect wife to escort about town on your perfect arm. There was no emotion—no real emotion. I hate that you were hurt—that you were scarred. But since you've met Finnea, for the first time in your life I can see that you truly feel. Hurt, anger, frustration. Love."

His heart pounded as he tried to deny her words. "I don't need you to play matchmaker, Mother," he stated, not bothering to explain that Finnea only wanted a fake engagement, not an actual marriage.

"Maybe, maybe not. But actually, I was just on my way to your house to talk to you." Suddenly she grew uncomfortable. "Your father told me . . . to tell you that it's time Mary live with you."

His body tensed. "She can't!"

"She can, and she will. Your father will brook no argument in this."

"The bastard!"

"Don't you dare say that. He's your father. And while I might hate this situation, I know he is right. Mary needs you whether you are willing to admit it or not."

His world spun.

Her voice softened and she stepped closer, her fingers reaching up and touching his scar as only Finnea had done before. "I love you, my dear, dear boy. But you've been handed circumstances that you must learn to deal with. It is time you stopped hiding away. Marry Finnea. Make a home for your child. She is only asking you to do what deep down you already want."

The party would start in less than forty-five minutes. Finnea had to find her mother and tell her there would be no announcement.

But when she hurried up the grand sweeping stairs of her family's home, inadequacy overwhelmed her at the sight of her mother and Penelope so at ease with each other, conferring over the last-minute details of the party.

"Everything is ready," Penelope told Leticia. "Once the guests start arriving, all you have to do is be your gracious self and I'll take care of everything else."

"Thank you, dear," Leticia said, her long gown a dreamy fluff of a sugary confection. "You have been indispensable to me these last weeks."

Finnea veered toward her room.

"Oh, Finnea, there you are," Leticia called out, her gown rustling. But she cut herself off abruptly as she took in the stained blue silk and the hair tumbling free of its moorings. "Oh my goodness, quickly, you must change! The guests will be here any minute."

Penelope looked at Finnea, then demurely lowered her gaze as she picked up her deep blue velvet skirt, which matched her eyes, and headed downstairs. Leticia took hold of Finnea's arm and propelled her toward her room.

"Mother, wait!"

"What is it, Finnea?" Leticia demanded.

"We need to talk."

"We can talk some other time. You're not presentable, and half of Boston is about to walk through the front door to hear the announcement of your engagement! And you will not announce anything looking like that."

"There isn't going to be an announcement."

"What?" The word reverberated in the long hallway.

"My engagement to Jeffrey is off."

"What do you mean?" she gasped.

"Just that. There will be no announcement."

"How could you let this happen?" Leticia's face distorted with outrage. "Everyone who is anyone in Boston will be here at any minute, and they are expecting to hear that you and Jeffrey are to be married!"

"It's too late for that."

"I should have known!" she cried, her voice shrill. "I should have known that it would never happen."

But then she sucked in her breath and calmed, leaving an eerie quiet that sent a shiver of foreboding up Finnea's spine.

Leticia's face suddenly relaxed and filled with a world of regret. She reached out and took her daughter's hand. "Do you understand how this isn't working?"

Finnea stood unmoving in the middle of the hallway, panic slipping over her like rain washing down the clear glass of a windowpane. She felt as if she were falling, drifting in air as if the world had been pulled out from beneath her. A free fall. Would it ever stop?

"What do you mean, Mother?" She asked the question very carefully, afraid that at any second she would crumble.

"Don't you see? You're unhappy. Nester is unhappy." Leticia hesitated. "It's too late to change the past, Finnea."

"What are you saying?"

"I think we both know that you don't belong here."

Finnea felt her entire body flinch as if she had been struck.

"Oh, Finnea, we've been kidding ourselves. You don't fit in here, no matter how hard you are trying."

Finnea was aware of the front door opening and the sound of guests arriving, the click of the latch, the low heels on marble, decorous hellos, wraps being taken. Leticia must have heard them, too, because her face transformed. She put on her perfect smile as if nothing had happened. Kind and genteel.

"We will discuss this further tomorrow. For now, I must see to the guests. We simply won't make an announcement; we will pretend as though there never was one planned. It is your birthday, after all."

Leticia stopped, suddenly awkward. "Happy birthday," she said with an uncertain kiss to the air beside Finnea's cheek.

Not one person had wished her a happy birthday until now. A consolation prize at the end of an awful day. But it wasn't the end yet, she reminded herself.

"We will make it through this party," her mother continued, stepping back. "Then we will talk."

Once her mother had gone, Finnea entered her bedroom. Panic threatened to swallow her whole. As soon as the door shut behind her she walked to the French doors that led to a balcony and pulled them open. The cold hit her first, harsh and biting, but she hardly noticed. With frigid winter air filling the room, catching in the draperies, she slid to the floor, her skirts billowing around her in a cloud of stained blue. She lay back on the thick rug like a child, the hand-knotted design of flowers forming a garland around her head. Unable to think, unable to feel, she stared up at the plastered ceiling, concentrating on the peaks and swirls of the white-icinged contours. Voices drifted up the stairs and down the halls, words that were muffled and fragmented by the carpeted floor.

She wanted to lie there forever, to never get up. She didn't want to go downstairs. But that wasn't her way. She would dress in the splendid gown her mother had chosen. If people were going to talk about her, let them talk about her to her face. Let them see that she was strong, not weak. She was African, after all. As her mother had just pointed out.

The house overflowed with guests, glittering and bedecked, jeweled in a way that Puritan Boston rarely saw. Men in white waistcoats and cutaway tails, women in shimmering gowns of the finest materials. Indeed, everyone who was anyone was in attendance. Leticia Winslet couldn't have asked for more. Except for the announcement of her daughter's engagement.

By the time Finnea came down, everyone had arrived. She steadied herself on the banister as she descended the stairs, trying to calm herself with the strands of music coming from the orchestra that played at the side of the room. Her mother was there, as were her grandmother and brother. But not a glimpse of Jeffrey, she realized with a sting of defeat. Of course he wasn't there, she reminded herself. She wouldn't have him.

Everyone in the room turned to look at her, the conversation breaking off as she entered, her foot on the bottom step. She had dressed with care in a stunning gown of soft gray velvet. Her mother's lady's maid had arranged her hair in an elegant style. Even she knew she looked beautiful. She could see it in the faces of the men, in the stiffening shoulders of the women—a sharp bristling like the ridge on an animal's neck.

Even in beauty and decorum she wasn't accepted.

The thought hit her suddenly, without warning.

But she was given no opportunity to take it in when Penelope entered the room. She looked stunning, a pale, icy beauty that would always be more fitting in this cool society than Finnea's wild features.

Penelope came forward, walking toward the stairs, but she bypassed Finnea without a glance and strode directly to Hannah.

"Mother Hannah," Penelope said with the familiarity that Finnea had never felt. "How lovely you look."

Hannah Grable, the queen among her people. Penelope as the granddaughter she wished she'd had. The heir to Hannah's throne. And Finnea's heart sank even further.

Hannah took Penelope's hand and allowed a kiss to her cheek. "Thank you, dear."

Still holding the older woman's hands, Penelope looked coldly back at Finnea. It was then that Finnea understood that no good could come of tonight. Penelope had clearly heard the engagement was off, and she relished what Finnea had not realized until now was a victory. An opponent who only now showed her colors.

"I see Jeffrey didn't arrive," Penelope said in a creamy drawl that everyone could hear. "Why is that, Finnea?"

It was like a physical blow. The women around the room glanced between Penelope and Finnea, waiting expectantly. Penelope couldn't let it go, couldn't let the evening slide by without playing her trump card.

It hit Finnea then—not sadness or lament but fury, white-hot fury for all she had tried to accomplish in this self-centered, limited world that was being tossed back in her face. She realized that next Penelope would ask about the announcement, and there was nothing she could do to stop her. Penelope didn't want to be usurped, never had.

"So tell us, Finnea," Penelope continued, "where *is* Jeffrey? Didn't you have a marriage announcement to make?"

Finnea raised her chin, fighting back the tremble she felt beginning in her soul, and looked her in the eye. "I won't be marrying Jeffrey."

The crowd murmured uneasily.

Penelope's smile was coy. "Why ever not?"

"Because she is marrying me."

The simple statement, spoken in a deep, rumbling voice, brought everything to an abrupt halt. One guest after another turned toward the arched entryway, until they stood silently. The crowd gaped but didn't say a word. They might have difficulty looking at him, but everyone there knew he was too important a man to cross.

"Matthew," Finnea barely whispered, emotion she didn't understand sweeping through her.

Matthew Hawthorne stepped into the grand room, tall and elegant. Impeccably dressed in white tie and black tails. He was beautiful, really. When he stood just so, it was easy to forget the scar. He did it in a way that made her think that he realized that fact. That he felt the need to hide even when he couldn't made her want to weep.

She knew he had rarely been out among people since the day he met his father at the street corner. He hadn't wanted to be seen. But here he was with all eyes focused on him.

"Ah," Penelope began, "how interesting to see you here, Mr.

Hawthorne. Have you come to fill in for Mr. Upton?" she asked with a meaningful look that everyone in the house could read.

Finnea stiffened as all eyes turned to stare at her, standing on the bottom step as if she were a china doll on display. But what took her breath was the furious look on Matthew's face as he stood like a statue.

"Why am I not surprised?" Penelope continued sarcastically. "I understand that Mr. Hawthorne has been doing a grand job of filling in for Mr. Upton. Is this a last-minute plan to save Finnea's reputation after you spent numerous days with her alone in your home?"

Penelope looked at Hannah with a knowingly raised brow. Finnea could see her disgrace in Hannah's eyes. Her grandmother understood that not only couldn't she keep a man but she had been alone with another, and Matthew had come here only to help her avoid total disgrace.

Hannah looked at Finnea, their eyes locking. Finnea braced herself for the biting remark.

But it didn't come.

In a moment Finnea would never forget, Hannah slowly took her hand away from Penelope, then pulled herself up to her full height, her own eyes like ice.

"Last-minute plan?" the older woman said, her voice commanding, her eyes fastening on the younger woman. "This is no last-minute plan, Penelope. I have known about it all along."

With the cool dignity of a queen, she stepped farther away, distancing herself from the woman. "Do you really think my granddaughter would be foolish enough to marry someone who only wants her for her money? Good God, no. In fact, just days ago your very own Nester fired the man. Don't you remember? You were sitting right there."

Penelope struggled to mask her surprise, and Nester choked.

"I heard it myself," Hannah added, looking at her grandson. "Didn't you fire Jeffrey Upton just the other day?"

"Well, yes, but—"

"I'm surprised you've forgotten, Penelope."

The tension was thick, filling the room. Hannah and Penelope stared at each other, and Finnea knew that Hannah was daring the younger woman to say another word. If Penelope did, she might win this battle, but she would lose the war. Her grandmother would see to it.

Tears of gratitude burned in Finnea's eyes. But her breath was swept away when Matthew turned to Hannah and said, "I may not be much to look at any longer, but I have wealth and I promise to care for your granddaughter with all my power."

Only when Matthew looked at Finnea and extended his hand to her did she see his uncertainty and his frustration. He was doing this, but he didn't want to.

Yet again, he was saving her. Her debts were mounting.

He was proving that he wasn't a coward, as she had so callously and unfairly thrown in his face. How could she be anything less?

"I would be proud to be your wife," she said, walking up and taking his hand.

Hannah picked up a glass of champagne. "To my granddaughter and her future husband."

The crowd gasped.

"May they enjoy a long and healthy life filled with joy."

The crowd began to talk at once, a din of noise. Hannah started to step away, but Finnea caught her arm. The woman looked down at the fingers that clutched her, then slowly met her eye.

"Why?" Finnea whispered, her voice barely steady.

Long seconds ticked by before Hannah raised her hand and laid it on top of Finnea's. "Because you are strong and brave. You have more courage in your little finger than Nester has in his entire body. I may not like this situation we find ourselves in, but you are my granddaughter. And Penelope had no right."

With that, she stepped away, leaving Matthew and Finnea alone among the crowd, cocooned against the noise.

"I appreciate what you are doing," Finnea said to him, her voice soft but strong in the clatter of talk all around them. "And rest assured, I will work quickly to deal with my inheritance problems. Then we can quietly break off the engagement, and you won't be bothered with me ever again."

He didn't respond, only looked at her in a way that was unnerving.

She chuckled uncomfortably. "You were quite convincing in your speech. If I didn't know better, I would have sworn you were serious."

"I am serious."

"What?" she gasped.

"I proposed and you accepted. I intend to marry you, Finnea."

"Now, Matthew, it was all for show."

"Boston doesn't know that, unless you would like me to gain their attention now and set them straight."

"But you can't!"

"I can," he said coldly. "And don't doubt that I will."

"Why?" she whispered.

"You once said that you owed me; now I've decided to call in that debt. We will marry, as we just announced. The fact is you need a husband." He hesitated. "And I need a mother for my child."

Child.

Her world tilted. "You have a child?" She could barely get the words past her lips.

"Yes. A daughter."

Her mind reeled. "How old?" was all she could ask.

"Six."

She pressed her eyes closed, feeling a strong sucking pull at her heart.

She had fled Africa to put memories of children behind her. Memories of a child named Isabel. Her precious child who would have been six years old this year if she had lived.

Part Three

The heart has its reasons which reason
knows nothing of.

Blaise Pascal

From the Journal of
Matthew Hawthorne

I thought I had left Africa behind forever, the unfamiliar desire—sharp, intense, not contained or polite—the emotion. But I realize now that in many ways I never left. I drew my Africa to me. I was still in that jungle, the canopy of trees and vines obscuring the sky. Finnea in my arms.

When I said we would marry, I saw her doubt. I felt it in my soul. It flickered in her eyes like fires burning just beyond the thick curtain of trees in the African forest. But once I admitted to myself that I wanted her, admitted that whatever had been dead inside me had opened up and started to breathe again whenever she was beside me, how could I let her go?

Chapter Thirteen

She couldn't do it.

Finnea walked up the long center aisle of Trinity Church, her gown a shimmering cloud of velvet and lace, a splash of weeping roses trailing from her hands. The priest waited at the altar, Matthew at his side, her family and his gathered together, and she knew with sinking certainty that she couldn't go through with this wedding—no matter what she owed him.

Finnea's eyes burned and her throat tightened. A child.

She hadn't thought . . .

It hadn't occurred to her . . .

How could she marry this man who expected her to be a mother to his child?

The church walls closed in around her, making it hard to breathe. Thick, hard-chiseled stones and gritty mortar blocked out the air. She had a sudden yearning for tall, dry grasses and wide-open spaces, a place where she could see forever and breathe. She longed for the smell of rain when it first hits dust, dry and sharp, tiny puffs filling the air.

A wave of anxiety nearly choked her. She had lost everything. Her dreams of her mother's love. Dreams of her family. She realized now that she had even lost herself as she tried to fit into a society that had no interest in her. Her dreams had been ripped apart, revealing that there was nothing here for her. Standing in the church, Finnea had no idea what was left.

Matthew?

He made her think of Africa. She had tried to outrun the pain, but by running away it was as if the loss had grown stronger, like wine fermenting in a barrel.

A mere three days had passed since her disastrous birthday.

Tongues had been wagging ever since. To make matters
worse, Matthew had insisted they marry quickly and had ob-
tained a special license, creating all the more titillating specu-
lation about their marriage.

Things had moved too fast for her to think straight. Before
she knew what was happening, she was walking up the church
aisle toward a man who made it clear that she had little choice
but to marry him, yet seemed angry about the very ultimatum
he had set before her.

But stripped of whatever illusion had remained about her
family, she knew she couldn't be at the mercy of Nester. She
felt trapped between her debt to Matthew and her need to free
herself from her brother.

She couldn't see any other solution. Matthew demanded
they marry immediately or not at all. Clearly he was willing to
do anything to gain a mother for his child.

But even when faced with the harsh reality of her brother,
Finnea didn't know how she could go through with the marriage. She might owe Matthew, but she couldn't tell him about
her past—about Isabel. That was a private pain she would
share with no one. Not even Matthew. And if she couldn't tell
him, how could she marry him?

But she had already agreed.

Finnea pressed her eyes closed for one long second, breathing deeply. Her shimmering gown was the same one she had
worn to the birthday gala, only now she wore a mantle of lace
that Emmaline Hawthorne had brought for her. "A gift," she
had said, "for my new daughter."

Swift, sweet joy shot through her, only dimmed by her own
mother's unrelenting disappointment.

Finnea looked up at the nave of the church. She sought
peace in the cathedral ceilings and carved stone pillars. She
sought courage from the scenes depicted in the stained-glass
windows before she focused on the priest.

The man looked ill at ease in his flowing robes of black and
white with hints of purple, though who could blame him,
based on the less-than-happy countenances of the wedding
party. Bradford Hawthorne stood like hard, cold marble in a

stiff black broadcloth jacket and creased trousers, his face unreadable. Even Emmaline Hawthorne, in a lovely gown of soft blue chintz and a cameo at her neck, looked as though she were having second thoughts.

Then there was Finnea's own family. Nester was angry at losing control over her shares, Leticia was weepy, and Hannah sat ramrod straight, her features implacable.

And Matthew's older brother. She looked at Grayson Hawthorne. He was the only person there she couldn't quite figure out. He stood like stone, much like his father. He didn't seem altogether opposed to the match, but rather confused and concerned by the sudden turn of events. The quiet solidarity between the brothers was apparent, and a flash of yearning swept through Finnea over the contrast between Matthew's brother and hers.

Finnea turned away from the thought as she continued up the aisle, turned away from the sudden burn of her eyes. And when she did, she saw Matthew's daughter, six-year-old Mary. A sweet child sitting next to Emmaline. The little girl had the blondest curls she had ever seen and round blue eyes, a rosebud mouth, and the face of an angel. She sat quietly, focused on a finely made porcelain doll, her small hand stroking the doll's hair as if trying to soothe it. Finnea knew in truth that Mary was trying to soothe herself.

Finnea's heart pounded. At any minute she felt as if she would scream, the scream she had held back, locked away for the past two years. She felt it bubble in her soul, begin to surge. Threatening. Oh, Isabel. Her dear sweet Isabel.

Finnea shrank from the memories, but her mind reeled with images that were far clearer than the scene around her.

"Mama . . ."

Finnea pressed her eyes closed. Please, not here. She turned her head as if she could turn away from the whispered word in her head.

"Oh, Mama, you are so funny!"

Finnea laughed into the clear spring day. "But you are funnier, my silly."

Everyone who saw them together had said they sounded just alike, just as they looked so much alike. The same red hair and bright green eyes. Even the way they walked was the same, hand in hand, cutting a path through the long, dry grasses.

"Do you love me, Mama?" Isabel asked suddenly one day.

Finnea stopped and bent down, her brow furrowed. "Of course I love you."

Isabel looked at her, large green eyes wide with intensity, the flowing native wrap so white against her sun-golden skin, and gently touched her mother's cheek with tiny hands as if memorizing the feel. "Only me?"

Finnea pulled her daughter close, her embrace fierce. "Yes, only you."

"Oh, Isabel."

The words choked her, and her head swam with pain and panic. She felt as if she were in a tunnel with no way out, the darkness sucking at her, pulling her in more deeply.

Her daughter was gone, taking what was left of her heart. How could she possibly love another?

Breaths coming in painful gasps, Finnea tore her gaze away from Mary. If she didn't escape, she knew she would scream. And if she started to scream now, she wasn't sure if she could ever stop.

But just when she would have gathered her skirts and fled down the aisle, she looked up at Matthew and saw an unexpected vulnerability barely hidden beneath his chiseled fierceness. He was certain she would flee, and somehow that hurt him. His face was turned just so, in that way that minimized the sight of his scar. That was when she realized she couldn't do it—she couldn't leave him at the altar after he had come to her aid yet again.

"Miss Winslet?" the priest prompted impatiently.

There were no alternatives. She owed him, though who would have guessed the price she would have to pay.

"Miss Winslet?"

In what seemed like only a flash of time, Finnea took the remaining steps to the altar, barely aware of the priest's words until he asked, "Do you take this man to be your lawfully wedded husband?"

Her head swam.

"Miss Winslet? Do you or don't you?"

"Yes. Yes, I do."

She only whispered the words, but they seemed to echo in the cavernous house of God. Bradford made some kind of disgruntled noise deep in his throat, Emmaline sighed, and Nester snorted. But what Finnea was most aware of was how she could actually feel Matthew ease.

"By the power vested in me, I now pronounce you man and wife. You may kiss the bride."

The words echoed in her mind, much as they echoed against the high ceilings. She looked at Matthew and took in this man, tall and stunningly handsome in his black formal jacket with cutaway tails, white tie, and waistcoat. Her husband.

Her breath caught at the look that came into his eyes. Dark. Possessive.

Her heart began to beat harder, and her lips parted. His gaze never left hers as his arm came around her, strong and secure, and he dipped his head. But a mere breath from her lips, he stopped. "You're mine now," he whispered for only her to hear, his voice like gravel. Then he covered her mouth with his own.

Despite the audience, the kiss was deep and demanding, and her fingers curled into the fine pleats of his waistcoat. His tongue twined with hers as one, his strong hand drifted to her lower back, pressing her close.

She went willingly, her body spinning with a sweet yearning that left her breathless. She was married. To this man— who alternately made her yearn, then made her need to run, just as he had in the jungle.

She was barely aware when the priest cleared his throat uncomfortably, and Grayson chuckled.

Red burst into her cheeks as Matthew stepped away, the look on his face bold and satisfied. Her body tingled with sensations she didn't understand, sensations that fought with the embarrassment. He had kissed her before with a sensuality and passion that melted her knees, but never with such utter possession.

She could hardly look away from him as the priest hurriedly

finished the ceremony, then dashed down the steps to the long aisle. He couldn't get away fast enough.

Emmaline was the first to approach them. Her eyes were filled with tears of either sadness or joy as she took Matthew's hand and pulled him close. "Congratulations, my dear son," she said softly, kissing him on the cheek.

Then she turned to Finnea and kissed her, too. Just when Finnea thought she would pull back, the woman whispered, "Make him happy. Please."

Emmaline retreated, all sign of tears gone, and was led away by her husband, who never said a word.

In the end, only Grayson and little Mary remained, the rest of the wedding party departing down the center aisle. Finnea watched them go with a mixture of envy and dismay.

"I apologize for our father," Grayson stated, his deep, rich voice resonating in the vacant space.

Finnea saw Matthew watch as Bradford departed. He clearly loved the man in spite of everything. But mixed with that love seemed to be a newly formed anger, as if he had been forced to reconsider his long-held assessment.

"But enough about our father," Grayson stated. He reached out and swept little Mary into his arms. The child glanced at Matthew, before burying her face in her uncle's shoulder.

Matthew's expression grew taut, but Grayson didn't notice. "I believe congratulations are in order." He turned to Matthew, his smile growing devilish. "May I kiss the bride?"

"A handshake will do."

Grayson burst out his laughter. "Now, now, little brother." He winked outrageously at Finnea, then glanced back at Matthew. "If Lucas were here, he'd steal a kiss. I, at least, have asked nicely."

Matthew scowled. "Have you heard from Lucas?"

"Yes. He wanted to be here. But you know how he and father are. Lucas didn't want to cause a scene."

Matthew nodded as if he understood.

"Now, about that kiss," Grayson added, his dark eyes glittering roguishly.

"That's enough from you," Matthew commanded, then reached out and pulled Finnea close.

Her heart kicked at the possessive gesture. She could feel the heat of Matthew and smell the clean, spicy aroma of him. No perfumes, like she had learned men in America so often wore. He smelled wonderful and rugged, and she found herself leaning against him—as if somehow he could protect her. With a start, she pushed away, realizing in that moment that for all his anger he made her feel safe.

She looked up at him, startled. How, when he had made it clear time and again that he wanted nothing to do with her, could he make her feel so safe?

Matthew didn't look any happier about the situation than she felt, but still he didn't let her go.

Soon enough Grayson left, leaving Matthew, Finnea, and Mary alone in the empty church. Feelings of safety fled.

If you dance with the devil, someday you'll pay.

Janji's words from long ago.

She had heard him say it countless times, but never understood it until now. She was married, to Matthew—a man she had failed to tell of her past, a man who didn't want her, or anyone. A man who wanted oblivion. He had warned her. But she had married him anyway. And now she stood before his daughter.

Long ago she had thought her heart could break no more. But standing in Trinity Church, she felt the tattered remains break apart completely.

How had she ever thought she could do this?

"I have a few rules, and if you follow them, I see no reason why we shouldn't get along."

Matthew eyed Finnea warily, as did Mary. They stood in the foyer of Dove's Way only minutes after the wedding ceremony.

Who was this straightforward, no-nonsense woman before him? he wondered as he stared at Finnea.

She was dressed in a proper gown, looking every inch the perfect lady. The only testament to her former wildness was in her eyes, vibrant and green like the African jungle. But combined with that vibrancy was a coldness—a distance she had erected between them that he didn't understand.

Matthew was hardly certain of what had transpired in the

church. He had been tired, his hand feeling like needles were stuck in it. He had barely managed to put the ring on her finger without shaking. His face hurt and his head throbbed, and now he found himself married. For better or for worse. And right now he was getting a full dose of worse.

"First," Finnea continued, addressing Mary, "if you're hungry, talk to Mr. Quincy. I don't cook."

Matthew's eyes went wide.

"Second," she added, casually smoothing the folds of her skirt, "if you go out, be sure to leave a note."

This time Mary's eyes went wide.

"You do write, don't you?" Finnea asked, worrying her lower lip. But she didn't wait for an answer. "And finally, don't wake me before noon unless you are seriously injured or physically ill." She thought for a minute, then nodded her head. "That's about it."

Matthew stared at his new wife much as his daughter did, stunned. He was sure at any moment the old Finnea, his Finnea, would burst out laughing and say it was all a joke. But this Finnea only turned away.

He caught her fingers, and for one fleeting moment he nearly laced them with his. He could feel her tremble, her eyes darkening with vulnerability. But before he could make sense of it, the defiance boldly surged back, making him doubt he had seen anything else.

She glanced down at the hand that held her before meeting his gaze. "Did I not make myself clear?"

Her voice held no weakness, no quaver, no trembling. His jaw muscles ticked. "Yes, you made yourself quite clear."

"Good." With that she walked away, her low heels clicking on marble, only stopping when she came to the bottom of the stairs. "I thought I'd take the yellow room I saw earlier. Could you have someone bring up my things?"

Matthew stood very still, his back rigid, his shoulders taut. The only sound in the house came from the tick of the hall clock and the occasional clatter of city traffic over cobbles beyond the door. She had chosen the room farthest from his own, and now she stared at him, daring him to contradict her choice.

He looked at her hard, anger ticking like a clock inside him. After long seconds, his gaze never wavering from hers, he called out.

"Quincy," he barked.

The butler came running, his coattails flapping. "Yes, sir?"

"Please have Miss—rather, Mrs.—Hawthorne's belongings taken to the yellow room."

"Of course, Mr. Hawthorne. I'll have them sent right up," he said, hurrying away as Finnea took the stairs.

Matthew and Mary watched her go. At length, Matthew turned to his daughter and started to explain, to offer some reassuring remark about this woman who was supposed to be her new mother.

But the instant he looked at her, she dropped her gaze to study her shoes, her doll held tightly in her arms. The gesture tore at his heart. He knew that she would look at anything as long as she didn't have to look at him.

He didn't trust himself to speak, unsure as he was of what would come out.

"May I be excused?" she whispered softly.

He nodded his head but then realized that since she wouldn't look at him she wasn't aware that he had answered.

"Yes," he said carefully, fighting back emotion. "Quincy will show you to your new room."

But before he could say anything else, she turned in her tiny black button boots and ran to the front door.

Mary couldn't get out of the house fast enough. She heard her father's shouts to come back.

"I will not," she whispered desperately, dashing away tears.

She hurried down the steps before he could reach her. Slipping through the yard of a house at the corner of Marlborough and Berkeley, Mary made her way to Commonwealth Avenue. Her steps didn't slow until she came to the street she had lived on her whole life. The world fell away with each step she took, until she was walking the path she knew by heart—knew each crack in the walkway, each rail of black wrought-iron fencing, the snow on the spikes looking like downy white hats.

A tall house of red brick with black shutters and a high

mansard roof stood out like a welcoming light. Home. Her real home.

Time went still, then swirled backward. Memories sprang to life. Real and vivid.

As if coming out of a bad dream, she hurried up the steps and was surprised when the knob on the front door was locked. Where was her mother?

She knocked, but no one answered. The curtains were drawn, everything quiet. She'd have to wait. Her mother was no doubt shopping or having tea.

She stared at the door. She didn't notice the long minutes that ticked by or the sun that began to set as she waited. Patiently. Her mother would come home.

Lights came on in the houses all around her, though her house remained dark. But still she waited, only sinking down onto the step when her legs grew weary, resting her head on her knees.

Matthew saw her from the corner. He stopped in his tracks, his throat tight. He had been everywhere. His parents', all through the Public Gardens and the Commons. Up and down each street of the Back Bay. But he had never guessed that she would come here, to this house where seven years ago he had brought his young wife, to this house where a year later he had shared the joy of their new daughter.

Never taking his eyes off his child, he walked up to the house that had been vacant now for nearly two years. When he turned up the flagstone path that led to the front door, Mary's head shot up. Their eyes locked and held.

"She's gone, baby," he said softly. "She's not coming back."

He watched as her blank stare flashed with devastation, then emptiness. He understood so well.

She closed her eyes, one tear squeezing through to roll down her cheek. "I know," she whispered.

But when he would have reached out to her, she dashed her tiny hand angrily across her face and raced back toward the house on Marlborough Street.

Chapter Fourteen

Breakfast the next morning was no better. As soon as Matthew walked into the dining room, Mary began to hum quietly, stroking her doll. Matthew stiffened and his heart sank. He hated this, hated that he didn't know how to bridge the gap between them. He would have turned on his heels and let her eat alone in peace if Finnea hadn't just walked into the room.

Something was different, he realized at the sight of her. Then he noticed that she wore the flowing white shirt of a hunter, the small, round, wooden buttons securely fastened to just below her neck. It was a shirt like the one she had worn on the train. She had tucked the tails of the shirt into the waist of a proper ladies' skirt that any Boston matron would be content to wear. The mix was startling. And provocative. The wildness mixed with propriety.

Matthew nearly chuckled at her defiance until a stab of pain burned through him when he reached to pull out her chair. His fingers tingled, and a dull ache throbbed through his arm and shoulder. When he glanced up, he found Finnea studying him curiously. Her brow furrowed, her head tilting slightly in confused consideration. For a second he was sure she had found him out, understood his damning weakness. But when he bit back the pain and held her chair with a bland smile in hopes of appearing casual, she seemed to shake away whatever confusion she had felt, and sat down.

It occurred to him that it would be harder to hide this damnable affliction with this woman and his daughter living with him. Of course some part of him had known it all along. But he had wanted Finnea, and he had pushed all other considerations from his mind.

The dining room was silent except for the crystalline clink of silver on china. Matthew sat back and drank his coffee, leaving his meal untouched. He didn't dare risk exposure by trying to eat. In the future, he decided, he would eat alone.

He studied her over sips of coffee. He knew she was uncomfortable. And Mary barely touched her food.

The silence stretched out as they picked at their meals.

It was Mary who finally asked to be excused just as Quincy entered.

"Don't you want some pancakes, Miss Mary?" the butler asked, a friendly smile pulling at his aged face. "I had Violet make your favorite."

"Thank you, Mr. Quincy, but I'm full." She looked at her father, then dropped her gaze as if for one brief second she had forgotten his face. "May I be excused?"

Long seconds ticked by. "Yes," he said finally.

As soon as Mary was gone, Finnea pushed up from her chair. "If you'll excuse me as well."

"No, I will not excuse you."

His voice was a quiet command, making Finnea stop in her tracks. She glanced at him from across the table. His face was lined with a warrior's hardness, the intensity of his gaze making her breath catch.

At length, he asked, "What is it about my daughter that upsets you? Or is it just me that you don't like?"

The question startled her. She hadn't expected him to broach the subject so directly. Her mind swam with possible answers, some true, some not.

How to tell him the truth?

How to explain her stupidity, her naïveté? How to explain the love she had felt for her daughter that made the foolishness of her conception insignificant? At least to her. But it mattered to everyone else. She had learned that in Africa.

Her father had been furious—furious at the man he had treated like a son, who in turn had betrayed his trust. But he had been furious at her as well, for stupidly giving in to a man

full of false love and gossamer-thin promises. Gatwith Neilander had charmed them all: her father, her, the natives. He
had arrived from Belgium with his reddish-blond hair and
laughing green eyes, and taught them better farming tech-
niques. Later, he had slipped away, having taught Finnea a
good deal more than that.

"You don't upset me, Matthew, nor does your daughter,"
she stated.

"Then what was that little display about when we got home
from the wedding?"

"I . . . I just felt it important to get off on the right foot."

"The right foot?" he asked, his tone stern. "Meaning you
wanted to let Mary know right away that you weren't interested in being a mother?"

Finnea cringed. She knew he was right, and she felt the heat
of embarrassment at the well-deserved recrimination. But
yesterday the words had come out before she could think. She
hadn't slept until noon in her life, but she had needed some
way to put distance between them, however artificial.

She watched as the hardness in his expression softened.

"Is it because I had another wife?"

Her heart kicked when he stood up from his chair. With the
predatory stride of a lion, he came around the table and gently
took her arm.

The feel of his fingers wrapping around her, the insistent
hum as blood rushed through her veins, his touch seeping into
her skin as he pulled her close.

"Is that it, Finn?" he asked, his voice low and rumbling.
"Are you upset that I had another wife?"

Embarrassment flashed through her. "Upset about another
wife?" God, did she seem so shallow? But the anger drained
away as quickly as it surfaced. Of course she was. Shallow and
awful.

"You are acting like your own mother, Finnea. Don't do that
to my daughter."

She locked away the hurt that his words caused. "But it's
true," she replied, barely able to get the words past the lump in
her throat. "I am my mother's child, after all. You've known
that all along. How can you expect me to be anything else?"

His blue eyes grew darker with intensity. "Because you are not your mother. You would never care more about society than your child. You would love her and care for her no matter what."

The words tore at her, twisted around her, strangled her. He didn't know how true they were. He also didn't know that in the end none of it had mattered.

"Since you know so much about it, *you* be the mother. You certainly don't need me."

She tried to pull away, but he wouldn't let her go. He studied her and she could tell he was looking deep, looking into her soul. She tried again to move away.

"But I do need you," he whispered, holding her there.

Tears sprang to life in her eyes as he pulled her closer.

His hand came up and cupped her cheek. "Mary needs you."

The thought of Isabel sprang to life in her mind.

"*We* need you," he added gruffly, his thumb brushing against her skin. "I know you aren't as cold as you're acting."

"But I am," she cried, the sob wrenching from her soul. "I am cold and hard! I can't do this! I thought I could, but I can't."

No one had told her how much she would love her child. No one had told her about the wonder she would experience at the feel of her daughter curled up in her arms, fresh from a bath— or how utterly destroyed she would be when she was gone.

He took hold of her shoulders and shook her gently but firmly. "You *can* do this, Finnea. You can be a wonderful mother. Just try!" His voice softened. "All I ask is that you try."

"No."

The single, obstinate word turned his blue eyes to chips of ice. "Why? Why won't you even try?"

Pride and defiance surged and she refused to let him see how she was hurting. "I told you I didn't want this marriage. I meant what I said. And I don't want you."

His eyes went blank, unfathomable depths resurfacing. "You might not have wanted a wedding ring, but you have proved on several occasions that you want me."

"That is not true!"

The words were barely out when he pulled her to him, his mouth descending on hers. His kiss was hard and punishing, but only for a moment. Almost instantly it turned soft and desperate. He murmured against her lips, stroking, urging her with his tongue, making her want to give in. He slid his hands down her sides, then up slowly, his fingers drifting along her back, his thumbs grazing her ribs.

He felt when she started to give in, felt when she started to melt against him. Her hands stopped pushing at him and curled into his shirt. His hands drifted low again, down her side, his thumbs curving around to skim over her abdomen, slipping beneath the thin white cotton of her skirt. He gently sucked her tongue into his mouth and she moaned, the innocent mewling sending a surge of blood to his groin. He was hard for her, hard and aching.

Cupping her round bottom, he pulled her up against his desire. "Do you feel how much I want you?"

At the words, he felt her stiffen in his arms. Tension flowed into her frame, and she tore her mouth away from his. "No!" she cried out.

He set her at arm's length. "Why? You want me, Finnea, but you keep pushing me away. Tell me why."

She tried to step away, but he held her there.

"Tell me, Finn, why?"

She stared at him for long seconds, her eyes desolate and darkened with despair. "Because."

"Because why?"

"Because I can't stand to feel!"

He expected many things, but not that. The words caught him in the stomach, words he understood so well. But every time he was near her, she made him feel. Desire, life. Hope.

Something flared inside him, twisting and hurting. Her ability to set herself apart was unbearable. She succeeded where he failed.

He wanted her to feel. He needed her to feel.

He had managed to numb himself in Africa, had begun to deaden the pain for all that he had lost. But since he met Finnea he had done nothing but feel, as if she were tearing him apart all over again.

She who had ripped open his heart wouldn't allow anyone around her to do the same.

Something had defeated her in Africa, he was sure of it now, but she refused to tell him what it was. And clearly her family had ripped her apart even more. Nonetheless, she stood there defiantly, building a wall around herself, standing strong against the pain.

But he needed her. And she needed him. For whatever reason, for whatever purpose. He accepted that now.

It was time she accepted it, too.

"You should have thought of that," he stated softly, "before you agreed to marry me."

He curled her closer, and her eyes went wary.

"I'm having your things moved out of the yellow room."

"Why?" she stammered.

"Because you're my wife, and from now on, you will sleep in the room that adjoins mine."

At the end of what seemed like an endless day, Finnea purposely made her way to the yellow room. The closer she got, the harder she prayed that Matthew hadn't followed through with his threat. But when she opened the door she knew right away that all of her belongings were gone.

A short, bubbly maid in a starched white apron appeared at her side.

"Mrs. Hawthorne, I just finished moving your things. I know you are just going to love the new room. It's so beautiful." The young girl giggled. "And Mr. Hawthorne is in his own room right next door."

Finnea's heart felt like lead in her chest. She walked down the hall as if she were walking toward an executioner's block. She couldn't afford this. But mixed with that knowledge was the clear memory of the touch of his lips, the graze of his fingers against her spine. Her breath grew shallow, and her skin tightened across her chest. Sensation tingled through her body as though Matthew were touching her now.

The door to her new room was open. A fire burned low on the hearth, filling the space with a welcoming glow. The ceiling was high, the walls papered with a delicate floral print. The perfect room for a lady.

"I've run your bath," the maid said. "Can I help you undress?"

"No. No, thank you."

Even after the maid departed, the door that must connect her room to the next remained closed. But only when Finnea sat down in front of the vanity and still she remained alone did her heart begin to settle. She waited for several minutes to pass, staring at the door's reflection in the mirror. And still it stayed firmly shut.

Relief and foolish disappointment mixed like wine with her blood. She went to the bath chamber that opened off the room. It looked like a private sanctuary. Marble tiles, hand-woven rugs, porcelain tub, beveled mirrors, a chaise, and even a commode. She wouldn't have to walk down the hall, as she had at her mother's house, or outside, as she had in Africa. A giddy pleasure raced through her at such a luxury.

She glanced between the steaming water in the tub and the connecting door. In an instant, she made her decision. Hurriedly, she brushed out her hair and pinned it on top of her head. After tossing her gown aside, she sank into the lavender-scented water until it lapped at her chin. Heaven.

She soaked until she felt the tension drain away. Steam rose up from the water, and she consciously put all thought from her mind.

She didn't know how long she soaked, but she was nearly asleep when she realized the water was cold. Quickly she washed and stepped out of the tub. She could see the door was still shut, and she breathed another sigh of relief at the thought that she could put off dealing with Matthew for another day.

But just when she pulled on a thin wrapper over her naked body, she stopped. Matthew sat in a wingback chair in front of the hearth, a crystal of brandy in his hand. He wore fine wool trousers and a white shirt, unbuttoned at the neck, revealing a glimpse of golden hair. His vest and coat were gone. He looked like a man at ease, at the end of the day, in the privacy of his bedchamber. Finnea's heart skipped a beat at the intimacy.

He looked up when she entered, and she could see his blue

eyes darken at the sight of her. The knowledge that he wanted her sent a tremor through her body. Her heart began to pound nervously and she forced a laugh.

"Fancy meeting you here," she offered. "Did you lose your way?"

His eyes darkened even more. "I lost my way a long time ago."

The words seared her soul, knowing that somehow he spoke a very deep truth.

She wanted out of there; she wanted him gone. She couldn't take his pain because there was nothing she could do about it. She couldn't ease his anger; she couldn't solve his problems with his father. She couldn't fill his need for a mother for his child.

"So much for jokes," she replied with a flippancy that even to her ears sounded false.

"Are you enjoying your new room?" he asked.

She shrugged as casually as she could. "A room is a room, a few walls, a floor, a ceiling, a bed—" She went still.

He glanced at the furniture mentioned, then back at her. "Come here, Finnea."

The words were a sensual command, making her body burn. "I'd rather not," she managed.

"I'd rather you did."

Her heart fluttered as he held out his hand, all casual pretense evaporating.

"I can't do this," she whispered, choked.

He stood, his chiseled body unfolding from the chair, so broad and tall that he blocked out the firelight. "You can, Finn, and you will."

Turning sharply, she intended to flee. But she hadn't gotten more than a few steps when he took her hand, pulling her back. His touch was gentle, though commanding, his eyes filled with all the emotion she refused to let herself feel.

He turned her around until she faced away from him, facing the fire. She stood woodenly as his hands trailed up her arms to her shoulders, then her hair, his fingers pulling the pins until the long strands tumbled free. His hands slid into her hair, his palms cradling her head, rubbing slowly.

"What are you doing?" she asked, holding herself perfectly still when she really wanted to lean back against him.

"I'm touching you." He leaned down and whispered in her ear. "I'm going to touch every inch of you."

Her stomach tensed.

"I'm going to touch your breasts," he added, his hands working their magic on her scalp. "I'm going to touch you between your legs, slip my fingers inside you until you're wet and slick and ready."

The knot in her stomach tightened, fighting with the sudden hot warmth that spread through her thighs.

"I'm going to show you how much you do feel, Finnea."

The words stabbed through the fog in her brain and she tried to jerk away. "Why are you doing this?" she gasped when his arm curled around her like a band of steel.

He seemed to pull a deep, jagged breath at the quick movement, pressing his lips to her head. "Because you are my wife," he said at last.

"But I don't want to be."

She felt him tense.

"Too late now," he whispered, his arm pulling her firmly back until her spine pressed against his chest.

He touched his lips to her hair; before parting the silk of her dressing gown. She gasped as slowly his hand slipped between the lapels, brushing against still-damp skin from the bath.

"Did you feel that?" he asked, his voice low and deep in her ear.

She jerked her head to the side, but it only brought her cheek up against his chest.

"I think you did."

His hand caressed her belly, sliding dangerously low, the tips of his long fingers grazing the tight curls between her legs, and her entire body burned.

"You feel, sweetheart," he stated.

His gentle touch made her want to weep.

"You're wrong," she replied, unable to say anything else. "I don't care enough to feel."

The motion of his hand stopped, hesitated as if he battled

within himself and he might cease his torment. But then a deep sound rumbled in his chest and his hand started again, this time moving higher, and her heart began to pound.

The silk lapels of the dressing gown fell apart completely, the long sash hanging at her sides. One large hand cupped her breast, pressing it high, his thumb brushing over the peak, making it taut.

"Still no feeling?" he asked.

"No," she whispered, her eyes closed.

Despite her plea, she tried to turn around, her body instinctively seeking what her mind didn't want. But he wouldn't let her, holding her captured against his chest as if he didn't want her to see him.

He buried his face in her hair as he palmed her breasts with both hands, gently rolling her taut nipples between his thumbs and forefingers. She felt dizzy and hot. Her head rolled on his chest as his hand drifted low. One hand still tantalized her breast, the other slipped between her legs as he had promised.

Her body began to move. She wanted to give in. But how could she? How could she open up her heart and body without shredding what little was left of her soul? She had given herself once. She couldn't do it again.

"Stop!" The word came out as a broken gasp. "Please. I can't do this."

He went still, his hands clasping her to him, though no longer in some attempt to arouse her. She had the fleeting thought that he was trying to fill her with strength.

"You can, Finn." He wrapped his arms around her shoulders. "Let me help you. I'm on your side. Don't you understand that?"

A shudder of emotion nearly undid her. She wanted to give in, to share her grief, and perhaps find out it wasn't so unendurable. But she knew that wasn't true. She could never forgive herself for not having saved her daughter.

"No, Matthew," she said so quietly that the words were nearly lost in the room. "I can't. This marriage is a mistake."

She felt the hot anger that flashed through him, but as soon as she had uttered the words she knew there was only one solution. She couldn't stay married to him because in truth she couldn't be the mother he had bargained for. She couldn't be a mother to his child any more than she could be a true wife.

"I am going to seek an annulment," she stated.

With barely controlled motions, he set her away from him and turned her around to look at him. His eyes burned like blue fire.

"There will be no annulment, now or ever," he stated with cold finality.

Then he was gone, disappearing through the doorway that separated their rooms.

Chapter Fifteen

Despite what Matthew had said, early the next morning Finnea sent a note explaining the situation regarding her shares of Winslet Ironworks to the man she knew had been her father's lawyer. She also asked that he see to her annulment. She pushed away the heaviness that came over her at the thought—pushed away the image that leaped into her mind of strong fingers splayed over her abdomen, then drifting lower.

Her breath came out in a trembling shudder. Sensation rippled through her body at the thought of how Matthew had touched her, his fingers on her nipples, his hand brushing over the curve of her flesh.

She pressed her eyes closed. She couldn't stay married to this man.

Later that day Finnea came downstairs for afternoon tea wearing another hunter's shirt, combined with a pair of low-heeled boots beneath her skirt. Her long, curling red hair was down, secured at her nape by a leather tie. Proper Boston attire was gone. She relished the freedom, relished the sense of self she felt returning after months of trying to be some-one she wasn't, hoping her mother could love her. Swept-up hair and perfect gowns having failed, she might as well be comfortable.

Her boots clicked against the tiled entry hall floor of Dove's Way, her stride determined. She entered the informal dining room and was awed by the large glass-paned doors looking out over the snow-covered gardens. The room was empty, ex-cept for the china, the silver-laden table, and Quincy.

"Good afternoon, Mrs. Hawthorne."

Finnea whirled around to look for Matthew's mother, only to realize he was talking to her.

Mrs. Hawthorne. Matthew's wife.

A wave of unexpected pleasure washed over her. But she brushed it away. She wouldn't be his wife for long.

"Good morning, Mr. Quincy."

She noticed that the man's normally ruddy cheeks were pale as he stood at attention by the side bar. "What's wrong? You don't look yourself."

The butler pressed his fingers experimentally against his cheek, then winced. "Nothing, Mrs. Hawthorne. Just a bit of a toothache."

She started toward him. "Let me have a look."

His eyes went wide, and he took a step back. "Whatever for?"

"I learned a bit about tooth ailments while I was growing up."

He warded her off as politely as he could. "Thank you, but I'm fine, Mrs. Hawthorne." He gestured toward the selection of finger sandwiches, cakes, and tea. "What can I get for you?"

She studied him for a second and decided not to push. "I can get it, Mr. Quincy, thank you," she said, distracted as she remembered the remedy Janji had always used to ease tooth pain.

She picked up a small plate of creamy bone china sprinkled with hand-painted flowers and thought of salt. A salt water wash. She retrieved a serving tong, recalling that one had to chew a fresh clove of garlic with the affected tooth, then pack the area with more salt and alum. She would make Mr. Quincy a concoction, but she wouldn't mention it until she had it mixed up and ready.

She glanced around the dining room. "Where is . . . are the others?"

"Miss Mary has already eaten and returned upstairs. Shall I call her?"

"No," she said hurriedly. "That won't be necessary."

He gave a brief, formal bow, then made to leave.

"And Mr. Hawthorne?" she asked before she could stop herself, the plate and silverware held suspended in the air.

Quincy halted, the creases in his weathered face deepening. "Mr. Hawthorne?" he asked, as if he had never heard of the man before.

Finnea looked at him oddly. "Yes, where is he? Will he be down soon?" She was certain she had heard him only minutes earlier just beyond the wall in his bedroom.

"Hmmm, well." He cleared his throat and seemed to search for words. "He's . . . out. Yes, out." He nodded his head. "Left at noon, he did."

Before she could ask for an explanation about the discrepancy, he hurried away, the graceful wooden door that led to the butler's pantry swinging shut in his wake.

"That was strange," she said to the empty room, tamping down the disappointment she felt at Matthew not being there.

It was ridiculous that she felt this way. She wanted him gone, but she was disappointed that he wasn't there. More proof that this situation was impossible.

Afternoon tea suddenly lost its appeal. She set the plate aside, then headed for the front door. She wanted out, out of the house, away from her thoughts.

The frigid February air beckoned to her, and she nearly ran to the door. But just as she was pulling on her coat, she noticed Mary precariously making her way down the stairs, dragging a suitcase behind her.

Thump, thump, thump. With her hair secured beneath a woolen hat, Mary came down each step, almost backward as she manhandled the traveling case that was very nearly as big as she.

"Mary!" Finnea exclaimed, frozen by surprise in the process of pulling on her winter wrap.

Mary whirled around and almost tumbled down the remaining step. Finnea automatically leaped forward to catch her, the child grabbing hold of her instinctively.

The feel of still-soft baby arms and shoulders teased Finnea's mind. For a moment she lost herself to the sensation, imagined the tiny arms wrapped around her neck in childish affection.

"Thank you for steadying me, ma'am," Mary stated with crisp formality. "I'm fine now."

Abruptly Finnea let go, then briskly secured her coat. "What are you doing?" she asked, hating the threat of tears that burned in her eyes.

Last night, Finnea had decided that affecting a kind but businesslike mien would be best in dealing with this child, a manner that wouldn't allow for bonds or attachments.

Mary raised her tiny chin and looked her in the eye. "I am running away. Then you won't have to worry about meals to cook or being woken up too early. And rest assured," she added in a voice far older than her meager years, "I planned to leave you a note. I *can* write."

Finnea blanched, her guilt over yesterday's display resurging. But which would be worse? she reasoned. Giving this innocent little girl false hope that she could be a true mother, or establishing a considerate but professional relationship? Yes, better to get things going as she intended they continue on—until the annulment came through.

She would be kind and polite. She would feed the child and clothe her, see to her needs. She would find what everyone referred to as a governess while she was waiting for her inheritance to be straightened out and for her annulment to come through. She could do no less. But first she had to convince the child to stay.

"Running away, is it? Good idea," Finnea said with a definite nod.

Mary's eyes went wide like tiny rounds of blue mint candy.

"In fact," Finnea continued, buttoning the last button on her coat and heading for the front door, "I think I'll do the same."

Mary didn't move, only stood at the bottom of the stairs, her traveling case lying on its side on the marble floor, her own coat fastened haphazardly to the top, the tiny boat buttons looking as if they were being tossed on a tempestuous sea.

At the door Finnea stopped, her hand on the heavily embossed brass knob. "Would you like to share a hired hack?" She twisted her lips and considered. "Or should we be economical and catch the trolley? If one is going to run away, one must start thinking about one's finances, I suppose."

Mary's brow furrowed. Obviously she had given little, if any, thought to finances.

But then Mary gave her head a vigorous little shake as if clearing her mind of half-witted thoughts. "*You* can't run away!"

Finnea focused on the child with the utmost seriousness. "Why ever not?"

"Well . . . because," Mary stammered, her mind churning for a suitable explanation.

"Just because?"

"Because you're a grown-up. Grown-ups don't run away."

"Really?" Finnea bit her lip and looked directly at the child. "Well, sometimes I don't do things right and I muck it all up. It's a bad habit of mine." Did the child understand? Did she hear the apology?

But of course it didn't matter, couldn't matter.

Finnea pulled back her shoulders. "Perhaps we could make a deal. I won't run away if you won't."

Mary considered her with dubious blue eyes, clearly wondering if she was serious or not. "Well, I suppose I could stay," she replied carefully. "But only if you will."

A poignant rush of emotion wrapped around Finnea's heart, twisting, hurting.

The desperation that had driven her to the front door in the first place grew and swelled. More than ever she wanted to escape, wanted to feel the bracing winter cold against her cheeks.

Without another word, she pulled the door open. A gust of wind rushed into the house, winter-dried leaves swirling in the frigid air, dancing on the ice and salt-crusted flagstone steps that marched down to the walkway below. Finnea stood, staring, memories of the past threatening. She saw Africa. She saw gentle warm winds and tiny arms wrapping around her neck.

"Where are you going?" Mary demanded, concern lacing her voice. "You said you weren't going to run away."

"I'm just going to the market to get a few things to make a concoction for Mr. Quincy's tooth. It shouldn't take long."

Mary eyed her doubtfully. "Maybe I should go with you."

In case you don't want to come back.

Finnea heard the words implied in the child's tone.

The clock chimed the hour, filling the foyer with the echoing bongs.

"Fine," Finnea said. "But you'd best do something about those buttons."

Mary dropped her head until her chin was planted in her chest, and she studied the front of her coat. With thickly gloved fingers, the child attempted to undo the misplaced boats, but the heavy wool was pulled too tight. She fumbled and fumbled some more. Then she looked up at Finnea in frustrated defeat. "I can't do it."

Finnea's mind went still, her heart pounding over the look on Mary's face. Leaning down, Finnea quickly started on the fastenings, concentrating on the boats as they slipped out of their moorings. She felt hot and crowded, like she was suffocating. Her own fingers stumbled before she finally had the buttons straightened. But when she started to push back, she found herself face-to-face with Mary, their eyes locked, so close she could make out the thick curl of white-blond lashes. And her eyes. So sweet, just like Isabel's.

"Thank you," Mary whispered.

Finnea's breath came out in a rush and she straightened abruptly. "Of course."

The streets were filled with carriages and trolleys, while women in gowns with hems brushing the ground hurried toward their homes. Mary and Finnea leaned into the wind as they headed down the granite-block walkway that lined Marlborough Street toward the Public Gardens. From there they would angle across the park in the direction of downtown, a lengthy trek under the best of circumstances, miserable in such wind and cold.

"Why don't we take a carriage?" Mary called out, the words muffled by the wind. "Now that we aren't running away, I suppose we have a nickel or two we could spare."

Finnea was taken in by the impish smile on Mary's cherub face. The teasing, the humor. The need to hug the child tight.

Finnea could only offer a crisp, efficient nod before she looked around. "I don't see a hired hack," was all she said, forcefully putting from her mind the child's crestfallen face that she didn't respond to the joke. "We'll look for one when we come out on Tremont Street."

They hunkered down and continued on. Thankfully, as soon as they walked through the stately gates into the Public Gardens, the trees, regardless of their barren state, and the tall evergreen bushes buffered the elements. Mary and Finnea continued on in relief.

The path had been shoveled, so they managed with relative ease. They walked side by side, Finnea slowing her stride to match Mary's.

"Where were you going to go when you ran away?" Finnea inquired.

Mary shrugged but didn't answer.

"Back to your grandmother's house?"

"No," the child said finally, glancing up. "I was thinking of taking a ship."

"Why did you want to go so far?" Finnea asked. "Wouldn't you miss all your friends?"

Mary bit her lip, then said, "Oh yes, I'd miss them. And they'd miss me as well. Terribly. I'm popular, you know. But if a person is going to run away, they should do it right and run far away."

Finnea thought of Matthew running to Africa. Was Mary the reason he had returned?

"Were you *really* going to run away?" Mary asked, breaking into her thoughts.

Finnea's step faltered and she looked at the child. Yes, yes, say yes. Maintain the professional, businesslike mien, keep the distance. "No," she said softly into the fading wind, unable to lie. "I wasn't really. It just seemed like the right thing to say at the time."

"I'm glad you weren't."

Relief and hope filled the child's eyes, and Finnea felt her heart twist even more. Her head swam and she wanted to scream as she wondered about her own child. Would she have still carried a doll? Would she have laughed with joy at the sight of all this snow?

The senseless wondering circled unchecked in her mind

like a whirling dervish until she thought she would go mad. She wanted to cease the endless replay of thoughts. They did no good, never had.

She looked out in the distance and saw the lagoon, the water frozen hard. The ice was empty of skaters, cold and beckoning. And just then the wind died down completely. The late afternoon sun broke through the clouds and danced on the surface of the tiny lake. Winter glistened on the tree branches.

Finnea took in the sight as if taking in a deep breath, swallowing back the scream that bubbled inside her. She didn't want to think, was tired of thinking; she wanted to lose herself.

She didn't have the razor-blade shoes the men wore on the ice, but she took a few determined steps toward the lagoon regardless, slowly at first, then faster and faster, until she ran.

"Finnea!" Mary cried out, but Finnea kept going, the wind pulling the tie from her uncovered hair.

She ran without stopping, straight for the lake, and barely broke her stride before she leaped out in her booted feet as she had longed to do since the first time she saw it. She hit the ice at a run, her head flung back, her arms extended at her sides like wings. Cold air stung her cheeks, bringing tears to her eyes as she slid across the lagoon.

Her cry of desperate release echoed in the snow-covered expanse, and for those few minutes time hung suspended and the endless circling of thoughts ceased. For one brief crystalline space of time, fear and panic didn't twist in her heart like a knife.

She ended up on the opposite side, her breath shallow, but from exertion, not panic. When she looked back, she saw Mary racing along the path, her tiny black-booted heels kicking up the back of her knee-length coat as she ran. She barreled over the footbridge and dashed off the path into the snow-covered grounds toward Finnea. Mary didn't stop until she stood in front of her. Only then did Finnea see the child's tears.

"What is it, Mary?" she asked, climbing awkwardly off the ice.

"Don't do that!" Mary raged.

Finnea was startled by the intensity. "Why not?"

"Because. Because it's stupid and silly . . . and my father wouldn't like it."

At this, Finnea scoffed. "True, but I'd have to say your father doesn't seem to like much of anything these days, now does he?"

Mary squeezed her eyes closed, and Finnea hated the stab of conscience she felt. She never meant to hurt the child, but obviously Mary thought the words applied to her.

"Oh, Mary," she said softly, coming forward. "Your father loves you." *Didn't he?*

"No, he doesn't!" she cried, her face mottled with blotches of red and tears. "And I don't care because I don't want him to love me. I hate him! I hate him! I wish he had never come back from Africa!"

Mary turned and fled, racing back the way she had come, leaving perfect footprints in the snow. Finnea stared at the tiny indentations until a gust of wind came up and erased them. But Mary and her tears could not be erased so easily. With a sigh, Finnea trudged through the snow to the path and followed her back to Dove's Way.

Matthew stood in his bedroom doorway, doing little to control his anger with his wife. He had received a letter from William Winslet's lawyer. On top of that, Mary had just charged past him down the hall, tears streaking her cheeks.

Seconds later Finnea hurried up the stairway, errant tendrils of red curling wildly around her face.

"What is wrong with Mary?" he demanded. He couldn't tell if she looked guilty or if she was just leery of him.

"She's upset."

"I can see that," he said carefully. "We made a deal. And that deal does not include you upsetting my daughter."

"But—"

"Nor does it include this," he stated, holding up an official-looking, cream-colored letter.

"What is it?" she asked warily.

"A letter from your father's solicitor."

"How dare he!"

Matthew turned on his heels and began to pace in front of the hearth in his room.

Indignant, Finnea followed him inside. "He had no right to contact you."

"Did you think he wouldn't? I am your husband. And beyond that, Jules Beetle happens to work for my brother."

"Mr. Beetle is a solicitor, not a saloon worker!"

His eyes narrowed. "Beetle works for Grayson, not Lucas. And Grayson is the senior partner of the firm which employs the man."

Finnea's face flashed red with anger. But he saw the anger fade when he came toward her. He raked his hand through his hair in frustration. "I told you before, and I tell you now for the last time, there will be no annulment. Not now, not ever. Do you understand?"

"What I understand is that you have no say in the matter. If Jules Beetle won't see to it, then I will find someone else who will."

He took a step closer, and she began to back out toward the hallway.

"On what grounds do you think any judge will consent if I don't agree?" he asked with a deceptive calm.

"On grounds that the marriage was not consummated."

His movement was swift and decisive. He caught her wrist and slammed the door shut. "I can remedy that quickly enough."

He pulled her close.

"Matthew," she said, her voice quavering, "what are you doing?"

"What I should have done last night." His eyes bored into her. "Undress."

Finnea took on a startled expression. "Good heavens, no!"

"You want to do this the hard way, fine by me."

She tried to escape, but he caught her against his chest. Pain seared through him. For one startling second everything seemed to cease—time, his frustration, his intent. Through the haze in his mind he could see her brow furrowed in confusion. But in the next second he pulled a deep, shuddering breath, his arm wrapping around her, and he could see her confusion evaporate, replaced by concern, this time for herself.

"A deal is a deal," he said, the words a breath against her skin.

Then he kissed her, his mouth coming down on hers. She tried to resist; he could feel her muscles go taut. But he couldn't stop the touch any more than he could stop himself from breathing.

"Kiss me, Finn," he demanded, suddenly more desperate than demanding.

She turned her head away from him.

He pulled back to look at her, the crook of one strong finger nudging her chin until she faced him. With an infinite slowness, he ran his hand down the length of her arm, and he felt a tremor race through her. Her lips parted on a puff of breath as her gaze dropped to his lips, bringing a surge of blood to his loins. "I don't want to do it this way, not in frustration."

"I don't want to do it at all," she whispered, her tone shaky.

"Are you sure?"

She looked away.

He backed her toward the bed, the thick draperies pulled open on the window that stood just beyond. With barely steady hands, he undid the long row of fastenings of her hunter's shirt. She opened her mouth to protest but snapped it shut when the tips of his fingers brushed her skin.

A glimpse of creamy flesh and a hint of cleavage were revealed where the soft muslin parted, taking his breath away. He stood for long moments and did nothing more than take her in.

A blush washed down her neck and shoulders, but she stood proud with her chin raised in challenge. It was always that way. She was always fighting.

Reverently, he brushed the material aside, then grazed his fingers against the swell of one breast. Her eyes fluttered closed.

"Do you feel that?"

"No," she replied, her voice little more than a whisper.

"I think you do."

"Think what you wish, I don't care enough to try and set you straight."

"Fine," he answered.

Her eyes met his in a blaze as he worked the fastenings of her skirt until it slid off into a puddle around her ankles. Only her chemise and petticoat remained, and a glimpse of pantaloons beneath.

Her spine was straight, and her eyes were cold. But still she wasn't defeated. The walls of her fortress remained securely in place, no breach to her armor despite the fact that she stood there in nothing more than undergarments.

Her strength slayed him. Her courage. Her beauty. Just as he remembered her in the jungle.

Long, golden rays of sunlight fell through the windows, washing over her. Full breasts with rose-dusted nipples. And while he couldn't see through the petticoats and pantaloons, he remembered well how her rounded hips gave way to long, shapely legs.

"Come here, Finn," he said, his voice a tender command.

Her eyes narrowed, and she started to step away. But he stayed her with his hand, a brush of palm down her arm. He stared at her, no longer understanding what he truly wanted from this defiant woman.

"Lie on the bed, Finnea," he said softly.

"Why?"

His gaze slid to her mouth. "Because I'm going to touch you just like I said, sweetheart." Facing her, he guided her closer to the bed with his body. "I'm going to kiss you and touch you until you are hot and slick with wanting."

The backs of her knees hit the mattress, and she sat down with a start. Her eyes went wild. But he didn't let up. He pressed her down until her red hair spilled across the coverlet.

Still standing, he leaned over her and planted one hand beside her head.

"Go on, then," she stated. "Get it over with. Do what you need to do so I can get on with my day."

As always, proud, defiant, never giving an inch. Would she ever?

He knew he should leave, knew he should walk out the door

and agree to her annulment. It was hard having her in the house with him, so close, so difficult to hide when his body was tired and weak, but he couldn't do without her. The fact was that when she wasn't making him crazy, she made him feel whole again. And because of that, he would have done anything for her—but let her go.

Leaning down, he gently caressed her firmly sealed lips with his tongue. "You taste like sunshine," he breathed against her.

"Thank you for that tidbit of information," she quipped, turning her head.

He chuckled quietly, his lips trailing across her cheek. "You're welcome. Sunshine and lemon. Tart. With just enough of a bite to make it worthwhile."

"We're a poet, are we?"

Despite her antagonistic tone, his lips lifted in a crooked smile. "Do you think?"

She snorted. "Hardly."

He laughed at that, then grew serious. "I would never hurt you, Finn."

He watched as her defiance shifted and changed to something more elusive. Dark and stormy.

"Does that mean you're going to let me go?" she asked.

He lowered himself on top of her in answer. "No, Finnea. You're my wife. Whether you want to be or not."

He kissed her, his lips dancing on her skin, and he could feel her tremble.

His kisses turned to nips as he worked his way down her body. His teeth grazed her skin and the fine cotton of her underclothes. Impatiently, he pulled off the chemise, before reaching beneath the petticoat and tugging her pantaloons down her legs.

She wouldn't look at him, so he dipped his head and laved one nipple with his tongue. Her breath caught and she jerked her head away, staring at the wall.

He groaned his satisfaction as the rose-colored tips pulled into tight buds. Red seared her cheeks as she bit her lip, and he knew she was keeping herself from moaning out loud.

"I hate you, you know that, don't you?" she whispered, the words an echo from that long night in the jungle.

He chuckled, much as he had all those months ago; he ran his tongue around first one nipple, then the other, his teeth gently grazing the tender flesh. Her breath grew shallow.

"Do you hate that?" he asked.

Her head was back and she swallowed hard. "Yes."

He smiled against her. "Liar."

He trailed down her body, from the sensitive swell between her breasts to the waistband of her fine linen petticoat. He went lower and lower until he was kneeling on the floor between her thighs. He didn't bother to take off her petticoat; he only slipped his hands under the hem and touched the bare silky flesh beneath.

"Stop!"

"Why, Finn? You said you didn't care enough to make me stop. Do you care now? Do you feel?" His smile disappeared. "Just say it, Finnea. Say you care, say that you feel."

Her eyes flashed with ire, but she remained stubbornly silent.

Determined, he skimmed his hands slowly up to her belly as he drew closer between her knees, the gauzy material of her undergarment bunching against his wrists as he watched her eyes flutter closed. Her mouth opened on a silent breath when the heel of his palm grazed the hairs that curled between her legs. Slowly, he brushed his hand back and forth.

"You feel, Finnea," he whispered. As if to prove his point, he dipped his head and tasted her.

"Matthew!" she gasped.

But her surprise was no match for his resolve. With the boldness of a man unwilling to give in, he pulled her knees up and came between them, then gently stroked the delicate folds of her womanhood with his fingers.

She sucked in her breath, and her hands fisted in the downy coverlet. Her body arched traitorously to his touch, and he spread her thighs against her waning resistance.

"God, you have such passion."

He planted her feet on the bed, cupping her hips and tasting again. Her hands flew up and grabbed his hair. But when he stroked and gently sucked, a deep strangled sound filled the room.

"Yes, Finn," he murmured against her. "Let go."

And she did.

The touch shattered her fortress. Her hips began to move, her determination not to feel giving way, nothing more than a faint memory. He laid one hand on her abdomen, his fingers splayed. With his tongue, he stroked her, brushing the tight nub hidden beneath the folds, her breath coming in short staccato bursts. Her fingers tangled in his hair as she began to whimper.

He knew she was close, and his heart surged. He wanted to bring her to release, needed to. Tilting her slightly, his own body throbbing and hard, he stroked her one long, lingering last time. With that she seemed to explode, her body quivering as she cried out his name.

Cupping her woman's flesh with his palm as her body convulsed, he murmured reassuring words. He stayed very still for a moment, then kissed the inside of her thigh when she had calmed. Finally, humbled and reverent, he stood and stretched out next to her, pulling her into his arms. Never had he been so moved by passion.

Minutes ticked by as they calmed.

"See, Finn, you do feel," he whispered later, stroking her hair.

Her eyes flashed open, and fire sparked to life. "Feel?" she demanded, the word choked and harsh as she jerked away from him, angrily batting down the thin remainder of her clothes. "Of course I feel. Don't you understand that? Don't you understand that I feel too much, for you, for this new life that has been one failure after the next, for Africa? God, I feel too much, and it's pulling me under."

The fire deserted her, leaving her spent. She squeezed her eyes closed and she bowed her head. "I'm tired of fighting, Matthew," she whispered so quietly that he nearly didn't hear. "I thought you understood that all along."

He sat stunned, realizing in a sharp, unrelenting moment that this was what he had set out to do. He had brought her to the dark, desolate place he knew so well. Shame and remorse wrapped around him.

He started to take her back into his arms, cherish her, whisper his apology. "Finn—"

But she pushed him away. "Don't, Matthew. I don't want to hear it." She scooted off the bed and reached for her clothes. "Please, just leave me alone. That's all I ask."

Words deserted him. How to explain the unexplainable. The unforgivable.

"I'm sorry, Finnea," he said, his voice filled with emotion.

She didn't answer. And who could blame her.

Angry at himself, he turned on his heels and quit the room. He slammed himself in the garden room and locked the door. God, what was happening to him?

Fire beat in his temples. He was drawn to a woman who wanted no part of him. A desire made worse by her nearness. Again, he cursed his stupidity for thinking this could ever work.

He had woken up on his bad side this morning, yet as the day progressed, he had begun to feel better. But whatever headway he had made was wiped out when he received the letter from Jules Beetle.

He picked up the paintbrush he had taken out of the box earlier, trying to block out the image of Finnea, her passion, as wild and intoxicating as the African jungles.

He wanted to paint, needed to paint, but his hand was weak. He felt like he did after a near accident. The warrior rush gone, leaving him shaky.

The smell of linseed oil filled the room. He relished the satiny feel of brush bristles against his fingers. He opened the tin of turpentine and welcomed the sharp sting in his nose.

He was going to paint.

Once and for all, he wanted to prove to himself that he could work—as if the act of painting could somehow prove that all was not lost.

With steadfast determination, he held the palette and paintbrush, then focused on the crisp white canvas. He concentrated, his hand extended. But half-formed images erased themselves in his mind. Color faded to black and white.

An annulment. The words clicked with finality in his brain. How could he deny her one if he couldn't do something as simple as paint?

But what if he could? What if he worked with diligence and proved that he could regain his life? What if he could put the pieces back together again, like pieces to a puzzle?

With quiet determination, he lifted the brush and focused on the canvas.

A sound startled Finnea in the night.

"Isabel?" she called out, more asleep than awake. "Is that you, baby?"

But then she truly woke, alone in her room, and a stark emptiness nearly choked her. Of course it wasn't Isabel. She had been dreaming.

Finnea rolled onto her side where she lay on the floor and looked out the window at the moon that flitted between scurrying clouds, tears slipping down and soaking into the pillowcase.

"Oh, Isabel," she whispered. "I miss you, baby. Do you know that I still love you? Do you know that I would never forget you?"

The night was still and quiet. She listened. But silence was all she heard.

She lay for long minutes until suddenly she heard the noise again. This time she realized it came from down the hall.

Very quietly, she pulled the blanket away and pushed up from the floor, wrapping herself in the cashmere robe her grandmother had given her as a wedding gift. Finnea peered down the hallway. A dim light was on in Mary's bedroom.

Shut the door. Go back to sleep. You'll be gone soon.

Her mind whirled frantically. But her heart propelled her forward. She stepped out into the hall and walked toward the glimmer of light.

But the child's bedroom was empty. Mary stood down the hall at a window in an alcove, staring out at the dark night. She wore a ruffled white-flannel nightgown and dainty velvet slippers on her feet. She looked like an angel with gently curling hair tumbling down her back. But then she shifted, and Finnea could see the tears streaming down her face.

"Mary?" she said quietly, struggling to keep her voice even and distant.

Mary turned with a start, pulling her doll close to her chest, and eyed Finnea warily.

"Did you have a bad dream?" Finnea asked, her voice gentle.

The little girl nodded her head and tugged her doll so close that Finnea thought it would rip apart.

"What was your dream about?"

Silent minutes ticked by as Mary's face screwed up with trauma. And just when Finnea thought she wouldn't answer at all, she burst out. "Please don't tell my father that I hate him."

Finnea's throat tightened, her eyes burned, and she barely held on to the distance she had put between them. When she spoke, the words were choked, tangled with emotions she did not want to feel. "Of course I won't tell him. I know you didn't mean it."

"I didn't, I really didn't."

"I know, Mary." Finnea had to wait for her voice to untangle from the tears that threatened. She pulled a deep, calming breath and searched for a smile. "Why don't you go back to bed and get some sleep. I'm sure everything will seem better in the morning."

"I can't sleep. I can't close my eyes. When I do, everything spins in my head."

Turn around and leave. Now. "What kind of things?" she whispered instead.

"I see my mother. And my father." Mary closed her eyes. "When we were happy. Before Mama died and Papa got hurt."

"Oh, Mary . . ." But her words trailed off. What could she say? She knew about those circling images, those relentless visions of a life that was no longer. "You have to get some sleep," she said at last.

The little girl looked at Finnea. "Will you go with me?"

Not knowing what else to do, she led the child back to her room. Finnea guided Mary straight to the bed, her hands barely touching tiny shoulders. She smoothed the covers, tightened the sheets, anything to keep busy, anything to maintain the distance. She had no ability to deal with this child's need. She couldn't, she thought, as she began to panic, her throat tight and burning.

Mary crawled onto the high feather mattress, and Finnea nodded her head decisively. With a quick tug and what she hoped was a kind smile, she tucked Mary in, then turned down the light.

She started to leave, but Mary unexpectedly caught her hand. Finnea stared at their fingers, entwined, Mary's so small and vulnerable.

"Don't leave me," Mary said so softly that Finnea barely heard her.

"Mama . . ."

Finnea couldn't breathe.

"Do you love me? Only me?"

Her hand was stiff inside the child's. She couldn't do this. She couldn't. She closed her eyes over the feel of Mary's hand. She wanted to jerk away, afraid she would break apart from loss and love and the knowledge that she would never see her own child again.

"Please," Mary whispered.

Fighting back tears, Finnea felt herself wrap her fingers tightly around Mary's, needing this child suddenly even more than the child needed her.

Sinking down, she sat on the edge of the bed. "I'm here, little one," she said, tears streaming down her cheeks in the dark. "There's nothing to be afraid of."

"Thank you," Mary murmured.

Finnea sat that way as the night slipped away, long past the time when Mary's breathing grew steady and deep. Looking at the child in sleep, Finnea disengaged their hands. And when she should have left, gone back to her own room and shut the door firmly between them, she lay down on the blankets beside Mary and gently wrapped the child in her arms.

"Sleep, baby," she whispered. "I won't leave you."

Chapter Sixteen

She dreamed of acacia trees and African grasses. She woke feeling disoriented, her mind filled with Matthew. With her heart beating out the wild rush of longing, she slowly slid her hand down her body along the same torturous path Matthew's lips had taken the day before, tracing the dips and curves with her fingertips, wanting to know what he had felt. In that moment when she was more asleep than awake, when a hazy scrim coated her mind, she was lost between the present and the past, lost in a place where nothing could hurt her.

But as the sun rose on the horizon, it burned the scrim away, leaving the stark colors of reality.

With a jerk, she ripped the covers back and pushed up from the floor. She needed a new lawyer. She would gain an annulment even if she had to go through every solicitor in Massachusetts. In the meantime, she had every intention of avoiding Matthew.

But two days later she determined she didn't have to try to avoid him at all. At night she slept alone in her room, the door between them remaining firmly shut. When she came down for meals in the mornings, the breakfast room was empty. She hadn't seen him once since the afternoon he had shattered her control.

She didn't like to think about the fact that by gaining an annulment she was defaulting on a debt she owed. But how could she remain in this house? Nothing had changed. And when she had pulled Mary into her arms the night of her bad dreams, Finnea had wanted nothing more than to stay. But it didn't matter what she wanted. She still couldn't be a mother; she had proven that once before in Africa.

"Good morning, Mrs. Hawthorne," the butler greeted as she came into the room.

"Good morning, Mr. Quincy. How is your tooth doing?" she asked, thankful for the diversion.

Quincy beamed, his hand pressing against his jaw experimentally. "It is much better. I barely feel it." He looked around, then leaned forward. "And my hand. That salve you made for me works wonders."

After dispensing the tooth concoction, Finnea had mixed garlic and thyme into a salve to heal an angry cut. Mary had come into the kitchen and had ended up helping with each step of the tedious process. The child seemed to absorb the purpose of each ingredient they used. Garlic to prevent infection. Thyme to soothe. Finnea had also told her how poplar bark reduced inflammation, lavender calmed nerves, and lemon balm reduced fevers. The list was endless, but Mary sat and listened with wide-eyed fascination.

A ripple of joy washed through her at the thought of Mary, a ripple of joy that she couldn't quite hold back.

"Where did you learn such remedies?" Quincy inquired.

"I spent time with the Katsu tribe's medicine man." She shrugged. "He frequently put me to work."

Quincy's eyes went wide. "You gave me a savage potion?"

Finnea stiffened and Quincy immediately was contrite.

"I mean, well, you see . . ."

"Savage as it may be, it worked, didn't it?"

His gray head tilted in thought. "Well, I guess it did." He grew serious. "I'm sorry, Mrs. Hawthorne."

She patted his arm. "Not to worry."

"I was wondering," he began hesitantly, when she started for the spread of luncheon fare, "about Violet."

"What is wrong?"

"Her ear. Perhaps you could . . ." His words trailed off awkwardly.

"I'll go see her now."

"But you should have your meal first."

Finnea grabbed a slice of hot bread. "I have it," she said, then headed for the kitchen.

Thirty minutes later Finnea hurried out the front door of Dove's Way. Just as she pulled on her heavy coat, she saw Mary sitting on the granite steps in the cold.

At the sound of the door, the child turned around. "Hello."

Finnea's heart skipped as she remembered the clean little-girl smell of a fresh bath and sweet, dry powder. "Hello, Mary."

"I thought I might go with you if you were going to run errands again."

Finnea fought the surge of emotion that made her want to smile. She needed to start looking for a governess to bring some order into Mary's life. But she wasn't sure where to start.

"Fine," she replied, trying for her best businesslike voice but failing. "We need some more garlic."

Mary wrinkled her nose as if she smelled garlic at its mere mention. "You sure use a lot of that stuff. What's it for this time?"

Finnea smiled. "To make a tincture to heal Violet's ear."

They walked for a few steps before suddenly Mary blurted, "Do you think you could heal my father?"

Finnea stilled and her heart wrenched in her chest. Heal Matthew? She didn't know how to heal herself, much less a man who wrapped his anger around him like clothes.

Or was it like armor? Like the warrior in the mosaic.

The thought hit her. Was he protecting himself by lashing out? But what would he be protecting himself from? People's reactions to his face? His father's callousness?

"Garlic isn't going to heal your father's scar any more than it can heal his anger."

Mary looked crushed and Finnea kicked herself.

"Though perhaps we could slip him a bit of garlic just to see," she added softly with a teasing smile, making Mary giggle.

They headed for the Public Gardens, walking side by side, neither saying a word. And it was much the same over the next few days, Finnea and Mary walking through the crowded shops of Boston, gathering herbs and oils, neither of them saying much, rather finding comfort in the routine.

The following day Finnea hurried out the front door, nearly calling her greeting to Mary in anticipation of seeing her. But the steps were empty. Disappointment hit her square in the chest, catching her off guard.

How had it happened?

She turned her face into the winter wind that blew in from the Charles River, the air cold and biting. She really hadn't needed to go out. They had enough garlic in the house to last for weeks, along with a good assortment of the many other herbs Janji had kept on hand.

Beyond that, Mr. Quincy and his small, discreet staff took care of the household's every need. There was no need to run errands. But somewhere along the line Finnea had gotten used to going out with Mary and working with her in the kitchen afterward as they made some new remedy for the staff.

Finnea started to return inside, the thought of walking through the cold streets alone unappealing. But just then the door flew back on its hinges and Mary dashed out, her gloved hands cramming her hat on her head.

"Sorry I'm late," she said, out of breath.

Finnea just stood for a moment, seared by the flash of unexpected joy.

"What's wrong?" Mary asked worriedly. "Are you mad that I'm late?"

"No," Finnea said softly, a heartfelt smile twisting on her lips. "Not mad at all."

"Good! Let's go."

And when Mary reached out and took Finnea's hand as if she had done it a thousand times before, Finnea didn't pull away.

They went to the marketplace at Faneuil Hall, then to the docks to see what fresh herbs and whatnots had just arrived, before finally searching tiny, cramped shops that catered to Chinese immigrants. They found long, knobby ginseng roots, along with giant green plantain leaves. They haggled over a half-dozen lemons imported from the south, and secured a fresh batch of yarrow leaves from a kind man from China who was a healer himself.

The day was glorious despite the bitter cold. A warmth surrounded them. But everything changed hours later as they made their way home, exhausted but euphoric over all of their finds. Not a block from Marlborough Street a small cluster of boys and girls were throwing snowballs. At the sight of the children, Finnea felt Mary tense, then try to veer off in another direction, but it was too late.

"There's Mary," called a young boy with sandy hair and freckles.

Mary froze and Finnea looked down at her in concern. "What is it?"

Mary jumped a bit as if she had forgotten Finnea was there. "Nothing's wrong."

Seeming to brace herself, Mary dropped Finnea's hand and went forward. She kept her head upright and walked steadily down the street toward Dove's Way.

Mary was a bit ahead of Finnea, and when the children started whispering things to the child, she couldn't hear what they said. She could only see that Mary looked straight ahead and continued on stoically.

Finnea remembered Mary saying she was very popular. Her brow furrowed in confusion as she followed along. It wasn't until Mary came to the granite steps leading to the front door that Finnea could make sense of the words.

"Mary Mary, Monster Mary," they chanted.

"What are you talking about?" Finnea demanded.

The children shrieked and wheeled around. At the sight of her they scattered, their daring laughter fluttering back in their wake as they raced away so fast that the long tails of their woolen mufflers flew out behind them.

She watched them go without seeing, trying to understand what had just happened. When she turned back, Mary dashed into the house.

Without thinking about shoulds or shouldn'ts, Finnea strode into Dove's Way, tossed her hat and coat aside, then hurried to the child's bedroom and knocked.

No answer.

She knocked again, the sound reverberating through the long hallway. "Mary, it's me, Finnea. Can I come in?"

Still no answer, but she could hear rustling inside. She opened the door and found Mary lying on the bed, facing the window, her doll pulled close.

"I'm sorry about what happened with those children," Finnea said, coming further into the room without closing the door.

Mary didn't reply.

"I'm sure they were just teasing."

"But they weren't!" she cried, rolling over in a tangle of skirts and petticoats. "They meant every word."

Then she started to cry, great gasping sobs.

Finnea went to her without thought, as if it were the most natural thing in the world to comfort this child. She came around the bed and sat down, pulling Mary into her arms, stroking her hair as if she were her daughter. "Shhh, shhh, it's going to be all right."

"But it isn't!" she said in a choking gasp. "It will never be all right again. My mama's gone and everyone hates me."

"No one hates you, Mary."

"Of course they do. You heard what they said. 'Mary, Mary, Monster Mary.' "

"You're not a monster!"

"*I'm* not a monster," she stated, pushing up. "But my father is! That's why they say it!"

It wasn't until then that they realized they weren't alone. A strange strangled sound erupted behind them. They turned quickly and found Matthew in the doorway, standing as still as stone. Once again he looked like *Mzungu Kichaa mwenye Kovu*. The Wild Man with the Scar. He looked fierce, his face chiseled, his gaze burning.

Mary gasped, then started to weep. She curled up on the bed. Finnea watched Matthew, who looked at Mary. Most of the time he hid his emotions well. But in that moment his feelings were etched on his face as clearly as his scar. For one startling moment Finnea saw the longing, the hurt—just as his daughter was hurting.

When he noticed that she was studying him, his face turned hard, as if a shield slipped over him. Without a word he turned and walked away.

She wanted to race after him, but first she had to focus on Mary.

For a moment, she was too afraid to move, too afraid to say the wrong thing. She stroked the child's hair as she cried into the pillow.

"Your father may be scarred, Mary, but he's not a monster."

Mary wrenched herself up. "But he's mean and angry! He acts different now."

Finnea let out a sigh. She couldn't deny Mary's words. She had thought before that Matthew must have once been a very happy man.

"Maybe so, but he's not angry with you," she said.

"That's not true! He *is* angry with me. Every time he sees me he is mad and angry."

Finnea didn't know how to counter the child's claim. But she knew then that she had to go to Matthew and demand once and for all that they talk about his anger. Talk about his daughter.

Finnea stroked Mary's hair until the child finally calmed.

Mary found her doll and pulled it close. "I guess now you know that I'm really not so popular."

Finnea felt the smile that trembled on her lips. "What do you mean, silly? You are hugely popular with me."

Mary looked up at her with tear-soaked eyes. "Really?" she whispered.

Finnea leaned close until their noses touched. "Really."

Flinging her arms around Finnea, Mary held tight. "Please don't ever leave me."

Finnea couldn't answer over the lump in her throat. She simply held the child for a few cherished moments before she cupped Mary's cheek. "We've had a full day. Why don't you rest before dinner."

Finnea left Mary and went in search of Matthew. Her stomach fluttered and the tingle of anticipation settled low.

She went straight to his suite of rooms and knocked. He didn't answer and there was no sound beyond the door.

As she headed downstairs, her footsteps were muffled by the yards-long oriental runner that stretched down the hall. She followed the design down the steps, concentrating on the tangle of vines that flowed to the first floor. The house was as silent as a tomb. The library was empty, as was Matthew's study. The west gallery stood quiet. But she stopped in her tracks when she came to the garden room.

He sat in front of his easel, long slanting rays of fading winter sun casting him in light as he stared, a paintbrush held forgotten in his hand. Not realizing that someone watched him, his defenses were down, and her brow furrowed at the sight of him. She realized then that he didn't look like a fierce warrior, as she had thought earlier. Rather, he looked haggard and drawn. He looked exhausted, as if he hadn't slept in days. She wondered if he had been sick and that was why she hadn't seen him.

Or could what he'd overheard cause this seemingly bone-deep weariness? It seemed like more than that. Something deeper, more complex.

Guilt plagued her. While she had asked Mr. Quincy where Matthew was, she had never pressed for a definite answer.

"Have you been ill?" she asked.

Matthew stood abruptly, spinning back to face her, and she saw the wildness. His height always surprised her, his massive shoulders and his golden hair, overlong, swept back from his forehead as if he had dragged his hands roughly through the strands. No, she thought without warning, it wasn't wildness in his eyes, it was panic. She straightened in confusion.

"I'm fine," he said forcefully.

"You don't look fine."

Instinctively, she started forward, intent on feeling his forehead for fever. But when she extended her hand, he grabbed it. They both froze, his blue eyes boring into her, until at length, he set her arm aside.

"I'm fine," he repeated.

She debated for a moment, then purposefully turned her attention to the easel, the momentum that had brought her here faltering. What did she truly know about this man? What did she know about his feelings for his daughter?

His drawing pad was turned to a blank sheet of paper. Charcoal pencils were lined up to the side. He yearned for his art—she knew it—but not once had she seen him attempt to draw or paint.

When she looked back from his supplies, she found him staring at her, studying her, and she grew uneasy.

"I wish I could paint you," he said, his voice gruff and low.

He watched her flinch, then grow wary. Her spine stiffened, her shoulders went back, and he would have smiled if the simple gesture didn't take such effort.

With each day that he tried to work he only got worse. It was getting more impossible to hide his affliction. He felt as if his carefully constructed facade were drifting apart like sawdust in water. All too frequently he woke up on his bad side, causing pain to shoot through him, his hand, his shoulder, his head.

Shame filled him, followed by rage. And fear.

She grew flustered. "Paint me? We've been over that, in the jungle. And the answer is still no."

He hadn't meant he would. He had only meant that he *wished* he could.

Frustration overwhelmed him, and when he turned away, he wasn't concentrating and he knocked into the easel clumsily. The pad wobbled, then tipped over, crashing into the neat line of pencils, which fell to the floor with a clatter. He reached out quickly in hopes of catching something, anything, but the fast movement sent pain searing up his arm.

He froze, trying to control his breath. His heart beat fast and his head pounded. With effort he focused on her.

"Did you interrupt me for a reason?" he asked tightly, wanting her gone.

He felt a flash of regret when her cheeks stained with embarrassment. But she didn't back down.

"Yes, I did. I want to speak to you about your daughter."

If possible, the pain intensified. He concentrated on the pencils lying like scattered play sticks on the floor. "I don't need you to talk to me about Mary."

She marched closer, whatever embarrassment she had felt clearly forgotten. "Don't you understand your daughter needs you?"

He opened his hand and closed it slowly, trying to ease the pain. "I'm providing for her."

"She needs your love, not your money!"

"No matter what I do, I can't erase the scar that scares her so much."

"Just try!" She pulled a deep breath. "You can start by loving her."

"I do love her!"

"Do you?"

"Of course I do! More than anything!"

"Then go to her. She has nightmares. She's scared. You could help her so much by going to her at night when she has those bad dreams."

"I *cause* the dreams!" he bellowed. "Don't you understand that?"

He started for the door, but she stormed after him. "Stop avoiding me!"

He turned back and looked at her, his head pounding furiously. "I thought that was what you wanted."

It was, but she didn't like hearing him say it. "I was talking about . . . this situation with Mary. Stop hiding."

"Now I'm hiding? Which is it, Finnea?"

"Both. You're avoiding the problems by hiding away."

"Is that so?" he asked, his tone lowering ominously.

"Yes! You hide from your daughter, from your family." She swept her arm toward his easel. "From your painting."

She saw the violence flare in his eyes, but she was too far gone to care.

"What would you have me do?" he asked murderously, his voice low and barely controlled.

"Spend time with Mary. And paint."

"I can't paint!" he suddenly burst out.

"You can't? Or you won't?"

His countenance was fierce, but for reasons that weren't clear, she couldn't let it go.

She raised her chin. "Are you afraid?"

He didn't respond.

"You said you wanted to paint me. Then do it," she challenged, posing in front of him. "Paint me."

He didn't move.

"Not enough inspiration after all?" she demanded with a relentless scoff. "Does this help?" She pulled the scarf away from her neck, showing a delicate V of skin.

His eyes trailed low, the blue darkening, but still he didn't move.

"Still not good enough?" she bit out. "Then how about this?" She unbuttoned her shirt, then ripped it off her back, standing before him in the hunter's pants she had donned that morning and a thin cotton chemise, her hair a wild red tumbling down her shoulders.

She could see his tension, but he stood like granite, only his hand opening and closing slowly at his side.

But she was too angry to care. "Should I take off more?"

When he didn't say a word, she started to jerk the chemise from the waist of her pants.

"Get out," he said, the words shaking with fury.

Her hands ceased to move and she met his gaze. "I will not. I will not leave this room until you stop making excuses! You say you love your daughter, but you won't go to her when she needs you. You say you want to paint. But you sit in front of the easel and do nothing!"

He started to pace, but his normal, casually predatory stride was gone, leaving his gait awkward and . . . and pained.

Her eyes narrowed in confusion as the thought hit her suddenly. He was in pain. "Matthew, are you—"

He cut her off. With a vicious curse, he wheeled around and ripped open the pad of paper.

She could see his body shudder. Life seemed to freeze inside her as she watched, dread filling her.

"Let me show you why I sit in front of the easel and do nothing."

He ripped a sheet free, the sudden, awkward movement sending a crystal vase flying to shatter on the floor. But Matthew gave it no notice. Her breath caught as he reached for a charcoal pencil, his long, chiseled fingers awkward and stumbling, his face pulled into a hideous mask.

"Matthew, don't," she said over the knot in her throat.

"Don't?" His laugh was haunted. "Too late for that, wife. You want to see the truth about your husband? I'll show you."

He held the pencil, and she could tell that his attention suddenly shifted as he concentrated. Truly concentrated. Slowly, he put the pencil to paper but could only manage an unsteady line. He growled his frustration, then started again. He used every ounce of his considerable strength to draw—just draw.

It was as if he had forgotten she was there. He focused on the task, drawing sketch after sketch, each one worse than the one before as he started working faster and faster, each stroke more frantic than the last until the lead snapped against the strain. With a ferocious roar, he leveled the easel, pencils and papers crashing to the floor in a flutter of paper and clatter of wood and lead.

Finnea stared at the ruined supplies, her heart pounding so hard, the sound filled her ears. How had she not understood? How had she not known that Matthew's anger was really about pain?

He didn't paint any longer because he couldn't. Physically he couldn't.

Guilt consumed her. Guilt and despair at all she had failed to see. She thought of the many times she should have noticed. On the train when she had fallen into his arm. At his parents' dinner party when he had clumsily knocked over his glass of wine. During their lessons. At the wedding. The times he had eaten slowly or not eaten at all. The times he had locked himself away for days at a time. Dear God, he had been locking himself away because he didn't want anyone to see he was in pain.

"Matthew."

His head was bowed, his chest heaving, his eyes closed.

"Matthew, talk to me."

"Get out."

"Matthew, please."

"Damn it, get out!"

She stopped, realizing she had to give him time—time that she needed to decide what to do, because she understood then how she could repay her debt after all.

She would find a way to heal Matthew, reunite him with his daughter, then be able to walk away from this marriage without losing what was left of her heart.

Chapter Seventeen

"Take off your shirt."

Matthew's head shot up and he stared at Finnea as if she had lost her mind.

It was nearly noon the next day, and she stood inside the door to his study. She hadn't had a drop of sleep, but she was exhilarated. She had spent the night making plans and writing out lists of all she would need. Earlier, she had searched out Mr. Quincy and given him the list of ingredients she sought. The butler had looked at her with eyes that glistened with relief and hope.

Barely taking the time to pull on a hat and coat, Quincy had dashed out of the house. Little more than an hour later he returned with the items he had been able to find. One more trip and he should have them all.

"What did you say?" Matthew asked.

"I said take off your shirt."

Matthew leaned back in his leather desk chair, no trace of the ferocious desperation from yesterday. Calmly he steepled his fingers, his golden brow tilting, his mouth crooking. "Well, well, Mrs. Hawthorne. Have you had second thoughts and now want to consummate our marriage after all?"

A blush rushed to her cheeks, but she ignored it. "I want to see your scars—all of them."

Plain and simple English. Blunt and to the point. Every trace of wry tilting brow and sensuality evaporated, replaced by a taut fierceness.

"No." He pushed up from his desk and headed for the door. But she stepped in front of him, blocking the way.

207

"Please," she said softly but with no less intensity. "I can help."

His nostrils flared.

She reached out and laid her hand gently on his bad arm. "But I can't do anything if you won't let me try."

He looked at the hand that touched him, and she felt the quiver of muscle beneath his skin. When he raised his eyes, he looked at her like a wolf caught in the iron jaw of a hunter's trap, his face lined with wariness, pain . . . and near-dead hope that indeed she could help.

They stood that way as the fire hissed and popped behind the grate. After long minutes ticked by and he still said nothing, she reached for the fastenings on his shirt. Forcing her fingers not to tremble, she eased each button from its mooring.

He never said a word, though his gaze never left her face, the close scrutiny unnerving. She persevered, but she nearly faltered altogether when she peeled the fine linen from his torso and saw the scars.

She counted silently, concentrating, anything for him not to see the devastation she felt. Dear God, how had she not understood?

After thinking about it all night, she had woken up certain she could help him. She had seen wounds in Africa, had seen the medicine man ease all sorts of pain. But nothing had prepared her for the sight of Matthew's scars.

They started at his shoulder and swept down his arm to his wrist, his hand left unscathed, making it possible to fool everyone into thinking he hadn't been wounded except for his face. The scar that ran through his eyebrow and cheek was actually only one long slash, but the scars on his body looked as if he had been dragged across broken glass, the wounds healing unevenly.

Carefully keeping her face blank, Finnea took in the knotted and tense muscles.

But what stunned her more was the beauty of the rest of him. A sculpted perfection, much like his face, that had been marred by tragedy. Her fingers itched to touch him, drift along his skin. She took a long, steadying breath at the sensation.

Following quickly on the heels of that awareness came awe

and respect. He had held himself together, showing no one the extent of his suffering. She was astounded that he had managed as well as he had. A lesser man would have given up long ago.

Just when she started to say something, she saw him tense, and a second later he tore his shirt from her hands.

"You've seen enough of the freak show," he snapped.

"No!" she cried, grabbing his arm without thinking.

Pain seared through him—she saw it, saw the cords of his neck bulge out and his face go white.

"I'm sorry," she gasped, leaping away.

He fell back in his chair, his eyes closed, his lips a thin bloodless line of pain. The room was silent and suddenly too hot. Finnea raged with guilt and ineffectiveness. She searched her mind for the right words to say. But it was Matthew who finally spoke.

"My guess is that garlic isn't going to solve my problem," he whispered, his eyes still closed.

She sucked in her breath.

"Yes," he said at the sound, "I know all about your doctoring. Even if Quincy hadn't regaled me with every one of your, as he put it, remarkable cures, I would have guessed something was up, since the house reeks of garlic."

"Oh, Matthew," she said, falling to her knees and taking his good hand. "I didn't think when I grabbed your arm."

With effort, he opened his eyes. Like a man moving in water, he lifted his hand and looked at it. "I've been to the best doctors in Boston. They say there is nothing to do but rest and let the wounds heal."

"Poppycock!"

Matthew's eyes narrowed. "What are you talking about?"

"That's a load of poppycock. You can't just let the wounds rest. You've had plenty of time to heal—and plenty of time for the muscles to grow weak from disuse."

The lines on Matthew's face hardened. "I've seen the best doctors in Boston."

"Yes, the same doctors who would stitch you up and leave you this way."

He recoiled as if she had hit him physically. "I'm sorry," she said with blunt efficiency.

"No need to be; you're only speaking the truth. They say I must be suffering from deterioration of the brain due to the blow to my head."

"That's absurd."

He eyed her, a hint of that earlier hope flaring to life, before he stamped it out. "My eyesight blurs. There is a tingling weakness in my right side making it impossible sometimes to do more than let my hand lie there like dead weight."

"Sometimes."

"What?"

"You said sometimes. Not always. I saw you pick up that pencil yesterday."

His lips thinned. "And you saw what I could do with it."

"Yes. I saw that you could pick it up and draw—"

He scoffed angrily.

"Don't you see, Matthew? Perhaps you didn't draw so well, but you *did* draw, proving that your arm is not dead weight. Sometimes it is *like* dead weight, which means that sometimes it's not. Are you following me?"

The hope flared again, a wavering flame, but it was there.

"If you were losing the use of your arm due to brain deterioration," she continued, "it would be consistent, and consistently become more useless." Surely.

Her mind reeled. She was in way over her head. What did she know of such things? Nothing. But she did know about scars and scar tissue and how easily the body could curl up on itself if it was not worked properly. She had to be right. She wouldn't think otherwise. And she couldn't let him see her doubt.

With careful but determined movements, she got to her feet and pried the shirt from his grasp. He watched her, wariness mixed with hope.

He sat in a high-backed chair of fine supple leather, and she found that it swiveled. She pushed it just so, until the sun illuminated the wounds. And then she touched him.

She felt more than heard his intake of breath. This time she hadn't hurt him—she understood that—but he must have felt that same shock of feeling she had experienced over the contact. He was so warm, and she wanted to press against him, seek his warmth. She knew if she stepped into his arms she would fit perfectly, like the missing piece of a puzzle.

Instead, she pulled her hands back and rubbed them together briskly to warm them. Then she touched him again.

With the delicacy of a butterfly, she traced the scars on his shoulder, wanting to understand their depths. When she felt some of the tension flow out of him, she touched him more firmly, feeling her way along the angry path down his arm.

The wounds had been deep, undoubtedly having severed muscles and tendons, the arm never given a chance to heal properly.

He seemed to hold his breath as she traced the scars, not a flicker of eyes or movement in his chest—until a knock sounded at the door.

He went rigid and grabbed for his shirt. "Who is it?" he demanded.

But Finnea didn't wait for an answer. She hurried to the door. "Did you get everything?" she asked in a rush of words when she found Quincy standing at attention.

He extended several branches of powdery blue-green leaves and grinned proudly. "Yes, madam. I have the eucalyptus right here."

"Grand!" She took the branches. "Give me a few minutes; then please have a tub of hot water drawn in Mr. Hawthorne's bath chamber."

Quincy went from proud to wary.

Matthew raised one dark blond brow. "Dare I ask what you plan to do with that?"

"You're going to take a bath."

The two men exchanged a glance before Quincy quickly left the room, and Matthew gave Finnea a look that heated her blood.

"Had I known this was the way to get you in my tub, I would have shown you my scars long ago," he quipped with a devilish twist of lips.

But he wasn't smiling thirty minutes later when he stood before the hot water.

"What are you doing?" she squeaked when she walked into the bath chamber off Matthew's bedroom, a vial of freshly pressed eucalyptus oil in her hand.

His shirt and shoes were gone, and he stilled in the process of reaching for the fastenings on his trousers. "I'm getting in the tub, as instructed."

"Without your clothes?"

He gave her a mischievous shrug. "That's usually how I do it."

She grimaced and blushed, mesmerized despite herself by the patch of golden hair on his chest that disappeared beneath the waist of his long pants.

"Is there a problem?" he asked, his voice rumbling along the hand-painted ceramic tiles.

Finnea felt moisture bead on her forehead and wrote it off to the stifling hot temperature in the room. "No, no problem. I wasn't thinking."

She poured in the oil, and the pungent scent of eucalyptus filled the room.

He coughed and eyed her, then made a sound much like a grunt.

His chest muscles rippled as he fumbled clumsily with the fastenings of his trousers. The hard creases returned to his face. She saw his pride mix with shame that he couldn't work the fastenings. Her heart went out to him, but she knew that her pity did him no good.

Briskly, as if all were right in the world, she strode right up to him and began to work the buttons of his pants as if she had done it every day of her life.

"I don't know how a body survives a winter in America," she said, keeping her voice light and steady as she slipped the first button free. "Snow, snow, snow." She undid another, then scoffed. "To think you said the snow would go away."

He didn't seem to breathe as she chattered, talking about everything and nothing, and eventually she felt him ease. But with the last fastening, her knuckles brushed against the strip of downy hair on his abdomen just as his trousers dropped to the floor.

Her chatter trailed off. He stood tall and sculpted, wearing only a snug pair of woolen drawers. Of their own volition, her eyes traveled the length of him, drifting low until she saw the undeniable evidence of his desire. Her eyes shot up, and she found him staring at her, his gaze as hot as the roaring fire behind him.

"I'd best stoke up the fire," she choked out, "while you get in the tub."

He stayed her, his large hand wrapping around her delicate wrist. "It's hot enough in here already."

Blood rushed to her cheeks. He had the amazing ability to do that to her.

"You are beautiful when you're embarrassed," he said softly, the back of one strong finger stroking her cheek.

"If you fancy red, I suppose," she breathed, thinking of her cheeks.

He took a long coil of her hair. "I do."

He started to pull her closer, but in the nick of time her senses returned.

"Get in the tub, Matthew," she said, slapping gently at the hands she wished all too clearly would touch her.

"I'd rather kiss you."

But she jumped out of his reach. "You don't really. You just want to avoid that hot water. Now get in."

Glowering, he turned back to the tub, eyeing it dubiously before he pulled the single tie at the waist of his drawers. The wool slipped down, revealing beautifully sculpted narrow hips. Curved and hard muscled. Perfect, no scars. Powerful thighs with golden hair.

Unable to move, she watched as he stepped into the tub, his body rippling.

Water splashed, followed immediately by, "Ahhgg! What are you trying to do, scald me?"

She blinked, then quickly hurried forward to test the water, bringing her inches away from him. They stared at each other.

"The water is fine," she managed, awkward and uncomfortable. "Stop complaining."

His lips pressed closed, and she regretted her words. He had done no complaining since the accident.

She sighed, sending up a silent prayer for guidance.

The tub was bigger than any tub she had seen since arriving in America. But even it wasn't large enough for Matthew. When he sank down, his knees popped up like tents.

"Now what?" he asked.

"You have to soak."

"What good will that do?" he demanded.

"It will loosen the muscles."

He grunted in response and sank a little lower until the water lapped at his chin.

"Stay in there for thirty minutes."

She started to leave, but his good hand reached out with surprising quickness, water flying everywhere as he took her hand. She could see the emotion, the darkness. And when he gently forced her to sit down on the little stool beside the tub, she wanted to weep for this man—for his pain, for his pride. But most of all for his bravery.

"I think I'll stay," she said with a crooked twist of her lips.

He gave a single nod of his head and a satisfied grunt, then sank back down and closed his eyes.

He was manageable enough at first, but after that he asked if he was done every few minutes.

With a growl of her own, she pushed up from the stool.

"Where are you going?" he demanded.

"To make you some tea."

"I don't want any tea. I'm too damn hot as it is."

"It's an herbal tea that will help you."

He studied her, his jaw set, but this time he didn't object when she headed for the door.

"You have fifteen more minutes," she called back. "Don't get out of there a second sooner."

In the kitchen, Mr. Quincy had all the supplies ready.

"Where's Mary?" she asked, looking around.

"I believe she is upstairs in her room. When I inquired after her she said she was tired."

Finnea knew better. Ever since she had told Mary the poultices and salves they were making were for Matthew, the child had suddenly been busy or tired and couldn't help. In truth, Finnea understood that Mary was determined to avoid her father at all costs.

Finnea sighed, but she knew she could only deal with things one step at a time.

She gathered the lavender and thyme she had mixed in oil earlier, which she would use on his scars. Then she quickly made tea from wood betony to ease the tension in his body. To reduce inflammation, she took the inner portion of poplar bark and mixed it with grated gingerroot, which would increase circulation.

Holding a measuring cup up to the light, she poured a generous amount of whiskey into a vial, then added the gingerroot and poplar bark. After heating the mixture slowly, she poured the herbs and alcohol into a batch of very thick oat porridge that she would spread over a strip of linen and use as a compress.

Quincy watched closely, then said, "I pray you can make a difference."

She smiled and patted the man's arm. "So do I."

With only minutes to go, she gathered the oil, compress, and teapot on a tray, then hurried upstairs. She stopped abruptly when she wheeled into the room to find him standing there, his back to her, a towel wrapped around his waist, moving his arm experimentally.

She could see him tense, but she knew that he felt a difference, slight as it was. He was not as stiff.

"I'm back," she said with a grin.

He turned to her with amazingly hopeful eyes, making him look like a child who had tasted the joy of sugar candy for the first time. "Look!" he said, demonstrating.

She leaned her shoulder against the doorjamb, the tray resting on her hip. "Very good."

His face shifted, and she watched as he grew determined, then headed back for the bath.

"I should stay in there longer," he stated.

Finnea's heart swelled and she chuckled with a wealth of emotion for this man. This amazing man.

But her thoughts were cut off when he got to the tub and dropped the towel from around his hips. Her mouth went dry.

"No!" she blurted out, the pots and vials clattering when she pushed away from the door.

He turned to face her. "Why not?"

But she hardly heard. He stood there, tall and strong, his shaft large and thick even in ease. She swallowed, her stomach fluttering at the sight. In Africa she had seen many men wearing little or nothing. But somehow with this man, in this room, it was different. The broad expanse of his shoulders, the taut, flat abdomen making the flutter in her stomach turn to something else, something like a tight coil.

"No such luck," she managed. "The water is the easy part. Now I'm going to work the muscles and scar tissue."

His brow furrowed as he studied her, clearly unconcerned about his naked state. "I don't like the sound of that."

"Have I led you astray so far?"

He moved his arm again as if having to remind himself. "All right. What do you want me to do?"

She pointed to his towel, at which he smiled a devilish smile, before securing it around his hips. Relieved and disappointed at the same time, she poured a cup of tea from a pot. "Drink this."

He eyed the pale-colored liquid. "Are you sure that's tea?"

"Of course I'm sure."

He did as she said, drinking it down so quickly that she was sure he must have scalded his tongue.

"Now what?" he asked, thrusting the cup out to her.

She gestured to a large chair in his bedroom. "I think it will be best if you sit over there."

If the bath chamber was big, the bedroom was enormous. A fire roared in the hearth, Persian carpets covered a parquet floor. The walls were lined with a rich wood wainscoting, topped by a deep-green, scrolled velvet that stretched to the ceiling. The effect was both striking and manly. And a bed. Giant and very present.

Vigorously, she rubbed a generous portion of oil between her hands, then touched his shoulder. She could feel he was tense. With careful strokes she swept her hands across his bad shoulder, working her way down his arm to his hand. She used one hand after the next, first easily, then gradually with more strength. The more he relaxed, the more pressure she applied. And soon she began to work in earnest.

She tested the range of movement in his hand and arm—minimal when extended at his side, fairly good when extended forward, which further explained his ability to move about in society with little to give him away. How many people walked around with their arms extended like wings?

After determining their flexibility, she slowly exercised the muscles, stretching them only slightly beyond their initial limits.

She started at his shoulder, stroking deeply, then down his arm, again and again, long sweeping motions, and his head fell back against the chair. She moved on to the forearm, dropping down onto a small upholstered stool just to the side of his chair, facing him at an angle, his arm extended between them. He groaned as she swept her ministrations down to his wrist and finally his hand. She worked each finger and his palm.

When she finished, there was an ease in his features that she had not seen since she had known him. She was quiet for a moment, just looking at this man, at his chiseled beauty.

She felt a sharp yearning to reach out and touch his face, run her fingers over his forehead and down the bridge of his nose. Then lower, just to feel, just to savor.

Her lips parted as her gaze drifted to his chest and that tantalizing swath of golden hair that trailed low until it disappeared beneath the white towel.

"Is that it?"

Her head snapped up and she found Matthew studying her.

"Yes," she blurted. "Now soak again. And drink more of that tea."

She glanced furtively around the stool until she found a towel to wipe the oil off her hands. Then she started to get up. But Matthew caught her arm, gently yet firmly.

He sat forward, his towel parting midthigh from his casual, all-too-male sprawled knees. Finnea had a fleeting glimpse of hard thighs and lower legs covered with golden hair before her gaze traveled up over chest and chin to meet probing blue eyes looking back, narrowed with emotion.

"Thank you," he said, having to clear his throat. "Thank you, Finn." His lips closed hard, and he nodded his head once, sharply, as if unable to say any more.

"You're welcome, Matthew," she whispered. Without thinking, she touched his cheek. "You're going to be fine."

The veins in his temples bulged and his jaw worked. Then he turned his head, turned his lips into her palm, and her breath caught.

She told herself to leave, to race out the door and never look back. But when he guided her up from the stool with maddening slowness, she went to him.

With exquisite care, he pulled her between his knees, his towel gathering against the waist of her skirt. As he drew her closer, he leaned back, bringing her with him until her body was secure between his thighs, the towel no longer separating them.

He brought his hands up, smoothed the hair back from her brow, and tipped her face to his.

"God, Finn," he groaned as he brushed his mouth against hers, his tongue seeking the crease between her lips.

The touch was teasing and intense, not a kiss, as his hand ran down her back. He pressed her closer, and she felt the evidence of his thick manhood growing hard and demanding. The tight coil of yearning throbbed deep and low inside of her as she remembered the afternoon he had broken through her control—as she remembered the feel of his tongue slipping between her legs.

His lips grazed the shell of her ear, then lower, trailing down to her neck. She was barely aware when he began working the buttons of her shirt, but when his lips drifted over the delicate skin beneath her collarbone, she gasped.

But she didn't pull away. She wrapped her arms around his shoulders, her head falling back, her mouth opening in soundless wonder.

"Touch me, Finn," he groaned.

And she did, as she had wanted to, in a way that had nothing to do with healing and everything to do with desire. She caressed his neck and shoulders before her hands trailed lower.

He slipped his hands beneath the layers of her clothes. His thumbs pressed against her abdomen, and his fingers curled around her sides. Slowly, he brought them up, over her burning skin, his fingers drifting forward to brush, just barely, over the sensitive peaks of her breasts. Sensation shuddered through her, and she felt the wet heat burn between her legs.

Carefully, he secured his arm around her waist, then came forward, taking her with him until he was on his knees and hands on the floor, she suddenly beneath him, the towel left behind in the chair. He kissed her forehead, then her cheek, his lips grazing lower as if he wanted to taste every inch of her. His hand slipped between the opening of her shirt and moved steadily downward until he cupped her breast beneath the chemise.

He palmed the swell, then bent to taste the skin revealed. Running his thumb across one tautening nipple, he looked at Finnea. "Do you understand how much I want you?"

So much. Too much. For now. But what about tomorrow?

She jerked away and scooted back.

"Finn," he breathed, his eyes still closed. "Don't do this. Not again."

"You're overdoing it," she said, breathless, grasping at any excuse.

She leaped to her feet, her heart racing unchecked. She would help him. But she wouldn't love him.

"You need to get back in the tub and soak longer." She raced for the door. "And remember to drink the rest of that tea."

Then she was gone, only the sound of his curse left to wrap around her as she fled.

Chapter Eighteen

Finnea dashed out of the house, her cheeks flushed, the insistent hum of blood rushing through her veins at the memory of Matthew's touch.

Carelessly buttoning her coat as she went, she half ran, half walked down Marlborough Street, then cut into the Public Gardens, the winter breeze stinging her cheeks as she tried to clear her head.

Oh Isabel, she cried silently. *Why aren't you here? Why couldn't things have been different?*

If only she could turn back the clock. If only she could do things over. She pressed her eyes closed. It was the "if onlys" that left her raw and aching.

She slipped on a patch of ice as she took the curving path toward the footbridge.

"Finnea!"

With a start she turned and found Mary racing toward her, the child's winter clothes wrapped so tightly around her that all that showed was the blue of her eyes.

"Wait for me," the child called out.

When she came up to her side, Finnea looked at her sternly. "I thought you were in your room. What are you doing in the Gardens?"

"You and I come here all the time."

"Yes, but we come here together. You shouldn't be out alone."

Finnea had yet to find a governess. She was failing to see to Mary's needs. The truth whirled around in her head maddeningly as they headed into the wind, neither speaking before they came around a bend to the frozen lagoon. Finnea felt frustrated and inadequate. She wanted solutions she didn't have.

A scream bubbled up inside her as a long ray of sun slanted out of the clouds and caught on the ice, beckoning like a friend.

She started to walk toward the lagoon, slowly, steadily.

"Finnea?" Mary called out nervously.

But she hardly heard as she began to walk faster, away from a world of things she didn't know how to handle. Her feelings for Matthew. Her responsibility to his daughter. The memory of her own.

With each step she took she went faster until she started to run. She hit the ice with a satisfying bang. Her hands came out as she skidded across the crystalline surface, her head thrown back, her hair fluttering behind her. For one pure and sacred moment, she was free. Free of fear, free of worry. Free of the little voice in her head that filled her with doubt.

On the opposite side of the lagoon, she slid to a halt. Mary got there at the same time, having run over the bridge and around. Tears spilled over on Mary's cheeks, her face a battlefield of emotion.

"I hate it when you do that!" the child cried, her voice echoing in the crisp, late-winter sky.

Finnea climbed off the ice with conviction spurring her on. She took Mary's hands and dropped to her knees before her. "Why, Mary?"

Finnea felt sure that there was something to this, something deep inside, and if she could dredge it up, surely she could help the child—no longer fail her.

Mary tried to pull away.

"No. Tell me why, Mary."

"Because it's dangerous! And it scares me," Mary cried through her tears.

"It's not dangerous. It's harmless and fun."

Finnea tried to pull her out on the ice. But Mary jerked away from her. "No! It is dangerous. I know! I saw my mother fall, and Daddy's friend Reynolds had to help her."

Finnea stilled at the mention of Matthew's first wife and her lover. "She was hurt?"

"Her knee. But I didn't see any blood." Mary dashed a blue mitten over her eyes, and her voice grew strained. "Though Reynolds had to kiss her to make it better. Mama said." She grew quiet. "He had to kiss her a lot." She looked at Finnea, her eyes desperate. "If we hadn't been on the ice, it never would have happened!"

And then Finnea understood Mary's fears. Of men kissing mothers. Of mothers unexpectedly dying. Of fathers suddenly changing. Life turning upside down. And somehow her world must have started tumbling out of control that day on the ice.

Finnea sighed. "Oh, Mary. You can't run away from things that scare you—like this ice, or children who tease you. Or your father."

Mary tried to pull free, but Finnea held her there.

"We can't bring your mother back, but your father is still here and he loves you."

"I told you, he doesn't!"

"You're wrong. He loves you very much."

Mary looked at her defiantly. "Why do you think that?"

Finnea pulled her into her arms, holding her tight, thinking of her promise to heal Matthew and his child, a promise to herself, a promise to fulfill a debt that she owed. "Because I saw it in his eyes. He loves you, Mary; he just doesn't know how to show it."

"You're just saying that."

"I'm not. It's the truth."

Pushing back, Mary looked at her, hope seeping in. "Are you sure?"

Laughter bubbled up over the tears that swelled in Finnea's throat. "I'm positive. He loves you, just as I know you love him. Show your father that you care, Mary. Show him by helping me make him better."

"Time to get up."

It was the next morning when Finnea walked into Matthew's room. Mary followed timidly behind her, a tray of all the concoctions, compresses, and teas they had made in her hands.

Matthew lay in the middle of the huge bed. "Go away," he

muttered into the downy pillow, dragging the covers over his head.

"Sorry, can't do it," Finnea replied, her voice chipper as she whipped back the heavy velvet curtains, bright, late-winter sunlight flooding every corner. "We have a lot of work ahead of us."

"You might, but I'm finished."

"Tsk, tsk. I never thought of you as a quitter."

Matthew only grunted. Then silence.

"Matthew?"

A weary sigh came from beneath the blankets. "I can't."

"Of course you can."

He lay there for long seconds.

"Matthew?" She walked up to the bed, concern knitting her brow.

"I can't move."

"What do you mean you can't move?"

"I hurt all over," he lamented with a groan.

Relief. It was nothing too serious, and she chuckled. "I told you that you overdid it yesterday."

With a sudden roar, Matthew whipped back the covers, his face contorted with pain. "I barely did anything!" he raged. "I'm an invalid! Do you hear me!"

Finnea remained still, shocked by the outburst, and then she thought of Mary. She turned to the child, who stood frozen, tiny knuckles whitening from her grip on the handles, before she wheeled away, her face a mask of terror. But the edge of the tray caught the doorjamb, and the concoctions and teas tumbled to the hardwood floor in a crash. Tears starting to flow, Mary fell to her knees as she tried to clean up the mess.

"Oh God. Mary," Matthew breathed.

At the words, Mary leaped up with a strangled cry and fled the room.

"Now look what you've done!" Finnea accused.

"Me?" he raged. "Why didn't you tell me she was here?"

"How was I supposed to know you were going to come out of the bed like an enraged bear?"

"How could you bring her here at all? I've told you she's afraid of me. Did you need proof for yourself?"

Finnea clasped her head in her hands. "No, no, I didn't think."

"Hell," Matthew said in a scathing tone. "You have a staggeringly dependable ability to not think."

"I'm sorry," she whispered. "But you can't blame Mary for being afraid of you. Have you ever tried to show her that you care?"

His face went hard.

"Have you?"

He wouldn't answer.

"Matthew, she loves you. She's afraid of you because she thinks you don't love her anymore."

He whipped around. "That's not true! I love her as I've always loved her."

"You know that. And I've tried to tell Mary that. But you need to show her. Especially now. Go to her, Matthew."

His eyes bored into her as he rubbed his bad shoulder. He looked every inch the Wild Man, and she thought he'd say no.

"It's time, Matthew."

His chest rose and fell.

"She's afraid of you, yes; I won't deny that. But it's not your scars that scare her."

With a strangled roar, he whipped a robe on over his nightclothes, sucking his breath through gritted teeth at the pain. Then he stormed out of the room.

Dear God, what had she done, she wondered, afraid that in his rage he was simply going to try to make a point.

Finnea followed behind him, racing to keep up. "Matthew, calm down. You're only going to make things worse if you act like this!"

But she need not have said anything. The minute he saw his daughter standing at the window in the hallway, holding her doll, all the anger swept out of him. His body grew quiet; his face filled with such intense love, it was painful to see.

"Mary," he whispered.

The child turned at the sound, and her eyes flared with fright.

Matthew faltered and Finnea began to panic. Was she wrong? Was Matthew right and she was only making things worse?

But Matthew wouldn't back away this time. "I'm sorry that I frightened you this morning."

Something flickered in Mary's face.

"I love you, princess," he said adamantly, his heart in his eyes. "I'm sorry I didn't tell you sooner."

Finnea willed Mary to race into her father's arms, to hug him tight, and wished the three of them would hold one another close like a family.

But Mary didn't race forward. And they weren't a family.

Mary watched him, her fear not so easily assuaged, and Finnea was crushed with foolish disappointment.

"Mary," Matthew said, "I was thinking."

The child pulled her doll closer.

"I see that it snowed last night," he persevered. "Remember what we used to do after a new snow?"

Her eyes danced with excitement before they dimmed. But still Matthew didn't give up.

"Let's go to the Public Gardens. Just like we used to."

Mary stood quietly, not uttering a word.

His lips crooked up at the corner. "It will be fun, I promise."

Mary's brow furrowed. "But you said you were hurting."

Finnea cringed, but Matthew surprised her even further when he smiled as if this tiny concession from his daughter was enough.

A laugh surged up in him, a sound both joyous and relieved as he glanced back at Finnea, then gave Mary a conspiratorial grin. "I'll soak in one of Finn's hair-raising baths, sure to scare away every malady known to man from the smell alone. After that we could go. How about that?"

Her tiny mouth twisted with indecision, and Finnea was sure Matthew held his breath. "Okay," the child finally whispered.

Matthew nodded and started to reach out but stopped himself when Mary flinched, covering his hurt with a smile. "Perfect. We'll meet in the foyer after lunch."

They left Dove's Way and headed for the park at a quarter past one, Matthew hiding his pain beneath his chiseled countenance. But Finnea knew better now.

The day was cold and sunny, the night's snow making everything look bright and clean. Upstairs, when Finnea had said that Matthew shouldn't be out in the cold, he waved off her comment. "This is what you wanted, isn't it?"

"Yes. I mean no."

"Which is it, Finnea?"

"I want you to spend time with Mary, yes, but inside, where you won't tax yourself."

He didn't look pleased with her comment, as if she had insulted him. "You said yourself that sitting around wasn't helping me."

"I didn't mean—"

"Besides," he cut her off, his voice growing oddly soft, "Mary and I always used to go to the park to build a snowman after a new snow. And there won't be many snows left. Spring is just around the corner. I want to go there with her now, just like before."

As if their world hadn't been turned upside down. How well Finnea understood the desire.

So they set out, the three of them bundled up and quiet, the only sound coming from the crunch of their footsteps over the shoveled walkway.

"Is that a new coat?" Matthew asked Mary.

Mary glanced down at herself and looked up, at first excited, then wary. But no longer with terror.

"Yes, it is. Grandmother bought it for me. It's made from a fine cheviot and is all the rage in Paris."

At the words, Matthew's expression grew tight. "You sound just like your mother."

Mary's step faltered and she peered up at her father. But he said nothing else, just looked straight ahead looking hard and fierce. Finnea could have kicked him.

"I think it is an absolutely smashing coat," she said.

But Mary wasn't appeased.

They continued on. At the entrance to the park, Matthew ushered them through the gate. They walked side by side, Mary quiet between them. After a few steps, Mary raced ahead.

Matthew stopped and stared at her back. "This isn't going well, is it?"

"What do you expect after that coat remark," Finnea stated.

"The last thing I want is for Mary to turn out like Kimberly."

"Good God! Mary is the sweetest child." She hesitated, then plunged ahead. "And regardless of how you feel about her mother, no child deserves to believe anything but the best about her parents. Either of them," she added pointedly.

He stared at her, his eyes like blue ice. But they both were caught off guard when Mary's unexpected laughter floated back to them and a snowball smacked Finnea square in the middle of her chest. Finnea stood dumbfounded with surprise, and Matthew started to laugh.

"Haven't you seen a snowball before?" he asked.

"A what?"

"A snowball!" Mary chimed, giggling.

"Yes, a snowball," Matthew added, tossing another at Finnea that was softly packed.

Finnea shook like a dog shaking off water.

Matthew and Mary exchanged a look, then burst out laughing.

"Let's get her," Matthew said in a mock whisper.

Finnea held out her hands to ward them off. But it was too late. They charged her, and before she could think she was lying on her back, staring up at a brilliantly blue sky.

"Oh my."

She didn't move, and Matthew and Mary exchanged another glance, this time of concern.

"Finnea?" Mary asked pensively.

No answer.

"Finnea!"

They dropped to their knees and leaned over her.

With that, Finnea let loose with two fully loaded hands, catching each of them in the face with snow.

After that it was a free-for-all. Tossing and rolling around, until each of them looked like powdered-sugar-covered cookie cutouts. They built a snowman and played snow bowling.

"Let's make snow angels!" Mary exclaimed.

Matthew helped Finnea up from the ground, then didn't let

go. He held her hands and pressed his forehead to hers. They stood locked together, a moment of perfect peace wrapped around them.

"Thank you, Mrs. Hawthorne," he whispered.

Pleasure and a sense of wondrous joy rushed to Finnea's cheeks.

"Come on, you two!"

Matthew dusted snow off Finnea's nose, then turned to Mary. "I think the two of you should make snow angels. I'm going to sit over here."

Instantly Finnea grew concerned. She could see the strain etched across his face. But when she would have said something, he quickly shook his head. "No, Finn. Not yet. Just a little while longer. Besides, I'm no angel," he joked. "And I want to watch."

Finnea was reluctant, but he shooed her away. "We'll leave after that," he promised.

Mary instructed Finnea in the fine art of falling back in a fresh patch of snow, then flapping arms and legs to form an angel. They dashed from new patch to new patch, covering the field with angels. It wasn't until they heard the not-quite-muffled groan that they snapped their heads up.

Matthew sat on the bench, his face transforming into a horrifying mask. Mary was confused. But Finnea could tell he was in terrible pain. She had come to recognize the look, though she didn't yet understand the cause.

Tripping over herself, Finnea raced toward Matthew, fear pushing her on. But just before she got to his side, she saw a rock fly out from the trees, catching Matthew in the neck. His face became ravaged with emotion. Impotent despair filled her as she glanced between Matthew and Mary, who hadn't moved.

The sound of laughter wafted over the snow and Mary's head swiveled. There, beyond the path in the distance, stood two little boys, still chuckling, still holding rocks in their hands. Finnea felt her stomach knot. How much did two people have to endure?

"Monster," the boys hissed.

Mary's face contorted and her lips began to tremble. She

started walking, much as she had that day when the children had taunted her. Then she started to run, tears streaming down her cheeks. But instead of passing Matthew by, she stopped in front of him and whirled toward the attackers.

"My father isn't a monster!" she cried out, her tiny voice echoing. "And I know that's you over there, Thaddeus Penhurst!"

Caught, Thaddeus's eyes went wide, and he and his friend dropped their ammunition and ran.

Mary turned to her father, her heart-shaped face grave and much too old for her years. "You *aren't* a monster, Daddy."

Daddy. Not Father.

"And I won't let them say another mean thing to you again."

Matthew sat very still, a single tear slipping down his cheek. He didn't speak, and Finnea knew that in that second he couldn't.

Chapter Nineteen

He went to her that night.

He found her standing beside her bed, wild red hair tumbling over her soft, white flannel nightdress, her hands pulling the sheet and covers back. She had dragged them all the way to the end of the mattress as if pulling them off. But at the sound of the door clicking open, she stopped, her full lips rounding in a silent O when she saw him.

What did she see? he wondered fleetingly. But he knew. She saw him, for whatever that was. She saw inside him, not the scar, not the anger. Had from the beginning.

How had he ever let her get away from him even for a second? Why hadn't he torn Matadi apart when he found her gone from the thatch-roofed hospital?

Perhaps because he was afraid, as she had accused him of being. Perhaps he was afraid of the person she saw in him. Afraid that he didn't want to be who he was—or who he had become. Once the layers of the onion are peeled back, they can't be put back on. Change is irreversible. And he hadn't wanted to change, hadn't wanted a new life—regardless of the fact that on the night he was scarred he had learned that his life had been shallow and worthless. But still, standing on a train in Africa, he would have given anything to have had that old life back. And what had that said about him?

He realized in that moment, standing at the connecting door to her bedroom, that she never would have given him a second glance had she met him before he was scarred—would have found him lacking.

The thought made him smile.

He gave little thought to the pillow that lay on the floor in the moonlight that streamed through the window. He walked toward her, his eyes never leaving hers.

He had waited. He had given her time. He couldn't wait any longer.

Taking her hand, he guided her back toward the doorway, a slice of his own room showing through. She walked a few steps, her bare feet padding on the carpet, before she let go of the covers she still held, the muslin and wool falling half on, half off the bed, looking like a spill of downy white.

He could feel her tremble, could see her green eyes darken when she saw his bed, and he wondered if she was remembering the day he had brought her to orgasm. Was she remembering the way her body had quivered with feeling? Could she still remember the feel of the blush of pleasure that had spread across her breasts when her body had shattered?

He guided her to the mattress and gently but firmly pressed her back when she tried to resist. Almost reluctantly, she lay back, then curled up on her side. He followed, stretching out next to her, pulling the covers over them, molding his body to hers, spooning her.

He could feel how tense she was in his arms, knew she was waiting, wondering, wanting, but telling herself she shouldn't. Wanting to flee. Wanting to stay.

Burying his face in her hair, breathing deeply, he pulled her close, his hand brushing over her body until he gently cupped her breast in the palm of his hand.

"Matthew?" she whispered, her voice a tremor.

"Shhh, Finn. Go to sleep."

She lay there for a moment, confused. Minutes ticked by until she finally must have realized that he wanted nothing of her other than her by his side. He felt when she relaxed then, felt when her body melded back into his.

And he slept.

Chapter Twenty

Two weeks later Finnea entered Matthew's room and found him staring at his face.

They had been working each day, soaking and stretching. Mary had been working tirelessly at Finnea's side downstairs, helping to make oils and teas, but the little girl was still hesitant around her father. There were no hugs or kisses. But occasionally she gave him a smile.

During those days Matthew never let out a word of pain or discouragement—about his injuries or Mary. He accepted her few smiles as if they were gifts from the gods, and he underwent every ministration to his wounds with nothing more than the bulge of cords on his neck or beads of sweat on his forehead. He endured the pain as he had endured the pain all this time. Stoically.

But this morning was different. When Finnea found him in front of the mirror, she knew he'd had a bad night.

"Good morning," she said.

He didn't speak. He sat carefully, staring at his reflection.

She came up behind him and looked at him in the mirror. "You are still such a striking man. The scar only makes you look fierce and ruggedly handsome," she whispered.

He drew a deep breath. "The loss of my looks has never bothered me."

"Then what?" she asked, wanting to know, needing to understand.

The expression on his face grew closed.

"Matthew, tell me, please."

"It was the loss of myself," he said finally.

He said the words slowly, and she knew each syllable cost him.

"When the glass exploded and that wooden beam crashed down on me, I didn't just lose the way I looked. I lost my identity." He scoffed. "Shallow, you say. Of course. But it had nothing to do with vanity. If I wasn't the handsome man with good humor and charm, who was I? If I wasn't my father's favorite or the one who made everyone laugh, who was I? And now, if I can't paint, what do I have left?"

"You have Mary."

He met her eyes in the mirror. "What about you, Finnea? Do I have you?"

Every night Matthew had taken her to his bed, pulling her into his arms as he curled up behind her, holding her tight until she could feel his breathing grow even and shallow. She relished the feel of him holding her. His large, solid body offered refuge at a time when she had given up on the possibility of such a thing.

But old habits die hard, and still she hadn't been able to sleep unless she was on the floor. Once he was asleep, she slipped out of bed and found peace in the moonlight, then slipped back before he woke in the morning.

Not once during those nights did he try to make love to her, only held her, as if keeping some unspoken promise that he wouldn't make her feel again until she was ready.

Each day all she could think about was Matthew, his daughter, and herself. The three of them together. Like a family. Could life be different? Was it possible they all were being offered a second chance?

Slowly she was bringing him back to his daughter. If she healed him also, could she be forgiven? Would her slate be wiped clean?

Could she ever forgive herself?

"What did all those doctors say about the scar on your face?" she asked instead, unable to answer his question. She didn't know the answer.

She watched as his jaw went hard. He jerked his head around to look at her. She could tell he wanted to demand an answer from her, but in the end he stopped himself.

"They said that unfortunately some scars don't heal as well as others. They said that there is a lot of scar tissue. That probably causes some of the pain, but . . ."

The words trailed off.

"But what?"

"But the searing pain must be caused by the blow to my head. They see no reason why a wound to my face would cause my head to ache and my vision to blur at times."

A shiver of doubt crept through her. Was she fooling herself? she wondered. Could it be that he had sustained damage to the brain, as the doctors believed?

But then his gaze caught hers in the mirror. She took in the clearness of his blue eyes, the knowledge. The sanity. And she refused to believe that there was anything wrong with his mind. It had to be something else.

"Sit down," she instructed.

He glanced at her wryly. "You get bossier all the time."

She smiled at him. "Please."

"Only if you sit with me." He took her hand, but she pulled away.

"Matthew, stop. You want to get better, don't you?"

"Holding you will make me feel better," he responded, reaching for her.

But she was too quick. "Sit still and behave."

His eyes changed when she pressed her fingers to the scar on his face. He sucked in his breath when she pressed deeply.

"I'm sorry," she whispered, but she didn't let up.

She moved along the red line, pressing, probing. Sweat began to drip down his face, down his back. And when she pressed again, she thought he would black out.

She gave him a second to steady himself, but when she tried to continue, his hand shot out and grabbed her wrist, gently but firmly. His breathing was labored, and he didn't say a word as she studied him.

"I think you should rest," she said finally.

Finnea left him then, her mind spinning with questions.

Something was not right, and she had a sneaking suspicion she knew what it was.

But before she did anything, she had to talk to his doctor,

though she knew she couldn't utter a word about it to Matthew. Not yet. Not until she was sure.

"Just who do you think you are to question my diagnosis?"

Finnea stared at Dr. Watson Phelps across the broad expanse of his neatly ordered desk. She had gotten his name from Mr. Quincy, and as soon as she had dressed in a respectable gown, she had slipped out of the house in search of the doctor.

He stood before her now, his face dangerously set.

"I am the wife of a man whom I believe has been misdiagnosed."

He scoffed. "And what credentials, pray tell, do you have that qualify you to make such a judgment?"

She raised her chin. What could she say? She had learned enough in America to know that the mention of neither Janji nor Africa would get her very far. But she had a hunch, and she wasn't willing to let it go.

"I take it you have none," he sneered. "I am the professional, madam. My opinion is sought by the most prominent of citizens." He looked down his nose at her, clearly angry that she had wasted his time. "Matthew Hawthorne has sustained an injury that is progressive and debilitating. The worst thing you can do is give the man false hope." He ushered her to the door. "Leave medical matters to men of medicine, madam, before you do more harm than good."

Outside on the crowded streets of Boston, the air was frigid. She had been told by no less than half a dozen people that spring was just around the corner, but she was having trouble believing it. It was as cold as ever, and the possibility that warmer weather would suddenly leap out at them seemed highly unlikely. But when she had expressed her disbelief, they had only chuckled and said she'd see.

She headed toward the Back Bay, giving little thought to the cold, her mind troubled and spinning over her conversation with the doctor. Dr. Phelps had been too quick to dismiss her theory, and why wouldn't he be? she realized. His reputation was at stake. He was the man who had tended Matthew after the accident.

Teeth set, Finnea went to Winslet Ironworks. It was the only place she could think to go to find the names of other doctors. She couldn't go to Matthew's parents and certainly not to her mother. And she couldn't imagine Nester would care enough to question her. But when she entered, she found Jeffrey instead.

"What are you doing here?" she asked, surprised.

He shrugged. "Who else was going to run this place? And at my age, what else am I going to do?"

Their conversation was tense and awkward, but she got a list of names. Just as she was leaving, he stopped her. "I'm sorry, Finnea. I really never meant to hurt you."

She could tell that he was sincere, and she nodded her head, wishing that the rest of life's troubles could be solved as easily.

Starting the next day, she set out to see each and every one on the list, in the afternoons, when Matthew locked himself away with his paints. But each doctor only looked at her as if she had gone mad. No one was willing to concede the possibility. No one was willing to get involved.

Doubt began to creep through her, trying to find a foothold in her determination. But just as she left the office of the last doctor on her list, the man's nurse nervously followed her out into the empty hallway and furtively handed her a slip of paper before she hurried back inside without a word.

Finnea stood dumbfounded, then slowly opened the note. The words were hastily scrawled.

Dr. Ethan Sanderling 301 Huntington Ave.

Twenty minutes later, a hired hack dropped her off in front of a wooden building in the South End. Inside, the office was small but clean, filled with men and women, children, all wounded and ill. She seemed to have found a doctor for the poor. After visiting office after plush office of Boston's finest doctors, Finnea wanted to flee this one.

But she stopped when a dividing curtain swung back and a man led out a patient. Finnea was sure he was the doctor.

He wore dark trousers, a waistcoat, and a white shirt with

the sleeves rolled up. He wasn't very tall, but he looked strong and kind, with unruly hair.

"Thank you, Dr. Sanderling," the patient said, clearly indebted.

The doctor smiled and nodded his head, then greeted several of the patients sitting in the waiting room. He knew most of them by name, telling each he would be with them as soon as possible.

"Now, who was here next?" he asked the group.

With no receptionist, Finnea expected bedlam. Instead, several patients looked thoughtful, while the others pointed at an elderly man.

"Jason Fowls is next."

Doctor Sanderling walked over and helped the man up, and just as he was turning, he noticed Finnea.

He straightened, though never losing hold of his patient.

"May I help you?" he asked, taking in her fine gown, surprise riddling his forehead.

"Yes," she began, having to clear her throat. "I am Mrs. Matthew Hawthorne, and I have come to consult with you about a certain condition."

She hated tossing out her married name as if that somehow made her special. But over the past several days she had learned the only way she could get the doctors to see her at all was to say who she was. The Hawthorne name got her out of waiting rooms and into offices so fast, her head spun.

This doctor merely nodded and gestured to the newly vacated seat. "I'll be with you as soon as I can."

She liked him immediately.

She liked the wait less.

He saw her two and a half hours later, at three in the afternoon.

"I hope you don't mind if I eat while we talk?" he began, taking a small tin pot from the top of the heating stove in the corner. "But if I don't eat now, I won't have a chance again until late this evening."

Ever practical, Finnea said, "Well, no, go right ahead."

"Now, what brings you to my humble establishment?" he asked, placing a linen square in his lap as if he were at a fine dinner party. "A Hawthorne has access to the best doctors in Boston."

"Do you mean to say you're not very good?" she blurted out before she could think.

The man chuckled. "I'd like to think that I'm better than most of the doctors in town. I trained with many of them." He grew serious. "But I can't sit by and let the poor and indigent go uncared for. Does that help?"

"Well, yes." She fidgeted.

"Good. Now for your concern."

While the man ate, Finnea explained her theory. When she came to the end, Ethan Sanderling sat back, his meal finished, his fingers steepled as he considered.

At any moment, Finnea was certain he would stand and accuse her of wasting his valuable time. Already she could hear the sounds of his waiting room growing crowded once again.

"I have to admit that your theory sounds far-fetched. I have no doubt that is why you are here. Everyone else must have run you out."

Finnea's heart sank, and she nodded, unable to lie. She pushed up from her seat.

"Hold on," the doctor said. "I'm not everyone else."

"Really?" She leaned closer, her gloved hands clutching the edge of the tabletop. "You don't think I'm crazy?"

He studied her intently. "I'm not sure what I think, Mrs. Hawthorne. But I'll have to see your husband to make that determination."

Racing home, her heart burgeoned with joy. But hope was cruelly dashed when she found Matthew in front of his easel, both hands pressed to his head, his face contorted with pain.

"Good God!" she cried, running forward. "What's wrong?"

He couldn't seem to talk, and she knew she had to get Matthew to Dr. Sanderling.

Had she been thinking, she would have waited until she had eased his pain to tell him about the doctor she had found. But she was so convinced of her assessment that she suddenly blurted it out. "There is a doctor I think you should see."

For one long moment Matthew didn't move or say a word.

He sat there. Then slowly he straightened and met her eye. He was pale and drawn, but his countenance grew dark. "Explain yourself."

"I found a doctor who is different from the rest."

"You went to see a doctor about me, without my knowledge?"

"It's not what you think; *he's* not what you think. Matthew, please see him."

"No."

"Matthew—"

"I said no. You had no right."

"But he's different! He isn't like the rest of them."

His expression was dangerous.

"Matthew, you have to see him. I'm certain I understand what is causing the pain. And Dr. Sanderling agrees that it's worth looking into. With the doctor's help, I believe we can alleviate the cause of your pain."

His eyes sparked with hope, battling with his anger that she had gone behind his back. She saw it, felt it.

"What do you think it is?" he said, his voice cautious.

She took a deep breath. "I believe some wood or glass from the accident is still in the wound."

He stared at her as if she had lost her mind. "What?" The word came out as an outraged burst of sound, his face a terrible mask of disbelief and dashed hope.

"Don't you see," she rushed on, "the only time you experience the tremendous pain is when you've had pressure against the scar. This doctor agrees it's possible. But he'll have to see you to determine if I'm right."

"You've pinned your hopes on some sort of debris?" he roared. His anger built and grew. "What kind of an idiotic idea is that?" He jerked off the chair, stalking across the room, shoving his hands through his hair. "Who in their right mind would believe that there is still something in the wound after so long?"

"Has anyone else come up with a better solution?" she demanded. "Just talk to him, Matthew," she pleaded. "His name is Dr. Sanderling and his office is tucked away in the South End on Huntington Avenue. No one has to see you go there."

"Damn it, didn't you hear what I just said? You're crazy. Crazier than me, apparently."

He grabbed her arm and pulled her roughly to him, his face still taut. "*Are* you crazy? Is that it, Finnea? Outlandish green and gold gowns. Hunter's clothes in Boston." He paused. "Sleeping on the floor."

Her eyes went wide.

"Yes, I know all about your habit of forgoing the comfort of a mattress and bed. I know all about your red hair spilling over pillows." His eyes grew unfathomable. "About glimpses of soft skin when your nightgown tangles around your legs."

"Stop this, Matthew," she said, her voice catching.

He drew her near, bending his head so close that his lips almost touched hers. "Stop what, Mrs. Hawthorne?"

She grew silent, then said, "Why is it that whenever I push into places that make you uncomfortable you try to scare me off by pretending to be someone you aren't? First after lunch with your father, now when faced with possible answers about your face. *Are* you afraid, Matthew?"

His eyes went wild with something she didn't understand. Fury? Fear? "I am not afraid!" he shouted.

Then his lips came down on hers, hard and demanding, as if to prove his words. There was no pleasure, only punishment. With a cry, she jerked her head to the side.

"I am not afraid," he repeated, his voice harsh. "But what about you? Why are you still pushing me away?" His grip tightened. "Why is that, Finn? Are *you* afraid? Afraid to tell me why you slip out of my bed at night even though I know you want me—or at least your body does."

The truth of his words sent mortification sizzling through her veins. Part of her knew that he was angry and disappointed and lashing out. But her heart began to pound nonetheless.

"Let me go, Matthew."

His eyes went hard and cold. "I asked you once before and you didn't answer. Answer me now. Did you really love Jeffrey? Is that it? Is that why you hold yourself apart from me?"

Jeffrey? Her stomach clenched. Didn't Matthew understand? She hadn't loved Jeffrey at all. That was why it would have been safe to marry him. Because she could afford to lose him.

But how would she survive if she lost Matthew? Or his daughter?

Dear God, how had it happened? She loved this man despite the fact that she couldn't afford to. Loved him with all her heart and soul. Loved his daughter. Wanted to be a part of their lives.

The truth of it staggered her. And made her feel guilty in turn—as if somehow she was being disloyal to Isabel.

"Damn it," he suddenly bellowed, crashing his fist into the wall. "Are you like Kimberly after all? Are you in love with another man?"

But she was given no time to answer when the tense quiet shattered. "Stop it!"

They wheeled around and found Mary. Tears streaked her cheeks.

"Stop fighting!" she cried. "I hate it when you fight. Just like you fought with Mama the night of the party."

Matthew went cold.

"Yes! I saw you and Mama in the cottage." Mary could barely talk through the sobs that racked her tiny body. "I know I was supposed to be in bed, but I wanted to see you so I snuck out and found you there. And I saw! I saw what Mama was doing with your friend."

Her cherub's face was mottled and red as she squeezed her eyes shut, trying to block out the images in her mind. "Now you know. Go ahead, punish me. Or leave me again if you like. But I won't be afraid anymore! I won't!"

In a whirl of skirts, Mary raced from the room, and seconds later she slammed out of the house.

For one stunned heartbeat Matthew and Finnea stared in shock.

"Oh God," Finnea breathed.

They dashed out the door, but Mary was too fast. She ran down the walkway toward the Public Gardens. Matthew and Finnea followed, racing through the gated entrance, then along the path that Finnea and Mary took almost every day.

Finnea's heart surged, then stilled in her chest when she saw a lone little figure standing before the lagoon, staring, her fingers clenched at her sides.

Finnea's breath caught because she understood all too clearly. "Please, no," she whispered, feeling the still-cold but rapidly warming air.

"Mary!" Matthew called out.

The child spun back to look at them. Even from this distance Finnea could see the blue eyes wide with fear and determination, tears streaming down her face.

"Mary, get away from there," Matthew demanded.

But she wouldn't move, and they were too far away.

"I'm not afraid!" the child cried out, her tiny voice reverberating in the barren trees.

Finnea broke into a dead run, but she was too late. Mary started to run as well, toward the lagoon that hints of spring had already touched.

"No!" Finnea screamed just as Mary hit the ice.

For one sparkling moment, Mary slid, her arms extended, her blonde hair free and flowing like a flag in the breeze. But in the next, a crack echoed ominously, snaking across the lake until the hard surface split into a million tiny pieces, and Mary broke through.

Matthew's shout was fierce and haunted, a warrior's battle cry as he pounded into the lagoon. Water and ice flew, breaking and churning as he made his way to his child.

He went under again and again, frantically searching. Finnea was in right behind him, and just as she reached his side he came up with Mary, her face already turning blue from cold and shock.

They trudged out of the water, then raced back to the house, Mary held securely in Matthew's arms as he crossed Arlington Street to Marlborough like a man possessed. When they finally entered the house, Quincy had the fire roaring.

"Little Mary," the older man gasped at the sight of the limp child in Matthew's embrace.

"We need hot water," Finnea instructed the butler. "I'll get dry towels."

Within minutes, they had the child in a tub to warm her rapidly. Matthew rubbed Mary's hands and feet with vigor while

Finnea held her up. Minutes later Mary started to murmur, the blue receding, replaced by the vibrant red of blood surging.

"We should dry her off now and hold her close to the fire," Finnea directed.

Matthew pulled the child out of the water and wrapped her in a thick flannel towel. He folded her securely to his chest and sat in front of the fire. He rocked her, even after the intense heat brought sweat soaking through his barely dried clothes.

"I think you should put her in bed now," Finnea said quietly.

Matthew nodded, and they went upstairs. Finnea quickly clothed her in a thick flannel nightdress while Matthew checked on the fire that burned in the grate. Then he returned to Mary's side and sat on the bed, ignoring the strain in his intensely aching body.

When Mary opened her eyes, the first person she saw was Matthew. It took the child a second to remember and understand. And when she did, terror swept over her face.

"Oh, Daddy, I'm sorry. Please don't be mad at me," she whispered, her lip quivering. "I didn't mean to see Mama in the cottage."

Matthew looked stunned by the words. Finnea could see the cords in his neck work until he pulled the child to him fiercely. "No, Mary. *I'm* sorry you had to see what happened that night. Dear God, I'm sorry I didn't understand sooner." He caressed her cheek and looked into her eyes. "Please don't be mad at *me*."

They clung together then, tightly, fiercely. The hug he had longed for, the love he had hoped to regain. Their tears mixing until it was unclear whose tears were whose.

Finnea felt her own tears, felt the tight vise of emotion around her throat until she thought she would break. When she was sure Mary was fine, she started out of the room.

"Finnea," Mary called out weakly.

Mary's pleasure was written on her face, and Finnea couldn't help her answering smile. "Yes?"

"Did you see? I did just like you said. I got out on the ice and I wasn't afraid."

Finnea's smile froze as hard as the ice had been in the dead of winter. "Yes, I saw," she managed. "You are a very brave little girl. Good night, sweetheart."

She saw the hard lines of confusion that came over Matthew's face. But she didn't wait for him to question her. She walked to her room with measured steps. She counted, concentrated, determined to make it behind closed doors. Once inside her bedroom, she went to the window. She refused to think—unable to think for fear of starting to scream, because just like before, she knew that if she started she would never stop.

Minutes later, Matthew came into the room. "What was that all about?" he asked in a low, commanding voice.

She didn't turn away from the window. "Mary wanted to prove that she wasn't afraid."

"By nearly getting herself killed? Where did she get such an idea? From you?"

"Yes."

"Good God! What exactly did you say to her?"

Finnea turned to him then. "All the wrong things."

She walked to the clothes cabinet and found the small satchel she had brought with her. Counting again, she began to pack her few belongings.

"What are you doing?" he asked tightly.

"I'm leaving." Simple, no emotion. She wouldn't look at him; she kept her hands busy.

"Why?" he demanded.

She stopped, afraid she would be sick. "I told you this wasn't going to work. I can't be a mother to your daughter. It's my fault that Mary fell through that ice. It's my fault that she went there."

"Finn," he said, reaching out to her.

She jerked away from his outstretched hands, her voice rising hysterically. "I'm the one that led her to the lagoon! I'm the one who raced out onto the ice! I'm the one who told her she couldn't run away from her fears when she told me she was afraid every time I slid across!"

Matthew reached for her again. "Finn."

But she slapped his hands away, dashing the tears from her eyes. "No! I led her there but never thought to teach her about ice and how it would melt, and how eventually it wouldn't be safe. I can't do this! I can't take care of your child!"

"Why?" He grabbed her arm and wheeled her around. "Damn it, tell me why?"

She met his gaze, and her sigh winged out of her on a defeated breath. "Because if I stay, I'll only manage to get your child killed."

"That's absurd," he burst out, his brow furrowed. "I've seen how you are with Mary. You're a wonderful mother."

The sadness in her face vanished, and she turned hard. Little did he know how untrue his words were.

"No," she said with deadly calm. "I am not a good mother. Or a good wife. My mother was right. I don't belong here. Not in this house, not in this city, or even in this country. I just didn't want to accept it."

"Don't say that!"

"I'm going to my mother's until I can determine what to do."

Matthew grabbed her and brought them face-to-face. "Finnea, I don't want you to go."

She wanted to throw her arms around him. How could she live without this man? But then her mind filled with the image of Mary falling through the ice—and of a dead child lying in her arms.

How could she stay?

She knew what he didn't—if she had been a good mother, Isabel would still be alive.

So she hardened her heart—for him and for his child. Not knowing what else to say, she replied harshly, "But I don't want to stay."

It was as if she had struck him, and it was only sheer force of will that kept her from throwing herself in his arms when he abruptly released her, pain and anger searing his face like a scar.

Chapter Twenty-one

Matthew stood before the canvas. White and blank, stretched so taut it felt like a drum. He didn't want to think, couldn't think. When he did, rage circled dangerously in his mind.

Bright sun streamed in through the long row of tall windows, falling over Matthew at his easel. Like a man obsessed, he became determined to paint, as if he could find truth and salvation in the rainbow hues arcing across the palette.

He picked up a paintbrush just as he had done every day for weeks. He held it in his hand. To no avail. While he had greater use of his muscles, he still hadn't painted—even on good days when his head didn't pound.

He stared, his mind as empty of vision and imagination as the canvas. Whatever had been inside him before that had made him paint, whatever it was from which he drew, was gone. He stood for long minutes, focusing, willing. Wishing. Until he threw the brush aside with a frustrated curse.

"Finnea!" he called without thinking, the word reverberating against the high ceilings. Reminding him she wasn't there.

He stopped in his tracks as people came running, the house seeming to shake from the footsteps dashing over hardwood floors and fine oriental carpets. Quincy raced up from the basement carrying a towel, his proper coat nowhere in sight, his elderly face lined with unexpected joy. Mary hurtled down the stairs from her bedroom. They came to a halt and glanced around, finding the room empty.

Matthew stood, implacable, willing his mind to a blank. He didn't say a word, but he could tell when Quincy understood what had happened. Mary, however, didn't comprehend.

"Where's Finnea?" Mary cried out, her joyous laughter filling the house as she threw open door after door in search of the woman she had missed desperately since she had left three days ago.

Quincy sighed his disappointment.

Mary stopped and looked at her father, the joy beginning to fade, replaced with confusion. "Where is she?"

The muscles in Matthew's jaw tightened. "I'm sorry, Mary. She's not here," he said, not knowing how to explain.

"But you called out to her, Daddy," she persisted.

Matthew dragged his paint-streaked hand through his tousled hair. "Yes, I did."

"Then she must be here. She must be hiding." She started away, heading for yet another closed door.

"No, princess, she's not here." He cleared his throat, wanting to be anywhere but in that room facing those questioning blue eyes. "You see, your silly father forgot for a second that she was gone." He shrugged, trying to seem casual. "Before I remembered, I called out to her."

Pain was replaced by a terrible understanding in her little-girl eyes. And then she reached out and took his hand. "Oh, Daddy, I do the same thing, too."

She walked away, with the grace and dignity of a queen, leaving the two grown men standing there staring after her.

"She's a strong one," Quincy murmured.

"Stronger than any little girl should have to be." Matthew's lips thinned. "Strong and brave, and she deserves a mother."

Without a hat or coat, Matthew stalked out the front door, deciding then and there to confront the woman who had promised to be just that.

He ignored the people who did double takes when he passed by. Anger and protectiveness pushed him on.

Only minutes later he came to Commonwealth Avenue and the Winslets' town house. He took up the brass ring and hammered it against the front door.

It seemed like forever before his sharp knock was answered.

"May I help you?" the butler asked in a droll tone.

"I'm here to see Mrs. Hawthorne."

The man looked confused.

"Finnea," Matthew clarified impatiently.

"Ah, yes. Miss Finnea. May I tell her who is calling?"

"Her husband," Matthew replied with a short, deep sound in his chest as he started forward.

But Hannah stepped into the foyer, raising a regal hand to stop him before he got inside. "Hello, Mr. Hawthorne. I assume you are here to see Finnea?" Her smile was shallow and didn't meet her eyes. "Unfortunately, she is out."

Matthew was nonplussed for one long second, before he narrowed his gaze. "Your butler just said he would tell her who was here. Now she is out?"

"Yes, he must have forgotten." She nodded meaningfully to the butler, and added a polite good day. And before Matthew could say another word, the door swung shut.

Matthew stared at the oak plank in disbelief. He'd had the door slammed in his face. He could hardly fathom the action. Never, even since the scandal, had he been turned away from anywhere, much less from a supposedly proper home.

Muttering a string of expletives, Matthew strode back to his own house and through the front door with a bang.

For three days he paced his study like a caged lion, telling himself he was angry because of Mary. He told himself he wanted to confront Finnea because she had made a promise, a promise she had failed to keep.

But with each day that passed, it became harder to believe his excuse. He wanted to see her. Needed to see her with an intensity that went beyond broken promises.

On the fourth day, Matthew gave up trying to understand his reasons for wanting to see her and returned to the house on Commonwealth Avenue. This time he was quicker than the butler. When the door started to crash closed, he flattened his good palm against the sturdy oak.

Matthew eyed the butler, then nearly cursed when he heard the recognizable click of sensible heels on marble.

"I see you have returned, Mr. Hawthorne," Hannah said.

"I am here to see Finnea." He enunciated each word with precision.

"And as I said before, my granddaughter is unavailable for visitors."

"I am not a visitor," he exploded. "She's my wife!"

The butler cringed and looked decidedly uncomfortable, but Hannah remained resolute. "Be that as it may, she doesn't want to see you."

They stared at each other, neither giving an inch. But short of physically pushing past the older woman, Matthew had little choice but to leave.

He stormed back to Dove's Way, slamming himself into the garden room. He stared at pencils and paintbrushes. Sketches lay discarded everywhere. Half-started canvases stood forgotten. Others stood like gaping blanks against the walls.

During those days, Matthew hardly saw Mary. She kept to herself, and he knew that Quincy was seeing to her needs. Something would have to change, though. Matthew knew it.

Finnea had been gone for over a week when he heard the noise. It was late and he was in his bedroom, still dressed. Sharp pains had begun to stab in his face, and he knew he would have another long sleepless night. When he heard the noise again, he walked out into the hallway to investigate.

He saw that Mary's door stood ajar, a dim light glowing inside. He remembered Finnea telling him Mary had nightmares. His first inclination was to call for Quincy. But he tamped down the need and went to his child.

She stood in the hallway before a large sweep of windows, looking out into the night.

His heart ticked at the sweetness of Mary. "Did you have a bad dream?" he asked softly into the silence.

She started and swung around, her long blond curls flying out around her shoulders.

When she saw it was him, she smiled sadly, as if expecting someone else, no doubt Finnea. Then she turned back to the window. He came up beside her and looked out. He could see a gaslight down below on the street, a circle of golden light around it, fighting off the dark.

"Do you have bad dreams often?" he asked without looking at her.

"No, just sometimes."

"Do you want to tell me about them?"

She hesitated, then said, "I'd rather not, thank you." As if she were sixty instead of six.

He searched his mind for how to deal with this child, how to be a father to her after so long.

"Is Finnea ever coming back?" she asked quietly.

He stiffened. "No, she's not," he finally answered. He could tell he had upset her. With a sigh he raked his hands through his hair. "I miss her, too."

She turned and looked at him. "Then why don't you bring her back?"

"It's not that simple, Mary."

"Why not?" she demanded.

"Because she doesn't want to return."

The words deflated her. "Oh, Daddy," she cried. "I miss her."

He knelt and opened his arms as she flew into them as she had a thousand times before—before their lives had changed so drastically. She cried against his shoulder, and he knew that she cried for so many things as he rocked her until her tears subsided.

Picking her up, he carried her back to her room and tucked her into bed. Sniffling, she hooked her elbows over the covers. The father in him began to resurface, old habits surging back.

"Do you want to tell me about your dreams now?" he asked, sitting down on the edge of the mattress.

Her gaze grew serious. She bit her lip as she considered if she should tell him or not. "I dream you're holding me," she whispered, dropping her gaze to her hands on the bed, "but all of a sudden you're gone and I'm all alone and everybody hates me."

His face furrowed with surprise and regret: surprise that he hadn't already known the answer, regret that she would ever dream such a thing.

With all the love he felt, he pulled her back into his arms and held her so close, he was afraid she might break. "God, Mary, I love you, and don't you forget that. I love you with all my heart. And I promise, I'll never leave you again."

* * *

Early the next morning, Matthew sat alone in the garden room. Mary was asleep upstairs. The servants were just beginning to stir in the lower regions of the house. And Finnea still hadn't returned. The fact was, she had wanted to go. Hadn't wanted to stay.

That made Matthew furious, or so he told himself in an attempt to explain away the twisting in his heart. He was angry for his daughter. Nothing more.

The room smelled of turpentine and linseed oil. Fine horsehair brushes and soft lead pencils lay out; paint was ready on a palette. But he couldn't concentrate.

Every few minutes his fingers found their way to his face. He pressed the scar experimentally, just a touch, then harder. Each time he could feel the sharp stab of pain.

Something left in the wound.

Matthew snorted his disdain into the quiet.

But then he pressed again, just enough to feel the pain beginning, making it harder and harder to discount Finnea's theory.

A discreet knock sounded on the door.

"Come in," he called out.

Quincy entered with a silver tray. "Your coffee, sir."

Ever since Finnea had walked out the door, Quincy had been disapprovingly quiet. So Matthew ignored him.

But just when the older man started for the door, he stopped him. "Quincy, I need you to do something for me."

The butler whirled around with hopeful eyes. "I know where she is," he blurted out.

Matthew's brow furrowed. "As do I, but that isn't what I'm talking about."

Disappointment clouded the older man's face.

"I want you to find someone else for me," Matthew explained.

Hours later, when the sun was setting on the horizon, Matthew's black lacquer landau pulled up in front of the wooden building in the South End.

After stepping down from the carriage, Matthew pushed through the door. The office was empty except for one man.

"Dr. Sanderling, I am Matthew Hawthorne. I believe my wife has spoken to you about my condition."

* * *

Mary peeked into the darkened room. A fire burned low, casting a dim light across the wood floor and thick carpet. Her father was sound asleep as she crept inside.

Quincy had explained that a doctor was making her father better. She was not so convinced. Sleeping, he looked worse than ever. And since he had arrived home yesterday afternoon, he had done nothing but sleep. She was worried.

People had a way of leaving her. First her mother, then her father for a while, now Finnea. Mary didn't want her father to leave her again, too.

But she had a plan regarding Finnea. She knew for a fact that Finnea hadn't gone to heaven like her mother. She had just gone a few blocks away. Mary had sneaked over and seen her through a window. But before she could do anything about that, her father had to wake up.

From the side of the bed, Mary peered closely at Matthew's sleeping form. She worried her lower lip as she studied him. There were cuts on his face that she didn't understand, new cuts over the old.

She tried to wake him to ask what had happened, but he didn't move, and her concern grew. After a moment she noticed a small bottle next to the bed. Laudanum. She recognized it, since her mother used to take the medicine all the time. "To calm my nerves," she had always explained.

Mary debated for a moment, then took the bottle. After pouring it down the sink, she hurried to the kitchen, remembering all the ingredients Finnea had used to make a salve for a wound.

Matthew woke. He felt groggy and his face was tight—but different. It took a moment for him to realize that the pain was nearly gone.

Instantly he brought his hand up to his cheek, then jerked it back when his fingers sunk into warm goo.

"What the devil?" he croaked.

"Careful, Daddy."

He stilled immediately and turned his head to find Mary

sitting beside his bed in a chair she must have dragged across the room.

She stood up and pressed him back to the bed with tiny hands, like some kind of miniature nurse. "You can't move too quickly or you might break open the stitches. But rest assured, I believe the doctor did a fine job."

Matthew blinked.

"Mr. Quincy explained what happened, and I have kept salves on the new cuts, to keep them from getting icky—I mean infected." She smiled proudly, as always, so much older than her years. "Dr. Sanderling was quite impressed when he came by to check on you. And now it's a good thing you're awake. You need to get out of bed and start moving around."

"You sound just like Finnea," he said without thinking, and immediately regretted his words.

But Mary only smiled. "I know, I was thinking the very same thing." She looked at him closely, a twinkle in her eye. "I was also thinking that it's time we win her back."

Matthew froze in the process of sitting up in bed, his heart hardening at the words.

"We can do it, Daddy. I'm sure."

Very slowly, Matthew swiveled around to look at his daughter. At the sight, his heart melted. Her blond curls, big blue eyes, and Cupid's-bow mouth. He was stunned by the surge of love he felt for her.

He hadn't allowed himself to think about it for so long. And if it hadn't been for Finnea, it was hard to say if he would ever have found his way back to his daughter. A staggering sense of gratitude washed over him.

He held his arms open, and Mary raced into them. He kissed her on the forehead. "So you think we can win her back, do you?"

"Oh yes!"

"Well, we will have to figure out a way to get past that butler over there, not to mention her grandmother," he muttered.

"That will be easy, Daddy, once we make a cake!"

"You think a cake is going to get us through the door?" His tone was skeptical.

"No one can turn away a present. It's rude!"

She didn't know Hannah Grable.

But then again, how could it hurt?

"All right, a cake it is. We'll send Quincy to the bakery."

"Oh no, Daddy! We have to make it ourselves. You and me. That way she will love it."

He wasn't so sure, but he couldn't bring himself to say no. "Fine," he said, determined that if his daughter made Finnea a cake, then by God the woman was going to accept it. He would see to that.

They started at noon the next day, after Mary pulled Matthew downstairs to the kitchen. Matthew couldn't remember when or if he had ever been to the nether regions of the house, but he knew for certain that he didn't know the first thing about how to work in it. Gleaming copper pots and pans hung from a massive chandelierlike structure in the ceiling. A huge, smooth-topped work area stood scrubbed and cleaned in the middle of the cavernous room. But it was warm and welcoming, and Mary seemed to know exactly what to do.

She pulled out bowls from cabinets, pointed to pans hanging from hooks, which he retrieved. She found spoons and measuring cups and an assortment of things that Matthew couldn't name. The clatter of glass and metal brought the cook from the pantry.

"Lord have mercy," the woman exclaimed as she bustled into the kitchen.

"Look, Violet," Mary said. "We are making a cake to bring Finnea back."

Violet glanced from Mary to Matthew. "Bring Miss Finnea back, you say?" She gave Matthew a decisive nod, adding, "And a nice bouquet of flowers wouldn't hurt while you're at it. A lady always loves flowers, she does."

"Now," Mary began, once Violet had returned to the pantry, "let's get started."

And they did, with Violet and Quincy coming and going, adding a bit of advice here and there. Matthew and Mary began by making a huge bowl of batter.

"Finnea will love this," Matthew said, handing a large spoon to his daughter.

Mary secured the large bowl in the crook of her arm and started to stir. "I think Finnea just plain loves to eat. And she doesn't care what anyone thinks of her, either."

His hand stilling in the process of measuring out a cup of sugar, Matthew glanced over at Mary. "Maybe now." He chuckled. "But when I first saw Finnea in Boston, it was at your grandmother's house, and she cared a great deal then. She was dressed like the perfect lady, in a stunning gown and jewels."

"*Our* Finnea?" she gasped.

Matthew laughed. "Yes, our Finnea." His smile faded to a line of remembrance. "I remember the very first time I saw her, I thought she was the most exceptional woman I had ever seen."

"Exceptional?" she asked, her brow furrowed in confusion. "You mean you thought she was pretty?"

Matthew gave a tilt of his head, before pouring a bit of sugar back into the canister when he got too much. "Pretty? Yes. But it was more than that. She was special." He looked over at his daughter. "On the night of the party, she ate a nasturtium."

"What's that?"

He chuckled. "A flower. Her mother was mortified. But Finnea handled herself with a grace that few women possess." He looked at his daughter. "The kind of grace you have, Mary."

It was as if he wanted to make up for lost time. He wanted her to know how he felt. But her response caught him off guard.

"Did my mother have that kind of grace?" she asked quietly.

His heart twisted at the memory of his wife. The fire and the pain. The betrayal.

But then he remembered Finnea telling him that no child should have to learn their parent isn't a good person.

A ghost of a smile touched his lips. A genuine smile as he dredged up different memories, of an earlier Kimberly.

"Yes," he said, his smile growing wider, "your mother had grace. Grace and beauty. And she loved you very much."

"Really?" Mary gasped with pleasure.

"Don't you remember her?"

"Yes, but sometimes it's hard."

He nodded his understanding as he made a decision. "Did I ever tell you about the time I first met your mother?"

"No," she breathed, rapt.

"Well," he began, as he held the bowl so she could stir the batter when her arm got tired. He told her about the day they met, and answered all the little-girl questions she had. They talked as they mixed the batter, then continued all through the baking and even as they spread thick chocolate icing all over the top.

The kitchen was toasty warm and filled with delicious smells. Mary was aglow with stories of a mother who had loved her. And when the cake was done, they stepped back to survey the finished product. Violet and Quincy stood with them as well.

Mary's eyes went wide.

"It's lopsided," she blurted, on the verge of tears.

Matthew panicked. He didn't want her to cry. He didn't want her to think she had failed. "I think it's a perfect cake. I think it looks grand."

"You're just saying that," she said, her lower lip trembling with defeat.

"I'm not," he insisted. He leaned down and turned her to face him. "It's perfect because you made it. And you know how Finnea is. She'll love it all the more because it's not like every other cake." And she'd better, he thought grimly. He would not allow his child to be hurt anymore.

Love burgeoned on Mary's cheeks. "You're right. That's all that matters."

He ruffled her hair. "Yes, that's all that matters."

"Now we must box it up to take over to her house." She smiled. "We will show her our cake. And your face."

He tensed.

"Oh, Daddy, she will be so pleased that you're getting better."

And he was. So much better that he could hardly believe it

was true. He felt as if a constant tension had been cut loose from his body.

They were interrupted when a sharp buzz sounded, indicating that the doorbell was ringing upstairs. Matthew and Mary gave it little thought when Quincy disappeared up the steps to answer the door. Only when he raced back down and said there was a visitor, the man's face lined with some emotion that neither of them could name, did their hearts stop.

"Finnea," Mary breathed, taking the word right out of Matthew's mouth.

He took her hand and they raced up the stairs, not hearing anything anyone was saying, only to stop dead in their tracks in the foyer. Disappointment mixed with confusion. Finnea hadn't returned.

Instead, they stared at a man, as tall as Matthew and as broad and powerful, his white flowing robes contrasting sharply with the brilliant black of his skin. Next to him was a large crate, the wooden slats across the top broken and askew as if it had traveled a long way. Straw stuck out and spilled a path on the marble tiles.

"He has just arrived from Africa, sir," Quincy explained. "For Mrs. Hawthorne."

"*Mbote,* Matthew," the man greeted solemnly without preamble. "I was told at the docks that I could find Finnea here."

"Janji," Matthew said through his surprise.

His long stride covered the distance, and the men shook hands in the African manner.

Then Janji looked around as if he expected Finnea to materialize. When she didn't, he turned back to Matthew. "Let me see her," he commanded.

Matthew stiffened. "She's not here. Why have you come for her?"

The African eyed him closely, and Matthew knew he was being sized up yet again—much as he had been sized up after Janji had lowered his gun, the lion lying dead only inches from Matthew's feet.

But that was a lifetime ago. His eyes narrowing, Matthew began to take the man's measure himself. At the gesture, the African grunted his approval.

"It is good to see you again, my friend," Janji said with a glimmer of a smile. "I promised Finnea I would make sure her cherished things arrived in America. I have kept my promise. I am here with her belongings."

"Look!" Mary exclaimed, pulling a handmade rag doll from the wood and straw.

"That isn't yours, Mary," Matthew said, and gently took the toy away.

But when he started to put it back, he noticed several other items.

Confusion shimmering through him, Matthew took out a tiny wooden horse and a carved ivory rattle. His movements were reluctant, but he understood at some primal level that this was important. This crate held the missing pieces to Finnea's darkness. The answer he had been searching for was right here.

"What are these?" he asked out loud, not understanding, though his heart had begun to pound.

Janji stood stoically.

"Damn it, Janji, tell me why you brought these toys to Finnea," he demanded.

The African met his eye. "It is not my story to tell. I am only here to deliver these things . . . and to see that she is safe. Take me to her now."

But Matthew was no longer listening. Thoughts raced through his head like a rush of howling wind. Then, placing one small toy in his pocket, he slammed out the front door and headed for Commonwealth Avenue. Even without the cake, this time he would not be turned away.

Chapter Twenty-two

Matthew hurtled up the front steps of the Winslet town house and had to hold himself back from breaking down the front door. He had to see Finnea and uncover once and for all the past that lurked in the recesses of her eyes. The past that he was sure now held her back . . . and kept them apart.

She hadn't wanted to leave, he realized with a curse; she had felt she had to go.

After he turned the knob to ring the bell inside, he paced as he waited for an answer, then banged again when no one answered quickly enough.

The butler finally pulled open the door, and at the look on Matthew's face, the man took a step back.

"Where is she?" he demanded.

"Miss Finnea is having dinner, sir," the man answered without having to be given a name. "But she is unavailable."

"Sorry, Bertram, but that isn't going to work this time." Matthew pushed past him as the man's long thin face pulled into sharp angles of surprise.

"Mr. Hawthorne, please!"

"What is going on out here?" Nester barked, stalking into the foyer with a square of white linen bunched in his hand as if he had gotten up from his seat so fast that he had forgotten to set his napkin aside.

At the sight of Matthew, his light green eyes narrowed angrily. "I demand you leave this instant!"

"Nice to see you, too, Nester," Matthew responded with a forbidding smile as he strode further into the house undeterred, his boot heels ringing on the marble tiles, gold gilt and sparkling crystal surrounding them. "I'm here to see Finnea."

"Don't you get it? She won't see you," he gloated. "She doesn't want to see you. So quit wasting our time and get the hell out of my house."

With a few long strides Matthew crossed the distance until he came to stand before the smaller man. Nester backed up automatically until he must have realized what he was doing and stopped, his chin rising.

"I said leave, Hawthorne."

"I'm afraid that is impossible. I'm going to see her, and I'm not leaving until I do."

Nester's white face flashed red, and a vein suddenly throbbed on his forehead. "Who do you think you are?"

"Her husband."

"Not for long!" he spat triumphantly. "I am seeing to the annulment myself."

Matthew felt as if he had taken a blow to the midsection. But close on the heels of that breath-sucking swell came cold, ruthless fury. He would not give her up. He would not lose her. Not again.

He took a step closer until he was only inches away from his brother-in-law. "If you see to anything, Winslet, you'll regret the day you were born."

"Is that a threat?"

"You bet. Now get out of my way."

The commotion brought Leticia Winslet out through a set of double doors. At the sight of Matthew, something flashed across her face. Relief? Joy? Matthew narrowed his eyes. He must have imagined it. If he was asked yet again to leave, he would defy this woman as well.

But Leticia surprised him. She turned to her son. "Do as the man said and step aside, Nester. He is here to see his wife." Turning her attention to Matthew, her gaze was intent. "My daughter is in the dining room. We were just about to have dinner." Her eyes sparked. "I think you should join us."

"What are you saying?" Nester cried.

"I'm saying that Mr. Hawthorne should join us for our meal."

Nester sputtered and fumed, then marched through the double doors.

Matthew looked at Leticia, suspicion filling his mind.

It must have shown on his face because she clasped her hands together, delicate gold bracelets jangling on her wrist as she held tightly. "My daughter is unhappy, Mr. Hawthorne. And I hate to see her in such a state."

This time Matthew was sure his suspicion showed. He felt his face harden ruthlessly at such an obvious lie. The woman had done everything but care about how her daughter felt.

"I know, I know," Leticia said with a weary sigh, her pale skin growing even paler. "You have no reason to believe that I care. But please try to, for Finnea's sake. And if nothing else, believe me when I say she is unhappy." She gestured toward the formal doors. "Go to her. See for yourself."

This time he was sure that genuine regret filled the woman's eyes, and Matthew wondered suddenly why Leticia Winslet had left Africa and never returned. What mother could leave a child behind and truly forget her? Was Leticia that sort of woman? Suddenly he wasn't so sure.

He extended his arm so Leticia would pass before him, after which he followed her into the dining room. The minute he stepped into the room he saw Finnea. The sight of her hit him hard. Her boldness, the vibrant life of her. After months of winter in Boston, the touch of gold in her skin had faded, leaving her features milk-white, made whiter by the intensity of her deep green eyes.

She wore a gown of dark blue velvet, simple but elegant, not Africa, but not entirely Boston either, as if she had found a style that was all her own. Looking at her, he was struck by how beautiful she was. And by how desperately he wanted her.

He took her in like a long, soothing sip of fine brandy. He watched as her lips fell open in a silent O at the sight of him, her eyes going wide with . . . something. But what? For one gratifying moment he was certain that she was glad to see him.

But then he caught sight of Jeffrey, sitting next to her at the table in his proper black coat. And the hard, tight fury he had felt before flashed through him.

Was that what she had wanted all along?

But as suddenly as the thought flitted through his head it

was gone. She was many things, but she had never been afraid of the truth. She didn't love Jeffrey Upton. And he would not let pride get in the way as it had when she left his house before. He would talk to her alone, show her the toy, and once and for all demand to know what had happened in Africa. If it was the last thing he did, he would talk to this woman, this woman that he loved.

Loved.

His spine straightened as the realization sank in. He loved her as he had never loved anyone in his life. He had known all along that he wanted her, that she filled the gaping hole in him somehow. But he had been too blind to see that it was more than that. Too afraid to believe it was more than that.

He had told her not to love him that night in the jungle because he didn't believe he could be loved. Not any longer. And he had wanted no more lies in his life.

But she had loved him anyway. For himself, with his scar, with his anger. He had known for some time that she had seen him for who he was, had sought him for that person. But he hadn't understood until now that she loved him—for him, not because he had saved her. Her feelings hadn't faded with time. He realized the truth in an instant.

And with that realization came another. It didn't matter what had happened in her past. He needed no explanation for the toys that had arrived in a broken crate on his floor. He loved her—just her, just as she was.

The force of understanding nearly drove him to his knees. He loved her. And he had never told her. He had never said the words that she needed to hear. More than that, he had tossed her love back in her face again and again.

His mind reeled at his stubborn refusal to accept the truth. He had come up with every excuse to explain away his behavior, when all the while he had behaved in that way he had because he loved her—but had pushed that love away.

Dear God, he had to tell her. Had to show her.

He addressed the group that was assembled around the table, but he only looked at Finnea. "I would like to speak to my wife."

He could see her swallow, then clear her throat to talk. "But

I don't wish to speak to you," she replied, making her mother gasp and Nester snicker.

Matthew didn't care about anyone else. His gaze bored into Finnea, seeking the truth, seeking her soul. With an arrogant nod, he said, "Fine. You don't have to speak to me, but you do have to suffer through my company for dinner."

Her head swung around to her mother.

"Yes, dear, didn't I tell you that I invited Mr. Hawthorne to join us?"

The woman didn't actually lie; she *had* invited him. Matthew wanted to dance the woman around the floor.

Finnea's head came back, and he saw something he was certain was fear race through her eyes.

"Get the hell out of here, Hawthorne," Nester raged, "before I send for the police."

"You'll send for no one, Nester," Leticia said crisply. "I will not have a dinner guest arrested in my home."

With that, Leticia directed Matthew to a vacant seat directly across from Finnea. Then, with a discreet nod of her head, she ordered a servant to bring another place setting.

Finnea dropped her gaze to her lap and seemed to panic as a serving maid hurriedly set a place of crystal and silver.

Dinner was served and the meal progressed in painful, awkward silence as Matthew racked his brain for some way to penetrate the wall Finnea had erected around herself. Clearly, she wasn't going to make this easy.

"Mary sends her regards," he offered.

Finnea's head came up with a start, her eyes hungry for news of his child. And Matthew was encouraged. "Yes, she's doing well. In fact, today we made a cake."

"You and Mary?" Finnea whispered.

"Yes, Mary and I made it." He chuckled in memory. "Though it came out of the oven a tad lopsided. But we made it for you, and I told her that you would love it no matter how it looked." His voice lowered gruffly. "You have a very special way of not caring about how something looks."

Finnea dropped her gaze and concentrated on the bowl of thick, steaming soup set before her, making it clear she didn't want to discuss it any further. But Matthew was determined. He would not give in.

He stared at her, his gaze steady on her bowed head. He willed her to look up.

Slowly she raised her head, her emerald eyes confused as if she didn't understand the pull on her.

"The cake was Mary's way of trying to win you back," he said, ignoring Nester's snort of disdain. "She said if we made it ourselves, with love, you would surely return."

He saw tears spring to life in her eyes, and her hands trembled as she returned them to her lap. Matthew wouldn't let up. He searched for a new approach. And that's when it came to him.

"Mrs. Winslet," he said casually to Leticia, "might I make a toast?"

"Well, yes, of course."

Everyone grew uncomfortable; Finnea's brow creased with confusion. Matthew looked directly at her, then reached out and with a steady and deliberate motion, picked up the delicate wineglass with his wounded hand.

Her eyes went wide when he didn't shake or tremble, and he knew that she understood instantly. Her gaze shot to his face, and she took in the rapidly healing wounds over his scars.

"You had it done?" she breathed.

"Had what done?" Nester demanded.

But neither Matthew nor Finnea explained.

"Yes," Matthew answered. "Dr. Sanderling said that I was a very fortunate man to have someone who so doggedly pursued what everyone else said was impossible."

"Oh, Matthew! I'm thrilled!"

"Thrilled enough to come home?" he asked softly, as if no one else were in the room.

Her elation shrank away and her face darkened. "No!" she suddenly blurted. "I can't go back. I told you I don't belong there."

She pushed up from her chair so abruptly that the chair tipped over with a crash. Her eyes were wild and she looked cornered. But when Matthew stood and started toward her, she fled.

"Good riddance," Nester called after her, then turned to Matthew. "Now if you'll leave, things will be perfect."

Hannah started to reprimand Nester, but Leticia stopped her mother. She turned to her cherished son, no longer simply impatient but angry, and wiped off his smug expression with her words. "Enough, Nester. I've had enough of your jealousy and vindictiveness. It's time you started acting your age." She pushed up from her chair with dignity and grace. "It's also time I had a long overdue talk with my daughter."

Leticia found Finnea in her bedroom, staring out into the night. Finnea heard the footsteps, but she didn't turn. She didn't know how much more she could take. A family that barely tolerated her. A child who made cakes to win her heart. And a man whom she loved but couldn't have.

A ship bound for Africa left in the morning. Her bags were packed. Ready except for a broken heart.

Her thoughts were interrupted when her mother started to speak. Finnea braced herself for a set-down.

"Stop being so angry," Leticia stated.

Confusion shimmered through Finnea's mind, and she looked back at her mother. "I'm not angry."

"Of course you are," Leticia replied, her normally smooth face lined with regret. "You're angry with me for leaving you."

Finnea turned back to the window abruptly.

"See, you are." Leticia came into the room. "You blame me for not returning." Her voice softened. "But it was your father who wouldn't let me. I tried once. I know, it was much later, but I did try. By then he no longer wanted me."

"That's not true. He despaired that you left us."

"Did he really say the words?"

Finnea's mind raced with memories, and she realized that he had never actually said the words. But she was sure she was right. She had been devastated by her mother's abandonment.

The thought hit her. *Her* abandonment.

She shook her head as if shaking cobwebs from her mind. Of course her father was devastated. His wife had left him and had taken his son. She would believe nothing else.

"After being apart for all those years, we were too different.

There no longer seemed to be any common ground. And your father didn't want me back."

"You're the one who broke your promise and didn't return. You didn't want me!" She sucked in her breath. "You didn't want him," she amended.

"Is that what he told you?"

"Yes." He *had* said her mother had broken her promise.

"I should have known," Leticia said on a sad sigh. She closed the distance that separated her from her child. "Look at me, Finnea."

Reluctantly, Finnea turned.

Leticia took her hands. "I made mistakes, but so did your father. Once I realized I needed to go back, I should have fought harder to return. But that doesn't mean I didn't love you. It only means I was weak."

Leticia reached up and touched Finnea's cheeks—a touch as soft and sweet as butter candy.

"I loved you then, Finnea, and I love you now. And it's a crime that I haven't shown you before. I don't deserve your forgiveness, but don't let your anger at me, or your trouble with the past, stand in the way of a man who cares for you."

Footsteps gained their attention, and they turned to find Matthew standing in the doorway. At the sight of the man, Leticia squeezed Finnea's hand and returned to the dining room.

"My mother's wrong," Finnea whispered, turning back to stare out the window. "My problem isn't my anger."

"I know," Matthew said, his voice solemn, wanting to pull her into his arms, to make things right, but knowing that he had to give her time. "I never thought it was about anger. Frustration, sadness. Abandonment, perhaps. But never anger. And I especially don't think that now, after Janji has arrived."

Finnea gasped and whirled around, her mouth slightly opened, her eyes wide with indescribable hope. "Janji is here? In Boston?"

"Yes." He searched her eyes, before pulling the toy from his pocket and extending it to her. "He has brought your belongings."

She staggered at the sight, and Matthew had to reach out

and steady her. When she met his gaze, he saw the darkness and the pain, no longer hidden by wildness or defiance.

"I want to see him," she whispered.

Nodding his head, Matthew took her hand and led her out the door. He would take her home. To Dove's Way. Where she belonged. He would help her deal with her past, then he would bind her to him with his love when no other restraint would hold her.

Chapter Twenty-three

Finnea flew out of the Winslet house. Matthew had to race to keep up, catching her hand and pulling her back to safety when she would have run into traffic.

Minutes later, they arrived on Marlborough Street. But when Finnea came to the front door, she stopped abruptly, bringing Matthew up short. She stared at the fine-grained wood, stared at the lion's-head knocker. But Matthew knew that wasn't what she saw.

"Are you sure it's Janji?" she asked quietly, afraid she was going to be disappointed.

"Yes," he replied solemnly. "I'm sure."

She closed her eyes for one brief second, as if praying, then carefully pushed through the door.

Once inside she remained quiet so that no one noticed her. She waited beneath the mosaic, the warrior holding the dove, her face a cipher as she took in the scene before her.

The massive man from Africa stood perfectly still, as if he hadn't moved a muscle since Matthew dashed out of the house. Mary stared at Janji from where she sat on the bottom step of the grand stairway, her elbows planted on her knees, her chin on her knuckles. The African stared back. Quincy paced and muttered.

"Janji," Finnea breathed.

The man turned to her, his expression fierce. His eyes traveled over her as a parent's inspecting a child. Then he smiled, a huge gleaming flash of white teeth.

"I see that my friend has taken good care of you," he said.

Finnea blushed but was given no time to respond when Mary swiveled around.

"Finnea!" The child raced across the foyer and threw her arms around her. "You're home."

Finnea touched Mary's head, and Matthew could see the tears forming in her eyes.

"Did you miss me?" Mary demanded.

"Yes, I missed you. Very much."

Mary let go abruptly and turned to Janji. "I win! You smiled."

Janji's smile grudgingly widened even more. "You would make a fine opponent in my land."

Mary beamed. This was the child he'd left behind, Matthew thought. Happy. Cheerful. Filled with love.

Finnea still hadn't moved, as if she didn't know what to expect from the visitor, until finally she came forward. Janji bowed his head formally when she stopped just in front of him.

"Bloody hell," she whispered through tears that had begun to slip down her cheeks. Then she threw her arms around him.

The man was clearly startled by the action.

"They hug all the time here, Janji," she said through a mixture of laughter and tears. "You'll have to get used to it if you plan to stay."

He stood stoically, then finally patted her awkwardly.

With a laugh and a sniffle, she moved back. "I have missed you, my friend."

"Yes," he said, clearly uncomfortable.

They went to the study, where a fire burned to ward off the chill of the spring night. They talked for hours, about the man's difficult trip to the Americas, about the oddness of this country. Matthew smiled as he listened, really seeing for the first time how strange Boston must seem to an outsider.

But then the talk turned to what had been happening with the tribe in Africa. Mary grew bored and slipped out of the room.

"Your *mundele* brother, Nester," Janji intoned, "is wanting to take our land away and sell it to another rich *mundele*."

"What?" Finnea demanded, leaning forward.

"Your brother is trying to sell your father's farm."

"I should have known he would try to do something like that," she raged. "And it's all my fault."

"Your fault?" Janji asked.

"Yes, my fault. I'm the one who told him about the farm. He knew nothing about it until I mentioned it. I should have known. Don't you worry. Nester will not get away with it. I'll deal with him as soon as I get back to the house."

Matthew didn't like the sound of that. She was home. She belonged here. And he wasn't about to let her leave again.

Beyond that, he didn't want her hurt anymore. Not by him. Not by Nester, and he could imagine how her brother would react to a plea from Finnea in regards to this farm. Matthew made a mental note to send word to Grayson first thing in the morning. His brother was one of the best lawyers around.

Suddenly Janji retrieved a satchel from the crate and extended it to Finnea.

"For you," the African said.

Matthew saw Finnea's breath catch and the tears that wiped away all laughter when she looked inside. With a strength that would have made a warrior proud, she reached over and laid her hand on Janji's. "Thank you, my friend. Thank you for bringing my memories to America."

"You are welcome." He hesitated. "Just so long as you don't let them hold you in the past."

She didn't answer. She pulled the satchel close to her chest, and Matthew knew her smile was forced. "I am tired," she said. "We will talk more in the morning."

Then she stood and Matthew knew she would head for the front door.

"You can't leave," Matthew stated.

"Why not?"

Matthew could feel Janji's eyes on him. *Because I don't want you to go.* But it was too soon for that. "Because—"

"Welcome home!"

The adults turned to the study entrance. Mary stood in the doorway, pushing a service cart that held the lopsided cake.

"Daddy and I made it just for you!"

For a moment, Mary's smile wavered and she bit her lip. "It didn't come out so good."

Matthew watched as tears sprang to life in Finnea's eyes; then she rushed forward and swept Mary close.

"It is a perfect cake. And I love it, just as I love you."

Mary traced the tears on Finnea's face. "And I love you."

The cake was served. Quincy and Violet shared a piece. Janji ate an entire slice and pronounced that he wanted more. Mary served the confection, doling out several slices that were sent to the servants in the kitchen.

But when the platter was empty, Finnea stood again. "It's getting late."

"Come on, Finnea," Mary said. "I'll walk with you upstairs."

Finnea's mouth fell open to protest, but Matthew met her eyes, willing her not to disappoint the child.

"Quincy will go to your mother's and get your things," he offered.

She started to balk; he could see it.

"Please," he added softly. "You have a guest, after all."

In the end she was convinced to stay. She gave Quincy instructions to have a room readied for Janji. Then she said good night and allowed Mary to pull her from the study, never losing her hold on the satchel.

Matthew started to go after her, to make sure that indeed she went upstairs instead of out the front door, but Janji spoke.

"You love her." It wasn't a question but a statement.

Matthew stared at the empty doorway, listening to her footsteps as she went up the stairs. "Yes, I do."

"I gambled when I sent her to you."

Matthew wheeled back.

"Yes, I sent her to you intentionally."

"But you told me it was cargo I was to look after, not a woman."

Janji smiled. "Yes."

"I knew I hadn't mistranslated." Matthew shook his head. "Why did you do it?"

"Because I believed. I believed she could heal you, and I knew if I told you it was a woman I was sending you, you wouldn't have agreed to take her—regardless of what you thought you owed me." The African hesitated. "But more than that, I believed you could heal her."

The truth hit Matthew square in the chest. She *had* healed him. But he hadn't even begun to understand her pain.

"I felt certain that I was right," Janji continued. He shook his head. "But now I see that she wants to return to Africa."

With a start, Matthew straightened. "When did she tell you that?"

"She didn't. I saw it in her eyes. In addition, she thinks she *is* going back."

"She is my wife," Matthew stated arrogantly, ignoring the fire of his heart. "She will stay with me." *And I will find a way to heal her.*

Janji's dark eyes were like fathomless pools, staring into him. "Good." As if he had understood the unspoken words. "She does not belong in Africa. At least not as a white woman alone. She must stay with you."

"She will," Matthew stated with a boldness that matched the wizened man's.

Janji actually chuckled at this. "You are good for her, even if she does not yet know it." The lightness faded. "But you must prove it to her."

Matthew would have been offended had anyone else said such a thing. But with this man he knew it was from the heart, for the good of Finnea, and he couldn't fault the man for that. Especially since he knew he was right.

After Quincy led Janji to a guest room, Matthew was left alone in the study. He stared at the flames, taking in all that he had learned, bits and pieces he had accumulated over the months he had known Finnea. Then he went to her.

He found her in the yellow room, standing at the window, looking out, the satchel opened on the bureau, a white baby's gown held in her arms. The room was dark except for the moonlight that streamed in.

"You had a daughter in Africa," he stated quietly, putting into words the conclusions he had drawn.

She didn't turn around, and for a moment he thought she hadn't heard.

But then she spoke, her words filled with an unfathomable sadness. "Her name was Isabel."

He came forward, stopping just behind her. "God, Finn, why didn't you tell me?"

She didn't answer his question but said, "She would be

Mary's age if she had lived." He could see her reflection in the window, could see her lips pull into a sad smile. "She would have loved Mary."

"Mary would have loved her . . . just as she loves you." He touched her shoulders, but at the contact she jerked away.

"No!"

But Matthew caught her, turning her determinedly around to face him. Her face was ravaged, streaked by tears. "What is it, Finnea?" he demanded. "Talk to me," he added, his voice fierce, needing to understand completely so he could help her. "You once said you couldn't stand to be touched, you couldn't stand to feel. Once and for all, tell me why."

She tried to jerk away, but he held her secure, his heart slamming against his chest, afraid of what she would say.

"Why won't you let me get close to you?" A thought spiraled into his mind, making him flinch. "Is it because you can't love anyone but Isabel's father? Is that what it has been all this time?"

Tears fell freely then, and he knew that as long as he lived he would never forget the look of utter devastation on her face.

"Isabel's father? Dear God, no. I can't stand to feel because I can't stand to be anything but sorry for having been a horrible mother," she cried softly.

His brow knitted. "You are a wonderful mother," he said, shaking her in earnestness. "I told you that before, and I meant it."

"I'm not! I couldn't keep my child safe—just as I couldn't keep Mary safe."

"What are you talking about?" he demanded.

He felt her go still, felt the will drain from her limbs. She looked out, staring off, seeing something very different from the walls that surrounded them. Just when he would have swept her up and cradled her, she spoke.

"I heard her cry."

"What?"

"I heard her cry. Just once, then she stopped. When I didn't hear her cry again, I went back to my work. I didn't go to her. Later, when I went in to check on her, she was dead. She choked. Choked! Choked on the button eye of her favorite stuffed bear." Her hands fisted; her face grew strained. "If I had noticed it was loose, or if I had gone when she cried, she would be alive! Do you understand?" she gasped, her eyes imploring him to see her brutal conclusion. "I could have saved her—should have saved her!"

A mountain of ifs that paralyze and make it impossible to truly live. How to counter that? How to help her move beyond?

He reached out to her, and when she tried to slap his hands away, he curled his fingers gently around her wrist and pulled her to him.

"No one can answer every cry, Finnea," he said softly against her skin.

"Maybe not, but a good mother answers all the right ones!"

Her tears became sobs, deep racking cries that Matthew could feel shudder through him when he cradled her against his chest. She fought him, but her strength was nothing compared to his. He held her, for the first time wondering if they could ever get beyond this.

He held her until her sobs trailed off and she collapsed against him. He stroked her hair, despairing.

"I don't belong here," she said hoarsely, forcefully putting distance between them. "I belong in Africa with Isabel."

He looked at her for an eternity. "Oh, Finn, Isabel is gone. You can't live in the past. You have to move beyond what you can't change. You taught me that. You taught Mary that, too. Lessons from a wonderful mother to a daughter."

Though she had stepped away, they were still so close that he could have easily touched her. But he didn't. He held back as desire surged through him—held back because what he felt was a deeper desire, a desperate desire to make things right, make her whole.

"I love you, Finnea," he whispered.

Her breath was ragged, and with that he couldn't hold back any longer. He pulled her to him. As soon as their bodies touched, her fingers fisted in his shirt as if she were afraid to let go, her forehead pressed hard against his chest.

"I love you with all my heart," he said, "as I have never loved anyone before."

Tilting her chin so he could see her face, he looked into her eyes, bright and green, desperate. He lined her jaw with his hands and pressed a kiss to her forehead before his fingers slid back to tangle in her hair.

"Finn," he breathed against her ear.

Tears burned in her eyes.

"Isabel will always be a part of you, Finn. But don't lock everyone else out."

"You don't understand."

His grip grew firm, intense. "Then explain it to me."

She stared at him, her teeth sinking into her lower lip. He could tell she was afraid. But he didn't know of what.

He started to push back, but her hand shot out and grabbed his wrist. "Don't leave me. Not again."

His heart slammed against his chest as he remembered the jungle. And when she reached up to him and whispered, "Hold me. Please," just as she had that day, he pushed answers and explanations from his mind.

He held her fiercely, and when he brushed his lips over hers she was lost. She clung to him, returning his kiss. Fiercely. Desperately. As if she couldn't get close enough.

"Sweet Finn."

His hands coiled in her hair, gently pulling her head back. He opened his mouth on her neck as his strong hands slipped down her spine, cupping her hips, pulling her up to the hard rigidness of his manhood. "I want to be inside you."

Her eyes flashed open, but he only swept her up in his arms and carried her to the bed. Gently but firmly he laid her down. "I'm going to make love to you, Finnea. I'm going to fill you as I was meant to."

Her eyes filled with trepidation, and she started to protest. But the words were cut off and her mouth fell open in a silent gasp when he grazed his fingers across the rosebud tips of her breasts, bringing them to taut peaks beneath the thin material of her gown.

"Let yourself feel," he said, his own urgency flaring at the banked passion he saw in her eyes.

And suddenly, it was as if she could do nothing less. He

grasped her wrists and pulled them above her head as he lowered his head to her breast, brushing the peak with his lips.

With maddening determination, he worked the fastenings of her gown, one by one, then started on her chemise when her gown had been discarded on the floor. He removed her clothes with slow, sensual strokes, lingering over the high, round breasts, the small, delicate waist, and the golden triangle of curls between her legs, bringing a sweet mewling sound from her lips.

"Finn," he murmured, his voice sounding hoarse and raw even to his own ears.

But he said nothing else, simply came over her and kissed her with the fierceness of long-held desire set free.

She gasped when his hard chest brushed ever so lightly against hers. He trailed his lips down her cheek to her neck, to her breasts. He palmed the fullness, then pulled one nipple deep in his mouth.

Her body trembled. "Matthew," she whispered.

"Yes, Finn." He said the words and trailed his lips even lower, letting go of her wrists. He kissed the outline of her ribs down to her abdomen. Then lower, pressing his lips to every inch of her body, until he stopped abruptly.

Unlike the day he shattered her control, he hadn't left any of her underclothes on. And he saw.

His body grew tense, and when he looked up her eyes bored into him, questioning. Vulnerable.

"Dear God," he breathed as he carefully, reverently touched the jagged proof on her inner thigh that she had been in the train wreck.

Instantly she tried to cover herself, but his large hands captured hers and moved them purposely away. With his throat oddly tight, he leaned down and pressed his lips to her scar.

She inhaled a sharp breath.

"You are so beautiful," he breathed against her skin.

He came up over her, lying on top of her, his weight supported by his elbows, his palms cradling her head as he looked deep into her eyes.

She turned her cheek into the mattress, but he wouldn't

allow it. He framed her head in his hands, forcing her to look at him. "We belong together. Do you understand that? Do you understand that it is all right to love again?"

He kissed her again, on her cheeks and eyelids and lips and ears, and she returned his kisses, matching his intensity.

Their love turned frantic. Her hands ripped at his belt and at the fastenings of his trousers. She gave a soft cry of frustration when her attempts were unsuccessful.

Another time he would have chuckled, but this time he was nearly moved to tears by her desire for him—the past giving up its strangling hold on her. He could feel it. Could feel the passion that the past had not allowed until now.

He kissed her again, smoothed her hair back from her face, and met her eyes. There was so much he wanted to say. His throat burned with the words he held back.

"Love me," she whispered when he did nothing more than look deep into her eyes.

With that he was lost. Her lips parted as he kissed her. He traced the line of her mouth with his tongue, savoring her sweetness. He kissed her again, hard and deep, his mouth slanting over hers. Pulling at his clothes, she groaned until he stepped away and freed himself from his trousers.

But when he started to come back to her, she shook her head no. He stood naked before her, his brow furrowed, his shaft thick and swollen with wanting her. She scooted to the edge of the bed on her knees so that she faced him.

"Let me touch you," she said.

Just as he had uttered to her.

And she did. Reaching out to cradle his sex.

He inhaled sharply, his eyes boring into her as she began to stroke the length of him. His body began to quiver as her hands grew bolder. Exerting every ounce of willpower he possessed, he held his body in check as he touched her cheek, slowly trailing the tips of his fingers down her naked flesh. He didn't stop until he came to the juncture between her thighs. This time she inhaled on a sharp breath when he slid his finger deep into her moist opening. And stroked. Slowly.

"Do you feel that, sweetheart?"

She caught a sob in her throat when he slipped two fingers inside her, filling her, nudging her thighs farther apart. And when he was sure she was ready and he knew he couldn't take much more, he gently pushed her back into the coverlet.

When he lay on top of her, their naked bodies pressed together, he grew still. She looked at him, her eyes questioning.

"We belong together," he whispered.

Then, with one powerful surge, he embedded himself fully inside her.

She cried out his name and he stopped, afraid he had hurt her. But she'd have none of that. She moved her hips, sending shivers of pleasure through his body the likes of which he had never experienced. He held her fragile form, carefully, moving slowly, until she urged him faster. Their hips came together, again and again, and he no longer thought to hold back.

Their lovemaking was primal, harkening back to Africa. The wildness. The passion. They tried to lose themselves in each other until they were lost, sensation coursing through each of them and they cried out.

For long minutes they lay entwined in the tangle of sheets. He kissed her forehead, then rolled over onto his back, bringing her with him. Matthew marveled at how content he was, how at ease, how whole he felt with this woman in his arms.

Silence surrounded them, perfect and complete.

But just when he thought she was asleep, she spoke. "I was about to be married."

"Ah, Finn. You don't have to say anything. I don't need to know any more than I do now." And he realized it was true.

"But I need to tell you. I believed Gatwith loved me, and I gave in to him the night before the wedding. I was young and swept away by his charm and dazzling smile."

He saw her angrily dash her tears away.

"I was a fool. After he satisfied his need, he went to my father as if nothing had happened. Can you imagine?" she said bitterly. "He actually slipped out of my room, then sat down with Father and sipped brandy as if earlier he had been doing nothing more than playing checkers with the natives." She looked away. "That night as a wedding gift my father gave Gatwith three highly valuable varieties of rubber tree saplings.

All of us could see that Gatwith had become a sort of son to my father. Gatwith took advantage of that. The valuable trees were all Gatwith needed to start a rubber plantation of his own." She shook her head. "That's what he wanted all along. He had asked to buy them when he first arrived because Father's variety was far superior to any in the world. God, how stupid I was. Gatwith didn't want me. He wanted to find a way to get the saplings. And once he had those, he had no reason to stay. He slipped away that night without a word. And there I stood the next day, dressed in a beautiful gown the tribeswomen had made for me, a garland in my hair, my father at my side, and not a groom to be found. He left me at the altar, he embarrassed my father, and when it became apparent that I was with child, I was shunned by everyone but Janji and his family. I could no longer go into town, where the Europeans were, and the missionary wouldn't let me go to church. I was an outcast. But worst of all, when Isabel was born, she was an outcast, too." She pressed her eyes closed. "She hardly seemed to notice. She had known nothing else. But I knew and it killed me inside." Her tears choked her, rage and despair strangling her.

"You must have hated Gatwith."

"Hate him?" Her eyes opened. "How could I hate the man who gave me Isabel?"

"You don't have to hate him—just hate what he did to you." He rocked her in his arms. "You are a better person than most people ever think of being."

"Isabel made me a better person. Isabel was so good and kind. You can see wisdom in a child if you really look." The words brought more tears. "I want her with me, here and now."

"She's always in your heart."

"But I want to see her. I want to see her burst of red hair and big green eyes. And the tiny freckles that dotted the bridge of her nose."

"She sounds like a tiny version of you."

He felt her smile against his chest. "That's what everyone said."

"Then she was a beauty."

"But she's gone," she finished on a whisper.

Gone, like so many people in her life, Matthew realized.

He stroked her hair. "I'll never leave you," he said solemnly. "You know that, don't you?"

He could tell she didn't believe him, but how could he blame her. "Time will prove me right, Finn."

She pressed close as if seeking his soul, and before long he could feel the even breathing that said she was asleep. The contentment that had filled him began to change. His heart began to pound with intensity. He wanted to paint. Needed to paint, and felt for the first time in months that he could, as he was meant to.

With a gentle kiss to Finnea's forehead, Matthew slipped out of bed. He threw on his clothes and went to the garden room in the darkened house. After shutting the door, he turned on the lights—every one of them, until every nook and corner was illuminated.

He pulled out a canvas, then tore through his tubes of paint until he had what he wanted. He began to work, without thinking.

He began to paint. No sketching. No preparation. Only the swift strokes of brush to canvas.

The movements were different, at first awkward and stilted. He realized in a startled space of time that despite how much progress he had made he would never paint the way he had before. But he realized as well that it didn't matter. He found a new rhythm. A new way to bring life to paint and canvas.

The world fell away and color sang in his mind. Images danced to life beneath his fingers like warriors dancing around a fire.

He worked for minutes, or maybe hours. He didn't know. Didn't care. He painted until he was finished—and knew that truly he was healed.

Finnea woke, the hint of morning touching the dark sky beyond the window.

She moved, just barely, and winced. She was amazed to find herself in a bed, not on the floor. And she had slept. Truly slept.

Last night came back to her with the tenderness from

lovemaking—and joy. Her body shimmered with feeling, for Matthew, for his daughter. For the possibility of moving beyond the past—without feeling as if she were somehow betraying Isabel.

She had told Matthew of her shame, told him her secrets, and had seen no condemnation in his eyes. He only loved her more for having shared her burden.

A stab of sadness snaked through her as she thought of her child.

Tears threatened. But she wouldn't let them come. Not after what she had shared with Matthew. She wanted to be with him now. To ensure that she had not imagined his love.

Wrapping herself back in the discarded clothes from last night, she went in search of Matthew.

The door to his bedroom stood ajar. But even in the early morning darkness she could tell he wasn't there—and that he hadn't slept in the bed.

Instinctively, she went downstairs, straight to the garden room, and found him, much as she had that first day on the train. Standing, staring out a window. But this time there was a bone-deep peace about him that had been missing before.

His beauty struck her. A beauty of soul and appearance, even with the scar. Or perhaps because of it.

She hadn't noticed last night that the swelling of his face had gone down, the redness subsided. But there had always been a fierceness that she hadn't realized wasn't part of his looks until now—now that it was gone. A tension caused by pain.

How had he withstood it?

Sudden uncertainty raced down her spine at the sight of him, this wonderful man whom she had loved for so long but had been unable to give in to. What if he regretted last night?

Fear raced through her. She wasn't ready for his response. She didn't think she could take another rejection.

She started to turn away.

"Come here," he said, his voice like gravel.

She looked back at him, and he held out his arm. Needing no other invitation, she raced to him and he curled her into his embrace.

He kissed her soundly, his lips lingering on hers, his tongue seeking entrance. She gave herself over to him, seeking just as he sought. A gasp shuddered through her when his hand slid lower and cupped her hips. He leaned back against the table, spreading his legs, pulling her to his hard desire.

"I want you," he whispered against her skin.

He kissed her deeply, groaning into her mouth. She clung to him, seeking his warmth.

But as suddenly as the kiss began, he stopped it.

"What is it?" she asked, pulling him close once again.

He smiled ruefully, then pressed his lips to her forehead. "As much as I would like to take you here and now, I need to give you time. I suspect you are sore this morning."

Finnea blushed at the truth of his words.

"God, you're beautiful," he whispered reverently. "What would I have done had you not gotten on that train?"

He hugged her to him so fiercely. She cherished the feeling. Cherished everything he made her feel.

They stood that way as the sun rose, the sky changing from a deep, rich purple, to muted shades of red and orange. That was when he set her back, holding her by the shoulders, and looked into her eyes. Just looked until she grew nervous.

"What is it, Matthew?"

"I'm going to have that show."

"What?" she gasped.

"A showing of my work. I know I can do it now. I'm ready. In fact, I am ready as I never was before."

"How do you know?"

Very slowly, he turned her around, his hands never leaving her, until she faced the canvas he had been working on.

At the sight, her breath caught and she froze.

Matthew wrapped his strong arms around her shoulders, pulling her back against his chest. "You've given me back my life, Finnea Hawthorne. First my daughter. Now my painting."

Emotion made it impossible for her to speak. Tears spilled down her cheeks.

His lips brushed against her hair. "I can't give you back your daughter, but I can give you her memory on canvas."

And he had. The painting was perfectly wrought, not in

minute detail, as his earlier work, but with an intensity and acuity that brought the child to life on canvas. The painting was both Finnea when she was young, and her daughter just before she died. The memory that had been fading, captured on canvas for eternity.

With trembling fingers, she reached out and nearly touched the drying lines of her daughter's face, gliding just over the surface, much as she had touched the lines of her own in the mirror, looking, seeking. And finally finding. Her place. Her daughter.

"I love you, Finnea. I love you with all my heart."

She turned and saw the tears that streaked her husband's face. Her heart swelling so much it hurt, she wrapped her arms around this man. "I love you," she whispered, her voice barely a rasp. "How can I ever thank you?"

"You already have, in ways that I am only now beginning to grasp. By loving me, by holding me, and by never leaving me again."

Chapter Twenty-four

Their love wrapped around them. Matthew spent his days painting and his nights making love to Finnea, then painting again until the sun came up. Only once did he leave the house without telling her, and that was to meet with Grayson in his downtown law office. Matthew had two matters he wanted his brother to look into. One thing needed saving, and another needed to be stopped once and for all. The farm and the annulment.

At home, Janji became a part of the family, teaching Mary about Africa, playing chess with Quincy. He also set out to learn everything he could about Boston.

Finnea took care of the arrangements for the show. Matthew had told her he would do it all, but she had insisted that she and Mary would make a project of finding just the right gallery for his work. After only a week of Finnea displaying the painting of Isabel, every reputable dealer in Boston wanted the show. None of them knew that the painting wasn't of Finnea as a child. But Finnea didn't want anyone to know otherwise.

"Why?" Matthew had asked her one night as she lay naked in his arms.

"Because I don't want to share. Call me selfish, but I want Isabel cherished, not dismissed and forgotten by people who never knew her."

She kissed the bare skin of his chest, rolling closer. "So I let them think what they want. And they want to think that the painting is of me." She looked up at him. "Is that so wrong?"

"No," he said, his voice rough as he pulled her on top of him, nudging her thighs apart.

He guided himself, then teased at her opening before sliding in, deep and full. She moved on him, and words were forgotten.

It was much the same every night. Long nights of love. Mornings with Finnea finding him gone, the new day filled with more artwork that took her breath away.

He painted her. He painted Mary. He painted everything that was in his mind, relishing the fact that he was painting again. He painted with a freedom that he had never experienced before. He had lost his talent once already and had survived. If it all went away again, he would still have himself. And that freed him. What he lost in detail, he made up for in a sense of depth he had never understood or expressed.

Two weeks before the show was scheduled, invitations went out. It was a week before the opening, after the paintings were hung in the downtown gallery renowned for the caliber of its artists, that critics were invited to preview the work. Then Finnea held her breath until the day of the event, when the reviews were supposed to run. Matthew only chuckled as if he didn't care one way or the other when she raced for the newspaper that morning. But his smile turned to satisfaction when she read aloud the words that described a quality and compassion that even jaded critics couldn't discount.

It was to be the night of all nights in Boston. Everyone who was anyone had been invited or had found a way to be at the show. And even Matthew's father, his mother had told him, planned to attend.

"He will see my work," Matthew said. "And he will see proof that I'm no longer an embarrassment to my family. That I can still be respected even after the scandal," he added with a kiss to Finnea's forehead. "With your help, my father will be proud."

Finnea hoped for her husband's sake that he was right.

The Matthew Hawthorne family dressed with care for the grand occasion. It had rained earlier, washing the city of daytime soot and grime, leaving a perfect crystal-clear sky dotted with thousands of stars.

Carriages pulled up to the gallery's canopied entrance. Gas lamps burned high, golden light spilling across the long red carpet that had been rolled out for the occasion. Liveried footmen stood at attention, helping the guests step down from black-enameled landaus and gold-trimmed barouches, everyone eager to get a glimpse of the wealthy Hawthorne and his art.

For days beforehand, Finnea had worried that people would flock to the gathering simply to gawk at Matthew and his face—this man they had called a monster. But once the guests were there, it was the paintings that they noticed.

Men and women alike marveled at the work. The colors that shimmered with life, the forms that awed.

Finnea looked across the room at her husband, joy filling her heart over the fact that the night was proving a huge success.

Mary sat on the stairway, looking like a fairy-tale princess, talking to her uncle, who sat beside her. Janji received nearly as much attention as the paintings, the guests thinking him an African king in his fine robes.

Dr. Sanderling was there, after graciously accepting Matthew's large donation for the Ethan Sanderling Clinic. Matthew had been adamant that the medical establishment be named after the doctor.

Emmaline Hawthorne mingled with the crowd, and Finnea could see the look of a proud mother as the older woman glanced from the paintings to her son. Even the Winslets were there. Nester and Penelope. Hannah reigning. And her mother, looking perfect and lovely.

Everything was going well, except that Bradford Hawthorne had yet to arrive. Would he stay away? Finnea wondered. Would he do that to his son?

She was on the verge of concluding the man would do just that, when the front door pushed open and Bradford entered.

Finnea saw Emmaline's quick and discreet prayer of thanks. Then she saw the joy that flashed over Matthew's face. It was that sight more than any other that made Finnea's heart begin to pound. She couldn't have said why. But like Emmaline, Finnea sent up a quick prayer, though hers had to do with Bradford Hawthorne not letting his son down. She might not like the man, but she wanted his approval for her husband.

He greeted and talked to the guests, his smile wide, his voice booming. He was a powerful man, and he seemed to be accepting of his son.

Thankfully her heart began to ease when the guests began to file out, leaving just family. It was only then, she realized, that Bradford started to move from painting to painting. Of her, of Mary. Of the three brothers. Emmaline was depicted. As was Bradford himself, a stunning work that showed the man with power and dignity.

But it was the canvases of Matthew, portrayed in a series of paintings that showed the progress of who Matthew had been and who he had become, which stopped Bradford. It was a depiction that could not fail to move any parent when taking in the sight of their child.

Bradford stood there, staring, and Finnea could see that Matthew was waiting, his pride etched on his face.

Bradford turned, and the room grew hushed. The father looked at his middle son, his favorite for so many years.

"Is this supposed to be art?" Bradford asked.

Emmaline gasped. Grayson abruptly stood from his place beside Mary, his eyes narrowing angrily.

Matthew grew very still, his eyes locked with his father's. To the casual eye, he looked no different than a few seconds before. But Finnea knew the truth.

Rage and fury consumed her, rage for her husband's sake, fury at the man who callously tossed love away as if it had no worth. Before anyone could speak, Finnea strode forward, her elegant gown swishing around her ankles like a storm-tossed sea.

"How dare you say such a thing," she snapped at the all-powerful Hawthorne patriarch.

The man raised a graying brow, his countenance set in steely lines that had intimidated some of the most powerful men in the world. But Finnea wasn't intimidated. She was furious.

"You call yourself a father?" she spat. "You don't deserve the love of my husband. He is good and kind, and a far better person than you will ever be."

Suddenly it was too much, and tears began to stream down

her cheeks. "He has honor and courage, where you are shallow and selfish. You are horrid, Bradford Hawthorne. And I hate you for hurting the man I love."

Her words reverberated against the high ceilings and tiled floors, trailing off until everyone who remained watched and waited.

"Don't cry, Finn."

She turned and found Matthew at her side. He stood there, strong and resolute, an odd smile pulling at his lips when she expected devastation.

"But," she began, before he cut her off.

"No buts. It doesn't matter."

"How can you say that?" she cried.

"Because it's true, though I only just realized it." He framed her face with his hands as if they were alone in the room. "You said not long ago that you didn't belong here. You don't, Finn."

Her brows furrowed and she was afraid she couldn't breathe. What did he mean? Did he think that if she were out of his life his father would accept him?

"You don't belong here, Finnea," he repeated, "and neither do I."

A collective gasp echoed through the cavernous room. Finnea was stunned, her mind trying to understand. But through the confusion, Finnea heard nearly soundless tears. Matthew must have heard them, too, because they both turned to find Mary standing to the side of the room, her face crumpling. She looked scared, afraid that her world was about to collapse yet again.

Finnea didn't know what to do, what to think. What was Matthew trying to say?

But then he extended his broad, strong hand to his daughter. "And Mary doesn't belong here either."

After a soundless, startled moment, the child raced across the wooden floor, running into her father's waiting arms. They stood clasped together, the three of them.

"We are a family," Matthew said softly, "and we belong together. But we don't belong here."

Part Four

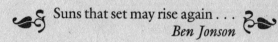

Suns that set may rise again . . .
Ben Jonson

Chapter Twenty-five

A cloud of steam burst from the train's engine stack as it crept out of Matadi. Excitement pinked Mary's cheeks as she hung her elbows over the metal sides of the open-air car. Her baby-fine hair caught in the wind as the train gathered momentum and sped away from the arid, boulder-strewn port town and headed into the jungle.

Finnea sat ramrod-straight, her fingers curled around the edge of the narrow wood-planked bench. Suddenly the train jarred, sending panic slicing through her veins. She stared straight ahead, her pulse racing.

"It's just a bump, Finn. You're okay."

Matthew pulled her close, gently taking her hands and twining her fingers with his. He kissed each knuckle as the train's motion settled out.

"You're going to make it home."

She eased at the sound of his voice, and when she looked up at him, she felt a wealth of emotion for this man. And she realized she was no longer afraid.

They were headed for the rubber plantation deep in the Congo. Janji had departed on a trade steamer a week before them, and would be there now waiting.

On the day they left Boston, Finnea stood with Matthew and Mary in front of Dove's Way. Their families were there, Grayson and even Lucas, standing shoulder to shoulder, each giving his brother an abrupt, fierce hug.

Emmaline cried quietly as Matthew pressed a kiss to her forehead. "One day we will return," he said gently. "But for now this is what we need to do."

Even Leticia got teary eyed, looking bemused by the emotion she was feeling. "It's as if we'd only just found each other," she said, dabbing her delicately wrought handkerchief to her nose.

"They are doing the right thing," Hannah said decisively, giving Finnea a quick, hard embrace. "And you heard that son-in-law of yours," she added to Leticia. "They'll come back."

The older woman's voice softened unexpectedly, and traitorous tears threatened. "We're all better off for your having come here. Remember that, child, and let that help you find your way back one day."

Even Nester looked off-kilter—not exactly sad, though not exactly immune either. Despite all the tension that had existed between them, Finnea hugged him. He blustered and squirmed until she let go. "Yes, well," he mumbled. He started away. But suddenly he stopped and looked back one last time, the corner of his lips crooking up into a fond smile. "Take care of yourself, little sis." Then he was gone.

But it was enough for Finnea.

She had left that world behind, left the mosaic that had given her hope in the beginning. But she would always remember the warrior and the dove. Dove's Way would always be a part of her. But she could no longer deny that her way home was to Africa.

They disembarked at the small rustic station where she had begun this journey a year ago. Matthew held tight to Mary's hand. She wanted to see everything, staring with open-mouthed amazement at the mahogany-colored women with woven baskets perched on their heads, who moved with the balance and grace of ballet dancers.

Animals were everywhere. Chickens and goats ran wild, taking refuge from the swarms of children that chased them in the dusty roads lined with brightly colored flowers and overgrown leaves of green.

Finnea could tell that Mary itched to join in the fun, but she stayed close to her father's side, not yet ready to venture too far away.

On the outskirts of the station, Matthew bought armloads

of flowers, then without a word started off down the dry, red-dirt road, petals trailing behind him as he went.

After a startled moment, Finnea and Mary raced to catch up. "What's the hurry?" they asked.

"The sun will be down soon."

Matthew strode on with determination, hard-carved muscles rippling beneath his hunter's clothes. Finnea chuckled. "Don't tell me you're afraid of what might come out in the dark."

He stopped, his arm snaking around her waist as he pulled her up against his chest. "Tonight I'll show you just how afraid I am of the dark." He brushed his lips against her hair. "But fear of the jungle isn't the reason I'm in a hurry. Come on."

He took off again.

"Daddy! You're going too fast!"

"It's not much farther, princess. You can make it."

Trees began to crowd the path, making it smaller and narrower as they went. But just when Mary would have stopped altogether, they came out into a clearing.

Mary gasped. And Finnea felt tears well in her eyes. She was home, finally.

Standing on a high point, they looked out to the west and could see the sun setting, a huge orange ball of fire sinking on the horizon. She had dreamed of this. Survived each day in the snow by imagining the feel of the heat on her skin.

"Thank you," she whispered.

Matthew smiled, then turned to Mary. "For you," he said, handing the child a colorful bouquet.

"And for you," he added to Finnea, filling her arms with rich red hibiscus and wild orchids.

"So many gifts. The sunset and now flowers."

A shout interrupted them. When they turned, Janji stood in the distance on the rough-hewn road that marked the final steps to the rubber plantation.

"Janji!" Mary cried out, waving her flowers in the air.

When he waved in return, she dashed down the path to him.

Finnea smiled and started to follow. But Matthew caught her hand.

"Before we go, I have something else for you." He dropped

the pack off his shoulder, reached inside, and pulled out a piece of paper. "This is for you."

Uncertain, she broke the seal and read the official-looking document. Her eyes scanned the lines once, then twice, before her head shot up.

"How is this possible? Nester said he wouldn't relinquish his shares."

"True, but he wasn't opposed to selling me the farm outright. It's yours, Finnea. Every acre, every tree."

Her face closed up. "No, Matthew. It's yours."

"What do you mean?"

"It doesn't work that way. You paid for it."

He considered her. "Ah, then that must mean Africa isn't mine?"

Her brow furrowed in bewilderment. "What are you talking about? Africa isn't anyone's."

"But it is. It's yours." His expression grew solemn. "In a manner of speaking, you paid for it. Here and in Boston."

She felt her heart kick.

He stepped closer and brushed an errant tendril of hair from her face. "You've given me your Africa—the beauty, the wildness. Now I am returning the favor and giving you the farm."

Pure, sheer happiness filled her soul. "Then it's ours, Matthew," she said. "Yours and mine and Mary's."

His warrior eyes grew fierce, his hand drifting down to the gentle curve of her belly. "And our child's."

At the words, Finnea felt excitement flare. *A child.*

A year ago she believed she would never again experience the feel of baby-soft arms holding her tight. But she had, with Mary, and she would again with their baby.

Doubt tried to fill her, and Matthew seemed to understand. "You *are* a good mother. And Isabel will always be with you."

Her lips pulled into a smile, and her excitement burst through. "We have so many plans to make. We need to fix a room for Mary, though my old room would be perfect for her. It has a beautiful window with lace curtains that overlooks a gazebo in the yard. Yes, I'm sure that will work. But we'll need another for the baby—"

"Hold on," he said with a chuckle. "We have plenty of time for house additions."

She slipped closer to him. "Yes, I suppose we do."

He ran his finger down her cheek, his face lined with emotion. "Have I told you recently how much I love you?"

She placed her hand over his heart and nodded, vibrant shades of African sun filling the world with orange and red. "Yes, you have. Every day. Just as I love you."

"We are forever, Finn, and I knew it the minute I saw you when you stepped on the train."

Finnea stepped back with a laugh. "You knew it that minute, did you? As I recall you were less than pleased to see me."

He shrugged like an errant schoolboy, his full smile crooked as he possessively pulled her back to him. "I *was* pleased. I just wasn't so good at showing it."

She laughed out loud, causing his smile to evaporate. Then one last time he reached down to his pack and pulled out a leather-bound volume.

Surprise filled her. "What is that?"

"A journal. I didn't always know how to show you that I cared, but I always wrote it down. I've written about you every day since I found you again in Boston. I love you, Finn. I have from the beginning." He held out the book. "This is for you. Proof of my love."

"Oh, Matthew, I don't need proof."

"Please."

With trembling hands, she took his gift and carefully flipped back the cover. She read the first entry and looked up at him, tears filling her eyes.

But he wouldn't let her say anything. He led her the last steps to the farm, and as soon as they had celebrated their homecoming with Janji and his family, she returned to the pages.

She read a bit each day, savoring each entry like a song or cherished poem, until she came to the end and found one blank page.

They had been there a week when Finnea looked up at Matthew as he entered their room. "You left one empty," she said from where she was sitting cross-legged on the bed, the book in her lap.

He took the leather-bound volume from her with a loving smile. "I have one entry left to write."

"When will you do it?" she demanded, her voice like a child's, filled with delight and impatience.

Matthew chuckled, his voice like gravel as he came toward her. "Soon. After that you can read it. But for now, I'm going to show you all the love I wrote about in those pages."

Finnea laughed as he tossed the journal aside. Stepping closer, he brushed his fingers against her skin until her laughter trailed off to desire. With a sound of deep satisfaction rumbling inside him, he held her in his hands, like the warrior and the dove.

From the Journal of
Matthew Hawthorne

You are with me now, my sweetest Finnea, on a farm in Africa. Mary is at our side, reaching out and taking your hand. And mine. Loving us as she loves her little brother, who follows her everywhere she goes.

We call him Chance because of what you said he has given us. Second chances. At love, at life, at living.

At night when you curl so securely against my side, you whisper that he looks just like me, handsome and beautiful. You look between us, seeing us as the same— as always, never seeing my scars.

Africa is our home now, the place where a man is nothing more than what he is inside—the place where my life truly began.

The past is still there, etched in my mind as much as on my face. But the edges have begun to wear away, like the edges of a stone washed smooth by the waves. For the first time I understand that sometimes hope is found in the least likely of places.

And the day you stepped on the train, I found my hope in you.

An interview with
Linda Francis Lee

Q: Can you give us a few words that you feel capture the
essence of *Dove's Way*?
A: Perhaps the best way to describe the book is part *My Fair
Lady*, part *Out of Africa*.

Q: How so?
A: I wanted to write a book about someone who steps into a
world that is completely foreign to her. A stranger in a strange
land. At the time, I was reading a great deal about Africa, and I
was mesmerized by its harsh, unforgiving beauty. But rather
than take an outsider to Africa, I got excited about the idea of
taking a woman who had been born in Boston, but raised in
the African Congo by her wanderlust father, and returning her
to Boston. On the outside, she looks like she belongs. But in
truth, she knows nothing about these people and their strict
and proper ways. I wanted to bring the beauty and freeness of
Africa to a rigid Boston society—and see what happened. As
you might imagine, the transition is a bumpy one. To try to
lessen the bumps, Finnea Winslet turns to Matthew Hawthorne, a Bostonian whom she met in Africa.

Q: How does Finnea meet Matthew?
A: She meets him on a train in Africa. After all my reading, I
couldn't forget the Congo Free State Railway, a rickety affair
built in the late 1800s that made its way precariously over the
most impassable parts of the Congo. If Finnea wanted to leave
the Congo, the most viable means of transportation to the
coast was on that railway. It is on the train that Finnea's and
Matthew's lives become inextricably intertwined.

Q: Both Africa and Boston are so vivid in the story. Have you ever lived in either place?

A: I haven't lived in Africa, and while I'm originally from Texas, in 1993, my husband and I moved to Boston for two and a half years. We moved in the fall, arriving in the city just in time for a record-breaking winter. I was raised on sunshine and bone-drying heat. A hundred plus inches of snow was quite a shock. But I loved Boston. Walking through the streets of the Back Bay or Beacon Hill, with cars kept away by the snow, I could so vividly see the town as it must have been in the late 1800s.

Q: What is your favorite part of writing?

A: I love finding that place where I lose myself in the world I have created—a place where the real world is pushed aside.

Q: Why historical fiction rather than contemporary, or nonfiction?

A: I have been fortunate enough to live in several places that are rich with history, cities that have worked hard to preserve their pasts—Texas, New York, Boston. I am always amazed to live among the very streets and houses, trees and cobbled paths that people lived among a hundred years ago, or two hundred years ago. In Texas, there are places where I would go that I could stand next to cottonwood trees that the conquistadors passed by four hundred years ago.

Q: What do you read for pleasure?

A: I read across the board. I read all types of fiction, as well as nonfiction, which generally leads me to the next occupation or residence of a new character. But there is nothing better than a wonderful story that is filled with romance. It's what I love reading the most, and it's what I hope to write.

Q: What kind of a writing schedule do you maintain?

A: I write five days a week, Monday through Friday. Though as I get closer to a deadline, I generally find myself doing little else besides writing and living in that imaginary world. Thank goodness for take-out and delivery food!

Q: Have you always written?
A: No, but as my mother is fond of saying, I always created stories in my head. I suspect that is a nice way of saying I spent too much time daydreaming!

Q: What is next?
A: *Dove's Way* is the first of a trilogy about three brothers. The Hawthorne brothers of Boston. After *Dove's Way* comes Grayson's story, *Swan's Grace*. It is the story of a man who is powerful and proper but is drawn to a woman who is a temptress one moment and an innocent the next. He is mesmerized by her loveliness—and shocked by her outrageousness. But he'll do whatever is necessary to make her his own. . . .

Turn the page
for a sneak peek at
Swan's Grace. . . .

On the heels of a triumphant tour in Europe, cellist Sophie Wentworth receives word from her father that he wants her to return home to Boston. She can't imagine why.

Regardless, while her entourage tells her not to go, Sophie has eagerly waited for the day her father would ask her to come home. She misses her father and the house she grew up in: Swan's Grace. But when Sophie and her friends arrive a week early, the house is closed and dark. No one is there. . . .

"This makes no sense," Sophie murmured.

She made her way through the first floor, pulling off her silk gloves, then her waist-length traveling jacket, tossing the item aside as she went. It felt so good to be there. Though she couldn't understand why no one was home.

Glancing around, everything looked the same, only somehow newer, she realized suddenly. But she wrote the changes off to time having passed, not to mention the dark.

Her thoughts were interrupted by the sudden commotion of booted steps on marble tiles which stopped abruptly, followed by Margaret's gasp from the foyer.

"I'd assume you were Conrad Wentworth," she heard Henry state in his favorite sarcastic lilt. "But you're a little young to have a full-grown daughter. Which begs the question, who are you?"

"A better question is, who are you?"

A man's voice, deep and low.

Sophie's head tilted and her mind raced. There was something familiar about the voice, but she couldn't place it.

Continuing her path through the hallway, she headed back to the foyer. But her steps faltered when she saw him.

Grayson Hawthorne. The oldest of the well-known Hawthorne brothers.

Her pulse slowed and she felt a shiver of awareness. It was always that way when she saw him. The astonishment that any man could be so striking. Sensual in a hard-chiseled way.

With his exacting glare pinning Henry to the spot, he stood in the flickering gaslight. He was a tall, commanding man with dark hair, longer than she remembered, swept back from his forehead. His jaw was strong, his shoulders sculpted beneath his four-button cutaway jacket that revealed fine woolen, perfectly creased trousers molded to his thighs in a way that made her heart beat slow.

Yes, it was Grayson Hawthorne. A stunning man. He was also the object of her most devoted girlhood infatuations.

Sophie remembered how as a child she had followed him around wherever he went with the tenacity of a bulldog. She was always in trouble, while he had always been kind and patient in a rolling-eyes sort of way. Indulgent of that odd duck Sophie Wentworth.

A fond smile pulled at her lips and she nearly shook her head in memory of the child she had once been. Had she really been such a peculiar sort?

"If you don't explain yourself," Grayson stated in hard, cold syllables, his gaze never wavering from little Henry, "I am going to send for the police."

"What is all this talk about the police?" Sophie asked, her smile growing wider as she strolled into the foyer in a swish of grosgrain silk.

Grayson turned at the sound, and stopped.

Their eyes met and held, and she knew he was as surprised to see her as she was to see him. But his astonishment was quickly contained behind a fathomless mask. Typical Grayson. Always the same, always ruthlessly contained. He was controlled, with a predatory grace, the lines of his body hard and well defined. His dark eyes were cool and considering, never allowing anyone to see what he felt.

Some months ago while she and her entourage had been in Paris, Margaret had received word from her cousin that Grayson had finally turned his attentions to choosing a wife. For half a second, Sophie had felt a young-girl wish that he would choose her. But she had just as quickly stamped out the thought. She would be no man's wife. Not even Grayson Hawthorne's. Or perhaps, especially not Grayson Hawthorne's.

It was rumored that the lady he chose had to be of unquestioned virtue, impeccable lineage, and high-minded principles. In short, the woman had to be as dull as the waters of Boston Harbor.

Sophie shuddered at the thought. Grayson Hawthorne

might be incredibly handsome and undeniably successful, but she had learned the night of her father's birthday party that he had become a man who would expect his wife to do as he wished, when he wished it, and without question.

She wondered who the poor woman was that Grayson had chosen to be his bride.

"Did you hear that, Sophie," Henry barked, "this brute has threatened to summon the police."

Margaret wrung her hands. "You can't call for the authorities for being in one's own house, surely."

Deandra scoffed, crushing her cigarette in an antique bowl. "I can see it now. PRODIGAL DAUGHTER TOSSED OUT OF HOME on the front page of every newspaper in town. It would be all over this rustic backwater by morning." Her green eyes narrowed in thought and she tapped her fingernail against the table. "No question that everyone would talk." Her finger stilled and she glanced at Sophie. "If you play your cards right, you just might get arrested. We couldn't pay for publicity like that."

Grayson's glacial stare locked on Deandra as if he didn't recognize *what* she was, much less who.

Sophie covered her burst of laughter with a cough. "Deandra, you are so bad."

"Isn't that what you pay me for?"

Sophie watched as Grayson slowly looked from person to person, finally fixing on her. Her heart gave a lurch and she felt an unaccustomed rush of heat as his gaze flicked over her.

His dark eyes narrowed. "Sophie?"

"Ding, ding, ding," she chimed, covering her fluttering heart with a laugh. "You win the prize."

One dark brow tilted sardonically, and for a second she would have sworn he almost smiled. But that was impossible. She knew that Grayson Hawthorne was not easily amused.

"You're here," he stated, his gaze never wavering. "And you're early."

"Ding, ding—right again. You are a veritable feast of correct answers tonight."

His brows flattened to hard lines.

"Alas," she continued undeterred as she sauntered forward,

her dainty heels clicking against the marble, "we caught an earlier ship out of France. A bucket of bolts held together with baling wire and twine, as far as I could see. But it got us here so I could surprise Father." She stopped abruptly as a thought occurred to her. "How did you know that I was coming home?"

For a second he seemed confused, or perhaps surprised by what she had said, then it was gone. "Your father told me."

"Ah well, that explains it. And since you know so much, why isn't my father here?" But the question trailed off, replaced by another. "Why are *you* here?"

His confusion resurfaced, then something dangerous flashed through his eyes. "Don't you know?"

They stared at each other, and she felt curiously off balance by the way he looked at her. His gaze was commanding. Strangely possessive.

"No, I don't know, Grayson. If I did, I wouldn't have asked."

His gaze burned into her, making her feel as if he had run his open palm over her skin. Her body tingled, and she was all too aware of this man.

She had liked it better when they were both young, coming and going from each other's houses as if they lived there. A smile teased at her lips as she remembered—her father with Grayson's father, smoking cigars in the study. Grayson's mother with her mother, sipping tea at Hawthorne House. Their parents had been the best of friends. And despite their age difference, she and Grayson had been friends, as well.

It had never been that way between her and his brothers, Matthew and Lucas. She had liked them well enough, but it was Grayson who drew her. But somehow as adults the ease they had shared as children had disappeared. The air between them now was charged, heated, just as it had been the night of her father's party.

"I live here," he said.

She blinked. "What?"

"I said I live here."

"You live here?" Her heart began to pound in a way that had nothing to do with strange possessiveness or burning gazes.

But she refused to give in to the rush of uncertainty. "Fallen on hard times have you?" she quipped, forcing the words from her mouth. "Sorry to hear it. But it's a big house. The more the merrier, I always say."

She had to find her father.

Gathering her long skirts, she started to turn away. But he caught her arm. His long, chiseled fingers curled with surprising gentleness just below her capped sleeve and she couldn't seem to look at anything else but his golden skin pressed against her own.

For one startled moment, she saw his hand, though it was a smaller, younger hand that she saw in her mind, brushing grit from her knee. Her dear, sweet Grayson. Her knight. The only person who had always been there for her—except once. When it mattered.

With the tip of his finger, he nudged her chin until their eyes met. "I am not a boarder, Sophie. I own Swan's Grace now. I thought you knew."

Every ounce of forced humor evaporated at the words, and she tugged her arm free. "That's absurd."

Silence, then: "I was led to believe Conrad talked to you about this." His eyes darkened even more, that dangerous flash resurfacing. "I bought the house from your father three months ago."

Her world spun and she couldn't seem to breathe. She hated the surety she heard in his voice.

But then she got ahold of herself. "That is ridiculous. It is not his house to sell."

"I'm afraid it was."

"It's mine!" A thread of panic flared in her voice.

"But it was in his name. The contract—"

"No!" she blurted out, cutting him off. "It was in his name, yes, but only because of some idiotic document I signed when I turned eighteen giving him control of my life." At the time, it had seemed a small price to pay for her freedom. A small price to pay to be allowed to leave Boston, leave the past, and attend Leipzig Music Conservatory in Germany. But her father never would have sold her house, she was sure.

Calm down, she told herself silently.

"Document or no, my father hasn't made a single attempt to involve himself in my life in years." As she said the words, she knew they were true, and the calm she fought for began to surface. "Clearly this is a misunderstanding. We will get it straightened out with my father in the morning."

She laughed, suddenly relieved. She reached across to him and patted his arm, regaining her composure. "Rest assured, if indeed some mistake has been made and money has changed hands, I will see to it that my father returns every penny."

His elegant panther's body grew still, and he considered her with cool, appraising eyes. He seemed to look into her. He had always been too good at reading her thoughts. It was all she could do not to close her eyes.

"The money isn't my concern."

"Well, good. Then there won't be any problems. In the meantime, we are exhausted. Come along, everyone."

The travelers started toward the stairs.

"Sophie," he stated, the word a quiet command.

At the bottom of the steps she turned back. "Yes?"

"You can't stay here."

Her heart leaped. They had no place else to go, but she couldn't tell him that. "Why not?"

The question stopped him. He stood for a moment and stared at her, this bold, commanding man, his handsome face shifting into hard, frustrated planes as he seemed to carry on some battle within himself.

"For now, let us just say that it isn't proper for an unmarried woman to sleep in the home of a bachelor," he replied evenly.

With that, a slow smile pulled across Sophie's lips, her equilibrium finally, truly restored. She ran the tips of her fingers provocatively down the sleeve of his dark suit coat. "So it *is* true. You really have turned into a fine prude."

Surprise flared on his face, though only briefly, before the muscles in his jaw tightened. Tension crackled in the air, and standing so close to him she could smell the deep, heated scent of sandalwood.

"Alas," she continued, stepping away abruptly, forcing a calm and bravado she did not feel, "I'm not terribly concerned about my reputation. But if you're concerned about yours, the Hotel Vendome isn't too far down the road. No doubt you could get a suitable room there."

Grayson slammed the brass knocker against the massive front door of the palatial sandstone and marble mansion on the Fens. The street was quiet, gaslights his only company. It was late. Much too late for a call. But Grayson wasn't about to wait until morning to confront Conrad Wentworth.

Impatiently, he banged the knocker again, pacing across the gray slate terrace until he heard fumbling inside. At length, the door pulled open a crack.

Raymond, the Wentworth butler, peered through the opening, his face creased with sleep, his trousers and waistcoat hastily thrown on, a candle and holder held up, casting a faint circle of light onto the front stoop.

"Mr. Hawthorne," the man said, alarmed.

"I'm here to see your employer."

Raymond stammered, stepping back, the door opening further. "But Mr. Wentworth has retired for the night."

"Then tell him to unretire."

The butler clearly didn't know what to make of the situation, but when Grayson stepped into the house, he didn't stop him.

Boot heels ringing on marble tiles, Grayson strode past two jewel-encrusted lions that perched in the foyer. Unlike most Bostonians, Conrad Wentworth wasn't opposed to displaying his wealth.

Wealth? Hell. If Conrad had bought fewer jewels for his house and his wife, they might not be in this situation.

Grayson was only glad he had learned about Conrad trying to sell Swan's Grace before it had gone to someone else. Though that certainly didn't help them now.

"But, sir—"

"Get him, Raymond."

The butler was saved from making a decision when a light came on at the top of the stairs.

"What is going on down there?"

Grayson turned to find Conrad Wentworth pulling on a silk robe over his nightshirt.

"Good God, Grayson. What is going on?"

"I want to know why the hell you signed a legal document selling your daughter's property without her consent."

Conrad halted on the stairs, then after a moment, continued on. When he came to the foyer, his slippered feet hit the tiles with a shuffle, and when he spoke, his voice was a study in calm as he smoothed his sleep-ruffled gray hair. "I signed that document because I had every right to."

Grayson pinned him with a glare. "You told me she was agreeable." He reined in his frustration as he stared at the older man. "And if you didn't tell her about the house, I can only surmise that you didn't tell her about the betrothal."

The house went quiet.

Conrad shifted his weight uncomfortably. With a wave of his hand, he sent the butler away, then he strode into a study off the foyer. The room was dark, but a gaslight quickly brightened the fine wood interior. He directed Grayson to one of the two wing-back chairs that faced a beautifully carved mahogany mantel. But Grayson wasn't interested in sitting.

Conrad cast a quick, nervous glance at him. "No, I haven't told her about the betrothal. But you are wrong about my authority. I am Sophie's father, and I have every right to guide her life."

"When she was younger, but not as an adult."

"Sophie is not just any adult. She has become a famous adult, and she was a child prodigy before that—the kind of woman of whom all sorts of people try to take advantage. I control a trust that was set up for her when her mother died. It includes Swan's Grace, and it gives me the right to make decisions regarding the direction of her life."

"If you felt so certain about this trust, why haven't you directed her before now?"

Conrad grimaced. "I've had other things on my mind."

"That is clear." Grayson seethed. "But she's your daughter."

"Sophie is not the only daughter I have!"

"Ah yes. Your new family. How could I forget."

Conrad flushed red, his stance growing defensive. "I was giving Sophie a chance to fulfill her dreams as a musician. She has become a success musically. That magazine article was proof of that."

The infamous article.

"But now it is time she returned home," Conrad continued, "to make a suitable life for herself. She's a woman, for mercy's sake. She can't be a musician forever. More than that, she certainly can't continue to travel around the world with that ill-assorted group of hangers-on the article mentioned. And I plan to tell her about the arrangements I've made just as soon as she arrives."

"Arrived," Grayson clarified impatiently. "Sophie is already here."

"What? She's not supposed to be here for another week!"

"Sophie is in Boston, at the Commonwealth Avenue house, expecting you." His jaw ticked. "Hell, Conrad, you didn't even bother to tell her you had moved."

The older man looked chagrined. "I had planned to explain that, too, when I picked her up at the harbor and brought her here to The Fens." The lines of his face softened. "I had planned to drive her around the Public Gardens, perhaps get out and walk over to see the skaters on the lagoon. I was going to tell her everything."

"And you think that would have been enough? A quick explanation during a stroll through the park? *After* the papers were signed?"

The softness evaporated and Conrad matched Grayson's anger. "She is twenty-four years old and it's time she learned that there is more to life than music. She needs guidance. And as her father it is my responsibility to see to her welfare. Therefore, I'm seeing to it now, and if I have to use that trust to get it done, then so be it. She will move in here where she belongs until she is married."

Grayson raked his hand through his hair. "God, what a mess." He looked at the older man with barely held patience. "Surely you understand that this is not the way to get your daughter to settle down. Sophie will only fight you." His gaze narrowed to slits of obsidian. "Which means she will also fight me."

"Let her fight. Whether she wants to admit it or not, I'm

doing what is best for her." Conrad gave a sharp tug to tighten the belted sash at his waist. "I will explain the situation to my daughter. I will go over there first thing in the morning."

"Tell her about the house," Grayson said, his temper under tight control. "But I don't want you making things worse by telling her about the betrothal." His eyes narrowed, and his voice took on a cold, hard edge. "I will tell her about our marriage myself. If she finds out that on top of everything else you betrothed her without her consent, she will be like a runaway horse with a bit between its teeth. She would reject the match simply to defy you."

"I am her father. She will not defy me!"

"Then you've forgotten what Sophie is like."

Conrad grumbled. "I haven't forgotten. She's as headstrong as they come. Always has been."

"My point exactly. Now I will have to untangle this mess."

Lance St. Leger is defying his destiny. The eldest son and heir to Castle Leger, he has returned from the army determined to continue his role as rakehell and black sheep. He is plagued by an infernal restlessness that cannot be appeased, perhaps because the St. Leger legacy of strange powers is most pronounced in Lance's own dubious gift. He calls it night drifting—his ability to separate his body from his soul, to spirit into the night while flesh and bone remain behind. And it is on one wild night's mad search for a magnificent stolen sword—the icon of the St. Leger power—that he finds her. . . .

THE NIGHT DRIFTER

Rosalind, a young, sheltered widow with a passion for the Arthurian legend, mistakes Lance's "drifting" soul for the ghost of Sir Lancelot. Seeing that she is in need of a champion, the St. Leger rogue assumes the role of the tragic knight, not knowing that this woman is his destiny, his perfect mate.

by Susan Carroll

But deep down in her heart, Rosalind is all too aware she is a mortal woman with very real desires that only a man of flesh and blood can fulfill—a man like Lance St. Leger. As a murderous enemy challenges the St. Leger power, Rosalind must tempt magic herself to save her beloved from the cold depths of eternal damnation.

Published by The Ballantine Publishing Group.
Available in bookstores everywhere.

PRINCE CHARMING

by Gaelen Foley

Destiny casts its hand one perfect moonlit night when Ascension's most elusive highwayman, the Masked Rider, chooses the wrong coach to rob. For inside is Rafael, the prince of the kingdom, renowned for his hot-blooded pursuits of women and other decadent pleasures. The failed raid leaves the equally notorious Masked Rider wounded and facing a hangman's noose. Then Rafe realizes his captive criminal is Lady Daniela Chiaramonte, a defiant beauty who torments him, awakening his senses and his heart as no woman has before.

Dani can only wonder if she's been delivered to heaven or hell once she agrees to marry the most desirable man in the Mediterranean—until forces of treachery threaten to destroy their tenuous alliance and bring down the throne itself. . . .

Published by The Ballantine Publishing Group.
Available at bookstores everywhere.

*"If you like to hoot with laughter and
have your heartstrings twanged, don't miss . . .
Maggie Osborne."*
—CATHERINE COULTER

SILVER LINING
by Maggie Osborne

As scruffy and rootless as the other prospectors searching for gold in the Rockies, Low Down wanted nothing in return for nursing a raggedy bunch through the pox. But when pressed to reveal her heart's wish, she admits, *"I want a baby."* Not a husband, not a forced marriage to the proud man who drew the scratched marble and became honor bound to marry her.

To be sure, Max McCord was easy on the eyes, but he loved another woman and dreamed of a different life. Yet they agreed to a temporary marriage that could end only in disaster. But can this strange twist of fate lead to the silver lining that both have been searching for?

Ask for SILVER LINING in your local bookstore.
Published by Ivy Books.